The Collected Shorter Supernatural & Weird Fiction of Algernon Blackwood Volume 1

Algernon Blackwood

The Collected Shorter Supernatural & Weird Fiction of Algernon Blackwood Volume 1

Thirteen Short Stories and Four Novelettes of the Strange and Unusual Including 'A Mysterious House', 'The Wood of the Dead', 'The Dance of Death', 'May Day Eve' and 'The Insanity of Jones'

Algernon Blackwood

The Collected Shorter Supernatural & Weird Fiction of Algernon Blackwood
Volume 1
Thirteen Short Stories and Four Novelettes of the Strange and Unusual Including 'A Mysterious House', 'The Wood of the Dead', 'The Dance of Death', 'May Day Eve' and 'The Insanity of Jones'
by Algernon Blackwood

Leonaur is an imprint of Oakpast Ltd

ISBN: 978-1-915234-90-2 (hardcover)
ISBN: 978-1-915234-91-9 (softcover)

http://www.leonaur.com

Publisher's Notes

The views expressed in this book are not necessarily those of the publisher.

Contents

A Mysterious House

Explanations are usually very tedious, and so without any introduction or perambulation I will plunge right into the midst of this uncanny story I am about to tell. . . . When, some fifteen years before the time of which I write, I was a schoolboy at Eton I made close friends with a fellow above me in the school, named Pellham. We were very great chums, and late on we went to Cambridge together, where my friend spent money and time in wasting both, while I read for holy orders, though I never actually entered the Church. Since that time, I had completely lost sight of him and he of me, and, with the exception of seeing his marriage in the papers, had no news at all of his whereabouts.

One morning, however, towards the close of September 1857, I received a letter from him, short, precise, and evidently written in a great hurry, asking me to go down and see him at his family seat just outside Norwich. I packed my bag and went that very same evening.

He met me himself at the station and drove me home. We hardly recognised each other at first sight, so much had we changed in appearance, both being on the dark side of thirty-five, but our individual characters had remained much the same and we were still to all appearance the best of friends. My friend was not very talkatively disposed, and I kept up a fire of questions until we drew up at the park gates.

Going up the drive to the house he brightened up considerably, and gave me plenty of information about himself and family. He was quite alone, I was surprised to hear, his wife and two daughters with an uncle of his having left for thew Continent two days previous.

After dinner he seemed quite the old 'Cambridge Undergrad' again, and once settled round the old-fashioned hearth, with cheroots and coffee, we talked on over the days spent at Eton and Cambridge.

We were just discussing our third edition of tobacco, when Pellham suddenly changed the subject, and said he would tell me now why he had written so shortly to me to pay him this unexpected visit. His face grew grave as he began by asking me if I was still a sceptic as regards ghostly manifestations.

'Indeed, I am,' was my answer; 'I have had no reason to change my views on the subject, and think exactly as I used to at Cambridge, when we so strongly differed; but I remember you then saying that, if ever in after years you should come across an opportunity of proving to me your ideas on the subject, you would write to me at once, and I also recollect giving my word that, if possible, I would come. But during the fifteen years that have since passed by I have bestowed little, if any, thought on the subject.'

'Exactly,' answered Pellham, with a grave smile that did not please me; 'but now I have at last heard of a case which will satisfy us both, I think, so I wrote to you to come down and fulfil your old promise by investigating it.'

'Well! Let me hear all bout it first,' I said cautiously. I certainly was not overjoyed to hear this news, for, though a sceptic to all intents and purposes, still 'ghosts' was a subject for which I had a certain fear, and the highest ambition of my life was not to investigate haunted houses and the like just because I had years ago promised I would should a chance occur. But I repressed my feelings and tried to look interested, which I was, and delighted, which I certainly was not.

Pellham then gave me a long account—thrilling enough too it was—of the case, which I have somewhat condensed in the following form. Some three or four years before, my friend had bought up a house which stood on the moorland about eight miles off. One morning before breakfast the tenant of the house, a Mr. Sherleigh (who was there with his family), suddenly burst into my friend's study without any ceremony, and, in great heat and excitement, shouted out the following words:

'You shall suffer for it, Lord Pellham, my wife mad, and the little boy killed with fright, because you didn't choose to warn us of the room next to the drawing-room, but you shall——.' Here the footman entered, and at a sign from his master led the excited and evidently cracked old man from the room, but not before he had crashed down some gold pieces on the table with: 'That's the last rent you'll get for that house, as sure as I am the last tenant.'

'Well,' continued my friend, 'that very day, now two years ago, I rode over there myself and the house was empty. The Sherleighs had left it, and since that day I have never been able to let it to anyone. Mr. Sherleigh, who was quite mad, poor fellow, threw himself before a train, and was cut to pieces, and Mrs. Sherleigh spread a report that it was haunted, and now no one will take it or even go near it, though it stands high and is in a very healthy position. Two nights ago,' he went on gravely, 'I was riding past the road which leads up to it, and through the trees I could see light in one of the upper rooms, and figures, or rather shadows, of a woman's figure, with something in her arms, kept crossing to and fro before the window-blind.

'I determined to go in and see what on earth it was, and tying my horse just outside I went in. In a minute or two I was close underneath the window where the light was still visible, and the shadow still moving to and fro with a horrible regularity. As I stood there, undecided, a feeling within warned me not to enter the house, so vivid, it was almost a soft voice that whispered in my ear. I heard no noise inside; the night air was moaning gently through the firtrees which surrounded the house on one side and nearly obscured the upper part of the window from view.

'I stooped down and picked up a large stone—it was a sharp-edged flint—and without any hesitation hurled it with all my might at the windowpane, some eight or ten feet from the ground. The stone went straight and struck the window on one of the wooden partitions, smashing the whole framework, glass and all, into a thousand splinters, many of which struck me where I stood. The result was awful and unexpected. The moment the stone touched the glass the lights quite disappeared, and in the blackness in which I was shrouded, the next minute, I could see hiding behind the broken corners of glass a dark face and form for a short instant, and then it went and all was pitch dark again.

'There I was among those gloomy pine trees hardly knowing which way to turn. The face I had caught a momentary glimpse of was the face of Mr. Sherleigh, whom I knew to be dead! My knees trembled. I tried to grope my way out of the wood, and stumbled from tree to tree, often striking my head against the low branches. In vain. With the weird light in the window as a guide, I had taken but a few minutes to come, but now all was dark and I could not find my way back again. I felt as if the dismal tree trunks were living things, which seemed to move.

'Suddenly I heard a noise on my left. I stopped and listened. Horror! I was still close to the window, and what I heard was a cracking and splintering of broken glass, as if someone from inside were slowly forcing their way out through the hole made by my stone! Was it he? The firtree next me suddenly shook violently, as if agitated by a powerful gust of wind, and then in a gleam of weird light I saw a long dark body hanging halfway out of the window, with black hair streaming down the shoulders. It raised one arm and slammed down something at my feet which fell with a rattle. And then hissed out: "There's the last rent you'll ever have for this house."

'I stood literally stupefied with horror, then a cold numb sensation came over me and I fell fainting on my face, but not until I heard my horse give a prolonged neigh and then his footsteps dying away in the distance on the hard moorland road. . . . When I recovered consciousness it was broad daylight. I was cold and damp; all night I had lain where I fell. I rose and limped, stiff and tired, to the place where I had tied my horse the night before, but no horse was there. And the horrible sound of his hoofs echoing away in the distance came back to me, and I shuddered as I thought of what I had seen.

'After a terrible trudge of three hours I reached home. A tremendous search had been made for me, of course, but no one dreamt of looking for me where I really was. The horse had found his way home, and I have never found out what frightened him so.'

My friend's account was over. He lit his cigar, which had gone out during the narrative, and settled himself comfortably in his chair, said, 'Well, old boy, that's a case I don't feel at all inclined to investigate by myself, but I'll do it with your aid. You know, a genuine sceptic is a great addition in such things, so we'll get to the bottom of it somehow.'

My feelings at that moment were not difficult to describe. I disliked the whole affair, and wanted heartily to get out of it; and yet something urged me to go through with it and show my friend that the house was all right, that imagination did it all, that the horse may have taken fright at anything, and that very possibly there really was someone in the house all the time, and imagination had done the rest. Such were the somewhat mixed thoughts in my mind at the time. However, in a few moments all was settled and we had agreed to go the following night, search the house first, and then sit up all night in the room next the drawing-room. Then we both went to our separate bedrooms to think the matter over and get a long sleep, as we neither expected to get any the following night.

Next morning at breakfast we both talked cheerfully about the coming night and how best to meet its requirements as regards food, etc. we agreed to take pistols for weapons, horses as a means of conveyance, and abundant food wherewith to fortify ourselves against a possible attack of ghosts.

The day drew on towards it close. It was very hot and sultry weather, and not a breath of wind stirred the murky atmosphere, as at 4.30 p.m. we bestrode our horses and made off in the direction of the 'White House.' A long gravel road, lonely in the extreme, led us across the wild uncultivated moorland for six or seven miles, then we saw a copse of firtrees which, my friend informed me, were the trees which sheltered one side of the house. In a few minutes we had passed through the front garden gate and were among the dark firtrees, and then as we turned a sharp corner the house burst full upon us.

It was square and ugly. Great staring windows in regular rows met our eyes and conveyed an unpleasant impression to the brain—at least, they did to mine. From the very next moment we had passed the front gate till I left the house the next morning, I felt a nasty sick sensation creep over me, a feeling of numbness and torpor which seemed to make the blood run thick and sluggish in my veins. The events of that night have remained engraven on my brain as with fire, and, though they happened years ago, I can see them now as vividly as then. Only an eye-witness can possibly describe them, should he wish to do justice to them, and so my feeble pen shall make the attempt.

It was about 6.30, and we had settled our horses in a barn outside for the night. There were only two walls to keep the barn in position, and these were simply a row of rotten posts, half-decayed in places, so we securely tied the horses, and, with a good supply of hay, left them for the night. We then approached the door and, after fumbling in the lock for some time, Pellham succeeded in opening it. A sickly, musty odour pervaded the hall, and the first thing we did after a thorough search, which revealed nothing, was to open all the doors and windows all over the house, so as to let in what little air there was.

Then we went upstairs into the little room next the drawing-room, where, according to Sherleigh, strange things had occurred. But the window was in pieces, and hardly an entire pane of glass was left, and we were forced to select another room on the same floor (*i.e.*, the second) and looking out to the same copse of pine trees, whose branches almost touched the glass, so close were they. It was a very ordinary room; a fireplace, no furniture but a rickety table and three chairs, one of which was broken.

The only disagreeable feature we noticed about the room was its gloominess; it was so very dark. The trees outside, as I have already said, were so close that the slightest breath of wind rustled their twigs against the window. We soon had six candles fixed and burning in different parts of the little room, and the blaze of light was still further increased by a roaring fire, on which a kettle was singing for tea, and eggs boiling in a saucepan, and at half-past seven we were in the middle of our first tea in a haunted house.

It was, indeed, less luxurious than the dinners I had been used to lately, but otherwise there was nothing to find fault with, and a little later the tea things were cleared away in a heap in a corner (where, by-the-by, they are to this day), and we were sitting round an empty table, smoking in silence. The door out into the passage was fast shut, but the window was wide open. The sun had sunk out of sight in a beautiful sky of wonderful colouring. Small fleecy clouds floating about caught the soft after-glow and looked unearthly as seen through the thick fir branches.

The faint red hue of the western sky looked like the reflection of some huge and distant conflagration, growing dimmer and fainter as the dark engines of the night played upon it, extinguishing the leaping flames and suffusing the sky with a red reflected glow. Not a breath of air stirred the trees. My friend had left the window and was poking and arranging the fire, with his back turned towards me. I was standing close to the window, looking at the fast-fading colours, when it seemed to me that the window sash was moving.

I looked closer. Yes! I was not mistaken. The lower half was gradually sinking; gradually and very quietly it went down. At first, I thought the weight had slipped and gone wrong, and the window was slipping down of its own accord; but when I saw the bolt pulled across and fastened as by an invisible hand, I thought differently. My first impulse was to immediately undo the bolt again and open the window, but on trying to move—good heavens! I found I had lost all power of motion and could not move a muscle of my body.

I was literally rooted to the ground. Neither could I move the muscles of my tongue or mouth; I could not speak or utter a sound. Pellham was still doing something to the fire, and I could hear him muttering to himself, though I could not distinguish any words. Suddenly, then. I felt the power of motion returning to me; my muscles were relaxing, and turning, though not without a considerable effort,

I walked to the fireplace. Pellham, then, for the first time noticed that the window was shut, and he made a remark about the closeness of the night, asking me why I had closed it.

'Hulloa,' he went on, before I had time to answer, 'by the gods above! What is happening to that window? Look—why it's moving!'

I turned. *The window was slowly being opened up again.*

Yes, sure enough it was. Slowly and steadily, it moved or was pushed up.

We could not believe our eyes; in half a minute the window was wide open again. I turned and looked at Pellham and he looked at me, and in dead silence we stared at one another, neither knowing what to say or wishing to break the silence. But at Length my friend spoke.

'I wish I were a sceptic, old man, like you are; sceptics are always safer in a place like this.'

'Yes,' I said, as cheerfully as I could, 'I feel safe enough, and what's more, I am convinced that the window was opened by human agency from outside.'

Pellham smiled, he knew as well as I that no human fingers could have fastened the bolt from the outside. 'Well,' he said briskly, 'perhaps you are right; come, let's examine the window.'

We rose and approached it, and my friend put his head and shoulders out into the air. It was very dark, and a strange oppressive stillness reigned outside, only broken by the gentle moaning sound of the night wind as it rustled through the trees and swept their branches like the strings of a lyre. I followed my friend's example, and together we peered out into the night. Soon my eyes rested on the ground below us, and at the base of one of the nearer pines I thought I could distinguish a black form, clinging, as it seemed, to the tree.

I pointed it out to Pellham, who failed to see anything, or at least said so; anyhow, I was glad to believe that my excited imagination was the real cause. We were still leaning out of the window in silence, when several of the trees, especially the one where I imagined I had seen the shape, were most violently agitated, as though by a mighty wind; but we felt not the slightest breath on our faces. At the same instant we heard a subdued shuffling sound in the room behind us, which seemed to come from the direction of the chimney. But neither of us referred to it as we slowly walked back to the fire and took up our places on either side on the two chairs, which were at the best very rickety.

'It isn't wise to leave the window open,' said my friend, suddenly, 'for if there really is anyone outside, they can see all and everything we do; while we, for our part, can see absolutely nothing of what goes on outside.'

I agreed, and walked up to the window, shutting it with a bang and firmly drawing the bolt.

'I've brought a book,' he went on, 'which I thought we might read out aloud in turn to relieve the dullness and the silence.'

He stopped speaking and looked at me, and at the same moment I raised my eyes to his face. To my intense horror and surprise, I noticed for the first time a long smear of blood, wet and crimson across his forehead. My horror was so great that for some seconds I could not find my tongue, and sat stupidly staring at him. At last, I gasped out:

'My dear fellow, what has happened to you, have you cut yourself?'

'Where? What do you mean?' he replied, looking round him with surprise.

For answer I took out my handkerchief, and wiping his brow, showed him the red stains. But as I stood there showing him this proof and as he was expressing his utter astonishment, I distinctly saw something that for the moment made the blood rush from the extremities and crowd into my head. Something seemed to tighten round my heart. I saw a large, gleaming knife and hand disappear into the air in the direction of the window. It was too much; my nerves failed me, and I dropped fainting to the floor.

★★★★★★★★★★

When I came to myself, I was lying where I fell by the fireplace. Pellham was sitting beside me.

'I thought you were dead,' he said, 'you've been unconscious for over an hour.' He said this in such a queer manner and laughed so fiendishly that I wondered what had happened to him during the interval. Had he seen something awful and gone mad? There was a strange light in his dark eyes and a leer on his lip. Just then he took up his book quite naturally and began to read aloud, every now and then he made a comment on what he was reading, quite sensibly too, and soon I began to think, as I sipped my brandy out of our flask, that I must have had a frightful dream. But there at my feet lay the blood-stained handkerchief, and I could not get over that. I glanced at his face; the smear had disappeared, and no scratch or wound was visible.

Pellham had not been reading long, perhaps some five or ten minutes, when we heard a strange noise outside among the trees, just audible above the death-like stillness of the autumn night. It was a confused voice like the low whispering of several persons, and as I listened, still weak from the last shock, the blood stood still in my veins. Pellham went on reading as usual. This struck me as very curious, for he must have heard the noise plainly; but I said nothing, and glancing at him I saw the same light in his eyes and the evil leer on his mouth, looking ugly in the flickering glare of the candles and firelight.

Suddenly we heard a tremendous noise outside, altogether drowning the first. The horses had broken loose and were tearing wildly past the house. Long and wild neighs rang out and died away, and we knew our horses were gone. Pellham was still reading, and as I looked at him a sudden and horrid thought flashed through my brain. It was this: had he anything to do with this? Was it possible? Before I had time to answer my question Pellham threw down the book and made for the door, locked it, drew out the key, and opening the window threw it far away among the trees. I then recognised the awful fact that I was alone with a madman.

I glanced at my watch; it was a quarter to one. Instead of one hour I must have been unconscious two at least. This was terrible in the extreme. He was a man of far more powerful physique than I, what was to be done? Pellham strode grinning up to the fire, went down on both knees and commenced blowing between the bars with all his might. I saw my chance, and quietly walking to the window, without a word I climbed out, and letting myself as far down as my arms would allow, I then let go and dropped. It was a distance of four or five feet, but in the darkness, I tumbled forward on my face.

As I rose, uninjured, I distinctly heard the sound of running feet close to me, but in my bewilderment, I could not make out clearly in which direction they were going; they only lasted a moment or two. But what a terrific sight met my gaze as I turned the corner of the house, and saw volumes of smoke pouring steadily out of the window and roof of the back portion of the house. Now and again a long flame, too, shot up to heaven.

'Good God!' I cried, 'the house is on fire.'

No wonder the horses had taken flight. But my poor friend, what could I do for him? The window was too high for me to climb in again, and the doors were locked. In a few minutes the flames would spread to this side of the house and the poor fellow would be burnt to death unless he had enough sense left to jump out of the window.

I hurried back to the spot where I had let myself down from the window, just in time to see the last scene of the most ghastly experience I have ever witnessed. Pellham was standing at the window. In his hand was a red-hot poker, and it was pointed at his throat, but the strain was too great for my nervous system and with a violent start *I woke up.*

★★★★★★★★★★

After our heavy tea we had both fallen asleep, just as we were in our chairs. Pellham was still snoring opposite me, and the light was stealing in through the window. It was morning, about half-past six. All the candles had burnt themselves out, and it was a wonder they had not set fire to the dry wood near them.

Twenty minutes later we had relit the fire and were discussing the remnant of eggs and coffee. Half an hour later we were riding home in the bright, crisp, morning air, and an hour and a half later we were in the middle of a second and far superior breakfast, during which I did *not* tell my dream, but during which we *did* agree that it had been the dullest and most uncomfortable night we had ever spent away from home.

A Haunted Island

The following events occurred on a small island of isolated position in a large Canadian lake, to whose cool waters the inhabitants of Montreal and Toronto flee for rest and recreation in the hot months. It is only to be regretted that events of such peculiar interest to the genuine student of the psychical should be entirely uncorroborated. Such unfortunately, however, is the case.

Our own party of nearly twenty had returned to Montreal that very day, and I was left in solitary possession for a week or two longer, in order to accomplish some important "reading" for the law which I had foolishly neglected during the summer.

It was late in September, and the big trout and *maskinonge* were stirring themselves in the depths of the lake, and beginning slowly to move up to the surface waters as the north winds and early frosts lowered their temperature. Already the maples were crimson and gold, and the wild laughter of the loons echoed in sheltered bays that never knew their strange cry in the summer.

With a whole island to oneself, a two-storey cottage, a canoe, and only the chipmunks, and the farmer's weekly visit with eggs and bread, to disturb one, the opportunities for hard reading might be very great. It all depends!

The rest of the party had gone off with many warnings to beware of Indians, and not to stay late enough to be the victim of a frost that thinks nothing of forty below zero. After they had gone, the loneliness of the situation made itself unpleasantly felt. There were no other islands within six or seven miles, and though the mainland forests lay a couple of miles behind me, they stretched for a very great distance unbroken by any signs of human habitation. But, though the island was completely deserted and silent, the rocks and trees that had echoed human laughter and voices almost every hour of the day for two months could not fail to retain some memories of it all; and I was not surprised to fancy I heard a shout or a cry as I passed from rock to rock, and more than once to imagine that I heard my own name called aloud.

In the cottage there were six tiny little bedrooms divided from one another by plain unvarnished partitions of pine. A wooden bedstead, a mattress, and a chair, stood in each room, but I only found two mirrors, and one of these was broken.

The boards creaked a good deal as I moved about, and the signs of occupation were so recent that I could hardly believe I was alone. I half expected to find someone left behind, still trying to crowd into a box more than it would hold. The door of one room was stiff, and refused for a moment to open, and it required very little persuasion to imagine someone was holding the handle on the inside, and that when it opened I should meet a pair of human eyes.

A thorough search of the floor led me to select as my own sleeping quarters a little room with a diminutive balcony over the verandah roof. The room was very small, but the bed was large, and had the best mattress of them all. It was situated directly over the sitting-room where I should live and do my "reading," and the miniature window looked out to the rising sun. With the exception of a narrow path which led from the front door and verandah through the trees to the boat-landing, the island was densely covered with maples, hemlocks, and cedars. The trees gathered in round the cottage so closely that the slightest wind made the branches scrape the roof and tap the wooden walls. A few moments after sunset the darkness became impenetrable, and ten yards beyond the glare of the lamps that shone through the sitting-room windows—of which there were four—you could not see an inch before your nose, nor move a step without running up against a tree.

The rest of that day I spent moving my belongings from my tent to the sitting-room, taking stock of the contents of the larder, and chopping enough wood for the stove to last me for a week. After that, just before sunset, I went round the island a couple of times in my canoe for precaution's sake. I had never dreamed of doing this before, but when a man is alone he does things that never occur to him when he is one of a large party.

How lonely the island seemed when I landed again! The sun was down, and twilight is unknown in these northern regions. The darkness comes up at once. The canoe safely pulled up and turned over on her face, I groped my way up the little narrow pathway to the verandah. The six lamps were soon burning merrily in the front room; but in the kitchen, where I "dined," the shadows were so gloomy, and the lamplight was so inadequate, that the stars could be seen peeping through the cracks between the rafters.

I turned in early that night. Though it was calm and there was no wind, the creaking of my bedstead and the musical gurgle of the water over the rocks below were not the only sounds that reached my ears. As I lay awake, the appalling emptiness of the house grew upon me. The corridors and vacant rooms seemed to echo innumerable footsteps, shufflings, the rustle of skirts, and a constant undertone of whispering. When sleep at length overtook me, the breathings and noises, however, passed gently to mingle with the voices of my dreams.

A week passed by, and the "reading" progressed favourably. On the tenth day of my solitude, a strange thing happened. I awoke after a good night's sleep to find myself possessed with a marked repugnance for my room. The air seemed to stifle me. The more I tried to define the cause of this dislike, the more unreasonable it appeared. There was something about the room that made me afraid. Absurd as it seems, this feeling clung to me obstinately while dressing, and more than once I caught myself shivering, and conscious of an inclination to get out of the room as quickly as possible. The more I tried to laugh it away, the more real it became; and when at last I was dressed, and went out into the passage, and downstairs into the kitchen, it was with feelings of relief, such as I might imagine would accompany one's escape from the presence of a dangerous contagious disease.

While cooking my breakfast, I carefully recalled every night spent in the room, in the hope that I might in some way connect the dislike I now felt with some disagreeable incident that had occurred in it. But the only thing I could recall was one stormy night when I suddenly awoke and heard the boards creaking so loudly in the corridor that I was convinced there were people in the house. So certain was I of this, that I had descended the stairs, gun in hand, only to find the doors and windows securely fastened, and the mice and black-beetles in sole possession of the floor. This was certainly not sufficient to account for the strength of my feelings.

The morning hours I spent in steady reading; and when I broke off in the middle of the day for a swim and luncheon, I was very much surprised, if not a little alarmed, to find that my dislike for the room had, if anything, grown stronger. Going upstairs to get a book, I experienced the most marked aversion to entering the room, and while within I was conscious all the time of an uncomfortable feeling that was half uneasiness and half apprehension. The result of it was that, instead of reading, I spent the afternoon on the water paddling and fishing, and when I got home about sundown, brought with me half a dozen delicious black bass for the supper-table and the larder.

As sleep was an important matter to me at this time, I had decided that if my aversion to the room was so strongly marked on my return as it had been before, I would move my bed down into the sitting-room, and sleep there. This was, I argued, in no sense a concession to an absurd and fanciful fear, but simply a precaution to ensure a good night's sleep. A bad night involved the loss of the next day's reading,—a loss I was not prepared to incur.

I accordingly moved my bed downstairs into a corner of the sitting-room facing the door, and was moreover uncommonly glad when the operation was completed, and the door of the bedroom closed finally upon the shadows, the silence, and the strange *fear* that shared the room with them.

The croaking stroke of the kitchen clock sounded the hour of eight as I finished washing up my few dishes, and closing the kitchen door behind me, passed into the front room. All the lamps were lit, and their reflectors, which I had polished up during the day, threw a blaze of light into the room.

Outside the night was still and warm. Not a breath of air was stirring; the waves were silent, the trees motionless, and heavy clouds hung like an oppressive curtain over the heavens. The darkness seemed to have rolled up with unusual swiftness, and not the faintest glow of colour remained to show where the sun had set. There was present in the atmosphere that ominous and overwhelming silence which so often precedes the most violent storms.

I sat down to my books with my brain unusually clear, and in my heart the pleasant satisfaction of knowing that five black bass were lying in the ice-house, and that tomorrow morning the old farmer would arrive with fresh bread and eggs. I was soon absorbed in my books.

As the night wore on the silence deepened. Even the chipmunks were still; and the boards of the floors and walls ceased creaking. I read on steadily till, from the gloomy shadows of the kitchen, came the hoarse sound of the clock striking nine. How loud the strokes sounded! They were like blows of a big hammer. I closed one book and opened another, feeling that I was just warming up to my work.

This, however, did not last long. I presently found that I was reading the same paragraphs over twice, simple paragraphs that did not require such effort. Then I noticed that my mind began to wander to other things, and the effort to recall my thoughts became harder with each digression. Concentration was growing momentarily more difficult. Presently I discovered that I had turned over two pages instead of one, and had not noticed my mistake until I was well down the page. This was becoming serious. What was the disturbing influence? It could not be physical fatigue. On the contrary, my mind was unusually alert, and in a more receptive condition than usual. I made a new and determined effort to read, and for a short time succeeded in giving my whole attention to my subject. But in a very few moments again I found myself leaning back in my chair, staring vacantly into space.

Something was evidently at work in my sub-consciousness. There was something I had neglected to do. Perhaps the kitchen door and windows were not fastened. I accordingly went to see, and found that they were! The fire perhaps needed attention. I went in to see, and found that it was all right! I looked at the lamps, went upstairs into every bedroom in turn, and then went round the house, and even into the ice-house. Nothing was wrong; everything was in its place. Yet something *was* wrong! The conviction grew stronger and stronger within me.

When I at length settled down to my books again and tried to read, I became aware, for the first time, that the room seemed growing cold. Yet the day had been oppressively warm, and evening had brought no relief. The six big lamps, moreover, gave out heat enough to warm the room pleasantly. But a chilliness, that perhaps crept up from the lake, made itself felt in the room, and caused me to get up to close the glass door opening on to the verandah.

For a brief moment I stood looking out at the shaft of light that fell from the windows and shone some little distance down the pathway, and out for a few feet into the lake.

As I looked, I saw a canoe glide into the pathway of light, and immediately crossing it, pass out of sight again into the darkness. It was perhaps a hundred feet from the shore, and it moved swiftly.

I was surprised that a canoe should pass the island at that time of night, for all the summer visitors from the other side of the lake had gone home weeks before, and the island was a long way out of any line of water traffic.

My reading from this moment did not make very good progress, for somehow the picture of that canoe, gliding so dimly and swiftly across the narrow track of light on the black waters, silhouetted itself against the background of my mind with singular vividness. It kept coming between my eyes and the printed page. The more I thought about it the more surprised I became. It was of larger build than any I had seen during the past summer months, and was more like the old Indian war canoes with the high curving bows and stern and wide beam. The more I tried to read, the less success attended my efforts; and finally I closed my books and went out on the verandah to walk up and down a bit, and shake the chilliness out of my bones.

The night was perfectly still, and as dark as imaginable. I stumbled down the path to the little landing wharf, where the water made the very faintest of gurgling under the timbers. The sound of a big tree falling in the mainland forest, far across the lake, stirred echoes in the heavy air, like the first guns of a distant night attack. No other sound disturbed the stillness that reigned supreme.

As I stood upon the wharf in the broad splash of light that followed me from the sitting-room windows, I saw another canoe cross the pathway of uncertain light upon the water, and disappear at once into the impenetrable gloom that lay beyond. This time I saw more distinctly than before. It was like the former canoe, a big birch-bark, with high-crested bows and stern and broad beam. It was paddled by two Indians, of whom the one in the stern—the steerer—appeared to be a very large man. I could see this very plainly; and though the second canoe was much nearer the island than the first, I judged that they were both on their way home to the Government Reservation, which was situated some fifteen miles away upon the mainland.

I was wondering in my mind what could possibly bring any Indians down to this part of the lake at such an hour of the night, when a third canoe, of precisely similar build, and also occupied by two Indians, passed silently round the end of the wharf. This time the canoe was very much nearer shore, and it suddenly flashed into my mind that the three canoes were in reality one and the same, and that only one canoe was circling the island!

This was by no means a pleasant reflection, because, if it were the correct solution of the unusual appearance of the three canoes in this lonely part of the lake at so late an hour, the purpose of the two men could only reasonably be considered to be in some way connected with myself. I had never known of the Indians attempting any violence upon the settlers who shared the wild, inhospitable country with them; at the same time, it was not beyond the region of possibility to suppose. . . . But then I did not care even to think of such hideous possibilities, and my imagination immediately sought relief in all manner of other solutions to the problem, which indeed came readily enough to my mind, but did not succeed in recommending themselves to my reason.

Meanwhile, by a sort of instinct, I stepped back out of the bright light in which I had hitherto been standing, and waited in the deep shadow of a rock to see if the canoe would again make its appearance. Here I could see, without being seen, and the precaution seemed a wise one.

After less than five minutes the canoe, as I had anticipated, made its fourth appearance. This time it was not twenty yards from the wharf, and I saw that the Indians meant to land. I recognised the two men as those who had passed before, and the steerer was certainly an immense fellow. It was unquestionably the same canoe. There could be no longer any doubt that for some purpose of their own the men had been going round and round the island for some time, waiting for an opportunity to land. I strained my eyes to follow them in the darkness, but the night had completely swallowed them up, and not even the faintest swish of the paddles reached my ears as the Indians plied their long and powerful strokes. The canoe would be round again in a few moments, and this time it was possible that the men might land. It was well to be prepared. I knew nothing of their intentions, and two to one (when the two are big Indians!) late at night on a lonely island was not exactly my idea of pleasant intercourse.

In a corner of the sitting-room, leaning up against the back wall, stood my Marlin rifle, with ten cartridges in the magazine and one lying snugly in the greased breech. There was just time to get up to the house and take up a position of defence in that corner. Without an instant's hesitation I ran up to the verandah, carefully picking my way among the trees, so as to avoid being seen in the light. Entering the room, I shut the door leading to the verandah, and as quickly as possible turned out every one of the six lamps. To be in a room so brilliantly lighted, where my every movement could be observed from outside, while I could see nothing but impenetrable darkness at every window, was by all laws of warfare an unnecessary concession to the enemy. And this enemy, if enemy it was to be, was far too wily and dangerous to be granted any such advantages.

I stood in the corner of the room with my back against the wall, and my hand on the cold rifle-barrel. The table, covered with my books, lay between me and the door, but for the first few minutes after the lights were out the darkness was so intense that nothing could be discerned at all. Then, very gradually, the outline of the room became visible, and the framework of the windows began to shape itself dimly before my eyes.

After a few minutes the door (its upper half of glass), and the two windows that looked out upon the front verandah, became specially distinct; and I was glad that this was so, because if the Indians came up to the house I should be able to see their approach, and gather something of their plans. Nor was I mistaken, for there presently came to my ears the peculiar hollow sound of a canoe landing and being carefully dragged up over the rocks. The paddles I distinctly heard being placed underneath, and the silence that ensued thereupon I rightly interpreted to mean that the Indians were stealthily approaching the house. . . .

While it would be absurd to claim that I was not alarmed—even frightened—at the gravity of the situation and its possible outcome, I speak the whole truth when I say that I was not overwhelmingly afraid for myself. I was conscious that even at this stage of the night I was passing into a psychical condition in which my sensations seemed no longer normal. Physical fear at no time entered into the nature of my feelings; and though I kept my hand upon my rifle the greater part of the night, I was all the time conscious that its assistance could be of little avail against the terrors that I had to face.

More than once I seemed to feel most curiously that I was in no real sense a part of the proceedings, nor actually involved in them, but that I was playing the part of a spectator—a spectator, moreover, on a psychic rather than on a material plane. Many of my sensations that night were too vague for definite description and analysis, but the main feeling that will stay with me to the end of my days is the awful horror of it all, and the miserable sensation that if the strain had lasted a little longer than was actually the case my mind must inevitably have given way.

Meanwhile I stood still in my corner, and waited patiently for what was to come. The house was as still as the grave, but the inarticulate voices of the night sang in my ears, and I seemed to hear the blood running in my veins and dancing in my pulses.

If the Indians came to the back of the house, they would find the kitchen door and window securely fastened. They could not get in there without making considerable noise, which I was bound to hear. The only mode of getting in was by means of the door that faced me, and I kept my eyes glued on that door without taking them off for the smallest fraction of a second.

My sight adapted itself every minute better to the darkness. I saw the table that nearly filled the room, and left only a narrow passage on each side. I could also make out the straight backs of the wooden chairs pressed up against it, and could even distinguish my papers and inkstand lying on the white oilcloth covering. I thought of the gay faces that had gathered round that table during the summer, and I longed for the sunlight as I had never longed for it before.

Less than three feet to my left the passage-way led to the kitchen, and the stairs leading to the bedrooms above commenced in this passage-way, but almost in the sitting-room itself. Through the windows I could see the dim motionless outlines of the trees: not a leaf stirred, not a branch moved.

A few moments of this awful silence, and then I was aware of a soft tread on the boards of the verandah, so stealthy that it seemed an impression directly on my brain rather than upon the nerves of hearing. Immediately afterwards a black figure darkened the glass door, and I perceived that a face was pressed against the upper panes. A shiver ran down my back, and my hair was conscious of a tendency to rise and stand at right angles to my head.

It was the figure of an Indian, broad-shouldered and immense; indeed, the largest figure of a man I have ever seen outside of a circus hall. By some power of light that seemed to generate itself in the brain, I saw the strong dark face with the aquiline nose and high cheek-bones flattened against the glass. The direction of the gaze I could not determine; but faint gleams of light as the big eyes rolled round and showed their whites, told me plainly that no corner of the room escaped their searching.

For what seemed fully five minutes the dark figure stood there, with the huge shoulders bent forward so as to bring the head down to the level of the glass; while behind him, though not nearly so large, the shadowy form of the other Indian swayed to and fro like a bent tree. While I waited in an agony of suspense and agitation for their next movement little currents of icy sensation ran up and down my spine and my heart seemed alternately to stop beating and then start off again with terrifying rapidity. They must have heard its thumping and the singing of the blood in my head! Moreover, I was conscious, as I felt a cold stream of perspiration trickle down my face, of a desire to scream, to shout, to bang the walls like a child, to make a noise, or do anything that would relieve the suspense and bring things to a speedy climax.

It was probably this inclination that led me to another discovery, for when I tried to bring my rifle from behind my back to raise it and have it pointed at the door ready to fire, I found that I was powerless to move. The muscles, paralysed by this strange fear, refused to obey the will. Here indeed was a terrifying complication!

There was a faint sound of rattling at the brass knob, and the door was pushed open a couple of inches. A pause of a few seconds, and it was pushed open still further. Without a sound of footsteps that was appreciable to my ears, the two figures glided into the room, and the man behind gently closed the door after him.

They were alone with me between the four walls. Could they see me standing there, so still and straight in my corner? Had they, perhaps, already seen me? My blood surged and sang like the roll of drums in an orchestra; and though I did my best to suppress my breathing, it sounded like the rushing of wind through a pneumatic tube.

My suspense as to the next move was soon at an end—only, however, to give place to a new and keener alarm. The men had hitherto exchanged no words and no signs, but there were general indications of a movement across the room, and whichever way they went they would have to pass round the table. If they came my way they would have to pass within six inches of my person.

While I was considering this very disagreeable possibility, I perceived that the smaller Indian (smaller by comparison) suddenly raised his arm and pointed to the ceiling. The other fellow raised his head and followed the direction of his companion's arm. I began to understand at last. They were going upstairs, and the room directly overhead to which they pointed had been until this night my bedroom. It was the room in which I had experienced that very morning so strange a sensation of fear, and but for which I should then have been lying asleep in the narrow bed against the window.

The Indians then began to move silently around the room; they were going upstairs, and they were coming round my side of the table. So stealthy were their movements that, but for the abnormally sensitive state of the nerves, I should never have heard them. As it was, their cat-like tread was distinctly audible. Like two monstrous black cats they came round the table toward me, and for the first time I perceived that the smaller of the two dragged something along the floor behind him. As it trailed along over the floor with a soft, sweeping sound, I somehow got the impression that it was a large dead thing with outstretched wings, or a large, spreading cedar branch. Whatever it was, I was unable to see it even in outline, and I was too terrified, even had I possessed the power over my muscles, to move my neck forward in the effort to determine its nature.

Nearer and nearer they came. The leader rested a giant hand upon the table as he moved. My lips were glued together, and the air seemed to burn in my nostrils. I tried to close my eyes, so that I might not see as they passed me; but my eyelids had stiffened, and refused to obey. Would they never get by me? Sensation seemed also to have left my legs, and it was as if I were standing on mere supports of wood or stone. Worse still, I was conscious that I was losing the power of balance, the power to stand upright, or even to lean backwards against the wall. Some force was drawing me forward, and a dizzy terror seized me that I should lose my balance, and topple forward against the Indians just as they were in the act of passing me.

Even moments drawn out into hours must come to an end some time, and almost before I knew it the figures had passed me and had their feet upon the lower step of the stairs leading to the upper bedrooms. There could not have been six inches between us, and yet I was conscious only of a current of cold air that followed them. They had not touched me, and I was convinced that they had not seen me. Even the trailing thing on the floor behind them had not touched my feet, as I had dreaded it would, and on such an occasion as this I was grateful even for the smallest mercies.

The absence of the Indians from my immediate neighbourhood brought little sense of relief. I stood shivering and shuddering in my corner, and, beyond being able to breathe more freely, I felt no whit less uncomfortable. Also, I was aware that a certain light, which, without apparent source or rays, had enabled me to follow their every gesture and movement, had gone out of the room with their departure. An unnatural darkness now filled the room, and pervaded its every corner so that I could barely make out the positions of the windows and the glass doors.

As I said before, my condition was evidently an abnormal one. The capacity for feeling surprise seemed, as in dreams, to be wholly absent.

My senses recorded with unusual accuracy every smallest occurrence, but I was able to draw only the simplest deductions.

The Indians soon reached the top of the stairs, and there they halted for a moment. I had not the faintest clue as to their next movement. They appeared to hesitate. They were listening attentively. Then I heard one of them, who by the weight of his soft tread must have been the giant, cross the narrow corridor and enter the room directly overhead—my own little bedroom. But for the insistence of that unaccountable dread I had experienced there in the morning, I should at that very moment have been lying in the bed with the big Indian in the room standing beside me.

For the space of a hundred seconds there was silence, such as might have existed before the birth of sound. It was followed by a long quivering shriek of terror, which rang out into the night, and ended in a short gulp before it had run its full course. At the same moment the other Indian left his place at the head of the stairs, and joined his companion in the bedroom. I heard the "thing" trailing behind him along the floor. A thud followed, as of something heavy falling, and then all became as still and silent as before.

It was at this point that the atmosphere, surcharged all day with the electricity of a fierce storm, found relief in a dancing flash of brilliant lightning simultaneously with a crash of loudest thunder. For five seconds every article in the room was visible to me with amazing distinctness, and through the windows I saw the tree trunks standing in solemn rows. The thunder pealed and echoed across the lake and among the distant islands, and the flood-gates of heaven then opened and let out their rain in streaming torrents.

The drops fell with a swift rushing sound upon the still waters of the lake, which leaped up to meet them, and pattered with the rattle of shot on the leaves of the maples and the roof of the cottage. A moment later, and another flash, even more brilliant and of longer duration than the first, lit up the sky from zenith to horizon, and bathed the room momentarily in dazzling whiteness. I could see the rain glistening on the leaves and branches outside. The wind rose suddenly, and in less than a minute the storm that had been gathering all day burst forth in its full fury.

Above all the noisy voices of the elements, the slightest sounds in the room overhead made themselves heard, and in the few seconds of deep silence that followed the shriek of terror and pain I was aware that the movements had commenced again. The men were leaving the room and approaching the top of the stairs. A short pause, and they began to descend. Behind them, tumbling from step to step, I could hear that trailing "thing" being dragged along. It had become ponderous!

I awaited their approach with a degree of calmness, almost of apathy, which was only explicable on the ground that after a certain point Nature applies her own anæsthetic, and a merciful condition of numbness supervenes. On they came, step by step, nearer and nearer, with the shuffling sound of the burden behind growing louder as they approached.

They were already half-way down the stairs when I was galvanised afresh into a condition of terror by the consideration of a new and horrible possibility. It was the reflection that if another vivid flash of lightning were to come when the shadowy procession was in the room, perhaps when it was actually passing in front of me, I should see everything in detail, and worse, be seen myself! I could only hold my breath and wait—wait while the minutes lengthened into hours, and the procession made its slow progress round the room.

The Indians had reached the foot of the staircase. The form of the huge leader loomed in the doorway of the passage, and the burden with an ominous thud had dropped from the last step to the floor. There was a moment's pause while I saw the Indian turn and stoop to assist his companion. Then the procession moved forward again, entered the room close on my left, and began to move slowly round my side of the table. The leader was already beyond me, and his companion, dragging on the floor behind him the burden, whose confused outline I could dimly make out, was exactly in front of me, when the cavalcade came to a dead halt. At the same moment, with the strange suddenness of thunderstorms, the splash of the rain ceased altogether, and the wind died away into utter silence.

For the space of five seconds my heart seemed to stop beating, and then the worst came. A double flash of lightning lit up the room and its contents with merciless vividness.

The huge Indian leader stood a few feet past me on my right. One leg was stretched forward in the act of taking a step. His immense shoulders were turned toward his companion, and in all their magnificent fierceness I saw the outline of his features. His gaze was directed upon the burden his companion was dragging along the floor; but his profile, with the big aquiline nose, high cheekbone, straight black hair and bold chin, burnt itself in that brief instant into my brain, never again to fade.

Dwarfish, compared with this gigantic figure, appeared the proportions of the other Indian, who, within twelve inches of my face, was stooping over the thing he was dragging in a position that lent to his person the additional horror of deformity. And the burden, lying upon a sweeping cedar branch which he held and dragged by a long stem, was the body of a white man. The scalp had been neatly lifted, and blood lay in a broad smear upon the cheeks and forehead.

Then, for the first time that night, the terror that had paralysed my muscles and my will lifted its unholy spell from my soul. With a loud cry I stretched out my arms to seize the big Indian by the throat, and, grasping only air, tumbled forward unconscious upon the ground.

I had recognised the body, and *the face was my own!*. . . .

It was bright daylight when a man's voice recalled me to consciousness. I was lying where I had fallen, and the farmer was standing in the room with the loaves of bread in his hands. The horror of the night was still in my heart, and as the bluff settler helped me to my feet and picked up the rifle which had fallen with me, with many questions and expressions of condolence, I imagine my brief replies were neither self-explanatory nor even intelligible.

That day, after a thorough and fruitless search of the house, I left the island, and went over to spend my last ten days with the farmer; and when the time came for me to leave, the necessary reading had been accomplished, and my nerves had completely recovered their balance.

On the day of my departure the farmer started early in his big boat with my belongings to row to the point, twelve miles distant, where a little steamer ran twice a week for the accommodation of hunters. Late in the afternoon I went off in another direction in my canoe, wishing to see the island once again, where I had been the victim of so strange an experience.

In due course I arrived there, and made a tour of the island. I also made a search of the little house, and it was not without a curious sensation in my heart that I entered the little upstairs bedroom. There seemed nothing unusual.

Just after I re-embarked, I saw a canoe gliding ahead of me around the curve of the island. A canoe was an unusual sight at this time of the year, and this one seemed to have sprung from nowhere. Altering my course a little, I watched it disappear around the next projecting point of rock. It had high curving bows, and there were two Indians in it. I lingered with some excitement, to see if it would appear again round the other side of the island; and in less than five minutes it came into view. There were less than two hundred yards between us, and the Indians, sitting on their haunches, were paddling swiftly in my direction.

I never paddled faster in my life than I did in those next few minutes. When I turned to look again, the Indians had altered their course, and were again circling the island.

The sun was sinking behind the forests on the mainland, and the crimson-coloured clouds of sunset were reflected in the waters of the lake, when I looked round for the last time, and saw the big bark canoe and its two dusky occupants still going round the island. Then the shadows deepened rapidly; the lake grew black, and the night wind blew its first breath in my face as I turned a corner, and a projecting bluff of rock hid from my view both island and canoe.

A Case of Eavesdropping

Jim Shorthouse was the sort of fellow who always made a mess of things. Everything with which his hands or mind came into contact issued from such contact in an unqualified and irremediable state of mess. His college days were a mess: he was twice rusticated. His schooldays were a mess: he went to half a dozen, each passing him on to the next with a worse character and in a more developed state of mess. His early boyhood was the sort of mess that copy-books and dictionaries spell with a big "M," and his babyhood—ugh! was the embodiment of howling, yowling, screaming mess.

At the age of forty, however, there came a change in his troubled life, when he met a girl with half a million in her own right, who consented to marry him, and who very soon succeeded in reducing his most messy existence into a state of comparative order and system.

Certain incidents, important and otherwise, of Jim's life would never have come to be told here but for the fact that in getting into his "messes" and out of them again he succeeded in drawing himself into the atmosphere of peculiar circumstances and strange happenings. He attracted to his path the curious adventures of life as unfailingly as meat attracts flies, and jam wasps. It is to the meat and jam of his life, so to speak, that he owes his experiences; his afterlife was all pudding, which attracts nothing but greedy children. With marriage the interest of his life ceased for all but one person, and his path became regular as the sun's instead of erratic as a comet's.

The first experience in order of time that he related to me shows that somewhere latent behind his disarranged nervous system there lay psychic perceptions of an uncommon order. About the age of twenty-two—I think after his second rustication—his father's purse and patience had equally given out, and Jim found himself stranded high and dry in a large American city. High and dry! And the only clothes that had no holes in them safely in the keeping of his uncle's wardrobe.

Careful reflection on a bench in one of the city parks led him to the conclusion that the only thing to do was to persuade the city editor of one of the daily journals that he possessed an observant mind and a ready pen, and that he could "do good work for your paper, sir, as a reporter." This, then, he did, standing at a most unnatural angle between the editor and the window to conceal the whereabouts of the holes.

"Guess we'll have to give you a week's trial," said the editor, who, ever on the lookout for good chance material, took on shoals of men in that way and retained on the average one man per shoal. Anyhow it gave Jim Shorthouse the wherewithal to sew up the holes and relieve his uncle's wardrobe of its burden.

Then he went to find living quarters; and in this proceeding his unique characteristics already referred to—what theosophists would call his Karma—began unmistakably to assert themselves, for it was in the house he eventually selected that this sad tale took place.

There are no "diggings" in American cities. The alternatives for small incomes are grim enough—rooms in a boarding-house where meals are served, or in a room-house where no meals are served—not even breakfast. Rich people live in palaces, of course, but Jim had nothing to do with "sich-like." His horizon was bounded by boarding-houses and room-houses; and, owing to the necessary irregularity of his meals and hours, he took the latter.

It was a large, gaunt-looking place in a side street, with dirty windows and a creaking iron gate, but the rooms were large, and the one he selected and paid for in advance was on the top floor. The landlady looked gaunt and dusty as the house, and quite as old. Her eyes were green and faded, and her features large.

"Waal," she twanged, with her electrifying Western drawl, "that's the room, if you like it, and that's the price I said. Now, if you want it, why, just say so; and if you don't, why, it don't hurt me any."

Jim wanted to shake her, but he feared the clouds of long-accumulated dust in her clothes, and as the price and size of the room suited him, he decided to take it.

"Anyone else on this floor?" he asked.

She looked at him queerly out of her faded eyes before she answered.

"None of my guests ever put such questions to me before," she said; "but I guess you're different. Why, there's no one at all but an old gent that's stayed here every bit of five years. He's over thar," pointing to the end of the passage.

"Ah! I see," said Shorthouse feebly. "So I'm alone up here?"

"Reckon you are, pretty near," she twanged out, ending the conversation abruptly by turning her back on her new "guest," and going slowly and deliberately downstairs.

The newspaper work kept Shorthouse out most of the night. Three times a week he got home at 1 a.m., and three times at 3 a.m. The room proved comfortable enough, and he paid for a second week. His unusual hours had so far prevented his meeting any inmates of the house, and not a sound had been heard from the "old gent" who shared the floor with him. It seemed a very quiet house.

One night, about the middle of the second week, he came home tired after a long day's work. The lamp that usually stood all night in the hall had burned itself out, and he had to stumble upstairs in the dark. He made considerable noise in doing so, but nobody seemed to be disturbed. The whole house was utterly quiet, and probably everybody was asleep. There were no lights under any of the doors. All was in darkness. It was after two o'clock.

After reading some English letters that had come during the day, and dipping for a few minutes into a book, he became drowsy and got ready for bed. Just as he was about to get in between the sheets, he stopped for a moment and listened. There rose in the night, as he did so, the sound of steps somewhere in the house below. Listening attentively, he heard that it was somebody coming upstairs—a heavy tread, and the owner taking no pains to step quietly. On it came up the stairs, tramp, tramp, tramp—evidently the tread of a big man, and one in something of a hurry.

At once thoughts connected somehow with fire and police flashed through Jim's brain, but there were no sounds of voices with the steps, and he reflected in the same moment that it could only be the old gentleman keeping late hours and tumbling upstairs in the darkness. He was in the act of turning out the gas and stepping into bed, when the house resumed its former stillness by the footsteps suddenly coming to a dead stop immediately outside his own room.

With his hand on the gas, Shorthouse paused a moment before turning it out to see if the steps would go on again, when he was startled by a loud knocking on his door. Instantly, in obedience to a curious and unexplained instinct, he turned out the light, leaving himself and the room in total darkness.

He had scarcely taken a step across the room to open the door, when a voice from the other side of the wall, so close it almost sounded in his ear, exclaimed in German, "Is that you, father? Come in."

The speaker was a man in the next room, and the knocking, after all, had not been on his own door, but on that of the adjoining chamber, which he had supposed to be vacant.

Almost before the man in the passage had time to answer in German, "Let me in at once," Jim heard someone cross the floor and unlock the door. Then it was slammed to with a bang, and there was audible the sound of footsteps about the room, and of chairs being drawn up to a table and knocking against furniture on the way. The men seemed wholly regardless of their neighbour's comfort, for they made noise enough to waken the dead.

"Serves me right for taking a room in such a cheap hole," reflected Jim in the darkness. "I wonder whom she's let the room to!"

The two rooms, the landlady had told him, were originally one. She had put up a thin partition—just a row of boards—to increase her income. The doors were adjacent, and only separated by the massive upright beam between them. When one was opened or shut the other rattled.

With utter indifference to the comfort of the other sleepers in the house, the two Germans had meanwhile commenced to talk both at once and at the top of their voices. They talked emphatically, even angrily. The words "Father" and "Otto" were freely used. Shorthouse understood German, but as he stood listening for the first minute or two, an eavesdropper in spite of himself, it was difficult to make head or tail of the talk, for neither would give way to the other, and the jumble of guttural sounds and unfinished sentences was wholly unintelligible. Then, very suddenly, both voices dropped together; and, after a moment's pause, the deep tones of one of them, who seemed to be the "father," said, with the utmost distinctness—

"You mean, Otto, that you refuse to get it?"

There was a sound of someone shuffling in the chair before the answer came. "I mean that I don't know how to get it. It is so much, father. It is *too* much. A part of it—"

"A part of it!" cried the other, with an angry oath, "a part of it, when ruin and disgrace are already in the house, is worse than useless. If you can get half you can get all, you wretched fool. Half-measures only damn all concerned."

"You told me last time—" began the other firmly, but was not allowed to finish. A succession of horrible oaths drowned his sentence, and the father went on, in a voice vibrating with anger—

"You know she will give you anything. You have only been married a few months. If you ask and give a plausible reason you can get all we want and more. You can ask it temporarily. All will be paid back. It will re-establish the firm, and she will never know what was done with it. With that amount, Otto, you know I can recoup all these terrible losses, and in less than a year all will be repaid. But without it. . . . You must get it, Otto. Hear me, you must. Am I to be arrested for the misuse of trust moneys? Is our honoured name to be cursed and spat on?" The old man choked and stammered in his anger and desperation.

Shorthouse stood shivering in the darkness and listening in spite of himself. The conversation had carried him along with it, and he had been for some reason afraid to let his neighbourhood be known. But at this point he realised that he had listened too long and that he must inform the two men that they could be overheard to every single syllable. So he coughed loudly, and at the same time rattled the handle of his door. It seemed to have no effect, for the voices continued just as loudly as before, the son protesting and the father growing more and more angry. He coughed again persistently, and also contrived purposely in the darkness to tumble against the partition, feeling the thin boards yield easily under his weight, and making a considerable noise in so doing. But the voices went on unconcernedly, and louder than ever. Could it be possible they had not heard?

By this time Jim was more concerned about his own sleep than the morality of overhearing the private scandals of his neighbours, and he went out into the passage and knocked smartly at their door. Instantly, as if by magic, the sounds ceased. Everything dropped into utter silence. There was no light under the door and not a whisper could be heard within. He knocked again, but received no answer.

"Gentlemen," he began at length, with his lips close to the keyhole and in German, "please do not talk so loud. I can overhear all you say in the next room. Besides, it is very late, and I wish to sleep."

He paused and listened, but no answer was forthcoming. He turned the handle and found the door was locked. Not a sound broke the stillness of the night except the faint swish of the wind over the skylight and the creaking of a board here and there in the house below. The cold air of a very early morning crept down the passage, and made him shiver. The silence of the house began to impress him disagreeably. He looked behind him and about him, hoping, and yet fearing, that something would break the stillness. The voices still seemed to ring on in his ears; but that sudden silence, when he knocked at the door, affected him far more unpleasantly than the voices, and put strange thoughts in his brain—thoughts he did not like or approve.

Moving stealthily from the door, he peered over the banisters into the space below. It was like a deep vault that might conceal in its shadows anything that was not good. It was not difficult to fancy he saw an indistinct moving to-and-fro below him. Was that a figure sitting on the stairs peering up obliquely at him out of hideous eyes? Was that a sound of whispering and shuffling down there in the dark halls and forsaken landings? Was it something more than the inarticulate murmur of the night?

The wind made an effort overhead, singing over the skylight, and the door behind him rattled and made him start. He turned to go back to his room, and the draught closed the door slowly in his face as if there were someone pressing against it from the other side. When he pushed it open and went in, a hundred shadowy forms seemed to dart swiftly and silently back to their corners and hiding-places. But in the adjoining room the sounds had entirely ceased, and Shorthouse soon crept into bed, and left the house with its inmates, waking or sleeping, to take care of themselves, while he entered the region of dreams and silence.

Next day, strong in the common sense that the sunlight brings, he determined to lodge a complaint against the noisy occupants of the next room and make the landlady request them to modify their voices at such late hours of the night and morning. But it so happened that she was not to be seen that day, and when he returned from the office at midnight it was, of course, too late.

Looking under the door as he came up to bed he noticed that there was no light, and concluded that the Germans were not in. So much the better. He went to sleep about one o'clock, fully decided that if they came up later and woke him with their horrible noises he would not rest till he had roused the landlady and made her reprove them with that authoritative twang, in which every word was like the lash of a metallic whip.

However, there proved to be no need for such drastic measures, for Shorthouse slumbered peacefully all night, and his dreams—chiefly of the fields of grain and flocks of sheep on the far-away farms of his father's estate—were permitted to run their fanciful course unbroken.

Two nights later, however, when he came home tired out, after a difficult day, and wet and blown about by one of the wickedest storms he had ever seen, his dreams—always of the fields and sheep—were not destined to be so undisturbed.

He had already dozed off in that delicious glow that follows the removal of wet clothes and the immediate snuggling under warm blankets, when his consciousness, hovering on the borderland between sleep and waking, was vaguely troubled by a sound that rose indistinctly from the depths of the house, and, between the gusts of wind and rain, reached his ears with an accompanying sense of uneasiness and discomfort. It rose on the night air with some pretence of regularity, dying away again in the roar of the wind to reassert itself distantly in the deep, brief hushes of the storm.

For a few minutes Jim's dreams were coloured only—tinged, as it were, by this impression of fear approaching from somewhere insensibly upon him. His consciousness, at first, refused to be drawn back from that enchanted region where it had wandered, and he did not immediately awaken. But the nature of his dreams changed unpleasantly. He saw the sheep suddenly run huddled together, as though frightened by the neighbourhood of an enemy, while the fields of waving corn became agitated as though some monster were moving uncouthly among the crowded stalks. The sky grew dark, and in his dream an awful sound came somewhere from the clouds. It was in reality the sound downstairs growing more distinct.

Shorthouse shifted uneasily across the bed with something like a groan of distress. The next minute he awoke, and found himself sitting straight up in bed—listening. Was it a nightmare? Had he been dreaming evil dreams, that his flesh crawled and the hair stirred on his head?

The room was dark and silent, but outside the wind howled dismally and drove the rain with repeated assaults against the rattling windows. How nice it would be—the thought flashed through his mind—if all winds, like the west wind, went down with the sun! They made such fiendish noises at night, like the crying of angry voices. In the daytime they had such a different sound. If only——

Hark! It was no dream after all, for the sound was momentarily growing louder, and its *cause* was coming up the stairs. He found himself speculating feebly what this cause might be, but the sound was still too indistinct to enable him to arrive at any definite conclusion.

The voice of a church clock striking two made itself heard above the wind. It was just about the hour when the Germans had commenced their performance three nights before. Shorthouse made up his mind that if they began it again he would not put up with it for very long. Yet he was already horribly conscious of the difficulty he would have of getting out of bed. The clothes were so warm and comforting against his back. The sound, still steadily coming nearer, had by this time become differentiated from the confused clamour of the elements, and had resolved itself into the footsteps of one or more persons.

"The Germans, hang 'em!" thought Jim. "But what on earth is the matter with me? I never felt so queer in all my life."

He was trembling all over, and felt as cold as though he were in a freezing atmosphere. His nerves were steady enough, and he felt no diminution of physical courage, but he was conscious of a curious sense of malaise and trepidation, such as even the most vigorous men have been known to experience when in the first grip of some horrible and deadly disease. As the footsteps approached this feeling of weakness increased. He felt a strange lassitude creeping over him, a sort of exhaustion, accompanied by a growing numbness in the extremities, and a sensation of dreaminess in the head, as if perhaps the consciousness were leaving its accustomed seat in the brain and preparing to act on another plane. Yet, strange to say, as the vitality was slowly withdrawn from his body, his senses seemed to grow more acute.

Meanwhile the steps were already on the landing at the top of the stairs, and Shorthouse, still sitting upright in bed, heard a heavy body brush past his door and along the wall outside, almost immediately afterwards the loud knocking of someone's knuckles on the door of the adjoining room.

Instantly, though so far not a sound had proceeded from within, he heard, through the thin partition, a chair pushed back and a man quickly cross the floor and open the door.

"Ah! it's you," he heard in the son's voice. Had the fellow, then, been sitting silently in there all this time, waiting for his father's arrival? To Shorthouse it came not as a pleasant reflection by any means.

There was no answer to this dubious greeting, but the door was closed quickly, and then there was a sound as if a bag or parcel had been thrown on a wooden table and had slid some distance across it before stopping.

"What's that?" asked the son, with anxiety in his tone.

"You may know before I go," returned the other gruffly. Indeed his voice was more than gruff: it betrayed ill-suppressed passion.

Shorthouse was conscious of a strong desire to stop the conversation before it proceeded any further, but somehow or other his will was not equal to the task, and he could not get out of bed. The conversation went on, every tone and inflexion distinctly audible above the noise of the storm.

In a low voice the father continued. Jim missed some of the words at the beginning of the sentence. It ended with: " . . . but now they've all left, and I've managed to get up to you. You know what I've come for." There was distinct menace in his tone.

"Yes," returned the other; "I have been waiting."

"And the money?" asked the father impatiently.

No answer.

"You've had three days to get it in, and I've contrived to stave off the worst so far—but tomorrow is the end."

No answer.

"Speak, Otto! What have you got for me? Speak, my son; for God's sake, tell me."

There was a moment's silence, during which the old man's vibrating accents seemed to echo through the rooms. Then came in a low voice the answer—

"I have nothing."

"Otto!" cried the other with passion, "nothing!"

"I can get nothing," came almost in a whisper.

"You lie!" cried the other, in a half-stifled voice. "I swear you lie. Give me the money."

A chair was heard scraping along the floor. Evidently the men had been sitting over the table, and one of them had risen. Shorthouse heard the bag or parcel drawn across the table, and then a step as if one of the men was crossing to the door.

"Father, what's in that? I must know," said Otto, with the first signs of determination in his voice. There must have been an effort on the son's part to gain possession of the parcel in question, and on the father's to retain it, for between them it fell to the ground. A curious rattle followed its contact with the floor. Instantly there were sounds of a scuffle. The men were struggling for the possession of the box. The elder man with oaths, and blasphemous imprecations, the other with short gasps that betokened the strength of his efforts. It was of short duration, and the younger man had evidently won, for a minute later was heard his angry exclamation.

"I knew it. Her jewels! You scoundrel, you shall never have them. It is a crime."

The elder man uttered a short, guttural laugh, which froze Jim's blood and made his skin creep. No word was spoken, and for the space of ten seconds there was a living silence. Then the air trembled with the sound of a thud, followed immediately by a groan and the crash of a heavy body falling over on to the table. A second later there was a lurching from the table on to the floor and against the partition that separated the rooms. The bed quivered an instant at the shock, but the unholy spell was lifted from his soul and Jim Shorthouse sprang out of bed and across the floor in a single bound. He knew that ghastly murder had been done—the murder by a father of his son.

With shaking fingers but a determined heart he lit the gas, and the first thing in which his eyes corroborated the evidence of his ears was the horrifying detail that the lower portion of the partition bulged unnaturally into his own room. The glaring paper with which it was covered had cracked under the tension and the boards beneath it bent inwards towards him. What hideous load was behind them, he shuddered to think.

All this he saw in less than a second. Since the final lurch against the wall not a sound had proceeded from the room, not even a groan or a footstep. All was still but the howl of the wind, which to his ears had in it a note of triumphant horror.

Shorthouse was in the act of leaving the room to rouse the house and send for the police—in fact his hand was already on the door-knob—when something in the room arrested his attention. Out of the corner of his eyes he thought he caught sight of something moving. He was sure of it, and turning his eyes in the direction, he found he was not mistaken.

Something was creeping slowly towards him along the floor. It was something dark and serpentine in shape, and it came from the place where the partition bulged. He stooped down to examine it with feelings of intense horror and repugnance, and he discovered that it was moving toward him from the *other side* of the wall. His eyes were fascinated, and for the moment he was unable to move. Silently, slowly, from side to side like a thick worm, it crawled forward into the room beneath his frightened eyes, until at length he could stand it no longer and stretched out his arm to touch it. But at the instant of contact he withdrew his hand with a suppressed scream. It was sluggish—and it was warm! and he saw that his fingers were stained with living crimson.

A second more, and Shorthouse was out in the passage with his hand on the door of the next room. It was locked. He plunged forward with all his weight against it, and, the lock giving way, he fell headlong into a room that was pitch dark and very cold. In a moment he was on his feet again and trying to penetrate the blackness. Not a sound, not a movement. Not even the sense of a presence. It was empty, miserably empty!

Across the room he could trace the outline of a window with rain streaming down the outside, and the blurred lights of the city beyond. But the room was empty, appallingly empty; and so still. He stood there, cold as ice, staring, shivering listening. Suddenly there was a step behind him and a light flashed into the room, and when he turned quickly with his arm up as if to ward off a terrific blow he found himself face to face with the landlady. Instantly the reaction began to set in.

It was nearly three o'clock in the morning, and he was standing there with bare feet and striped pyjamas in a small room, which in the merciful light he perceived to be absolutely empty, carpetless, and without a stick of furniture, or even a window-blind. There he stood staring at the disagreeable landlady. And there she stood too, staring and silent, in a black wrapper, her head almost bald, her face white as chalk, shading a sputtering candle with one bony hand and peering over it at him with her blinking green eyes. She looked positively hideous.

"Waal?" she drawled at length, "I heard yer right enough. Guess you couldn't sleep! Or just prowlin' round a bit—is that it?"

The empty room, the absence of all traces of the recent tragedy, the silence, the hour, his striped pyjamas and bare feet—everything together combined to deprive him momentarily of speech. He stared at her blankly without a word.

"Waal?" clanked the awful voice.

"My dear woman," he burst out finally, "there's been something awful—" So far his desperation took him, but no farther. He positively stuck at the substantive.

"Oh! there hasn't been nothin'," she said slowly still peering at him. "I reckon you've only seen and heard what the others did. I never can keep folks on this floor long. Most of 'em catch on sooner or later—that is, the ones that's kind of quick and sensitive. Only you being an Englishman I thought you wouldn't mind. Nothin' really happens; it's only thinkin' like."

Shorthouse was beside himself. He felt ready to pick her up and drop her over the banisters, candle and all.

"Look there," he said, pointing at her within an inch of her blinking eyes with the fingers that had touched the oozing blood; "look there, my good woman. Is that only thinking?"

She stared a minute, as if not knowing what he meant.

"I guess so," she said at length.

He followed her eyes, and to his amazement saw that his fingers were as white as usual, and quite free from the awful stain that had been there ten minutes before. There was no sign of blood. No amount of staring could bring it back. Had he gone out of his mind? Had his eyes and ears played such tricks with him? Had his senses become false and perverted? He dashed past the landlady, out into the passage, and gained his own room in a couple of strides. Whew! . . . the partition no longer bulged. The paper was not torn. There was no creeping, crawling thing on the faded old carpet.

"It's all over now," drawled the metallic voice behind him. "I'm going to bed again."

He turned and saw the landlady slowly going downstairs again, still shading the candle with her hand and peering up at him from time to time as she moved. A black, ugly, unwholesome object, he thought, as she disappeared into the darkness below, and the last flicker of her candle threw a queer-shaped shadow along the wall and over the ceiling.

Without hesitating a moment, Shorthouse threw himself into his clothes and went out of the house. He preferred the storm to the horrors of that top floor, and he walked the streets till daylight. In the evening he told the landlady he would leave next day, in spite of her assurances that nothing more would happen.

"It never comes back," she said—"that is, not after he's killed."

Shorthouse gasped.

"You gave me a lot for my money," he growled.

"Waal, it aren't my show," she drawled. "I'm no spirit medium. You take chances. Some'll sleep right along and never hear nothin'. Others, like yourself, are different and get the whole thing."

"Who's the old gentleman?—does he hear it?" asked Jim.

"There's no old gentleman at all," she answered coolly. "I just told you that to make you feel easy like in case you did hear anythin'. You were all alone on the floor."

"Say now," she went on, after a pause in which Shorthouse could think of nothing to say but unpublishable things, "say now, do tell, did you feel sort of cold when the show was on, sort of tired and weak, I mean, as if you might be going to die?"

"How can I say?" he answered savagely; "what I felt God only knows."

"Waal, but He won't tell," she drawled out. "Only I was wonderin' how you really did feel, because the man who had that room last was found one morning in bed—"

"In bed?"

"He was dead. He was the one before you. Oh! You don't need to get rattled so. You're all right. And it all really happened, they do say. This house used to be a private residence some twenty-five years ago, and a German family of the name of Steinhardt lived here. They had a big business in Wall Street, and stood 'way up in things."

"Ah!" said her listener.

"Oh yes, they did, right at the top, till one fine day it all bust and the old man skipped with the boodle—"

"Skipped with the boodle?"

"That's so," she said; "got clear away with all the money, and the son was found dead in his house, committed soocide it was thought. Though there was some as said he couldn't have stabbed himself and fallen in that position. They said he was murdered. The father died in prison. They tried to fasten the murder on him, but there was no motive, or no evidence, or no somethin'. I forget now."

"Very pretty," said Shorthouse.

"I'll show you somethin' mighty queer any-ways," she drawled, "if you'll come upstairs a minute. I've heard the steps and voices lots of times; they don't pheaze me any. I'd just as lief hear so many dogs barkin'. You'll find the whole story in the newspapers if you look it up—not what goes on here, but the story of the Germans. My house would be ruined if they told all, and I'd sue for damages."

They reached the bedroom, and the woman went in and pulled up the edge of the carpet where Shorthouse had seen the blood soaking in the previous night.

"Look thar, if you feel like it," said the old hag. Stooping down, he saw a dark, dull stain in the boards that corresponded exactly to the shape and position of the blood as he had seen it.

That night he slept in a hotel, and the following day sought new quarters. In the newspapers on file in his office after a long search he found twenty years back the detailed story, substantially as the woman had said, of Steinhardt & Co.'s failure, the absconding and subsequent arrest of the senior partner, and the suicide, or murder, of his son Otto. The landlady's room-house had formerly been their private residence.

The Empty House

Certain houses, like certain persons, manage somehow to proclaim at once their character for evil. In the case of the latter, no particular feature need betray them; they may boast an open countenance and an ingenuous smile; and yet a little of their company leaves the unalterable conviction that there is something radically amiss with their being: that they are evil. Willy nilly, they seem to communicate an atmosphere of secret and wicked thoughts which makes those in their immediate neighbourhood shrink from them as from a thing diseased.

And, perhaps, with houses the same principle is operative, and it is the aroma of evil deeds committed under a particular roof, long after the actual doers have passed away, that makes the gooseflesh come and the hair rise. Something of the original passion of the evil-doer, and of the horror felt by his victim, enters the heart of the innocent watcher, and he becomes suddenly conscious of tingling nerves, creeping skin, and a chilling of the blood. He is terror-stricken without apparent cause.

There was manifestly nothing in the external appearance of this particular house to bear out the tales of the horror that was said to reign within. It was neither lonely nor unkempt. It stood, crowded into a corner of the square, and looked exactly like the houses on either side of it. It had the same number of windows as its neighbours; the same balcony overlooking the gardens; the same white steps leading up to the heavy black front door; and, in the rear, there was the same narrow strip of green, with neat box borders, running up to the wall that divided it from the backs of the adjoining houses. Apparently, too, the number of chimney pots on the roof was the same; the breadth and angle of the eaves; and even the height of the dirty area railings.

And yet this house in the square, that seemed precisely similar to its fifty ugly neighbours, was as a matter of fact entirely different—horribly different.

Wherein lay this marked, invisible difference is impossible to say. It cannot be ascribed wholly to the imagination, because persons who had spent some time in the house, knowing nothing of the facts, had declared positively that certain rooms were so disagreeable they would rather die than enter them again, and that the atmosphere of the whole house produced in them symptoms of a genuine terror; while the series of innocent tenants who had tried to live in it and been forced to decamp at the shortest possible notice, was indeed little less than a scandal in the town.

When Shorthouse arrived to pay a "weekend" visit to his Aunt Julia in her little house on the seafront at the other end of the town, he found her charged to the brim with mystery and excitement. He had only received her telegram that morning, and he had come anticipating boredom; but the moment he touched her hand and kissed her apple-skin wrinkled cheek, he caught the first wave of her electrical condition. The impression deepened when he learned that there were to be no other visitors, and that he had been telegraphed for with a very special object.

Something was in the wind, and the "something" would doubtless bear fruit; for this elderly spinster aunt, with a mania for psychical research, had brains as well as will power, and by hook or by crook she usually managed to accomplish her ends. The revelation was made soon after tea, when she sidled close up to him as they paced slowly along the seafront in the dusk.

"I've got the keys," she announced in a delighted, yet half awesome voice. "Got them till Monday!"

"The keys of the bathing-machine, or—?" he asked innocently, looking from the sea to the town. Nothing brought her so quickly to the point as feigning stupidity.

"Neither," she whispered. "I've got the keys of the haunted house in the square—and I'm going there tonight."

Shorthouse was conscious of the slightest possible tremor down his back. He dropped his teasing tone. Something in her voice and manner thrilled him. She was in earnest.

"But you can't go alone—" he began.

"That's why I wired for you," she said with decision.

He turned to look at her. The ugly, lined, enigmatical face was alive with excitement. There was the glow of genuine enthusiasm round it like a halo. The eyes shone. He caught another wave of her excitement, and a second tremor, more marked than the first, accompanied it.

"Thanks, Aunt Julia," he said politely; "thanks awfully."

"I should not dare to go quite alone," she went on, raising her voice; "but with you I should enjoy it immensely. You're afraid of nothing, I know."

"Thanks *so* much," he said again. "Er—is anything likely to happen?"

"A great deal *has* happened," she whispered, "though it's been most cleverly hushed up. Three tenants have come and gone in the last few months, and the house is said to be empty for good now."

In spite of himself Shorthouse became interested. His aunt was so very much in earnest.

"The house is very old indeed," she went on, "and the story—an unpleasant one—dates a long way back. It has to do with a murder committed by a jealous stableman who had some affair with a servant in the house. One night he managed to secrete himself in the cellar, and when everyone was asleep, he crept upstairs to the servants' quarters, chased the girl down to the next landing, and before anyone could come to the rescue threw her bodily over the banisters into the hall below."

"And the stableman—?"

"Was caught, I believe, and hanged for murder; but it all happened a century ago, and I've not been able to get more details of the story."

Shorthouse now felt his interest thoroughly aroused; but, though he was not particularly nervous for himself, he hesitated a little on his aunt's account.

"On one condition," he said at length.

"Nothing will prevent my going," she said firmly; "but I may as well hear your condition."

"That you guarantee your power of self-control if anything really horrible happens. I mean—that you are sure you won't get too frightened."

"Jim," she said scornfully, "I'm not young, I know, nor are my nerves; but *with you* I should be afraid of nothing in the world!"

This, of course, settled it, for Shorthouse had no pretensions to being other than a very ordinary young man, and an appeal to his vanity was irresistible. He agreed to go.

Instinctively, by a sort of sub-conscious preparation, he kept himself and his forces well in hand the whole evening, compelling an accumulative reserve of control by that nameless inward process of gradually putting all the emotions away and turning the key upon them—a process difficult to describe, but wonderfully effective, as all men who have lived through severe trials of the inner man well understand. Later, it stood him in good stead.

But it was not until half-past ten, when they stood in the hall, well in the glare of friendly lamps and still surrounded by comforting human influences, that he had to make the first call upon this store of collected strength. For, once the door was closed, and he saw the deserted silent street stretching away white in the moonlight before them, it came to him clearly that the real test that night would be in dealing with *two fears* instead of one. He would have to carry his aunt's fear as well as his own. And, as he glanced down at her sphinx-like countenance and realised that it might assume no pleasant aspect in a rush of real terror, he felt satisfied with only one thing in the whole adventure—that he had confidence in his own will and power to stand against any shock that might come.

Slowly they walked along the empty streets of the town; a bright autumn moon silvered the roofs, casting deep shadows; there was no breath of wind; and the trees in the formal gardens by the sea-front watched them silently as they passed along. To his aunt's occasional remarks Shorthouse made no reply, realising that she was simply surrounding herself with mental buffers—saying ordinary things to prevent herself thinking of extra-ordinary things. Few windows showed lights, and from scarcely a single chimney came smoke or sparks. Shorthouse had already begun to notice everything, even the smallest details. Presently they stopped at the street corner and looked up at the name on the side of the house full in the moonlight, and with one accord, but without remark, turned into the square and crossed over to the side of it that lay in shadow.

"The number of the house is thirteen," whispered a voice at his side; and neither of them made the obvious reference, but passed across the broad sheet of moonlight and began to march up the pavement in silence.

It was about half-way up the square that Shorthouse felt an arm slipped quietly but significantly into his own, and knew then that their adventure had begun in earnest, and that his companion was already yielding imperceptibly to the influences against them. She needed support.

A few minutes later they stopped before a tall, narrow house that rose before them into the night, ugly in shape and painted a dingy white. Shutterless windows, without blinds, stared down upon them, shining here and there in the moonlight. There were weather streaks in the wall and cracks in the paint, and the balcony bulged out from the first floor a little unnaturally. But, beyond this generally forlorn appearance of an unoccupied house, there was nothing at first sight to single out this particular mansion for the evil character it had most certainly acquired.

Taking a look over their shoulders to make sure they had not been followed, they went boldly up the steps and stood against the huge black door that fronted them forbiddingly. But the first wave of nervousness was now upon them, and Shorthouse fumbled a long time with the key before he could fit it into the lock at all. For a moment, if truth were told, they both hoped it would not open, for they were a prey to various unpleasant emotions as they stood there on the threshold of their ghostly adventure.

Shorthouse, shuffling with the key and hampered by the steady weight on his arm, certainly felt the solemnity of the moment. It was as if the whole world—for all experience seemed at that instant concentrated in his own consciousness—were listening to the grating noise of that key. A stray puff of wind wandering down the empty street woke a momentary rustling in the trees behind them, but otherwise this rattling of the key was the only sound audible; and at last it turned in the lock and the heavy door swung open and revealed a yawning gulf of darkness beyond.

With a last glance at the moonlit square, they passed quickly in, and the door slammed behind them with a roar that echoed prodigiously through empty halls and passages. But, instantly, with the echoes, another sound made itself heard, and Aunt Julia leaned suddenly so heavily upon him that he had to take a step backwards to save himself from falling.

A man had coughed close beside them—so close that it seemed they must have been actually by his side in the darkness.

With the possibility of practical jokes in his mind, Shorthouse at once swung his heavy stick in the direction of the sound; but it met nothing more solid than air. He heard his aunt give a little gasp beside him.

"There's someone here," she whispered; "I heard him."

"Be quiet!" he said sternly. "It was nothing but the noise of the front door."

"Oh! get a light—quick!" she added, as her nephew, fumbling with a box of matches, opened it upside down and let them all fall with a rattle on to the stone floor.

The sound, however, was not repeated; and there was no evidence of retreating footsteps. In another minute they had a candle burning, using an empty end of a cigar case as a holder; and when the first flare had died down he held the impromptu lamp aloft and surveyed the scene. And it was dreary enough in all conscience, for there is nothing more desolate in all the abodes of men than an unfurnished house dimly lit, silent, and forsaken, and yet tenanted by rumour with the memories of evil and violent histories.

They were standing in a wide hall-way; on their left was the open door of a spacious dining-room, and in front the hall ran, ever narrowing, into a long, dark passage that led apparently to the top of the kitchen stairs. The broad uncarpeted staircase rose in a sweep before them, everywhere draped in shadows, except for a single spot about half-way up where the moonlight came in through the window and fell on a bright patch on the boards.

This shaft of light shed a faint radiance above and below it, lending to the objects within its reach a misty outline that was infinitely more suggestive and ghostly than complete darkness. Filtered moonlight always seems to paint faces on the surrounding gloom, and as Shorthouse peered up into the well of darkness and thought of the countless empty rooms and passages in the upper part of the old house, he caught himself longing again for the safety of the moonlit square, or the cosy, bright drawing-room they had left an hour before. Then realising that these thoughts were dangerous, he thrust them away again and summoned all his energy for concentration on the present.

"Aunt Julia," he said aloud, severely, "we must now go through the house from top to bottom and make a thorough search."

The echoes of his voice died away slowly all over the building, and in the intense silence that followed he turned to look at her. In the candle-light he saw that her face was already ghastly pale; but she dropped his arm for a moment and said in a whisper, stepping close in front of him—

"I agree. We must be sure there's no one hiding. That's the first thing."

She spoke with evident effort, and he looked at her with admiration.

"You feel quite sure of yourself? It's not too late—"

"I think so," she whispered, her eyes shifting nervously toward the shadows behind. "Quite sure, only one thing—"

"What's that?"

"You must never leave me alone for an instant."

"As long as you understand that any sound or appearance must be investigated at once, for to hesitate means to admit fear. That is fatal."

"Agreed," she said, a little shakily, after a moment's hesitation. "I'll try—"

Arm in arm, Shorthouse holding the dripping candle and the stick, while his aunt carried the cloak over her shoulders, figures of utter comedy to all but themselves, they began a systematic search.

Stealthily, walking on tip-toe and shading the candle lest it should betray their presence through the shutterless windows, they went first into the big dining-room. There was not a stick of furniture to be seen. Bare walls, ugly mantel-pieces and empty grates stared at them. Everything, they felt, resented their intrusion, watching them, as it were, with veiled eyes; whispers followed them; shadows flitted noiselessly to right and left; something seemed ever at their back, watching, waiting an opportunity to do them injury.

There was the inevitable sense that operations which went on when the room was empty had been temporarily suspended till they were well out of the way again. The whole dark interior of the old building seemed to become a malignant Presence that rose up, warning them to desist and mind their own business; every moment the strain on the nerves increased.

Out of the gloomy dining-room they passed through large folding doors into a sort of library or smoking-room, wrapt equally in silence, darkness, and dust; and from this they regained the hall near the top of the back stairs.

Here a pitch black tunnel opened before them into the lower regions, and—it must be confessed—they hesitated. But only for a minute. With the worst of the night still to come it was essential to turn from nothing. Aunt Julia stumbled at the top step of the dark descent, ill lit by the flickering candle, and even Shorthouse felt at least half the decision go out of his legs.

"Come on!" he said peremptorily, and his voice ran on and lost itself in the dark, empty spaces below.

"I'm coming," she faltered, catching his arm with unnecessary violence.

They went a little unsteadily down the stone steps, a cold, damp air meeting them in the face, close and mal-odorous. The kitchen, into which the stairs led along a narrow passage, was large, with a lofty ceiling. Several doors opened out of it—some into cupboards with empty jars still standing on the shelves, and others into horrible little ghostly back offices, each colder and less inviting than the last. Black beetles scurried over the floor, and once, when they knocked against a deal table standing in a corner, something about the size of a cat jumped down with a rush and fled, scampering across the stone floor into the darkness. Everywhere there was a sense of recent occupation, an impression of sadness and gloom.

Leaving the main kitchen, they next went towards the scullery. The door was standing ajar, and as they pushed it open to its full extent Aunt Julia uttered a piercing scream, which she instantly tried to stifle by placing her hand over her mouth. For a second Shorthouse stood stock-still, catching his breath. He felt as if his spine had suddenly become hollow and someone had filled it with particles of ice.

Facing them, directly in their way between the doorposts, stood the figure of a woman. She had dishevelled hair and wildly staring eyes, and her face was terrified and white as death.

She stood there motionless for the space of a single second. Then the candle flickered and she was gone—gone utterly—and the door framed nothing but empty darkness.

"Only the beastly jumping candle-light," he said quickly, in a voice that sounded like someone else's and was only half under control. "Come on, aunt. There's nothing there."

He dragged her forward. With a clattering of feet and a great appearance of boldness they went on, but over his body the skin moved as if crawling ants covered it, and he knew by the weight on his arm that he was supplying the force of locomotion for two. The scullery was cold, bare, and empty; more like a large prison cell than anything else. They went round it, tried the door into the yard, and the windows, but found them all fastened securely. His aunt moved beside him like a person in a dream. Her eyes were tightly shut, and she seemed merely to follow the pressure of his arm. Her courage filled him with amazement. At the same time he noticed that a certain odd change had come over her face, a change which somehow evaded his power of analysis.

"There's nothing here, aunty," he repeated aloud quickly. "Let's go upstairs and see the rest of the house. Then we'll choose a room to wait up in."

She followed him obediently, keeping close to his side, and they locked the kitchen door behind them. It was a relief to get up again. In the hall there was more light than before, for the moon had travelled a little further down the stairs. Cautiously they began to go up into the dark vault of the upper house, the boards creaking under their weight.

On the first floor they found the large double drawing-rooms, a search of which revealed nothing. Here also was no sign of furniture or recent occupancy; nothing but dust and neglect and shadows. They opened the big folding doors between front and back drawing-rooms and then came out again to the landing and went on upstairs.

They had not gone up more than a dozen steps when they both simultaneously stopped to listen, looking into each other's eyes with a new apprehension across the flickering candle flame. From the room they had left hardly ten seconds before came the sound of doors quietly closing. It was beyond all question; they heard the booming noise that accompanies the shutting of heavy doors, followed by the sharp catching of the latch.

"We must go back and see," said Shorthouse briefly, in a low tone, and turning to go downstairs again.

Somehow she managed to drag after him, her feet catching in her dress, her face livid.

When they entered the front drawing-room it was plain that the folding doors had been closed—half a minute before. Without hesitation Shorthouse opened them. He almost expected to see someone facing him in the back room; but only darkness and cold air met him. They went through both rooms, finding nothing unusual. They tried in every way to make the doors close of themselves, but there was not wind enough even to set the candle flame flickering. The doors would not move without strong pressure. All was silent as the grave. Undeniably the rooms were utterly empty, and the house utterly still.

"It's beginning," whispered a voice at his elbow which he hardly recognised as his aunt's.

He nodded acquiescence, taking out his watch to note the time. It was fifteen minutes before midnight; he made the entry of exactly what had occurred in his notebook, setting the candle in its case upon the floor in order to do so. It took a moment or two to balance it safely against the wall.

Aunt Julia always declared that at this moment she was not actually watching him, but had turned her head towards the inner room, where she fancied she heard something moving; but, at any rate, both positively agreed that there came a sound of rushing feet, heavy and very swift—and the next instant the candle was out!

But to Shorthouse himself had come more than this, and he has always thanked his fortunate stars that it came to him alone and not to his aunt too. For, as he rose from the stooping position of balancing the candle, and before it was actually extinguished, a face thrust itself forward so close to his own that he could almost have touched it with his lips. It was a face working with passion; a man's face, dark, with thick features, and angry, savage eyes. It belonged to a common man, and it was evil in its ordinary normal expression, no doubt, but as he saw it, alive with intense, aggressive emotion, it was a malignant and terrible human countenance.

There was no movement of the air; nothing but the sound of rushing feet—stockinged or muffled feet; the apparition of the face; and the almost simultaneous extinguishing of the candle.

In spite of himself, Shorthouse uttered a little cry, nearly losing his balance as his aunt clung to him with her whole weight in one moment of real, uncontrollable terror. She made no sound, but simply seized him bodily. Fortunately, however, she had seen nothing, but had only heard the rushing feet, for her control returned almost at once, and he was able to disentangle himself and strike a match.

The shadows ran away on all sides before the glare, and his aunt stooped down and groped for the cigar case with the precious candle. Then they discovered that the candle had not been *blown* out at all; it had been *crushed* out. The wick was pressed down into the wax, which was flattened as if by some smooth, heavy instrument.

How his companion so quickly overcame her terror, Shorthouse never properly understood; but his admiration for her self-control increased tenfold, and at the same time served to feed his own dying flame—for which he was undeniably grateful. Equally inexplicable to him was the evidence of physical force they had just witnessed. He at once suppressed the memory of stories he had heard of "physical mediums" and their dangerous phenomena; for if these were true, and either his aunt or himself was unwittingly a physical medium, it meant that they were simply aiding to focus the forces of a haunted house already charged to the brim. It was like walking with unprotected lamps among uncovered stores of gun-powder.

So, with as little reflection as possible, he simply relit the candle and went up to the next floor. The arm in his trembled, it is true, and his own tread was often uncertain, but they went on with thoroughness, and after a search revealing nothing they climbed the last flight of stairs to the top floor of all.

Here they found a perfect nest of small servants' rooms, with broken pieces of furniture, dirty cane-bottomed chairs, chests of drawers, cracked mirrors, and decrepit bedsteads. The rooms had low sloping ceilings already hung here and there with cobwebs, small windows, and badly plastered walls—a depressing and dismal region which they were glad to leave behind.

It was on the stroke of midnight when they entered a small room on the third floor, close to the top of the stairs, and arranged to make themselves comfortable for the remainder of their adventure. It was absolutely bare, and was said to be the room—then used as a clothes closet—into which the infuriated groom had chased his victim and finally caught her. Outside, across the narrow landing, began the stairs leading up to the floor above, and the servants' quarters where they had just searched.

In spite of the chilliness of the night there was something in the air of this room that cried for an open window. But there was more than this. Shorthouse could only describe it by saying that he felt less master of himself here than in any other part of the house. There was something that acted directly on the nerves, tiring the resolution, enfeebling the will. He was conscious of this result before he had been in the room five minutes, and it was in the short time they stayed there that he suffered the wholesale depletion of his vital forces, which was, for himself, the chief horror of the whole experience.

They put the candle on the floor of the cupboard, leaving the door a few inches ajar, so that there was no glare to confuse the eyes, and no shadow to shift about on walls and ceiling. Then they spread the cloak on the floor and sat down to wait, with their backs against the wall.

Shorthouse was within two feet of the door on to the landing; his position commanded a good view of the main staircase leading down into the darkness, and also of the beginning of the servants' stairs going to the floor above; the heavy stick lay beside him within easy reach.

The moon was now high above the house. Through the open window they could see the comforting stars like friendly eyes watching in the sky. One by one the clocks of the town struck midnight, and when the sounds died away the deep silence of a windless night fell again over everything. Only the boom of the sea, far away and lugubrious, filled the air with hollow murmurs.

Inside the house the silence became awful; awful, he thought, because any minute now it might be broken by sounds portending terror. The strain of waiting told more and more severely on the nerves; they talked in whispers when they talked at all, for their voices aloud sounded queer and unnatural. A chilliness, not altogether due to the night air, invaded the room, and made them cold. The influences against them, whatever these might be, were slowly robbing them of self-confidence, and the power of decisive action; their forces were on the wane, and the possibility of real fear took on a new and terrible meaning. He began to tremble for the elderly woman by his side, whose pluck could hardly save her beyond a certain extent.

He heard the blood singing in his veins. It sometimes seemed so loud that he fancied it prevented his hearing properly certain other sounds that were beginning very faintly to make themselves audible in the depths of the house. Every time he fastened his attention on these sounds, they instantly ceased. They certainly came no nearer. Yet he could not rid himself of the idea that movement was going on somewhere in the lower regions of the house.

The drawing-room floor, where the doors had been so strangely closed, seemed too near; the sounds were further off than that. He thought of the great kitchen, with the scurrying black-beetles, and of the dismal little scullery; but, somehow or other, they did not seem to come from there either. Surely they were not *outside* the house!

Then, suddenly, the truth flashed into his mind, and for the space of a minute he felt as if his blood had stopped flowing and turned to ice.

The sounds were not downstairs at all; they were *upstairs*—upstairs, somewhere among those horrid gloomy little servants' rooms with their bits of broken furniture, low ceilings, and cramped windows—upstairs where the victim had first been disturbed and stalked to her death.

And the moment he discovered where the sounds were, he began to hear them more clearly. It was the sound of feet, moving stealthily along the passage overhead, in and out among the rooms, and past the furniture.

He turned quickly to steal a glance at the motionless figure seated beside him, to note whether she had shared his discovery. The faint candle-light coming through the crack in the cupboard door, threw her strongly-marked face into vivid relief against the white of the wall. But it was something else that made him catch his breath and stare again. An extraordinary something had come into her face and seemed to spread over her features like a mask; it smoothed out the deep lines and drew the skin everywhere a little tighter so that the wrinkles disappeared; it brought into the face—with the sole exception of the old eyes—an appearance of youth and almost of childhood.

He stared in speechless amazement—amazement that was dangerously near to horror. It was his aunt's face indeed, but it was her face of forty years ago, the vacant innocent face of a girl. He had heard stories of that strange effect of terror which could wipe a human countenance clean of other emotions, obliterating all previous expressions; but he had never realised that it could be literally true, or could mean anything so simply horrible as what he now saw. For the dreadful signature of overmastering fear was written plainly in that utter vacancy of the girlish face beside him; and when, feeling his intense gaze, she turned to look at him, he instinctively closed his eyes tightly to shut out the sight.

Yet, when he turned a minute later, his feelings well in hand, he saw to his intense relief another expression; his aunt was smiling, and though the face was deathly white, the awful veil had lifted and the normal look was returning.

"Anything wrong?" was all he could think of to say at the moment. And the answer was eloquent, coming from such a woman.

"I feel cold—and a little frightened," she whispered.

He offered to close the window, but she seized hold of him and begged him not to leave her side even for an instant.

"It's upstairs, I know," she whispered, with an odd half laugh; "but I can't possibly go up."

But Shorthouse thought otherwise, knowing that in action lay their best hope of self-control.

He took the brandy flask and poured out a glass of neat spirit, stiff enough to help anybody over anything. She swallowed it with a little shiver. His only idea now was to get out of the house before her collapse became inevitable; but this could not safely be done by turning tail and running from the enemy. Inaction was no longer possible; every minute he was growing less master of himself, and desperate, aggressive measures were imperative without further delay. Moreover, the action must be taken *towards* the enemy, not away from it; the climax, if necessary and unavoidable, would have to be faced boldly. He could do it now; but in ten minutes he might not have the force left to act for himself, much less for both!

Upstairs, the sounds were meanwhile becoming louder and closer, accompanied by occasional creaking of the boards. Someone was moving stealthily about, stumbling now and then awkwardly against the furniture.

Waiting a few moments to allow the tremendous dose of spirits to produce its effect, and knowing this would last but a short time under the circumstances, Shorthouse then quietly got on his feet, saying in a determined voice—

"Now, Aunt Julia, we'll go upstairs and find out what all this noise is about. You must come too. It's what we agreed."

He picked up his stick and went to the cupboard for the candle. A limp form rose shakily beside him breathing hard, and he heard a voice say very faintly something about being "ready to come." The woman's courage amazed him; it was so much greater than his own; and, as they advanced, holding aloft the dripping candle, some subtle force exhaled from this trembling, white-faced old woman at his side that was the true source of his inspiration. It held something really great that shamed him and gave him the support without which he would have proved far less equal to the occasion.

They crossed the dark landing, avoiding with their eyes the deep black space over the banisters. Then they began to mount the narrow staircase to meet the sounds which, minute by minute, grew louder and nearer. About half-way up the stairs Aunt Julia stumbled and Shorthouse turned to catch her by the arm, and just at that moment there came a terrific crash in the servants' corridor overhead. It was instantly followed by a shrill, agonised scream that was a cry of terror and a cry for help melted into one.

Before they could move aside, or go down a single step, someone came rushing along the passage overhead, blundering horribly, racing madly, at full speed, three steps at a time, down the very staircase where they stood. The steps were light and uncertain; but close behind them sounded the heavier tread of another person, and the staircase seemed to shake.

Shorthouse and his companion just had time to flatten themselves against the wall when the jumble of flying steps was upon them, and two persons, with the slightest possible interval between them, dashed past at full speed. It was a perfect whirlwind of sound breaking in upon the midnight silence of the empty building.

The two runners, pursuer and pursued, had passed clean through them where they stood, and already with a thud the boards below had received first one, then the other. Yet they had seen absolutely nothing—not a hand, or arm, or face, or even a shred of flying clothing.

There came a second's pause. Then the first one, the lighter of the two, obviously the pursued one, ran with uncertain footsteps into the little room which Shorthouse and his aunt had just left. The heavier one followed. There was a sound of scuffling, gasping, and smothered screaming; and then out on to the landing came the step—of a single person *treading weightily*.

A dead silence followed for the space of half a minute, and then was heard a rushing sound through the air. It was followed by a dull, crashing thud in the depths of the house below—on the stone floor of the hall.

Utter silence reigned after. Nothing moved. The flame of the candle was steady. It had been steady the whole time, and the air had been undisturbed by any movement whatsoever. Palsied with terror, Aunt Julia, without waiting for her companion, began fumbling her way downstairs; she was crying gently to herself, and when Shorthouse put his arm round her and half carried her he felt that she was trembling like a leaf. He went into the little room and picked up the cloak from the floor, and, arm in arm, walking very slowly, without speaking a word or looking once behind them, they marched down the three flights into the hall.

In the hall they saw nothing, but the whole way down the stairs they were conscious that someone followed them; step by step; when they went faster IT was left behind, and when they went more slowly IT caught them up. But never once did they look behind to see; and at each turning of the staircase they lowered their eyes for fear of the following horror they might see upon the stairs above.

With trembling hands Shorthouse opened the front door, and they walked out into the moonlight and drew a deep breath of the cool night air blowing in from the sea.

Smith: An Episode in a Lodging-House

"When I was a medical student," began the doctor, half turning towards his circle of listeners in the firelight, "I came across one or two very curious human beings; but there was one fellow I remember particularly, for he caused me the most vivid, and I think the most uncomfortable, emotions I have ever known.

"For many months I knew Smith only by name as the occupant of the floor above me. Obviously his name meant nothing to me. Moreover I was busy with lectures, reading, cliniques and the like, and had little leisure to devise plans for scraping acquaintance with any of the other lodgers in the house. Then chance brought us curiously together, and this fellow Smith left a deep impression upon me as the result of our first meeting.

"At the time the strength of this first impression seemed quite inexplicable to me, but looking back at the episode now from a standpoint of greater knowledge I judge the fact to have been that he stirred my curiosity to an unusual degree, and at the same time awakened my sense of horror—whatever that may be in a medical student—about as deeply and permanently as these two emotions were capable of being stirred at all in the particular system and set of nerves called ME.

"How he knew that I was interested in the study of languages was something I could never explain, but one day, quite unannounced, he came quietly into my room in the evening and asked me point-blank if I knew enough Hebrew to help him in the pronunciation of certain words.

"He caught me along the line of least resistance, and I was greatly flattered to be able to give him the desired information; but it was only when he had thanked me and was gone that I realised I had been in the presence of an unusual individuality. For the life of me I could not quite seize and label the peculiarities of what I felt to be a very striking personality, but it was borne in upon me that he was a man apart from his fellows, a mind that followed a line leading away from ordinary human intercourse and human interests, and into regions that left in his atmosphere something remote, rarefied, chilling.

"The moment he was gone I became conscious of two things—an intense curiosity to know more about this man and what his real interests were, and secondly, the fact that my skin was crawling and that my hair had a tendency to rise."

The doctor paused a moment here to puff hard at his pipe, which, however, had gone out beyond recall without the assistance of a match; and in the deep silence, which testified to the genuine interest of his listeners, someone poked the fire up into a little blaze, and one or two others glanced over their shoulders into the dark distances of the big hall.

"On looking back," he went on, watching the momentary flames in the grate, "I see a short, thick-set man of perhaps forty-five, with immense shoulders and small, slender hands. The contrast was noticeable, for I remember thinking that such a giant frame and such slim finger bones hardly belonged together. His head, too, was large and very long, the head of an idealist beyond all question, yet with an unusually strong development of the jaw and chin. Here again was a singular contradiction, though I am better able now to appreciate its full meaning, with a greater experience in judging the values of physiognomy. For this meant, of course, an enthusiastic idealism balanced and kept in check by will and judgment—elements usually deficient in dreamers and visionaries.

"At any rate, here was a being with probably a very wide range of possibilities, a machine with a pendulum that most likely had an unusual length of swing.

"The man's hair was exceedingly fine, and the lines about his nose and mouth were cut as with a delicate steel instrument in wax. His eyes I have left to the last. They were large and quite changeable, not in colour only, but in character, size, and shape. Occasionally they seemed the eyes of someone else, if you can understand what I mean, and at the same time, in their shifting shades of blue, green, and a nameless sort of dark grey, there was a sinister light in them that lent to the whole face an aspect almost alarming. Moreover, they were the most luminous optics I think I have ever seen in any human being.

"There, then, at the risk of a wearisome description, is Smith as I saw him for the first time that winter's evening in my shabby student's rooms in Edinburgh. And yet the real part of him, of course, I have left untouched, for it is both indescribable and unget-at-able. I have spoken already of an atmosphere of warning and aloofness he carried about with him. It is impossible further to analyse the series of little shocks his presence always communicated to my being; but there was that about him which made me instantly on the *qui vive* in his presence, every nerve alert, every sense strained and on the watch. I do not mean that he deliberately suggested danger, but rather that he brought forces in his wake which automatically warned the nervous centres of my system to be on their guard and alert.

"Since the days of my first acquaintance with this man I have lived through other experiences and have seen much I cannot pretend to explain or understand; but, so far in my life, I have only once come across a human being who suggested a disagreeable familiarity with unholy things, and who made me feel uncanny and 'creepy' in his presence; and that unenviable individual was Mr. Smith.

"What his occupation was during the day I never knew. I think he slept until the sun set. No one ever saw him on the stairs, or heard him move in his room during the day. He was a creature of the shadows, who apparently preferred darkness to light. Our landlady either knew nothing, or would say nothing. At any rate she found no fault, and I have since wondered often by what magic this fellow was able to convert a common landlady of a common lodging-house into a discreet and uncommunicative person. This alone was a sign of genius of some sort.

"'He's been here with me for years—long before you come, an' I don't interfere or ask no questions of what doesn't concern me, as long as people pays their rent,' was the only remark on the subject that I ever succeeded in winning from that quarter, and it certainly told me nothing nor gave me any encouragement to ask for further information.

"Examinations, however, and the general excitement of a medical student's life for a time put Mr. Smith completely out of my head. For a long period he did not call upon me again, and for my part, I felt no courage to return his unsolicited visit.

"Just then, however, there came a change in the fortunes of those who controlled my very limited income, and I was obliged to give up my ground-floor and move aloft to more modest chambers on the top of the house. Here I was directly over Smith, and had to pass his door to reach my own.

"It so happened that about this time I was frequently called out at all hours of the night for the maternity cases which a fourth-year student takes at a certain period of his studies, and on returning from one of these visits at about two o'clock in the morning I was surprised to hear the sound of voices as I passed his door. A peculiar sweet odour, too, not unlike the smell of incense, penetrated into the passage.

"I went upstairs very quietly, wondering what was going on there at this hour of the morning. To my knowledge Smith never had visitors. For a moment I hesitated outside the door with one foot on the stairs. All my interest in this strange man revived, and my curiosity rose to a point not far from action. At last I might learn something of the habits of this lover of the night and the darkness.

"The sound of voices was plainly audible, Smith's predominating so much that I never could catch more than points of sound from the other, penetrating now and then the steady stream of his voice. Not a single word reached me, at least, not a word that I could understand, though the voice was loud and distinct, and it was only afterwards that I realised he must have been speaking in a foreign language.

"The sound of footsteps, too, was equally distinct. Two persons were moving about the room, passing and repassing the door, one of them a light, agile person, and the other ponderous and somewhat awkward. Smith's voice went on incessantly with its odd, monotonous droning, now loud, now soft, as he crossed and re-crossed the floor. The other person was also on the move, but in a different and less regular fashion, for I heard rapid steps that seemed to end sometimes in stumbling, and quick sudden movements that brought up with a violent lurching against the wall or furniture.

"As I listened to Smith's voice, moreover, I began to feel afraid. There was something in the sound that made me feel intuitively he was in a tight place, and an impulse stirred faintly in me—very faintly, I admit—to knock at the door and inquire if he needed help.

"But long before the impulse could translate itself into an act, or even before it had been properly weighed and considered by the mind, I heard a voice close beside me in the air, a sort of hushed whisper which I am certain was Smith speaking, though the sound did not seem to have come to me through the door. It was close in my very ear, as though he stood beside me, and it gave me such a start, that I clutched the banisters to save myself from stepping backwards and making a clatter on the stairs.

"'There is nothing you can do to help me,' it said distinctly, 'and you will be much safer in your own room.'

"I am ashamed to this day of the pace at which I covered the flight of stairs in the darkness to the top floor, and of the shaking hand with which I lit my candles and bolted the door. But, there it is, just as it happened.

"This midnight episode, so odd and yet so trivial in itself, fired me with more curiosity than ever about my fellow-lodger. It also made me connect him in my mind with a sense of fear and distrust. I never saw him, yet I was often, and uncomfortably, aware of his presence in the upper regions of that gloomy lodging-house. Smith and his secret mode of life and mysterious pursuits, somehow contrived to awaken in my being a line of reflection that disturbed my comfortable condition of ignorance. I never saw him, as I have said, and exchanged no sort of communication with him, yet it seemed to me that his mind was in contact with mine, and some of the strange forces of his atmosphere filtered through into my being and disturbed my equilibrium. Those upper floors became haunted for me after dark, and, though outwardly our lives never came into contact, I became unwillingly involved in certain pursuits on which his mind was centred. I felt that he was somehow making use of me against my will, and by methods which passed my comprehension.

"I was at that time, moreover, in the heavy, unquestioning state of materialism which is common to medical students when they begin to understand something of the human anatomy and nervous system, and jump at once to the conclusion that they control the universe and hold in their forceps the last word of life and death. I 'knew it all,' and regarded a belief in anything beyond matter as the wanderings of weak, or at best, untrained minds. And this condition of mind, of course, added to the strength of this upsetting fear which emanated from the floor below and began slowly to take possession of me.

"Though I kept no notes of the subsequent events in this matter, they made too deep an impression for me ever to forget the sequence in which they occurred. Without difficulty I can recall the next step in the adventure with Smith, for adventure it rapidly grew to be."

The doctor stopped a moment and laid his pipe on the table behind him before continuing. The fire had burned low, and no one stirred to poke it. The silence in the great hall was so deep that when the speaker's pipe touched the table the sound woke audible echoes at the far end among the shadows.

"One evening, while I was reading, the door of my room opened and Smith came in. He made no attempt at ceremony. It was after ten o'clock and I was tired, but the presence of the man immediately galvanised me into activity. My attempts at ordinary politeness he thrust on one side at once, and began asking me to vocalise, and then pronounce for him, certain Hebrew words; and when this was done he abruptly inquired if I was not the fortunate possessor of a very rare Rabbinical Treatise, which he named.

"How he knew that I possessed this book puzzled me exceedingly; but I was still more surprised to see him cross the room and take it out of my bookshelf almost before I had had time to answer in the affirmative. Evidently he knew exactly where it was kept. This excited my curiosity beyond all bounds, and I immediately began asking him questions; and though, out of sheer respect for the man, I put them very delicately to him, and almost by way of mere conversation, he had only one reply for the lot. He would look up at me from the pages of the book with an expression of complete comprehension on his extraordinary features, would bow his head a little and say very gravely—

"'That, of course, is a perfectly proper question,'—which was absolutely all I could ever get out of him.

"On this particular occasion he stayed with me perhaps ten or fifteen minutes. Then he went quickly downstairs to his room with my Hebrew Treatise in his hand, and I heard him close and bolt his door.

"But a few moments later, before I had time to settle down to my book again, or to recover from the surprise his visit had caused me, I heard the door open, and there stood Smith once again beside my chair. He made no excuse for his second interruption, but bent his head down to the level of my reading lamp and peered across the flame straight into my eyes.

"'I hope,' he whispered, 'I hope you are never disturbed at night?'

"'Eh?' I stammered, 'disturbed at night? Oh no, thanks, at least, not that I know of—'

"'I'm glad,' he replied gravely, appearing not to notice my confusion and surprise at his question. 'But, remember, should it ever be the case, please let me know at once.'

"And he was gone down the stairs and into his room again.

"For some minutes I sat reflecting upon his strange behaviour. He was not mad, I argued, but was the victim of some harmless delusion that had gradually grown upon him as a result of his solitary mode of life; and from the books he used, I judged that it had something to do with mediæval magic, or some system of ancient Hebrew mysticism. The words he asked me to pronounce for him were probably 'Words of Power,' which, when uttered with the vehemence of a strong will behind them, were supposed to produce physical results, or set up vibrations in one's own inner being that had the effect of a partial lifting of the veil.

"I sat thinking about the man, and his way of living, and the probable effects in the long-run of his dangerous experiments, and I can recall perfectly well the sensation of disappointment that crept over me when I realised that I had labelled his particular form of aberration, and that my curiosity would therefore no longer be excited.

"For some time I had been sitting alone with these reflections—it may have been ten minutes or it may have been half an hour—when I was aroused from my reverie by the knowledge that someone was again in the room standing close beside my chair. My first thought was that Smith had come back again in his swift, unaccountable manner, but almost at the same moment I realised that this could not be the case at all. For the door faced my position, and it certainly had not been opened again.

"Yet, someone was in the room, moving cautiously to and fro, watching me, almost touching me. I was as sure of it as I was of myself, and though at the moment I do not think I was actually afraid, I am bound to admit that a certain weakness came over me and that I felt that strange disinclination for action which is probably the beginning of the horrible paralysis of real terror. I should have been glad to hide myself, if that had been possible, to cower into a corner, or behind a door, or anywhere so that I could not be watched and observed.

"But, overcoming my nervousness with an effort of the will, I got up quickly out of my chair and held the reading lamp aloft so that it shone into all the corners like a searchlight.

"The room was utterly empty! It was utterly empty, at least, to the *eye*, but to the nerves, and especially to that combination of sense perception which is made up by all the senses acting together, and by no one in particular, there was a person standing there at my very elbow.

"I say 'person,' for I can think of no appropriate word. For, if it *was* a human being, I can only affirm that I had the overwhelming conviction that it was *not*, but that it was some form of life wholly unknown to me both as to its essence and its nature. A sensation of gigantic force and power came with it, and I remember vividly to this day my terror on realising that I was close to an invisible being who could crush me as easily as I could crush a fly, and who could see my every movement while itself remaining invisible.

"To this terror was added the certain knowledge that the 'being' kept in my proximity for a definite purpose. And that this purpose had some direct bearing upon my well-being, indeed upon my life, I was equally convinced; for I became aware of a sensation of growing lassitude as though the vitality were being steadily drained out of my body. My heart began to beat irregularly at first, then faintly. I was conscious, even within a few minutes, of a general drooping of the powers of life in the whole system, an ebbing away of self-control, and a distinct approach of drowsiness and torpor.

"The power to move, or to think out any mode of resistance, was fast leaving me, when there rose, in the distance as it were, a tremendous commotion. A door opened with a clatter, and I heard the peremptory and commanding tones of a human voice calling aloud in a language I could not comprehend. It was Smith, my fellow-lodger, calling up the stairs; and his voice had not sounded for more than a few seconds, when I felt something withdrawn from my presence, from my person, indeed from my *very skin*. It seemed as if there was a rushing of air and some large creature swept by me at about the level of my shoulders. Instantly the pressure on my heart was relieved, and the atmosphere seemed to resume its normal condition.

"Smith's door closed quietly downstairs, as I put the lamp down with trembling hands. What had happened I do not know; only, I was alone again and my strength was returning as rapidly as it had left me.

"I went across the room and examined myself in the glass. The skin was very pale, and the eyes dull. My temperature, I found, was a little below normal and my pulse faint and irregular. But these smaller signs of disturbance were as nothing compared with the feeling I had—though no outward signs bore testimony to the fact—that I had narrowly escaped a real and ghastly catastrophe. I felt shaken, somehow, shaken to the very roots of my being."

The doctor rose from his chair and crossed over to the dying fire, so that no one could see the expression on his face as he stood with his back to the grate, and continued his weird tale.

"It would be wearisome," he went on in a lower voice, looking over our heads as though he still saw the dingy top floor of that haunted Edinburgh lodging-house; "it would be tedious for me at this length of time to analyse my feelings, or attempt to reproduce for you the thorough examination to which I endeavoured then to subject my whole being, intellectual, emotional, and physical. I need only mention the dominant emotion with which this curious episode left me—the indignant anger against myself that I could ever have lost my self-control enough to come under the sway of so gross and absurd a delusion. This protest, however, I remember making with all the emphasis possible. And I also remember noting that it brought me very little satisfaction, for it was the protest of my reason only, when all the rest of my being was up in arms against its conclusions.

"My dealings with the 'delusion,' however, were not yet over for the night; for very early next morning, somewhere about three o'clock, I was awakened by a curiously stealthy noise in the room, and the next minute there followed a crash as if all my books had been swept bodily from their shelf on to the floor.

"But this time I was not frightened. Cursing the disturbance with all the resounding and harmless words I could accumulate, I jumped out of bed and lit the candle in a second, and in the first dazzle of the flaring match—but before the wick had time to catch—I was certain I *saw* a dark grey shadow, of ungainly shape, and with something more or less like a human head, drive rapidly past the side of the wall farthest from me and disappear into the gloom by the angle of the door.

"I waited one single second to be sure the candle was alight, and then dashed after it, but before I had gone two steps, my foot stumbled against something hard piled up on the carpet and I only just saved myself from falling headlong. I picked myself up and found that all the books from what I called my 'language shelf' were strewn across the floor. The room, meanwhile, as a minute's search revealed, was quite empty. I looked in every corner and behind every stick of furniture, and a student's bedroom on a top floor, costing twelve shillings a week, did not hold many available hiding-places, as you may imagine.

"The crash, however, was explained. Some very practical and physical force had thrown the books from their resting-place. That, at least, was beyond all doubt. And as I replaced them on the shelf and noted that not one was missing, I busied myself mentally with the sore problem of how the agent of this little practical joke had gained access to my room, and then escaped again. *For my door was locked and bolted.*

"Smith's odd question as to whether I was disturbed in the night, and his warning injunction to let him know at once if such were the case, now of course returned to affect me as I stood there in the early morning, cold and shivering on the carpet; but I realised at the same moment how impossible it would be for me to admit that a more than usually vivid nightmare could have any connection with himself. I would rather stand a hundred of these mysterious visitations than consult such a man as to their possible cause.

"A knock at the door interrupted my reflections, and I gave a start that sent the candle grease flying.

"'Let me in,' came in Smith's voice.

"I unlocked the door. He came in fully dressed. His face wore a curious pallor. It seemed to me to be under the skin and to shine through and almost make it luminous. His eyes were exceedingly bright.

"I was wondering what in the world to say to him, or how he would explain his visit at such an hour, when he closed the door behind him and came close up to me—uncomfortably close.

"'You should have called me at once,' he said in his whispering voice, fixing his great eyes on my face.

"I stammered something about an awful dream, but he ignored my remark utterly, and I caught his eye wandering next—if any movement of those optics can be described as 'wandering'—to the bookshelf. I watched him, unable to move my gaze from his person. The man fascinated me horribly for some reason. Why, in the devil's name, was he up and dressed at three in the morning? How did he know anything had happened unusual in my room? Then his whisper began again.

"'It's your amazing vitality that causes you this annoyance,' he said, shifting his eyes back to mine.

"I gasped. Something in his voice or manner turned my blood into ice.

"'That's the real attraction,' he went on. 'But if this continues one of us will have to leave, you know.'

"I positively could not find a word to say in reply. The channels of speech dried up within me. I simply stared and wondered what he would say next. I watched him in a sort of dream, and as far as I can remember, he asked me to promise to call him sooner another time, and then began to walk round the room, uttering strange sounds, and making signs with his arms and hands until he reached the door. Then he was gone in a second, and I had closed and locked the door behind him.

"After this, the Smith adventure drew rapidly to a climax. It was a week or two later, and I was coming home between two and three in the morning from a maternity case, certain features of which for the time being had very much taken possession of my mind, so much so, indeed, that I passed Smith's door without giving him a single thought.

"The gas jet on the landing was still burning, but so low that it made little impression on the waves of deep shadow that lay across the stairs. Overhead, the faintest possible gleam of grey showed that the morning was not far away. A few stars shone down through the skylight. The house was still as the grave, and the only sound to break the silence was the rushing of the wind round the walls and over the roof. But this was a fitful sound, suddenly rising and as suddenly falling away again, and it only served to intensify the silence.

"I had already reached my own landing when I gave a violent start. It was automatic, almost a reflex action in fact, for it was only when I caught myself fumbling at the door handle and thinking where I could conceal myself quickest that I realised a voice had sounded close beside me in the air. It was the same voice I had heard before, and it seemed to me to be calling for help. And yet the very same minute I pushed on into the room, determined to disregard it, and seeking to persuade myself it was the creaking of the boards under my weight or the rushing noise of the wind that had deceived me.

"But hardly had I reached the table where the candles stood when the sound was unmistakably repeated: 'Help! help!' And this time it was accompanied by what I can only describe as a vivid tactile hallucination. I was touched: the *skin* of my arm was clutched by fingers.

"Some compelling force sent me headlong downstairs as if the haunting forces of the whole world were at my heels. At Smith's door I paused. The force of his previous warning injunction to seek his aid without delay acted suddenly and I leant my whole weight against the panels, little dreaming that I should be called upon to give help rather than to receive it.

"The door yielded at once, and I burst into a room that was so full of a choking vapour, moving in slow clouds, that at first I could distinguish nothing at all but a set of what seemed to be huge shadows passing in and out of the mist. Then, gradually, I perceived that a red lamp on the mantelpiece gave all the light there was, and that the room which I now entered for the first time was almost empty of furniture.

"The carpet was rolled back and piled in a heap in the corner, and upon the white boards of the floor I noticed a large circle drawn in black of some material that emitted a faint glowing light and was apparently smoking. Inside this circle, as well as at regular intervals outside it, were curious-looking designs, also traced in the same black, smoking substance. These, too, seemed to emit a feeble light of their own.

"My first impression on entering the room had been that it was full of—*people*, I was going to say; but that hardly expresses my meaning *Beings*, they certainly were, but it was borne in upon me beyond the possibility of doubt, that they were not human beings. That I had caught a momentary glimpse of living, intelligent entities I can never doubt, but I am equally convinced, though I cannot prove it, that these entities were from some other scheme of evolution altogether, and had nothing to do with the ordinary human life, either incarnate or discarnate.

"But, whatever they were, the visible appearance of them was exceedingly fleeting. I no longer saw anything, though I still felt convinced of their immediate presence. They were, moreover, of the same order of life as the visitant in my bedroom of a few nights before, and their proximity to my atmosphere in numbers, instead of singly as before, conveyed to my mind something that was quite terrible and overwhelming. I fell into a violent trembling, and the perspiration poured from my face in streams.

"They were in constant motion about me. They stood close to my side; moved behind me; brushed past my shoulder; stirred the hair on my forehead; and circled round me without ever actually touching me, yet always pressing closer and closer. Especially in the air just over my head there seemed ceaseless movement, and it was accompanied by a confused noise of whispering and sighing that threatened every moment to become articulate in words. To my intense relief, however, I heard no distinct words, and the noise continued more like the rising and falling of the wind than anything else I can imagine.

"But the characteristic of these 'Beings' that impressed me most strongly at the time, and of which I have carried away the most permanent recollection, was that each one of them possessed what seemed to be a *vibrating centre* which impelled it with tremendous force and caused a rapid whirling motion of the atmosphere as it passed me. The air was full of these little vortices of whirring, rotating force, and whenever one of them pressed me too closely I felt as if the nerves in that particular portion of my body had been literally drawn out, absolutely depleted of vitality, and then immediately replaced—but replaced dead, flabby, useless.

"Then, suddenly, for the first time my eyes fell upon Smith. He was crouching against the wall on my right, in an attitude that was obviously defensive, and it was plain he was in extremities. The terror on his face was pitiable, but at the same time there was another expression about the tightly clenched teeth and mouth which showed that he had not lost all control of himself. He wore the most resolute expression I have ever seen on a human countenance, and, though for the moment at a fearful disadvantage, he looked like a man who had confidence in himself, and, in spite of the working of fear, was waiting his opportunity.

"For my part, I was face to face with a situation so utterly beyond my knowledge and comprehension, that I felt as helpless as a child, and as useless.

"'Help me back—quick—into that circle,' I heard him half cry, half whisper to me across the moving vapours.

"My only value appears to have been that I was not afraid to act. Knowing nothing of the forces I was dealing with I had no idea of the deadly perils risked, and I sprang forward and caught him by the arms. He threw all his weight in my direction, and by our combined efforts his body left the wall and lurched across the floor towards the circle.

"Instantly there descended upon us, out of the empty air of that smoke-laden room, a force which I can only compare to the pushing, driving power of a great wind pent up within a narrow space. It was almost explosive in its effect, and it seemed to operate upon all parts of my body equally. It fell upon us with a rushing noise that filled my ears and made me think for a moment the very walls and roof of the building had been torn asunder. Under its first blow we staggered back against the wall, and I understood plainly that its purpose was to prevent us getting back into the circle in the middle of the floor.

"Pouring with perspiration, and breathless, with every muscle strained to the very utmost, we at length managed to get to the edge of the circle, and at this moment, so great was the opposing force, that I felt myself actually torn from Smith's arms, lifted from my feet, and twirled round in the direction of the windows as if the wheel of some great machine had caught my clothes and was tearing me to destruction in its revolution.

"But, even as I fell, bruised and breathless, against the wall, I saw Smith firmly upon his feet in the circle and slowly rising again to an upright position. My eyes never left his figure once in the next few minutes.

"He drew himself up to his full height. His great shoulders squared themselves. His head was thrown back a little, and as I looked I saw the expression on his face change swiftly from fear to one of absolute command. He looked steadily round the room and then his voice began to *vibrate*. At first in a low tone, it gradually rose till it assumed the same volume and intensity I had heard that night when he called up the stairs into my room.

"It was a curiously increasing sound, more like the swelling of an instrument than a human voice; and as it grew in power and filled the room, I became aware that a great change was being effected slowly and surely. The confusion of noise and rushings of air fell into the roll of long, steady vibrations not unlike those caused by the deeper pedals of an organ. The movements in the air became less violent, then grew decidedly weaker, and finally ceased altogether. The whisperings and sighings became fainter and fainter, till at last I could not hear them at all; and, strangest of all, the light emitted by the circle, as well as by the designs round it, increased to a steady glow, casting their radiance upwards with the weirdest possible effect upon his features. Slowly, by the power of his voice, behind which lay undoubtedly a genuine knowledge of the occult manipulation of sound, this man dominated the forces that had escaped from their proper sphere, until at length the room was reduced to silence and perfect order again.

"Judging by the immense relief which also communicated itself to my nerves I then felt that the crisis was over and Smith was wholly master of the situation.

"But hardly had I begun to congratulate myself upon this result, and to gather my scattered senses about me, when, uttering a loud cry, I saw him leap out of the circle and fling himself into the air—as it seemed to me, into the empty air. Then, even while holding my breath for dread of the crash he was bound to come upon the floor, I saw him strike with a dull thud against a solid body in mid-air, and the next instant he was wrestling with some ponderous thing that was absolutely invisible to me, and the room shook with the struggle.

"To and fro *they* swayed, sometimes lurching in one direction, sometimes in another, and always in horrible proximity to myself, as I leaned trembling against the wall and watched the encounter.

"It lasted at most but a short minute or two, ending as suddenly as it had begun. Smith, with an unexpected movement, threw up his arms with a cry of relief. At the same instant there was a wild, tearing shriek in the air beside me and something rushed past us with a noise like the passage of a flock of big birds. Both windows rattled as if they would break away from their sashes. Then a sense of emptiness and peace suddenly came over the room, and I knew that all was over.

"Smith, his face exceedingly white, but otherwise strangely composed, turned to me at once.

"'God!—if you hadn't come—You deflected the stream; broke it up—' he whispered. 'You saved me.'"

The doctor made a long pause. Presently he felt for his pipe in the darkness, groping over the table behind us with both hands. No one spoke for a bit, but all dreaded the sudden glare that would come when he struck the match. The fire was nearly out and the great hall was pitch dark.

But the story-teller did not strike that match. He was merely gaining time for some hidden reason of his own. And presently he went on with his tale in a more subdued voice.

"I quite forget," he said, "how I got back to my own room. I only know that I lay with two lighted candles for the rest of the night, and the first thing I did in the morning was to let the landlady know I was leaving her house at the end of the week.

"Smith still has my Rabbinical Treatise. At least he did not return it to me at the time, and I have never seen him since to ask for it."

A Suspicious Gift

Blake had been in very low water for months—almost under water part of the time—due to circumstances he was fond of saying were no fault of his own; and as he sat writing in his room on "third floor back" of a New York boarding-house, part of his mind was busily occupied in wondering when his luck was going to turn again.

It was his room only in the sense that he paid the rent. Two friends, one a little Frenchman and the other a big Dane, shared it with him, both hoping eventually to contribute something towards expenses, but so far not having accomplished this result. They had two beds only, the third being a mattress they slept upon in turns, a week at a time. A good deal of their irregular "feeding" consisted of oatmeal, potatoes, and sometimes eggs, all of which they cooked on a strange utensil they had contrived to fix into the gas jet.

Occasionally, when dinner failed them altogether, they swallowed a little raw rice and drank hot water from the bathroom on the top of it, and then made a wild race for bed so as to get to sleep while the sensation of false repletion was still there. For sleep and hunger are slight acquaintances as they well knew. Fortunately all New York houses are supplied with hot air, and they only had to open a grating in the wall to get a plentiful, if not a wholesome amount of heat.

Though loneliness in a big city is a real punishment, as they had severally learnt to their cost, their experiences, three in a small room for several months, had revealed to them horrors of quite another kind, and their nerves had suffered according to the temperament of each. But, on this particular evening, as Blake sat scribbling by the only window that was not cracked, the Dane and the Frenchman, his companions in adversity, were in wonderful luck. They had both been asked out to a restaurant to dine with a friend who also held out to one of them a chance of work and remuneration. They would not be back till late, and when they did come they were pretty sure to bring in supplies of one kind or another. For the Frenchman never could resist the offer of a glass of absinthe, and this meant that he would be able to help himself plentifully from the free-lunch counters, with which all New York bars are furnished, and to which any purchaser of a drink is entitled to help himself and devour on the spot or carry away casually in his hand for consumption elsewhere.

Thousands of unfortunate men get their sole subsistence in this way in New York, and experience soon teaches where, for the price of a single drink, a man can take away almost a meal of chip potatoes, sausage, bits of bread, and even eggs. The Frenchman and the Dane knew their way about, and Blake looked forward to a supper more or less substantial before pulling his mattress out of the cupboard and turning in upon the floor for the night.

Meanwhile he could enjoy a quiet and lonely evening with the room all to himself.

In the daytime he was a reporter on an evening newspaper of sensational and lying habits. His work was chiefly in the police courts; and in his spare hours at night, when not too tired or too empty, he wrote sketches and stories for the magazines that very rarely saw the light of day on their printed and paid-for sentences. On this particular occasion he was deep in a most involved tale of a psychological character, and had just worked his way into a sentence, or set of sentences, that completely baffled and muddled him.

He was fairly out of his depth, and his brain was too poorly supplied with blood to invent a way out again. The story would have been interesting had he written it simply, keeping to facts and feelings, and not diving into difficult analysis of motive and character which was quite beyond him. For it was largely autobiographical, and was meant to describe the adventures of a young Englishman who had come to grief in the usual manner on a Canadian farm, had then subsequently become bar-keeper, sub-editor on a Methodist magazine, a teacher of French and German to clerks at twenty-five cents per hour, a model for artists, a super on the stage, and, finally, a wanderer to the goldfields.

Blake scratched his head, and dipped the pen in the inkpot, stared out through the blindless windows, and sighed deeply. His thoughts kept wandering to food, beefsteak and steaming vegetables. The smell of cooking that came from a lower floor through the broken windows was a constant torment to him. He pulled himself together and again attacked the problem.

" . . . for with some people," he wrote, "the imagination is so vivid as to be almost an extension of consciousness. . . ." But here he stuck absolutely. He was not quite sure what he meant by the words, and how to finish the sentence puzzled him into blank inaction. It was a difficult point to decide, for it seemed to come in appropriately at this point in his story, and he did not know whether to leave it as it stood, change it round a bit, or take it out altogether. It might just spoil its chances of being accepted: editors were such clever men. But, to re-write the sentence was a grind, and he was so tired and sleepy. After all, what did it matter? People who were clever would force a meaning into it; people who were not clever would pretend—he knew of no other classes of readers. He would let it stay, and go on with the action of the story. He put his head in his hands and began to think hard.

His mind soon passed from thought to reverie. He fell to wondering when his friends would find work and relieve him of the burden—he acknowledged it as such—of keeping them, and of letting another man wear his best clothes on alternate Sundays. He wondered when his "luck" would turn. There were one or two influential people in New York whom he could go and see if he had a dress suit and the other conventional uniforms. His thoughts ran on far ahead, and at the same time, by a sort of double process, far behind as well.

His home in the "old country" rose up before him; he saw the lawn and the cedars in sunshine; he looked through the familiar windows and saw the clean, swept rooms. His story began to suffer; the psychological masterpiece would not make much progress unless he pulled up and dragged his thoughts back to the treadmill. But he no longer cared; once he had got as far as that cedar with the sunshine on it, he never could get back again. For all he cared, the troublesome sentence might run away and get into someone else's pages, or be snuffed out altogether.

There came a gentle knock at the door, and Blake started. The knock was repeated louder. Who in the world could it be at this late hour of the night? On the floor above, he remembered, there lived another Englishman, a foolish, second-rate creature, who sometimes came in and made himself objectionable with endless and silly chatter. But he was an Englishman for all that, and Blake always tried to treat him with politeness, realising that he was lonely in a strange land. But tonight, of all people in the world, he did not want to be bored with Perry's cackle, as he called it, and the "Come in" he gave in answer to the second knock had no very cordial sound of welcome in it.

However, the door opened in response, and the man came in. Blake did not turn round at once, and the other advanced to the centre of the room, but *without speaking*. Then Blake knew it was not his enemy, Perry, and turned round.

He saw a man of about forty standing in the middle of the carpet, but standing sideways so that he did not present a full face. He wore an overcoat buttoned up to the neck, and on the felt hat which he held in front of him fresh raindrops glistened. In his other hand he carried a small black bag. Blake gave him a good look, and came to the conclusion that he might be a secretary, or a chief clerk, or a confidential man of sorts. He was a shabby-respectable-looking person. This was the sum-total of the first impression, gained the moment his eyes took in that it was *not* Perry; the second impression was less pleasant, and reported at once that something was wrong.

Though otherwise young and inexperienced, Blake—thanks, or curses, to the police court training—knew more about common criminal blackguardism than most men of fifty, and he recognised that there was somewhere a suggestion of this undesirable world about the man. But there was more than this. There was something singular about him, something far out of the common, though for the life of him Blake could not say wherein it lay. The fellow was out of the ordinary, and in some very undesirable manner.

All this, that takes so long to describe, Blake saw with the first and second glance. The man at once began to speak in a quiet and respectful voice.

"Are you Mr. Blake?" he asked.

"I am."

"Mr. Arthur Blake?"

"Yes."

"Mr. Arthur *Herbert* Blake?" persisted the other, with emphasis on the middle name.

"That is my full name," Blake answered simply, adding, as he remembered his manners; "but won't you sit down, first, please?"

The man advanced with a curious sideways motion like a crab and took a seat on the edge of the sofa. He put his hat on the floor at his feet, but still kept the bag in his hand.

"I come to you from a well-wisher," he went on in oily tones, without lifting his eyes. Blake, in his mind, ran quickly over all the people he knew in New York who might possibly have sent such a man, while waiting for him to supply the name. But the man had come to a full stop and was waiting too.

"A well-wisher of *mine*?" repeated Blake, not knowing quite what else to say.

"Just so," replied the other, still with his eyes on the floor. "A well-wisher of yours."

"A man or—" he felt himself blushing, "or a woman?"

"That," said the man shortly, "I cannot tell you."

"You can't tell me!" exclaimed the other, wondering what was coming next, and who in the world this mysterious well-wisher could be who sent so discreet and mysterious a messenger.

"I cannot tell you the name," replied the man firmly. "Those are my instructions. But I bring you something from this person, and I am to give it to you, to take a receipt for it, and then to go away without answering any questions."

Blake stared very hard. The man, however, never raised his eyes above the level of the second china knob on the chest of drawers opposite. The giving of a receipt sounded like money. Could it be that some of his influential friends had heard of his plight? There were possibilities that made his heart beat. At length, however, he found his tongue, for this strange creature was determined apparently to say nothing more until he had heard from him.

"Then, what have you got for me, please?" he asked bluntly.

By way of answer the man proceeded to open the bag. He took out a parcel wrapped loosely in brown paper, and about the size of a large book. It was tied with string, and the man seemed unnecessarily long untying the knot. When at last the string was off and the paper unfolded, there appeared a series of smaller packages inside. The man took them out very carefully, almost as if they had been alive, Blake thought, and set them in a row upon his knees. They were dollar bills. Blake, all in a flutter, craned his neck forward a little to try and make out their denomination. He read plainly the figures 100.

"There are ten thousand dollars here," said the man quietly.

The other could not suppress a little cry.

"And they are for you."

Blake simply gasped. "Ten thousand dollars!" he repeated, a queer feeling growing up in his throat. "*Ten thousand.* Are you sure? I mean—you mean they are for *me*?" he stammered. He felt quite silly with excitement, and grew more so with every minute, as the man maintained a perfect silence. Was it not a dream? Wouldn't the man put them back in the bag presently and say it was a mistake, and they were meant for somebody else? He could not believe his eyes or his ears. Yet, in a sense, it was possible. He had read of such things in books, and even come across them in his experience of the courts—the erratic and generous philanthropist who is determined to do his good deed and to get no thanks or acknowledgment for it.

Still, it seemed almost incredible. His troubles began to melt away like bubbles in the sun; he thought of the other fellows when they came in, and what he would have to tell them; he thought of the German landlady and the arrears of rent, of regular food and clean linen, and books and music, of the chance of getting into some respectable business, of—well, of as many things as it is possible to think of when excitement and surprise fling wide open the gates of the imagination.

The man, meanwhile, began quietly to count over the packages aloud from one to ten, and then to count the bills in each separate packet, also from one to ten. Yes, there were ten little heaps, each containing ten bills of a hundred-dollar denomination. That made ten thousand dollars. Blake had never seen so much money in a single lump in his life before; and for many months of privation and discomfort he had not known the "feel" of a twenty-dollar note, much less of a hundred-dollar one. He heard them crackle under the man's fingers, and it was like crisp laughter in his ears. The bills were evidently new and unused.

But, side by side with the excitement caused by the shock of such an event, Blake's caution, acquired by a year of vivid New York experience, was meanwhile beginning to assert itself. It all seemed just a little too much out of the likely order of things to be quite right. The police courts had taught him the amazing ingenuity of the criminal mind, as well as something of the plots and devices by which the unwary are beguiled into the dark places where blackmail may be levied with impunity. New York, as a matter of fact, just at that time was literally undermined with the secret ways of the blackmailers, the green-goods men, and other police-protected abominations; and the only weak point in the supposition that this was part of some such proceeding was the selection of himself—a poor newspaper reporter—as a victim. It did seem absurd, but then the whole thing was so out of the ordinary, and the thought once having entered his mind, was not so easily got rid of. Blake resolved to be very cautious.

The man meanwhile, though he never appeared to raise his eyes from the carpet, had been watching him closely all the time.

"If you will give me a receipt I'll leave the money at once," he said, with just a vestige of impatience in his tone, as if he were anxious to bring the matter to a conclusion as soon as possible.

"But you say it is quite impossible for you to tell me the name of my well-wisher, or why *she* sends me such a large sum of money in this extraordinary way?"

"The money is sent to you because you are in need of it," returned the other; "and it is a present without conditions of any sort attached. You have to give me a receipt only to satisfy the sender that it has reached your hands. The money will never be asked of you again."

Blake noticed two things from this answer: first, that the man was not to be caught into betraying the sex of the well-wisher; and secondly, that he was in some hurry to complete the transaction. For he was now giving reasons, attractive reasons, why he should accept the money and make out the receipt.

Suddenly it flashed across his mind that if he took the money and gave the receipt *before a witness*, nothing very disastrous could come of the affair. It would protect him against blackmail, if this was, after all, a plot of some sort with blackmail in it; whereas, if the man were a madman, or a criminal who was getting rid of a portion of his ill-gotten gains to divert suspicion, or if any other improbable explanation turned out to be the true one, there was no great harm done, and he could hold the money till it was claimed, or advertised for in the newspapers. His mind rapidly ran over these possibilities, though, of course, under the stress of excitement, he was unable to weigh any of them properly; then he turned to his strange visitor again and said quietly—

"I will take the money, although I must say it seems to me a very unusual transaction, and I will give you for it such a receipt as I think proper under the circumstances."

"A proper receipt is all I want," was the answer.

"I mean by that a receipt before a proper witness—"

"Perfectly satisfactory," interrupted the man, his eyes still on the carpet. "Only, it must be dated, and headed with your address here in the correct way."

Blake could see no possible objection to this, and he at once proceeded to obtain his witness. The person he had in his mind was a Mr. Barclay, who occupied the room above his own; an old gentleman who had retired from business and who, the landlady always said, was a miser, and kept large sums secreted in his room. He was, at any rate, a perfectly respectable man and would make an admirable witness to a transaction of this sort. Blake made an apology and rose to fetch him, crossing the room in front of the sofa where the man sat, in order to reach the door. As he did so, he saw for the first time the *other side* of his visitor's face, the side that had been always so carefully turned away from him.

There was a broad smear of blood down the skin from the ear to the neck. It glistened in the gaslight.

Blake never knew how he managed to smother the cry that sprang to his lips, but smother it he did. In a second he was at the door, his knees trembling, his mind in a sudden and dreadful turmoil.

His main object, so far as he could recollect afterwards, was to escape from the room as if he had noticed nothing, so as not to arouse the other's suspicions. The man's eyes were always on the carpet, and probably, Blake hoped, he had not noticed the consternation that must have been written plainly on his face. At any rate he had uttered no cry.

In another second he would have been in the passage, when suddenly he met a pair of wicked, staring eyes fixed intently and with a cunning smile upon his own. It was the other's face in the mirror calmly watching his every movement.

Instantly, all his powers of reflection flew to the winds, and he thought only upon the desirability of getting help at once. He tore upstairs, his heart in his mouth. Barclay must come to his aid. This matter was serious—perhaps horribly serious. Taking the money, or giving a receipt, or having anything at all to do with it became an impossibility. Here was crime. He felt certain of it.

In three bounds he reached the next landing and began to hammer at the old miser's door as if his very life depended on it. For a long time he could get no answer. His fists seemed to make no noise. He might have been knocking on cotton wool, and the thought dashed through his brain that it was all just like the terror of a nightmare.

Barclay, evidently, was still out, or else sound asleep. But the other simply could not wait a minute longer in suspense. He turned the handle and walked into the room. At first he saw nothing for the darkness, and made sure the owner of the room was out; but the moment the light from the passage began a little to disperse the gloom, he saw the old man, to his immense relief, lying asleep on the bed.

Blake opened the door to its widest to get more light and then walked quickly up to the bed. He now saw the figure more plainly, and noted that it was dressed and lay only upon the outside of the bed. It struck him, too, that he was sleeping in a very odd, almost an unnatural, position.

Something clutched at his heart as he looked closer. He stumbled over a chair and found the matches. Calling upon Barclay the whole time to wake up and come downstairs with him, he blundered across the floor, a dreadful thought in his mind, and lit the gas over the table. It seemed strange that there was no movement or reply to his shouting. But it no longer seemed strange when at length he turned, in the full glare of the gas, and saw the old man lying huddled up into a ghastly heap on the bed, his throat cut across from ear to ear.

And all over the carpet lay new dollar bills, crisp and clean like those he had left downstairs, and strewn about in little heaps.

For a moment Blake stood stock-still, bereft of all power of movement. The next, his courage returned, and he fled from the room and dashed downstairs, taking five steps at a time. He reached the bottom and tore along the passage to his room, determined at any rate to seize the man and prevent his escape till help came.

But when he got to the end of the little landing he found that his door had been closed. He seized the handle, fumbling with it in his violence. It felt slippery and kept turning under his fingers without opening the door, and fully half a minute passed before it yielded and let him in headlong.

At the first glance he saw the room was empty, and the man gone!

Scattered upon the carpet lay a number of the bills, and beside them, half hidden under the sofa where the man had sat, he saw a pair of gloves—thick, leathern gloves—and a butcher's knife. Even from the distance where he stood the blood-stains on both were easily visible.

Dazed and confused by the terrible discoveries of the last few minutes, Blake stood in the middle of the room, overwhelmed and unable to think or move. Unconsciously he must have passed his hand over his forehead in the natural gesture of perplexity, for he noticed that the skin felt wet and sticky. His hand was covered with blood! And when he rushed in terror to the looking-glass, he saw that there was a broad red smear across his face and forehead. Then he remembered the slippery handle of the door and knew that it had been carefully moistened!

In an instant the whole plot became clear as daylight, and he was so spellbound with horror that a sort of numbness came over him and he came very near to fainting. He was in a condition of utter helplessness, and had anyone come into the room at that minute and called him by name he would simply have dropped to the floor in a heap.

"If the police were to come in now!" The thought crashed through his brain like thunder, and at the same moment, almost before he had time to appreciate a quarter of its significance, there came a loud knocking at the front door below. The bell rang with a dreadful clamour; men's voices were heard talking excitedly, and presently heavy steps began to come up the stairs in the direction of his room.

It *was* the police!

And all Blake could do was to laugh foolishly to himself—and wait till they were upon him. He could not move nor speak. He stood face to face with the evidence of his horrid crime, his hands and face smeared with the blood of his victim, and there he was standing when the police burst open the door and came noisily into the room.

"Here it is!" cried a voice he knew. "Third floor back! And the fellow caught red-handed!"

It was the man with the bag leading in the two policemen.

Hardly knowing what he was doing in the fearful stress of conflicting emotions, he made a step forward. But before he had time to make a second one, he felt the heavy hand of the law descend upon both shoulders at once as the two policemen moved up to seize him. At the same moment a voice of thunder cried in his ear—

"Wake up, man! Wake up! Here's the supper, and good news too!"

Blake turned with a start in his chair and saw the Dane, very red in the face, standing beside him, a hand on each shoulder, and a little further back he saw the Frenchman leering happily at him over the end of the bed, a bottle of beer in one hand and a paper package in the other.

He rubbed his eyes, glancing from one to the other, and then got up sleepily to fix the wire arrangement on the gas jet to boil water for cooking the eggs which the Frenchman was in momentary danger of letting drop upon the floor.

Keeping His Promise

It was eleven o'clock at night, and young Marriott was locked into his room, cramming as hard as he could cram. He was a "Fourth Year Man" at Edinburgh University and he had been ploughed for this particular examination so often that his parents had positively declared they could no longer supply the funds to keep him there.

His rooms were cheap and dingy, but it was the lecture fees that took the money. So Marriott pulled himself together at last and definitely made up his mind that he would pass or die in the attempt, and for some weeks now he had been reading as hard as mortal man can read. He was trying to make up for lost time and money in a way that showed conclusively he did not understand the value of either. For no ordinary man—and Marriott was in every sense an ordinary man—can afford to drive the mind as he had lately been driving his, without sooner or later paying the cost.

Among the students he had few friends or acquaintances, and these few had promised not to disturb him at night, knowing he was at last reading in earnest. It was, therefore, with feelings a good deal stronger than mere surprise that he heard his doorbell ring on this particular night and realised that he was to have a visitor. Some men would simply have muffled the bell and gone on quietly with their work. But Marriott was not this sort. He was nervous. It would have bothered and pecked at his mind all night long not to know who the visitor was and what he wanted. The only thing to do, therefore, was to let him in—and out again—as quickly as possible.

The landlady went to bed at ten o'clock punctually, after which hour nothing would induce her to pretend she heard the bell, so Marriott jumped up from his books with an exclamation that augured ill for the reception of his caller, and prepared to let him in with his own hand.

The streets of Edinburgh town were very still at this late hour—it was late for Edinburgh—and in the quiet neighbourhood of F—— Street, where Marriott lived on the third floor, scarcely a sound broke the silence. As he crossed the floor, the bell rang a second time, with unnecessary clamour, and he unlocked the door and passed into the little hallway with considerable wrath and annoyance in his heart at the insolence of the double interruption.

"The fellows all know I'm reading for this exam. Why in the world do they come to bother me at such an unearthly hour?"

The inhabitants of the building, with himself, were medical students, general students, poor Writers to the Signet, and some others whose vocations were perhaps not so obvious. The stone staircase, dimly lighted at each floor by a gas-jet that would not turn above a certain height, wound down to the level of the street with no pretence at carpet or railing. At some levels it was cleaner than at others. It depended on the landlady of the particular level.

The acoustic properties of a spiral staircase seem to be peculiar. Marriott, standing by the open door, book in hand, thought every moment the owner of the footsteps would come into view. The sound of the boots was so close and so loud that they seemed to travel disproportionately in advance of their cause. Wondering who it could be, he stood ready with all manner of sharp greetings for the man who dared thus to disturb his work. But the man did not appear. The steps sounded almost under his nose, yet no one was visible.

A sudden queer sensation of fear passed over him—a faintness and a shiver down the back. It went, however, almost as soon as it came, and he was just debating whether he would call aloud to his invisible visitor, or slam the door and return to his books, when the cause of the disturbance turned the corner very slowly and came into view.

It was a stranger. He saw a youngish man short of figure and very broad. His face was the colour of a piece of chalk and the eyes, which were very bright, had heavy lines underneath them. Though the cheeks and chin were unshaven and the general appearance unkempt, the man was evidently a gentleman, for he was well dressed and bore himself with a certain air. But, strangest of all, he wore no hat, and carried none in his hand; and although rain had been falling steadily all the evening, he appeared to have neither overcoat nor umbrella.

A hundred questions sprang up in Marriott's mind and rushed to his lips, chief among which was something like "Who in the world are you?" and "What in the name of heaven do you come to me for?" But none of these questions found time to express themselves in words, for almost at once the caller turned his head a little so that the gas light in the hall fell upon his features from a new angle. Then in a flash Marriott recognised him.

"Field! Man alive! Is it you?" he gasped.

The Fourth Year Man was not lacking in intuition, and he perceived at once that here was a case for delicate treatment. He divined, without any actual process of thought, that the catastrophe often predicted had come at last, and that this man's father had turned him out of the house. They had been at a private school together years before, and though they had hardly met once since, the news had not failed to reach him from time to time with considerable detail, for the family lived near his own and between certain of the sisters there was great intimacy. Young Field had gone wild later, he remembered hearing about it all—drink, a woman, opium, or something of the sort—he could not exactly call to mind.

"Come in," he said at once, his anger vanishing. "There's been something wrong, I can see. Come in, and tell me all about it and perhaps I can help—" He hardly knew what to say, and stammered a lot more besides. The dark side of life, and the horror of it, belonged to a world that lay remote from his own select little atmosphere of books and dreamings. But he had a man's heart for all that.

He led the way across the hall, shutting the front door carefully behind him, and noticed as he did so that the other, though certainly sober, was unsteady on his legs, and evidently much exhausted. Marriott might not be able to pass his examinations, but he at least knew the symptoms of starvation—acute starvation, unless he was much mistaken—when they stared him in the face.

"Come along," he said cheerfully, and with genuine sympathy in his voice. "I'm glad to see you. I was going to have a bite of something to eat, and you're just in time to join me."

The other made no audible reply, and shuffled so feebly with his feet that Marriott took his arm by way of support. He noticed for the first time that the clothes hung on him with pitiful looseness. The broad frame was literally hardly more than a frame. He was as thin as a skeleton. But, as he touched him, the sensation of faintness and dread returned. It only lasted a moment, and then passed off, and he ascribed it not unnaturally to the distress and shock of seeing a former friend in such a pitiful plight.

"Better let me guide you. It's shamefully dark—this hall. I'm always complaining," he said lightly, recognising by the weight upon his arm that the guidance was sorely needed, "but the old cat never does anything except promise." He led him to the sofa, wondering all the time where he had come from and how he had found out the address. It must be at least seven years since those days at the private school when they used to be such close friends.

"Now, if you'll forgive me for a minute," he said, "I'll get supper ready—such as it is. And don't bother to talk. Just take it easy on the sofa. I see you're dead tired. You can tell me about it afterwards, and we'll make plans."

The other sat down on the edge of the sofa and stared in silence, while Marriott got out the brown loaf, scones, and huge pot of marmalade that Edinburgh students always keep in their cupboards. His eyes shone with a brightness that suggested drugs, Marriott thought, stealing a glance at him from behind the cupboard door. He did not like yet to take a full square look. The fellow was in a bad way, and it would have been so like an examination to stare and wait for explanations. Besides, he was evidently almost too exhausted to speak. So, for reasons of delicacy—and for another reason as well which he could not exactly formulate to himself—he let his visitor rest apparently unnoticed, while he busied himself with the supper. He lit the spirit lamp to make cocoa, and when the water was boiling he drew up the table with the good things to the sofa, so that Field need not have even the trouble of moving to a chair.

"Now, let's tuck in," he said, "and afterwards we'll have a pipe and a chat. I'm reading for an exam, you know, and I always have something about this time. It's jolly to have a companion."

He looked up and caught his guest's eyes directed straight upon his own. An involuntary shudder ran through him from head to foot. The face opposite him was deadly white and wore a dreadful expression of pain and mental suffering.

"By Gad!" he said, jumping up, "I quite forgot. I've got some whisky somewhere. What an ass I am. I never touch it myself when I'm working like this."

He went to the cupboard and poured out a stiff glass which the other swallowed at a single gulp and without any water. Marriott watched him while he drank it, and at the same time noticed something else as well—Field's coat was all over dust, and on one shoulder was a bit of cobweb. It was perfectly dry; Field arrived on a soaking wet night without hat, umbrella, or overcoat, and yet perfectly dry, even dusty. Therefore he had been under cover. What did it all mean? Had he been hiding in the building? . . .

It was very strange. Yet he volunteered nothing; and Marriott had pretty well made up his mind by this time that he would not ask any questions until he had eaten and slept. Food and sleep were obviously what the poor devil needed most and first—he was pleased with his powers of ready diagnosis—and it would not be fair to press him till he had recovered a bit.

They ate their supper together while the host carried on a running one-sided conversation, chiefly about himself and his exams and his "old cat" of a landlady, so that the guest need not utter a single word unless he really wished to—which he evidently did not! But, while he toyed with his food, feeling no desire to eat, the other ate voraciously. To see a hungry man devour cold scones, stale oatcake, and brown bread laden with marmalade was a revelation to this inexperienced student who had never known what it was to be without at least three meals a day. He watched in spite of himself, wondering why the fellow did not choke in the process.

But Field seemed to be as sleepy as he was hungry. More than once his head dropped and he ceased to masticate the food in his mouth. Marriott had positively to shake him before he would go on with his meal. A stronger emotion will overcome a weaker, but this struggle between the sting of real hunger and the magical opiate of overpowering sleep was a curious sight to the student, who watched it with mingled astonishment and alarm. He had heard of the pleasure it was to feed hungry men, and watch them eat, but he had never actually witnessed it, and he had no idea it was like this. Field ate like an animal—gobbled, stuffed, gorged. Marriott forgot his reading, and began to feel something very much like a lump in his throat.

"Afraid there's been awfully little to offer you, old man," he managed to blurt out when at length the last scone had disappeared, and the rapid, one-sided meal was at an end. Field still made no reply, for he was almost asleep in his seat. He merely looked up wearily and gratefully.

"Now you must have some sleep, you know," he continued, "or you'll go to pieces. I shall be up all night reading for this blessed exam. You're more than welcome to my bed. Tomorrow we'll have a late breakfast and—and see what can be done—and make plans—I'm awfully good at making plans, you know," he added with an attempt at lightness.

Field maintained his "dead sleepy" silence, but appeared to acquiesce, and the other led the way into the bedroom, apologising as he did so to this half-starved son of a baronet—whose own home was almost a palace—for the size of the room. The weary guest, however, made no pretence of thanks or politeness. He merely steadied himself on his friend's arm as he staggered across the room, and then, with all his clothes on, dropped his exhausted body on the bed. In less than a minute he was to all appearances sound asleep.

For several minutes Marriott stood in the open door and watched him; praying devoutly that he might never find himself in a like predicament, and then fell to wondering what he would do with his unbidden guest on the morrow. But he did not stop long to think, for the call of his books was imperative, and happen what might, he must see to it that he passed that examination.

Having again locked the door into the hall, he sat down to his books and resumed his notes on *materia medica* where he had left off when the bell rang. But it was difficult for some time to concentrate his mind on the subject. His thoughts kept wandering to the picture of that white-faced, strange-eyed fellow, starved and dirty, lying in his clothes and boots on the bed. He recalled their schooldays together before they had drifted apart, and how they had vowed eternal friendship—and all the rest of it. And now! What horrible straits to be in. How could any man let the love of dissipation take such hold upon him?

But one of their vows together Marriott, it seemed, had completely forgotten. Just now, at any rate, it lay too far in the background of his memory to be recalled.

Through the half-open door—the bedroom led out of the sitting-room and had no other door—came the sound of deep, long-drawn breathing, the regular, steady breathing of a tired man, so tired that, even to listen to it made Marriott almost want to go to sleep himself.

"He needed it," reflected the student, "and perhaps it came only just in time!"

Perhaps so; for outside the bitter wind from across the Forth howled cruelly and drove the rain in cold streams against the window-panes, and down the deserted streets. Long before Marriott settled down again properly to his reading, he heard distantly, as it were, through the sentences of the book, the heavy, deep breathing of the sleeper in the next room.

A couple of hours later, when he yawned and changed his books, he still heard the breathing, and went cautiously up to the door to look round.

At first the darkness of the room must have deceived him, or else his eyes were confused and dazzled by the recent glare of the reading lamp. For a minute or two he could make out nothing at all but dark lumps of furniture, the mass of the chest of drawers by the wall, and the white patch where his bath stood in the centre of the floor.

Then the bed came slowly into view. And on it he saw the outline of the sleeping body gradually take shape before his eyes, growing up strangely into the darkness, till it stood out in marked relief—the long black form against the white counterpane.

He could hardly help smiling. Field had not moved an inch. He watched him a moment or two and then returned to his books. The night was full of the singing voices of the wind and rain. There was no sound of traffic; no hansoms clattered over the cobbles, and it was still too early for the milk carts. He worked on steadily and conscientiously, only stopping now and again to change a book, or to sip some of the poisonous stuff that kept him awake and made his brain so active, and on these occasions Field's breathing was always distinctly audible in the room.

Outside, the storm continued to howl, but inside the house all was stillness. The shade of the reading lamp threw all the light upon the littered table, leaving the other end of the room in comparative darkness. The bedroom door was exactly opposite him where he sat. There was nothing to disturb the worker, nothing but an occasional rush of wind against the windows, and a slight pain in his arm.

This pain, however, which he was unable to account for, grew once or twice very acute. It bothered him; and he tried to remember how, and when, he could have bruised himself so severely, but without success.

At length the page before him turned from yellow to grey, and there were sounds of wheels in the street below. It was four o'clock. Marriott leaned back and yawned prodigiously. Then he drew back the curtains. The storm had subsided and the Castle Rock was shrouded in mist. With another yawn he turned away from the dreary outlook and prepared to sleep the remaining four hours till breakfast on the sofa. Field was still breathing heavily in the next room, and he first tiptoed across the floor to take another look at him.

Peering cautiously round the half-opened door his first glance fell upon the bed now plainly discernible in the grey light of morning. He stared hard. Then he rubbed his eyes. Then he rubbed his eyes again and thrust his head farther round the edge of the door. With fixed eyes he stared harder still, and harder.

But it made no difference at all. He was staring into an empty room.

The sensation of fear he had felt when Field first appeared upon the scene returned suddenly, but with much greater force. He became conscious, too, that his left arm was throbbing violently and causing him great pain. He stood wondering, and staring, and trying to collect his thoughts. He was trembling from head to foot.

By a great effort of the will he left the support of the door and walked forward boldly into the room.

There, upon the bed, was the impress of a body, where Field had lain and slept. There was the mark of the head on the pillow, and the slight indentation at the foot of the bed where the boots had rested on the counterpane. And there, plainer than ever—for he was closer to it—was *the breathing*!

Marriott tried to pull himself together. With a great effort he found his voice and called his friend aloud by name!

"Field! Is that you? Where are you?"

There was no reply; but the breathing continued without interruption, coming directly from the bed. His voice had such an unfamiliar sound that Marriott did not care to repeat his questions, but he went down on his knees and examined the bed above and below, pulling the mattress off finally, and taking the coverings away separately one by one. But though the sounds continued there was no visible sign of Field, nor was there any space in which a human being, however small, could have concealed itself. He pulled the bed out from the wall, but the sound *stayed where it was*. It did not move with the bed.

Marriott, finding self-control a little difficult in his weary condition, at once set about a thorough search of the room. He went through the cupboard, the chest of drawers, the little alcove where the clothes hung—everything. But there was no sign of anyone. The small window near the ceiling was closed; and, anyhow, was not large enough to let a cat pass. The sitting-room door was locked on the inside; he could not have got out that way. Curious thoughts began to trouble Marriott's mind, bringing in their train unwelcome sensations. He grew more and more excited; he searched the bed again till it resembled the scene of a pillow fight; he searched both rooms, knowing all the time it was useless,—and then he searched again. A cold perspiration broke out all over his body; and the sound of heavy breathing, all this time, never ceased to come from the corner where Field had lain down to sleep.

Then he tried something else. He pushed the bed back exactly into its original position—and himself lay down upon it just where his guest had lain. But the same instant he sprang up again in a single bound. The breathing was close beside him, almost on his cheek, and between him and the wall! Not even a child could have squeezed into the space.

He went back into his sitting-room, opened the windows, welcoming all the light and air possible, and tried to think the whole matter over quietly and clearly. Men who read too hard, and slept too little, he knew were sometimes troubled with very vivid hallucinations. Again he calmly reviewed every incident of the night; his accurate sensations; the vivid details; the emotions stirred in him; the dreadful feast—no single hallucination could ever combine all these and cover so long a period of time. But with less satisfaction he thought of the recurring faintness, and curious sense of horror that had once or twice come over him, and then of the violent pains in his arm. These were quite unaccountable.

Moreover, now that he began to analyse and examine, there was one other thing that fell upon him like a sudden revelation: *During the whole time Field had not actually uttered a single word!* Yet, as though in mockery upon his reflections, there came ever from that inner room the sound of the breathing, long-drawn, deep, and regular. The thing was incredible. It was absurd.

Haunted by visions of brain fever and insanity, Marriott put on his cap and macintosh and left the house. The morning air on Arthur's Seat would blow the cobwebs from his brain; the scent of the heather, and above all, the sight of the sea. He roamed over the wet slopes above Holyrood for a couple of hours, and did not return until the exercise had shaken some of the horror out of his bones, and given him a ravening appetite into the bargain.

As he entered he saw that there was another man in the room, standing against the window with his back to the light. He recognised his fellow-student Greene, who was reading for the same examination.

"Read hard all night, Marriott," he said, "and thought I'd drop in here to compare notes and have some breakfast. You're out early?" he added, by way of a question. Marriott said he had a headache and a walk had helped it, and Greene nodded and said "Ah!" But when the girl had set the steaming porridge on the table and gone out again, he went on with rather a forced tone, "Didn't know you had any friends who drank, Marriott?"

This was obviously tentative, and Marriott replied drily that he did not know it either.

"Sounds just as if some chap were 'sleeping it off' in there, doesn't it, though?" persisted the other, with a nod in the direction of the bedroom, and looking curiously at his friend. The two men stared steadily at each other for several seconds, and then Marriott said earnestly—

"Then you hear it too, thank God!"

"Of course I hear it. The door's open. Sorry if I wasn't meant to."

"Oh, I don't mean that," said Marriott, lowering his voice. "But I'm awfully relieved. Let me explain. Of course, if you hear it too, then it's all right; but really it frightened me more than I can tell you. I thought I was going to have brain fever, or something, and you know what a lot depends on this exam. It always begins with sounds, or visions, or some sort of beastly hallucination, and I—"

"Rot!" ejaculated the other impatiently. "What *are* you talking about?"

"Now, listen to me, Greene," said Marriott, as calmly as he could, for the breathing was still plainly audible, "and I'll tell you what I mean, only don't interrupt." And thereupon he related exactly what had happened during the night, telling everything, even down to the pain in his arm. When it was over he got up from the table and crossed the room.

"You hear the breathing now plainly, don't you?" he said. Greene said he did. "Well, come with me, and we'll search the room together." The other, however, did not move from his chair.

"I've been in already," he said sheepishly; "I heard the sounds and thought it was you. The door was ajar—so I went in."

Marriott made no comment, but pushed the door open as wide as it would go. As it opened, the sound of breathing grew more and more distinct.

"*Someone* must be in there," said Greene under his breath.

"*Someone* is in there, but *where*?" said Marriott. Again he urged his friend to go in with him. But Greene refused point-blank; said he had been in once and had searched the room and there was nothing there. He would not go in again for a good deal.

They shut the door and retired into the other room to talk it all over with many pipes. Greene questioned his friend very closely, but without illuminating result, since questions cannot alter facts.

"The only thing that ought to have a proper, a logical, explanation is the pain in my arm," said Marriott, rubbing that member with an attempt at a smile. "It hurts so infernally and aches all the way up. I can't remember bruising it, though."

"Let me examine it for you," said Greene. "I'm awfully good at bones in spite of the examiners' opinion to the contrary." It was a relief to play the fool a bit, and Marriott took his coat off and rolled up his sleeve.

"By George, though, I'm bleeding!" he exclaimed. "Look here! What on earth's this?"

On the forearm, quite close to the wrist, was a thin red line. There was a tiny drop of apparently fresh blood on it. Greene came over and looked closely at it for some minutes. Then he sat back in his chair, looking curiously at his friend's face.

"You've scratched yourself without knowing it," he said presently.

"There's no sign of a bruise. It must be something else that made the arm ache."

Marriott sat very still, staring silently at his arm as though the solution of the whole mystery lay there actually written upon the skin.

"What's the matter? I see nothing very strange about a scratch," said Greene, in an unconvincing sort of voice. "It was your cuff links probably. Last night in your excitement—"

But Marriott, white to the very lips, was trying to speak. The sweat stood in great beads on his forehead. At last he leaned forward close to his friend's face.

"Look," he said, in a low voice that shook a little. "Do you see that red mark? I mean *underneath* what you call the scratch?"

Greene admitted he saw something or other, and Marriott wiped the place clean with his handkerchief and told him to look again more closely.

"Yes, I see," returned the other, lifting his head after a moment's careful inspection. "It looks like an old scar."

"It *is* an old scar," whispered Marriott, his lips trembling. "*Now* it all comes back to me."

"All what?" Greene fidgeted on his chair. He tried to laugh, but without success. His friend seemed bordering on collapse.

"Hush! Be quiet, and—I'll tell you," he said. "*Field made that scar.*"

For a whole minute the two men looked each other full in the face without speaking.

"Field made that scar!" repeated Marriott at length in a louder voice.

"Field! You mean—last night?"

"No, not last night. Years ago—at school, with his knife. And I made a scar in his arm with mine." Marriott was talking rapidly now.

"We exchanged drops of blood in each other's cuts. He put a drop into my arm and I put one into his—"

"In the name of heaven, what for?"

"It was a boys' compact. We made a sacred pledge, a bargain. I remember it all perfectly now. We had been reading some dreadful book and we swore to appear to one another—I mean, whoever died first swore to show himself to the other. And we sealed the compact with each other's blood. I remember it all so well—the hot summer afternoon in the playground, seven years ago—and one of the masters caught us and confiscated the knives—and I have never thought of it again to this day—"

"And you mean—" stammered Greene.

But Marriott made no answer. He got up and crossed the room and lay down wearily upon the sofa, hiding his face in his hands.

Greene himself was a bit non-plussed. He left his friend alone for a little while, thinking it all over again. Suddenly an idea seemed to strike him. He went over to where Marriott still lay motionless on the sofa and roused him. In any case it was better to face the matter, whether there was an explanation or not. Giving in was always the silly exit.

"I say, Marriott," he began, as the other turned his white face up to him. "There's no good being so upset about it. I mean—if it's all an hallucination we know what to do. And if it isn't—well, we know what to think, don't we?"

"I suppose so. But it frightens me horribly for some reason," returned his friend in a hushed voice. "And that poor devil—"

"But, after all, if the worst is true and—and that chap *has* kept his promise—well, he has, that's all, isn't it?"

Marriott nodded.

"There's only one thing that occurs to me," Greene went on, "and that is, are you quite sure that—that he really ate like that—I mean that he actually *ate anything at all*?" he finished, blurting out all his thought.

Marriott stared at him for a moment and then said he could easily make certain. He spoke quietly. After the main shock no lesser surprise could affect him.

"I put the things away myself," he said, "after we had finished. They are on the third shelf in that cupboard. No one's touched 'em since."

He pointed without getting up, and Greene took the hint and went over to look.

"Exactly," he said, after a brief examination; "just as I thought. It was partly hallucination, at any rate. The things haven't been touched. Come and see for yourself."

Together they examined the shelf. There was the brown loaf, the plate of stale scones, the oatcake, all untouched. Even the glass of whisky Marriott had poured out stood there with the whisky still in it.

"You were feeding—no one," said Greene "Field ate and drank nothing. He was not there at all!"

"But the breathing?" urged the other in a low voice, staring with a dazed expression on his face.

Greene did not answer. He walked over to the bedroom, while Marriott followed him with his eyes. He opened the door, and listened. There was no need for words. The sound of deep, regular breathing came floating through the air. There was no hallucination about that, at any rate. Marriott could hear it where he stood on the other side of the room.

Greene closed the door and came back. "There's only one thing to do," he declared with decision. "Write home and find out about him, and meanwhile come and finish your reading in my rooms. I've got an extra bed."

"Agreed," returned the Fourth Year Man; "there's no hallucination about that exam; I must pass that whatever happens."

And this was what they did.

It was about a week later when Marriott got the answer from his sister. Part of it he read out to Greene—she wrote:

> It is curious, that in your letter you should have enquired after Field. It seems a terrible thing, but you know only a short while ago Sir John's patience became exhausted, and he turned him out of the house, they say without a penny. Well, what do you think? He has killed himself. At least, it looks like suicide. Instead of leaving the house, he went down into the cellar and simply starved himself to death. . . . They're trying to suppress it, of course, but I heard it all from my maid, who got it from

their footman. . . . They found the body on the 14th and the doctor said he had died about twelve hours before. . . . He was dreadfully thin. . . .

"Then he died on the 13th," said Greene.
Marriott nodded.
"That's the very night he came to see you."
Marriott nodded again.

The Wood of the Dead

One summer, in my wanderings with a knapsack, I was at luncheon in the room of a wayside inn in the western country, when the door opened and there entered an old rustic, who crossed close to my end of the table and sat himself down very quietly in the seat by the bow window. We exchanged glances, or, properly speaking, nods, for at the moment I did not actually raise my eyes to his face, so concerned was I with the important business of satisfying an appetite gained by tramping twelve miles over a difficult country.

The fine warm rain of seven o'clock, which had since risen in a kind of luminous mist about the tree tops, now floated far overhead in a deep blue sky, and the day was settling down into a blaze of golden light. It was one of those days peculiar to Somerset and North Devon, when the orchards shine and the meadows seem to add a radiance of their own, so brilliantly soft are the colourings of grass and foliage.

The innkeeper's daughter, a little maiden with a simple country loveliness, presently entered with a foaming pewter mug, enquired after my welfare, and went out again. Apparently she had not noticed the old man sitting in the settle by the bow window, nor had he, for his part, so much as once turned his head in our direction.

Under ordinary circumstances I should probably have given no thought to this other occupant of the room; but the fact that it was supposed to be reserved for my private use, and the singular thing that he sat looking aimlessly out of the window, with no attempt to engage me in conversation, drew my eyes more than once somewhat curiously upon him, and I soon caught myself wondering why he sat there so silently, and always with averted head.

He was, I saw, a rather bent old man in rustic dress, and the skin of his face was wrinkled like that of an apple; corduroy trousers were caught up with a string below the knee, and he wore a sort of brown fustian jacket that was very much faded. His thin hand rested upon a stoutish stick. He wore no hat and carried none, and I noticed that his head, covered with silvery hair, was finely shaped and gave the impression of something noble.

Though rather piqued by his studied disregard of my presence, I came to the conclusion that he probably had something to do with the little hostel and had a perfect right to use this room with freedom, and I finished my luncheon without breaking the silence and then took the settle opposite to smoke a pipe before going on my way.

Through the open window came the scents of the blossoming fruit trees; the orchard was drenched in sunshine and the branches danced lazily in the breeze; the grass below fairly shone with white and yellow daisies, and the red roses climbing in profusion over the casement mingled their perfume with the sweetly penetrating odour of the sea.

It was a place to dawdle in, to lie and dream away a whole afternoon, watching the sleepy butterflies and listening to the chorus of birds which seemed to fill every corner of the sky. Indeed, I was already debating in my mind whether to linger and enjoy it all instead of taking the strenuous pathway over the hills, when the old rustic in the settle opposite suddenly turned his face towards me for the first time and began to speak.

His voice had a quiet dreamy note in it that was quite in harmony with the day and the scene, but it sounded far away, I thought, almost as though it came to me from outside where the shadows were weaving their eternal tissue of dreams upon the garden floor. Moreover, there was no trace in it of the rough quality one might naturally have expected, and, now that I saw the full face of the speaker for the first time, I noted with something like a start that the deep, gentle eyes seemed far more in keeping with the timbre of the voice than with the rough and very countrified appearance of the clothes and manner. His voice set pleasant waves of sound in motion towards me, and the actual words, if I remember rightly, were—

"You are a stranger in these parts?" or "Is not this part of the country strange to you?"

There was no "sir," nor any outward and visible sign of the deference usually paid by real country folk to the town-bred visitor, but in its place a gentleness, almost a sweetness, of polite sympathy that was far more of a compliment than either.

I answered that I was wandering on foot through a part of the country that was wholly new to me, and that I was surprised not to find a place of such idyllic loveliness marked upon my map.

"I have lived here all my life," he said, with a sigh, "and am never tired of coming back to it again."

"Then you no longer live in the immediate neighbourhood?"

"I have moved," he answered briefly, adding after a pause in which his eyes seemed to wander wistfully to the wealth of blossoms beyond the window; "but I am almost sorry, for nowhere else have I found the sunshine lie so warmly, the flowers smell so sweetly, or the winds and streams make such tender music. . . ."

His voice died away into a thin stream of sound that lost itself in the rustle of the rose-leaves climbing in at the window, for he turned his head away from me as he spoke and looked out into the garden. But it was impossible to conceal my surprise, and I raised my eyes in frank astonishment on hearing so poetic an utterance from such a figure of a man, though at the same time realising that it was not in the least inappropriate, and that, in fact, no other sort of expression could have properly been expected from him.

"I am sure you are right," I answered at length, when it was clear he had ceased speaking; "or there is something of enchantment here—of real fairy-like enchantment—that makes me think of the visions of childhood days, before one knew anything of—of—"

I had been oddly drawn into his vein of speech, some inner force compelling me. But here the spell passed and I could not catch the thoughts that had a moment before opened a long vista before my inner vision.

"To tell you the truth," I concluded lamely, "the place fascinates me and I am in two minds about going further—"

Even at this stage I remember thinking it odd that I should be talking like this with a stranger whom I met in a country inn, for it has always been one of my failings that to strangers my manner is brief to surliness. It was as though we were figures meeting in a dream, speaking without sound, obeying laws not operative in the everyday working world, and about to play with a new scale of space and time perhaps.

But my astonishment passed quickly into an entirely different feeling when I became aware that the old man opposite had turned his head from the window again, and was regarding me with eyes so bright they seemed almost to shine with an inner flame. His gaze was fixed upon my face with an intense ardour, and his whole manner had suddenly become alert and concentrated. There was something about him I now felt for the first time that made little thrills of excitement run up and down my back. I met his look squarely, but with an inward tremor.

"Stay, then, a little while longer," he said in a much lower and deeper voice than before; "stay, and I will teach you something of the purpose of my coming."

He stopped abruptly. I was conscious of a decided shiver.

"You have a special purpose then—in coming back?" I asked, hardly knowing what I was saying.

"To call away someone," he went on in the same thrilling voice, "someone who is not quite ready to come, but who is needed elsewhere for a worthier purpose." There was a sadness in his manner that mystified me more than ever.

"You mean—?" I began, with an unaccountable access of trembling.

"I have come for someone who must soon move, even as I have moved."

He looked me through and through with a dreadfully piercing gaze, but I met his eyes with a full straight stare, trembling though I was, and I was aware that something stirred within me that had never stirred before, though for the life of me I could not have put a name to it, or have analysed its nature. Something lifted and rolled away. For one single second I understood clearly that the past and the future exist actually side by side in one immense Present; that it was *I* who moved to and fro among shifting, protean appearances.

The old man dropped his eyes from my face, and the momentary glimpse of a mightier universe passed utterly away. Reason regained its sway over a dull, limited kingdom.

"Come tonight," I heard the old man say, "come to me tonight into the Wood of the Dead. Come at midnight—"

Involuntarily I clutched the arm of the settle for support, for I then felt that I was speaking with someone who knew more of the real things that are and will be, than I could ever know while in the body, working through the ordinary channels of sense—and this curious half-promise of a partial lifting of the veil had its undeniable effect upon me.

The breeze from the sea had died away outside, and the blossoms were still. A yellow butterfly floated lazily past the window. The song of the birds hushed—I smelt the sea—I smelt the perfume of heated summer air rising from fields and flowers, the ineffable scents of June and of the long days of the year—and with it, from countless green meadows beyond, came the hum of myriad summer life, children's voices, sweet pipings, and the sound of water falling.

I knew myself to be on the threshold of a new order of experience—of an ecstasy. Something drew me forth with a sense of inexpressible yearning towards the being of this strange old man in the window seat, and for a moment I knew what it was to taste a mighty and wonderful sensation, and to touch the highest pinnacle of joy I have ever known. It lasted for less than a second, and was gone; but in that brief instant of time the same terrible lucidity came to me that had already shown me how the past and future exist in the present, and I realised and understood that pleasure and pain are one and the same force, for the joy I had just experienced included also all the pain I ever had felt, or ever could feel. . . .

The sunshine grew to dazzling radiance, faded, passed away. The shadows paused in their dance upon the grass, deepened a moment, and then melted into air. The flowers of the fruit trees laughed with their little silvery laughter as the wind sighed over their radiant eyes the old, old tale of its personal love. Once or twice a voice called my name. A wonderful sensation of lightness and power began to steal over me.

Suddenly the door opened and the innkeeper's daughter came in. By all ordinary standards, her's was a charming country loveliness, born of the stars and wildflowers, of moonlight shining through autumn mists upon the river and the fields; yet, by contrast with the higher order of beauty I had just momentarily been in touch with, she seemed almost ugly. How dull her eyes, how thin her voice, how vapid her smile, and insipid her whole presentment.

For a moment she stood between me and the occupant of the window seat while I counted out the small change for my meal and for her services; but when, an instant later, she moved aside, I saw that the settle was empty and that there was no longer anyone in the room but our two selves.

This discovery was no shock to me; indeed, I had almost expected it, and the man had gone just as a figure goes out of a dream, causing no surprise and leaving me as part and parcel of the same dream without breaking of continuity. But, as soon as I had paid my bill and thus resumed in very practical fashion the thread of my normal consciousness, I turned to the girl and asked her if she knew the old man who had been sitting in the window seat, and what he had meant by the Wood of the Dead.

The maiden started visibly, glancing quickly round the empty room, but answering simply that she had seen no one. I described him in great detail, and then, as the description grew clearer, she turned a little pale under her pretty sunburn and said very gravely that it must have been the ghost.

"Ghost! What ghost?"

"Oh, the village ghost," she said quietly, coming closer to my chair with a little nervous movement of genuine alarm, and adding in a lower voice, "He comes before a death, they say!"

It was not difficult to induce the girl to talk, and the story she told me, shorn of the superstition that had obviously gathered with the years round the memory of a strangely picturesque figure, was an interesting and peculiar one.

The inn, she said, was originally a farmhouse, occupied by a yeoman farmer, evidently of a superior, if rather eccentric, character, who had been very poor until he reached old age, when a son died suddenly in the Colonies and left him an unexpected amount of money, almost a fortune.

The old man thereupon altered no whit his simple manner of living, but devoted his income entirely to the improvement of the village and to the assistance of its inhabitants; he did this quite regardless of his personal likes and dislikes, as if one and all were absolutely alike to him, objects of a genuine and impersonal benevolence. People had always been a little afraid of the man, not understanding his eccentricities, but the simple force of this love for humanity changed all that in a very short space of time; and before he died he came to be known as the Father of the Village and was held in great love and veneration by all.

A short time before his end, however, he began to act queerly. He spent his money just as usefully and wisely, but the shock of sudden wealth after a life of poverty, people said, had unsettled his mind. He claimed to see things that others did not see, to hear voices, and to have visions. Evidently, he was not of the harmless, foolish, visionary order, but a man of character and of great personal force, for the people became divided in their opinions, and the vicar, good man, regarded and treated him as a "special case." For many, his name and atmosphere became charged almost with a spiritual influence that was not of the best. People quoted texts about him; kept when possible out of his way, and avoided his house after dark. None understood him, but though the majority loved him, an element of dread and mystery became associated with his name, chiefly owing to the ignorant gossip of the few.

A grove of pine trees behind the farm—the girl pointed them out to me on the slope of the hill—he said was the Wood of the Dead, because just before anyone died in the village he saw them walk into that wood, singing. None who went in ever came out again. He often mentioned the names to his wife, who usually published them to all the inhabitants within an hour of her husband's confidence; and it was found that the people he had seen enter the wood—died.

On warm summer nights he would sometimes take an old stick and wander out, hatless, under the pines, for he loved this wood, and used to say he met all his old friends there, and would one day walk in there never to return. His wife tried to break him gently off this habit, but he always had his own way; and once, when she followed and found him standing under a great pine in the thickest portion of the grove, talking earnestly to someone she could not see, he turned and rebuked her very gently, but in such a way that she never repeated the experiment, saying—

"You should never interrupt me, Mary, when I am talking with the others; for they teach me, remember, wonderful things, and I must learn all I can before I go to join them."

This story went like wild-fire through the village, increasing with every repetition, until at length everyone was able to give an accurate description of the great veiled figures the woman declared she had seen moving among the trees where her husband stood. The innocent pine-grove now became positively haunted, and the title of "Wood of the Dead" clung naturally as if it had been applied to it in the ordinary course of events by the compilers of the Ordnance Survey.

On the evening of his ninetieth birthday the old man went up to his wife and kissed her. His manner was loving, and very gentle, and there was something about him besides, she declared afterwards, that made her slightly in awe of him and feel that he was almost more of a spirit than a man.

He kissed her tenderly on both cheeks, but his eyes seemed to look right through her as he spoke.

"Dearest wife," he said, "I am saying goodbye to you, for I am now going into the Wood of the Dead, and I shall not return. Do not follow me, or send to search, but be ready soon to come upon the same journey yourself."

The good woman burst into tears and tried to hold him, but he easily slipped from her hands, and she was afraid to follow him. Slowly she saw him cross the field in the sunshine, and then enter the cool shadows of the grove, where he disappeared from her sight.

That same night, much later, she woke to find him lying peacefully by her side in bed, with one arm stretched out towards her, *dead*. Her story was half believed, half doubted at the time, but in a very few years afterwards it evidently came to be accepted by all the countryside. A funeral service was held to which the people flocked in great numbers, and everyone approved of the sentiment which led the widow to add the words, "The Father of the Village," after the usual texts which appeared upon the stone over his grave.

This, then, was the story I pieced together of the village ghost as the little innkeeper's daughter told it to me that afternoon in the parlour of the inn.

"But you're not the first to say you've seen him," the girl concluded; "and your description is just what we've always heard, and that window, they say, was just where he used to sit and think, and think, when he was alive, and sometimes, they say, to cry for hours together."

"And would you feel afraid if you had seen him?" I asked, for the girl seemed strangely moved and interested in the whole story.

"I think so," she answered timidly. "Surely, if he spoke to me. He did speak to *you*, didn't he, sir?" she asked after a slight pause.

"He said he had come for someone."

"Come for someone," she repeated. "Did he say—" she went on falteringly.

"No, he did not say for whom," I said quickly, noticing the sudden shadow on her face and the tremulous voice.

"Are you really sure, sir?"

"Oh, quite sure," I answered cheerfully. "I did not even ask him." The girl looked at me steadily for nearly a whole minute as though there were many things she wished to tell me or to ask. But she said nothing, and presently picked up her tray from the table and walked slowly out of the room.

Instead of keeping to my original purpose and pushing on to the next village over the hills, I ordered a room to be prepared for me at the inn, and that afternoon I spent wandering about the fields and lying under the fruit trees, watching the white clouds sailing out over the sea. The Wood of the Dead I surveyed from a distance, but in the village I visited the stone erected to the memory of the "Father of the Village"—who was thus, evidently, no mythical personage—and saw also the monuments of his fine unselfish spirit: the schoolhouse he built, the library, the home for the aged poor, and the tiny hospital.

That night, as the clock in the church tower was striking half-past eleven, I stealthily left the inn and crept through the dark orchard and over the hayfield in the direction of the hill whose southern slope was clothed with the Wood of the Dead. A genuine interest impelled me to the adventure, but I also was obliged to confess to a certain sinking in my heart as I stumbled along over the field in the darkness, for I was approaching what might prove to be the birth-place of a real country myth, and a spot already lifted by the imaginative thoughts of a considerable number of people into the region of the haunted and ill-omened.

The inn lay below me, and all round it the village clustered in a soft black shadow unrelieved by a single light. The night was moonless, yet distinctly luminous, for the stars crowded the sky. The silence of deep slumber was everywhere; so still, indeed, that every time my foot kicked against a stone I thought the sound must be heard below in the village and waken the sleepers.

I climbed the hill slowly, thinking chiefly of the strange story of the noble old man who had seized the opportunity to do good to his fellows the moment it came his way, and wondering why the causes that operate ceaselessly behind human life did not always select such admirable instruments. Once or twice a night-bird circled swiftly over my head, but the bats had long since gone to rest, and there was no other sign of life stirring.

Then, suddenly, with a singular thrill of emotion, I saw the first trees of the Wood of the Dead rise in front of me in a high black wall. Their crests stood up like giant spears against the starry sky; and though there was no perceptible movement of the air on my cheek I heard a faint, rushing sound among their branches as the night breeze passed to and fro over their countless little needles. A remote, hushed murmur rose overhead and died away again almost immediately; for in these trees the wind seems to be never absolutely at rest, and on the calmest day there is always a sort of whispering music among their branches.

For a moment I hesitated on the edge of this dark wood, and listened intently. Delicate perfumes of earth and bark stole out to meet me. Impenetrable darkness faced me. Only the consciousness that I was obeying an order, strangely given, and including a mighty privilege, enabled me to find the courage to go forward and step in boldly under the trees.

Instantly the shadows closed in upon me and "something" came forward to meet me from the centre of the darkness. It would be easy enough to meet my imagination half-way with fact, and say that a cold hand grasped my own and led me by invisible paths into the unknown depths of the grove; but at any rate, without stumbling, and always with the positive knowledge that I was going straight towards the desired object, I pressed on confidently and securely into the wood. So dark was it that, at first, not a single star-beam pierced the roof of branches overhead; and, as we moved forward side by side, the trees shifted silently past us in long lines, row upon row, squadron upon squadron, like the units of a vast, soundless army.

And, at length, we came to a comparatively open space where the trees halted upon us for a while, and, looking up, I saw the white river of the sky beginning to yield to the influence of a new light that now seemed spreading swiftly across the heavens.

"It is the dawn coming," said the voice at my side that I certainly recognised, but which seemed almost like a whispering from the trees, "and we are now in the heart of the Wood of the Dead."

We seated ourselves on a moss-covered boulder and waited the coming of the sun. With marvellous swiftness, it seemed to me, the light in the east passed into the radiance of early morning, and when the wind awoke and began to whisper in the tree tops, the first rays of the risen sun fell between the trunks and rested in a circle of gold at our feet.

"Now, come with me," whispered my companion in the same deep voice, "for time has no existence here, and that which I would show you is already *there*!"

We trod gently and silently over the soft pine needles. Already the sun was high over our heads, and the shadows of the trees coiled closely about their feet. The wood became denser again, but occasionally we passed through little open bits where we could smell the hot sunshine and the dry, baked pine needles. Then, presently, we came to the edge of the grove, and I saw a hayfield lying in the blaze of day, and two horses basking lazily with switching tails in the shafts of a laden hay-waggon.

So complete and vivid was the sense of reality, that I remember the grateful realisation of the cool shade where we sat and looked out upon the hot world beyond.

The last pitchfork had tossed up its fragrant burden, and the great horses were already straining in the shafts after the driver, as he walked slowly in front with one hand upon their bridles. He was a stalwart fellow, with sunburned neck and hands. Then, for the first time, I noticed, perched aloft upon the trembling throne of hay, the figure of a slim young girl. I could not see her face, but her brown hair escaped in disorder from a white sun-bonnet, and her still browner hands held a well-worn hay rake. She was laughing and talking with the driver, and he, from time to time, cast up at her ardent glances of admiration—glances that won instant smiles and soft blushes in response.

The cart presently turned into the roadway that skirted the edge of the wood where we were sitting. I watched the scene with intense interest and became so much absorbed in it that I quite forgot the manifold, strange steps by which I was permitted to become a spectator.

"Come down and walk with me," cried the young fellow, stopping a moment in front of the horses and opening wide his arms. "Jump! and I'll catch you!"

"Oh, oh," she laughed, and her voice sounded to me as the happiest, merriest laughter I had ever heard from a girl's throat. "Oh, oh! that's all very well. But remember I'm Queen of the Hay, and I must ride!"

"Then I must come and ride beside you," he cried, and began at once to climb up by way of the driver's seat. But, with a peal of silvery laughter, she slipped down easily over the back of the hay to escape him, and ran a little way along the road. I could see her quite clearly, and noticed the charming, natural grace of her movements, and the loving expression in her eyes as she looked over her shoulder to make sure he was following. Evidently, she did not wish to escape for long, certainly not for ever.

In two strides the big, brown swain was after her, leaving the horses to do as they pleased. Another second and his arms would have caught the slender waist and pressed the little body to his heart. But, just at that instant, the old man beside me uttered a peculiar cry. It was low and thrilling, and it went through me like a sharp sword.

HE had called her by her own name—and she had heard.

For a second she halted, glancing back with frightened eyes. Then, with a brief cry of despair, the girl swerved aside and dived in swiftly among the shadows of the trees.

But the young man saw the sudden movement and cried out to

her passionately—

"Not that way, my love! Not that way! It's the Wood of the Dead!"

She threw a laughing glance over her shoulder at him, and the wind caught her hair and drew it out in a brown cloud under the sun. But the next minute she was close beside me, lying on the breast of my companion, and I was certain I heard the words repeatedly uttered with many sighs: "Father, you called, and I have come. And I come willingly, for I am very, very tired."

At any rate, so the words sounded to me, and mingled with them I seemed to catch the answer in that deep, thrilling whisper I already knew: "And you shall sleep, my child, sleep for a long, long time, until it is time for you to begin the journey again."

In that brief second of time I had recognised the face and voice of the innkeeper's daughter, but the next minute a dreadful wail broke from the lips of the young man, and the sky grew suddenly as dark as night, the wind rose and began to toss the branches about us, and the whole scene was swallowed up in a wave of utter blackness.

Again the chill fingers seemed to seize my hand, and I was guided by the way I had come to the edge of the wood, and crossing the hayfield still slumbering in the starlight, I crept back to the inn and went to bed.

A year later I happened to be in the same part of the country, and the memory of the strange summer vision returned to me with the added softness of distance. I went to the old village and had tea under the same orchard trees at the same inn.

But the little maid of the inn did not show her face, and I took occasion to enquire of her father as to her welfare and her whereabouts.

"Married, no doubt," I laughed, but with a strange feeling that clutched at my heart.

"No, sir," replied the innkeeper sadly, "not married—though she was just going to be—but dead. She got a sunstroke in the hayfields, just a few days after you were here, if I remember rightly, and she was gone from us in less than a week."

Skeleton Lake: An Episode in Camp

The utter loneliness of our moose-camp on Skeleton Lake had impressed us from the beginning—in the Quebec backwoods, five days by trail and canoe from civilisation—and perhaps the singular name contributed a little to the sensation of eeriness that made itself felt in the camp circle when once the sun was down and the late October mists began rising from the lake and winding their way in among the tree trunks.

For, in these regions, all names of lakes and hills and islands have their origin in some actual event, taking either the name of a chief participant, such as Smith's Ridge, or claiming a place in the map by perpetuating some special feature of the journey or the scenery, such as Long Island, Deep Rapids, or Rainy Lake.

All names thus have their meaning and are usually pretty recently acquired, while the majority are self-explanatory and suggest human and pioneer relations. Skeleton Lake, therefore, was a name full of suggestion, and though none of us knew the origin or the story of its birth, we all were conscious of a certain lugubrious atmosphere that haunted its shores and islands, and but for the evidences of recent moose tracks in its neighbourhood we should probably have pitched our tents elsewhere.

For several hundred miles in any direction we knew of only one other party of whites. They had journeyed up on the train with us, getting in at North Bay, and hailing from Boston way. A common goal and object had served by way of introduction. But the acquaintance had made little progress. This noisy, aggressive Yankee did not suit our fancy much as a possible neighbour, and it was only a slight intimacy between his chief guide, Jake the Swede, and one of our men that kept the thing going at all. They went into camp on Beaver Creek, fifty miles and more to the west of us.

But that was six weeks ago, and seemed as many months, for days and nights pass slowly in these solitudes and the scale of time changes wonderfully. Our men always seemed to know by instinct pretty well "whar them other fellows was movin'," but in the interval no one had come across their trails, or once so much as heard their rifle shots.

Our little camp consisted of the professor, his wife, a splendid shot and keen woods-woman, and myself. We had a guide apiece, and hunted daily in pairs from before sunrise till dark.

It was our last evening in the woods, and the professor was lying in my little wedge tent, discussing the dangers of hunting alone in couples in this way. The flap of the tent hung back and let in fragrant odours of cooking over an open wood fire; everywhere there were bustle and preparation, and one canoe already lay packed with moose horns, her nose pointing southwards.

"If an accident happened to one of them," he was saying, "the survivor's story when he returned to camp would be entirely unsupported evidence, wouldn't it? Because, you see—"

And he went on laying down the law after the manner of professors, until I became so bored that my attention began to wander to pictures and memories of the scenes we were just about to leave: Garden Lake, with its hundred islands; the rapids out of Round Pond; the countless vistas of forest, crimson and gold in the autumn sunshine; and the starlit nights we had spent watching in cold, cramped positions for the wary moose on lonely lakes among the hills. The hum of the professor's voice in time grew more soothing. A nod or a grunt was all the reply he looked for. Fortunately, he loathed interruptions. I think I could almost have gone to sleep under his very nose; perhaps I did sleep for a brief interval.

Then it all came about so quickly, and the tragedy of it was so unexpected and painful, throwing our peaceful camp into momentary confusion, that now it all seems to have happened with the uncanny swiftness of a dream.

First, there was the abrupt ceasing of the droning voice, and then the running of quick little steps over the pine needles, and the confusion of men's voices; and the next instant the professor's wife was at the tent door, hatless, her face white, her hunting bloomers bagging at the wrong places, a rifle in her hand, and her words running into one another anyhow.

"Quick, Harry! It's Rushton. I was asleep and it woke me. Something's happened. You must deal with it!"

In a second we were outside the tent with our rifles.

"My God!" I heard the professor exclaim, as if he had first made the discovery. "It *is* Rushton!"

I saw the guides helping—dragging—a man out of a canoe. A brief space of deep silence followed in which I heard only the waves from the canoe washing up on the sand; and then, immediately after, came the voice of a man talking with amazing rapidity and with odd gaps between his words. It was Rushton telling his story, and the tones of his voice, now whispering, now almost shouting, mixed with sobs and solemn oaths and frequent appeals to the Deity, somehow or other struck the false note at the very start, and before any of us guessed or knew anything at all. Something moved secretly between his words, a shadow veiling the stars, destroying the peace of our little camp, and touching us all personally with an undefinable sense of horror and distrust.

I can see that group to this day, with all the detail of a good photograph: standing half-way between the firelight and the darkness, a slight mist rising from the lake, the frosty stars, and our men, in silence that was all sympathy, dragging Rushton across the rocks towards the camp fire. Their *moccasins* crunched on the sand and slipped several times on the stones beneath the weight of the limp, exhausted body, and I can still see every inch of the pared cedar branch he had used for a paddle on that lonely and dreadful journey.

But what struck me most, as it struck us all, was the limp exhaustion of his body compared to the strength of his utterance and the tearing rush of his words. A vigorous driving-power was there at work, forcing out the tale, red-hot and throbbing, full of discrepancies and the strangest contradictions; and the nature of this driving-power I first began to appreciate when they had lifted him into the circle of firelight and I saw his face, grey under the tan, terror in the eyes, tears too, hair and beard awry, and listened to the wild stream of words pouring forth without ceasing.

I think we all understood then, but it was only after many years that anyone dared to confess what he thought.

There was Matt Morris, my guide; Silver Fizz, whose real name was unknown, and who bore the title of his favourite drink; and huge Hank Milligan—all ears and kind intention; and there was Rushton, pouring out his ready-made tale, with ever-shifting eyes, turning from face to face, seeking confirmation of details none had witnessed but himself—and *one other.*

Silver Fizz was the first to recover from the shock of the thing, and to realise, with the natural sense of chivalry common to most genuine back-woodsmen, that the man was at a terrible disadvantage. At any rate, he was the first to start putting the matter to rights.

"Never mind telling it just now," he said in a gruff voice, but with real gentleness; "get a bite t'eat first and then let her go afterwards. Better have a horn of whisky too. It ain't all packed yet, I guess."

"Couldn't eat or drink a thing," cried the other. "Good Lord, don't you see, man, I want to *talk* to someone first? I want to get it out of me to someone who can answer—answer. I've had nothing but trees to talk with for three days, and I can't carry it alone any longer. Those cursed, silent trees—I've told it 'em a thousand times. Now, just see here, it was this way. When we started out from camp—"

He looked fearfully about him, and we realised it was useless to stop him. The story was bound to come, and come it did.

Now, the story itself was nothing out of the way; such tales are told by the dozen round any camp fire where men who have knocked about in the woods are in the circle. It was the way he told it that made our flesh creep. He was near the truth all along, but he was skimming it, and the skimming took off the cream that might have saved his soul.

Of course, he smothered it in words—odd words, too—melodramatic, poetic, out-of-the-way words that lie just on the edge of frenzy. Of course, too, he kept asking us each in turn, scanning our faces with those restless, frightened eyes of his, "What would *you* have done?" "What else could I do?" and "Was that *my* fault?" But that was nothing, for he was no milk-and-water fellow who dealt in hints and suggestions; he told his story boldly, forcing his conclusions upon us as if we had been so many wax cylinders of a phonograph that would repeat accurately what had been told us, and these questions I have mentioned he used to emphasise any special point that he seemed to think required such emphasis.

The fact was, however, the picture of what had actually happened was so vivid still in his own mind that it reached ours by a process of telepathy which he could not control or prevent. All through his true-false words this picture stood forth in fearful detail against the shadows behind him. He could not veil, much less obliterate, it. We knew; and, I always thought, *he knew that we knew.*

The story itself, as I have said, was sufficiently ordinary. Jake and himself, in a nine-foot canoe, had upset in the middle of a lake, and had held hands across the upturned craft for several hours, eventually cutting holes in her ribs to stick their arms through and grasp hands lest the numbness of the cold water should overcome them. They were miles from shore, and the wind was drifting them down upon a little island. But when they got within a few hundred yards of the island, they realised to their horror that they would after all drift past it.

It was then the quarrel began. Jake was for leaving the canoe and swimming. Rushton believed in waiting till they actually had passed the island and were sheltered from the wind. Then they could make the island easily by swimming, canoe and all. But Jake refused to give in, and after a short struggle—Rushton admitted there was a struggle—got free from the canoe—and disappeared *without a single cry.*

Rushton held on and proved the correctness of his theory, and finally made the island, canoe and all, after being in the water over five hours. He described to us how he crawled up on to the shore, and fainted at once, with his feet lying half in the water; how lost and terrified he felt upon regaining consciousness in the dark; how the canoe had drifted away and his extraordinary luck in finding it caught again at the end of the island by a projecting cedar branch. He told us that the little axe—another bit of real luck—had caught in the thwart when the canoe turned over, and how the little bottle in his pocket holding the emergency matches was whole and dry. He made a blazing fire and searched the island from end to end, calling upon Jake in the darkness, but getting no answer; till, finally, so many half-drowned men seemed to come crawling out of the water on to the rocks, and vanish among the shadows when he came up with them, that he lost his nerve completely and returned to lie down by the fire till the daylight came.

He then cut a bough to replace the lost paddles, and after one more useless search for his lost companion, he got into the canoe, fearing every moment he would upset again, and crossed over to the mainland. He knew roughly the position of our camping place, and after paddling day and night, and making many weary portages, without food or covering, he reached us two days later.

This, more or less, was the story, and we, knowing whereof he spoke, knew that every word was literally true, and at the same time went to the building up of a hideous and prodigious lie.

Once the recital was over, he collapsed, and Silver Fizz, after a general expression of sympathy from the rest of us, came again to the rescue.

"But now, Mister, you jest *got* to eat and drink whether you've a mind to, or no."

And Matt Morris, cook that night, soon had the fried trout and bacon, and the wheat cakes and hot coffee passing round a rather silent and oppressed circle. So we ate round the fire, ravenously, as we had eaten every night for the past six weeks, but with this difference: that there was one among us who was more than ravenous—and he gorged.

In spite of all our devices he somehow kept himself the centre of observation. When his tin mug was empty, Morris instantly passed the tea-pail; when he began to mop up the bacon grease with the dough on his fork, Hank reached out for the frying pan; and the can of steaming boiled potatoes was always by his side. And there was another difference as well: he was sick, terribly sick before the meal was over, and this sudden nausea after food was more eloquent than words of what the man had passed through on his dreadful, foodless, ghost-haunted journey of forty miles to our camp. In the darkness he thought he would go crazy, he said. There were voices in the trees, and figures were always lifting themselves out of the water, or from behind boulders, to look at him and make awful signs. Jake constantly peered at him through the underbrush, and everywhere the shadows were moving, with eyes, footsteps, and following shapes.

We tried hard to talk of other things, but it was no use, for he was bursting with the rehearsal of his story and refused to allow himself the chances we were so willing and anxious to grant him. After a good night's rest he might have had more self-control and better judgment, and would probably have acted differently. But, as it was, we found it impossible to help him.

Once the pipes were lit, and the dishes cleared away, it was useless to pretend any longer. The sparks from the burning logs zigzagged upwards into a sky brilliant with stars. It was all wonderfully still and peaceful, and the forest odours floated to us on the sharp autumn air. The cedar fire smelt sweet and we could just hear the gentle wash of tiny waves along the shore. All was calm, beautiful, and remote from the world of men and passion. It was, indeed, a night to touch the soul, and yet, I think, none of us heeded these things. A bull-moose might almost have thrust his great head over our shoulders and have escaped unnoticed. The death of Jake the Swede, with its sinister setting, was the real presence that held the centre of the stage and compelled attention.

"You won't p'raps care to come along, Mister," said Morris, by way of a beginning; "but I guess I'll go with one of the boys here and have a hunt for it."

"Sure," said Hank. "Jake an' I done some biggish trips together in the old days, and I'll do that much for'm."

"It's deep water, they tell me, round them islands," added Silver Fizz; "but we'll find it, sure pop,—if it's thar."

They all spoke of the body as "it."

There was a minute or two of heavy silence, and then Rushton again burst out with his story in almost the identical words he had used before. It was almost as if he had learned it by heart. He wholly failed to appreciate the efforts of the others to let him off.

Silver Fizz rushed in, hoping to stop him, Morris and Hank closely following his lead.

"I once knew another travellin' partner of his," he began quickly; "used to live down Moosejaw Rapids way—"

"Is that so?" said Hank.

"Kind o' useful sort er feller," chimed in Morris.

All the idea the men had was to stop the tongue wagging before the discrepancies became so glaring that we should be forced to take notice of them, and ask questions. But, just as well try to stop an angry bull-moose on the run, or prevent Beaver Creek freezing in mid-winter by throwing in pebbles near the shore. Out it came! And, though the discrepancy this time was insignificant, it somehow brought us all in a second face to face with the inevitable and dreaded climax.

"And so I tramped all over that little bit of an island, hoping he might somehow have gotten in without my knowing it, and always thinking I *heard that awful last cry of his* in the darkness—and then the night dropped down impenetrably, like a damn thick blanket out of the sky, and—"

All eyes fell away from his face. Hank poked up the logs with his boot, and Morris seized an ember in his bare fingers to light his pipe, although it was already emitting clouds of smoke. But the professor caught the ball flying.

"I thought you said he sank without a cry," he remarked quietly, looking straight up into the frightened face opposite, and then riddling mercilessly the confused explanation that followed.

The cumulative effect of all these forces, hitherto so rigorously repressed, now made itself felt, and the circle spontaneously broke up, everybody moving at once by a common instinct. The professor's wife left the party abruptly, with excuses about an early start next morning. She first shook hands with Rushton, mumbling something about his comfort in the night.

The question of his comfort, however, devolved by force of circumstances upon myself, and he shared my tent. Just before wrapping up in my double blankets—for the night was bitterly cold—he turned and began to explain that he had a habit of talking in his sleep and hoped I would wake him if he disturbed me by doing so.

Well, he did talk in his sleep—and it disturbed me very much indeed. The anger and violence of his words remain with me to this day, and it was clear in a minute that he was living over again some portion of the scene upon the lake. I listened, horror-struck, for a moment or two, and then understood that I was face to face with one of two alternatives: I must continue an unwilling eavesdropper, or I must waken him. The former was impossible for me, yet I shrank from the latter with the greatest repugnance; and in my dilemma I saw the only way out of the difficulty and at once accepted it.

Cold though it was, I crawled stealthily out of my warm sleeping-bag and left the tent, intending to keep the old fire alight under the stars and spend the remaining hours till daylight in the open.

As soon as I was out I noticed at once another figure moving silently along the shore. It was Hank Milligan, and it was plain enough what he was doing: he was examining the holes that had been cut in the upper ribs of the canoe. He looked half ashamed when I came up with him, and mumbled something about not being able to sleep for the cold. But, there, standing together beside the over-turned canoe, we both saw that the holes were far too small for a man's hand and arm and could not possibly have been cut by two men hanging on for their lives in deep water. Those holes had been made afterwards.

Hank said nothing to me and I said nothing to Hank, and presently he moved off to collect logs for the fire, which needed replenishing, for it was a piercingly cold night and there were many degrees of frost.

Three days later Hank and Silver Fizz followed with stumbling footsteps the old Indian trail that leads from Beaver Creek to the southwards. A hammock was slung between them, and it weighed heavily. Yet neither of the men complained; and, indeed, speech between them was almost nothing. Their thoughts, however, were exceedingly busy, and the terrible secret of the woods which formed their burden weighed far more heavily than the uncouth, shifting mass that lay in the swinging hammock and tugged so severely at their shoulders.

They had found "it" in four feet of water not more than a couple of yards from the lee shore of the island. And in the back of the head was a long, terrible wound which no man could possibly have inflicted upon himself.

The Strange Adventures of a Private Secretary in New York

1

It was never quite clear to me how Jim Shorthouse managed to get his private secretaryship; but, once he got it, he kept it, and for some years he led a steady life and put money in the savings bank.

One morning his employer sent for him into the study, and it was evident to the secretary's trained senses that there was something unusual in the air.

"Mr. Shorthouse," he began, somewhat nervously, "I have never yet had the opportunity of observing whether or not you are possessed of personal courage."

Shorthouse gasped, but he said nothing. He was growing accustomed to the eccentricities of his chief. Shorthouse was a Kentish man; Sidebotham was "raised" in Chicago; New York was the present place of residence.

"But," the other continued, with a puff at his very black cigar, "I must consider myself a poor judge of human nature in future, if it is not one of your strongest qualities."

The private secretary made a foolish little bow in modest appreciation of so uncertain a compliment. Mr. Jonas B. Sidebotham watched him narrowly, as the novelists say, before he continued his remarks.

"I have no doubt that you are a plucky fellow and—" He hesitated, and puffed at his cigar as if his life depended upon it keeping alight.

"I don't think I'm afraid of anything in particular, sir—except women," interposed the young man, feeling that it was time for him to make an observation of some sort, but still quite in the dark as to his chief's purpose.

"Humph!" he grunted. "Well, there are no women in this case so far as I know. But there may be other things that—that hurt more."

"Wants a special service of some kind, evidently," was the secretary's reflection. "Personal violence?" he asked aloud.

"Possibly (*puff*), in fact (*puff, puff*) probably."

Shorthouse smelt an increase of salary in the air. It had a stimulating effect.

"I've had some experience of that article, sir," he said shortly; "but I'm ready to undertake anything in reason."

"I can't say how much reason or unreason there may prove to be in this particular case. It all depends."

Mr. Sidebotham got up and locked the door of his study and drew down the blinds of both windows. Then he took a bunch of keys from his pocket and opened a black tin box. He ferreted about among blue and white papers for a few seconds, enveloping himself as he did so in a cloud of blue tobacco smoke.

"I feel like a detective already," Shorthouse laughed.

"Speak low, please," returned the other, glancing round the room. "We must observe the utmost secrecy. Perhaps you would be kind enough to close the registers," he went on in a still lower voice. "Open registers have betrayed conversations before now."

Shorthouse began to enter into the spirit of the thing. He tiptoed across the floor and shut the two iron gratings in the wall that in America houses supply hot air and are termed "registers." Mr. Sidebotham had meanwhile found the paper he was looking for. He held it in front of him and tapped it once or twice with the back of his right hand as if it were a stage letter and himself the villain of the melodrama.

"This is a letter from Joel Garvey, my old partner," he said at length. "You have heard me speak of him."

The other bowed. He knew that many years before Garvey & Sidebotham had been well known in the Chicago financial world. He knew that the amazing rapidity with which they accumulated a fortune had only been surpassed by the amazing rapidity with which they had immediately afterwards disappeared into space. He was further aware—his position afforded facilities—that each partner was still to some extent in the other's power, and that each wished most devoutly that the other would die.

The sins of his employer's early years did not concern him, however. The man was kind and just, if eccentric; and Shorthouse, being in New York, did not probe to discover more particularly the sources whence his salary was so regularly paid. Moreover, the two men had grown to like each other and there was a genuine feeling of trust and respect between them.

"I hope it's a pleasant communication, sir," he said in a low voice.

"Quite the reverse," returned the other, fingering the paper nervously as he stood in front of the fire.

"Blackmail, I suppose."

"Precisely." Mr. Sidebotham's cigar was not burning well; he struck a match and applied it to the uneven edge, and presently his voice spoke through clouds of wreathing smoke.

"There are valuable papers in my possession bearing his signature. I cannot inform you of their nature; but they are extremely valuable *to me*. They belong, as a matter of fact, to Garvey as much as to me. Only I've got them—"

"I see."

"Garvey writes that he wants to have his signature removed—wants to cut it out with his own hand. He gives reasons which incline me to consider his request—"

"And you would like me to take him the papers and see that he does it?"

"And bring them back again with you," he whispered, screwing up his eyes into a shrewd grimace.

"And bring them back again with me," repeated the secretary. "I understand perfectly."

Shorthouse knew from unfortunate experience more than a little of the horrors of blackmail. The pressure Garvey was bringing to bear upon his old enemy must be exceedingly strong. That was quite clear. At the same time, the commission that was being entrusted to him seemed somewhat quixotic in its nature. He had already "enjoyed" more than one experience of his employer's eccentricity, and he now caught himself wondering whether this same eccentricity did not sometimes go—further than eccentricity.

"I cannot read the letter to you," Mr. Sidebotham was explaining, "but I shall give it into your hands. It will prove that you are my—er—my accredited representative. I shall also ask you not to read the package of papers. The signature in question you will find, of course, on the last page, at the bottom."

There was a pause of several minutes during which the end of the cigar glowed eloquently.

"Circumstances compel me," he went on at length almost in a

whisper, "or I should never do this. But you understand, of course, the thing is a ruse. Cutting out the signature is a mere pretence. It is nothing. *What Garvey wants are the papers themselves.*"

The confidence reposed in the private secretary was not misplaced. Shorthouse was as faithful to Mr. Sidebotham as a man ought to be to the wife that loves him.

The commission itself seemed very simple. Garvey lived in solitude in the remote part of Long Island. Shorthouse was to take the papers to him, witness the cutting out of the signature, and to be specially on his guard against any attempt, forcible or otherwise, to gain possession of them. It seemed to him a somewhat ludicrous adventure, but he did not know all the facts and perhaps was not the best judge.

The two men talked in low voices for another hour, at the end of which Mr. Sidebotham drew up the blinds, opened the registers and unlocked the door.

Shorthouse rose to go. His pockets were stuffed with papers and his head with instructions; but when he reached the door he hesitated and turned.

"Well?" said his chief.

Shorthouse looked him straight in the eye and said nothing.

"The personal violence, I suppose?" said the other. Shorthouse bowed.

"I have not seen Garvey for twenty years," he said; "all I can tell you is that I believe him to be occasionally of unsound mind. I have heard strange rumours. He lives alone, and in his lucid intervals studies chemistry. It was always a hobby of his. But the chances are twenty to one against his attempting violence. I only wished to warn you—in case—I mean, so that you may be on the watch."

He handed his secretary a Smith and Wesson revolver as he spoke. Shorthouse slipped it into his hip pocket and went out of the room.

A drizzling cold rain was falling on fields covered with half-melted snow when Shorthouse stood, late in the afternoon, on the platform of the lonely little Long Island station and watched the train he had just left vanish into the distance.

It was a bleak country that Joel Garvey, Esq., formerly of Chicago, had chosen for his residence and on this particular afternoon it presented a more than usually dismal appearance. An expanse of flat fields covered with dirty snow stretched away on all sides till the sky dropped down to meet them. Only occasional farm buildings broke the monotony, and the road wound along muddy lanes and beneath dripping trees swathed in the cold raw fog that swept in like a pall of the dead from the sea.

It was six miles from the station to Garvey's house, and the driver of the rickety buggy Shorthouse had found at the station was not communicative. Between the dreary landscape and the drearier driver he fell back upon his own thoughts, which, but for the spice of adventure that was promised, would themselves have been even drearier than either. He made up his mind that he would waste no time over the transaction. The moment the signature was cut out he would pack up and be off. The last train back to Brooklyn was 7.15; and he would have to walk the six miles of mud and snow, for the driver of the buggy had refused point-blank to wait for him.

For purposes of safety, Shorthouse had done what he flattered himself was rather a clever thing. He had made up a second packet of papers identical in outside appearance with the first. The inscription, the blue envelope, the red elastic band, and even a blot in the lower left-hand corner had been exactly reproduced. Inside, of course, were only sheets of blank paper. It was his intention to change the packets and to let Garvey see him put the sham one into the bag. In case of violence the bag would be the point of attack, and he intended to lock it and throw away the key. Before it could be forced open and the deception discovered there would be time to increase his chances of escape with the real packet.

It was five o'clock when the silent Jehu pulled up in front of a half-broken gate and pointed with his whip to a house that stood in its own grounds among trees and was just visible in the gathering gloom. Shorthouse told him to drive up to the front door but the man refused.

"I ain't runnin' no risks," he said; "I've got a family."

This cryptic remark was not encouraging, but Shorthouse did not pause to decipher it. He paid the man, and then pushed open the rickety old gate swinging on a single hinge, and proceeded to walk up the drive that lay dark between close-standing trees. The house soon came into full view. It was tall and square and had once evidently been white, but now the walls were covered with dirty patches and there were wide yellow streaks where the plaster had fallen away. The windows stared black and uncompromising into the night. The garden was overgrown with weeds and long grass, standing up in ugly patches beneath their burden of wet snow. Complete silence reigned over all. There was not a sign of life. Not even a dog barked. Only, in the distance, the wheels of the retreating carriage could be heard growing fainter and fainter.

As he stood in the porch, between pillars of rotting wood, listening to the rain dripping from the roof into the puddles of slushy snow, he was conscious of a sensation of utter desertion and loneliness such as he had never before experienced. The forbidding aspect of the house had the immediate effect of lowering his spirits. It might well have been the abode of monsters or demons in a child's wonder tale, creatures that only dared to come out under cover of darkness. He groped for the bell-handle, or knocker, and finding neither, he raised his stick and beat a loud tattoo on the door. The sound echoed away in an empty space on the other side and the wind moaned past him between the pillars as if startled at his audacity. But there was no sound of approaching footsteps and no one came to open the door. Again he beat a tattoo, louder and longer than the first one; and, having done so, waited with his back to the house and stared across the unkempt garden into the fast gathering shadows.

Then he turned suddenly, and saw that the door was standing ajar. It had been quietly opened and a pair of eyes were peering at him round the edge. There was no light in the hall beyond and he could only just make out the shape of a dim human face.

"Does Mr. Garvey live here?" he asked in a firm voice.

"Who are you?" came in a man's tones.

"I'm Mr. Sidebotham's private secretary. I wish to see Mr. Garvey on important business."

"Are you expected?"

"I suppose so," he said impatiently, thrusting a card through the opening. "Please take my name to him at once, and say I come from Mr. Sidebotham on the matter Mr. Garvey wrote about."

The man took the card, and the face vanished into the darkness, leaving Shorthouse standing in the cold porch with mingled feelings of impatience and dismay. The door, he now noticed for the first time, was on a chain and could not open more than a few inches. But it was the manner of his reception that caused uneasy reflections to stir within him—reflections that continued for some minutes before they were interrupted by the sound of approaching footsteps and the flicker of a light in the hall.

The next instant the chain fell with a rattle, and gripping his bag tightly, he walked into a large ill-smelling hall of which he could only just see the ceiling. There was no light but the nickering taper held by the man, and by its uncertain glimmer Shorthouse turned to examine him. He saw an undersized man of middle age with brilliant, shifting eyes, a curling black beard, and a nose that at once proclaimed him a Jew. His shoulders were bent, and, as he watched him replacing the chain, he saw that he wore a peculiar black gown like a priest's cassock reaching to the feet.

It was altogether a lugubrious figure of a man, sinister and funereal, yet it seemed in perfect harmony with the general character of its surroundings. The hall was devoid of furniture of any kind, and against the dingy walls stood rows of old picture frames, empty and disordered, and odd-looking bits of wood-work that appeared doubly fantastic as their shadows danced queerly over the floor in the shifting light.

"If you'll come this way, Mr. Garvey will see you presently," said the Jew gruffly, crossing the floor and shielding the taper with a bony hand. He never once raised his eyes above the level of the visitor's waistcoat, and, to Shorthouse, he somehow suggested a figure from the dead rather than a man of flesh and blood. The hall smelt decidedly ill.

All the more surprising, then, was the scene that met his eyes when the Jew opened the door at the further end and he entered a room brilliantly lit with swinging lamps and furnished with a degree of taste and comfort that amounted to luxury. The walls were lined with handsomely bound books, and armchairs were arranged round a large mahogany desk in the middle of the room. A bright fire burned in the grate and neatly framed photographs of men and women stood on the mantelpiece on either side of an elaborately carved clock. French windows that opened like doors were partially concealed by warm red curtains, and on a sideboard against the wall stood decanters and glasses, with several boxes of cigars piled on top of one another. There was a pleasant odour of tobacco about the room. Indeed, it was in such glowing contrast to the chilly poverty of the hall that Shorthouse already was conscious of a distinct rise in the thermometer of his spirits.

Then he turned and saw the Jew standing in the doorway with his eyes fixed upon him, somewhere about the middle button of his waistcoat. He presented a strangely repulsive appearance that somehow could not be attributed to any particular detail, and the secretary associated him in his mind with a monstrous black bird of prey more than anything else.

"My time is short," he said abruptly; "I hope Mr. Garvey will not keep me waiting."

A strange flicker of a smile appeared on the Jew's ugly face and vanished as quickly as it came. He made a sort of deprecating bow by way of reply. Then he blew out the taper and went out, closing the door noiselessly behind him.

Shorthouse was alone. He felt relieved. There was an air of obsequious insolence about the old Jew that was very offensive. He began to take note of his surroundings. He was evidently in the library of the house, for the walls were covered with books almost up to the ceiling. There was no room for pictures. Nothing but the shining backs of well-bound volumes looked down upon him. Four brilliant lights hung from the ceiling and a reading lamp with a polished reflector stood among the disordered masses of papers on the desk.

The lamp was not lit, but when Shorthouse put his hand upon it he found it was *warm*. The room had evidently only just been vacated.

Apart from the testimony of the lamp, however, he had already felt, without being able to give a reason for it, that the room had been occupied a few moments before he entered. The atmosphere over the desk seemed to retain the disturbing influence of a human being; an influence, moreover, so recent that he felt as if the cause of it were still in his immediate neighbourhood. It was difficult to realise that he was quite alone in the room and that somebody was not in hiding. The finer counterparts of his senses warned him to act as if he were being observed; he was dimly conscious of a desire to fidget and look round, to keep his eyes in every part of the room at once, and to conduct himself generally as if he were the object of careful human observation.

How far he recognised the cause of these sensations it is impossible to say; but they were sufficiently marked to prevent his carrying out a strong inclination to get up and make a search of the room. He sat quite still, staring alternately at the backs of the books, and at the red curtains; wondering all the time if he was really being watched, or if it was only the imagination playing tricks with him.

A full quarter of an hour passed, and then twenty rows of volumes suddenly shifted out towards him, and he saw that a door had opened in the wall opposite. The books were only sham backs after all, and when they moved back again with the sliding door, Shorthouse saw the figure of Joel Garvey standing before him.

Surprise almost took his breath away. He had expected to see an unpleasant, even a vicious apparition with the mark of the beast unmistakably upon its face; but he was wholly unprepared for the elderly, tall, fine-looking man who stood in front of him—well-groomed, refined, vigorous, with a lofty forehead, clear grey eyes, and a hooked nose dominating a clean shaven mouth and chin of considerable character—a distinguished looking man altogether.

"I'm afraid I've kept you waiting, Mr. Shorthouse," he said in a pleasant voice, but with no trace of a smile in the mouth or eyes. "But the fact is, you know, I've a mania for chemistry, and just when you were announced I was at the most critical moment of a problem and was really compelled to bring it to a conclusion."

Shorthouse had risen to meet him, but the other motioned him to resume his seat. It was borne in upon him irresistibly that Mr. Joel Garvey, for reasons best known to himself, was deliberately lying, and he could not help wondering at the necessity for such an elaborate misrepresentation. He took off his overcoat and sat down.

"I've no doubt, too, that the door startled you," Garvey went on, evidently reading something of his guest's feelings in his face. "You probably had not suspected it. It leads into my little laboratory. Chemistry is an absorbing study to me, and I spend most of my time there." Mr. Garvey moved up to the armchair on the opposite side of the fireplace and sat down.

Shorthouse made appropriate answers to these remarks, but his mind was really engaged in taking stock of Mr. Sidebotham's old-time partner. So far there was no sign of mental irregularity and there was certainly nothing about him to suggest violent wrong-doing or coarseness of living. On the whole, Mr. Sidebotham's secretary was most pleasantly surprised, and, wishing to conclude his business as speedily as possible, he made a motion towards the bag for the purpose of opening it, when his companion interrupted him quickly—

"You are Mr. Sidebotham's *private* secretary, are you not?" he asked.

Shorthouse replied that he was. "Mr. Sidebotham," he went on to explain, "has entrusted me with the papers in the case and I have the honour to return to you your letter of a week ago." He handed the letter to Garvey, who took it without a word and deliberately placed it in the fire. He was not aware that the secretary was ignorant of its contents, yet his face betrayed no signs of feeling. Shorthouse noticed, however, that his eyes never left the fire until the last morsel had been consumed. Then he looked up and said, "You are familiar then with the facts of this most peculiar case?"

Shorthouse saw no reason to confess his ignorance.

"I have all the papers, Mr. Garvey," he replied, taking them out of the bag, "and I should be very glad if we could transact our business as speedily as possible. If you will cut out your signature I—"

"One moment, please," interrupted the other. "I must, before we proceed further, consult some papers in my laboratory. If you will allow me to leave you alone a few minutes for this purpose we can conclude the whole matter in a very short time."

Shorthouse did not approve of this further delay, but he had no option than to acquiesce, and when Garvey had left the room by the private door he sat and waited with the papers in his hand. The minutes went by and the other did not return. To pass the time he thought of taking the false packet from his coat to see that the papers were in order, and the move was indeed almost completed, when something—he never knew what—warned him to desist. The feeling again came over him that he was being watched, and he leaned back in his chair with the bag on his knees and waited with considerable impatience for the other's return. For more than twenty minutes he waited, and when at length the door opened and Garvey appeared, with profuse apologies for the delay, he saw by the clock that only a few minutes still remained of the time he had allowed himself to catch the last train.

"Now I am completely at your service," he said pleasantly; "you must, of course, know, Mr. Shorthouse, that one cannot be too careful in matters of this kind—especially," he went on, speaking very slowly and impressively, "in dealing with a man like my former partner, whose mind, as you doubtless may have discovered, is at times very sadly affected."

Shorthouse made no reply to this. He felt that the other was watching him as a cat watches a mouse.

"It is almost a wonder to me," Garvey added, "that he is still at large. Unless he has greatly improved it can hardly be safe for those who are closely associated with him."

The other began to feel uncomfortable. Either this was the other side of the story, or it was the first signs of mental irresponsibility.

"All business matters of importance require the utmost care in my opinion, Mr. Garvey," he said at length, cautiously.

"Ah! then, as I thought, you have had a great deal to put up with from him," Garvey said, with his eyes fixed on his companion's face. "And, no doubt, he is still as bitter against me as he was years ago when the disease first showed itself?"

Although this last remark was a deliberate question and the questioner was waiting with fixed eyes for an answer, Shorthouse elected to take no notice of it. Without a word he pulled the elastic band from the blue envelope with a snap and plainly showed his desire to conclude the business as soon as possible. The tendency on the other's part to delay did not suit him at all.

"But never personal violence, I trust, Mr. Shorthouse," he added.

"Never."

"I'm glad to hear it," Garvey said in a sympathetic voice, "very glad to hear it. And now," he went on, "if you are ready we can transact this little matter of business before dinner. It will only take a moment."

He drew a chair up to the desk and sat down, taking a pair of scissors from a drawer. His companion approached with the papers in his hand, unfolding them as he came. Garvey at once took them from him, and after turning over a few pages he stopped and cut out a piece of writing at the bottom of the last sheet but one.

Holding it up to him Shorthouse read the words "Joel Garvey" in faded ink.

"There! That's my signature," he said, "and I've cut it out. It must be nearly twenty years since I wrote it, and now I'm going to burn it."

He went to the fire and stooped over to burn the little slip of paper, and while he watched it being consumed Shorthouse put the real papers in his pocket and slipped the imitation ones into the bag. Garvey turned just in time to see this latter movement.

"I'm putting the papers back," Shorthouse said quietly; "you've done with them, I think."

"Certainly," he replied as, completely deceived, he saw the blue envelope disappear into the black bag and watched Shorthouse turn the key. "They no longer have the slightest interest for me." As he spoke he moved over to the sideboard, and pouring himself out a small glass of whisky asked his visitor if he might do the same for him. But the visitor declined and was already putting on his overcoat when Garvey turned with genuine surprise on his face.

"You surely are not going back to New York tonight, Mr. Shorthouse?" he said, in a voice of astonishment.

"I've just time to catch the 7.15 if I'm quick."

"But I never heard of such a thing," Garvey said. "Of course I took it for granted that you would stay the night."

"It's kind of you," said Shorthouse, "but really I must return tonight. I never expected to stay."

The two men stood facing each other. Garvey pulled out his watch.

"I'm exceedingly sorry," he said; "but, upon my word, I took it for granted you would stay. I ought to have said so long ago. I'm such a lonely fellow and so little accustomed to visitors that I fear I forgot my manners altogether. But in any case, Mr. Shorthouse, you cannot catch the 7.15, for it's already after six o'clock, and that's the last train tonight." Garvey spoke very quickly, almost eagerly, but his voice sounded genuine.

"There's time if I walk quickly," said the young man with decision, moving towards the door. He glanced at his watch as he went. Hitherto he had gone by the clock on the mantelpiece. To his dismay he saw that it was, as his host had said, long after six. The clock was half an hour slow, and he realised at once that it was no longer possible to catch the train.

Had the hands of the clock been moved back intentionally? Had he been purposely detained? Unpleasant thoughts flashed into his brain and made him hesitate before taking the next step. His employer's warning rang in his ears. The alternative was six miles along a lonely road in the dark, or a night under Garvey's roof. The former seemed a direct invitation to catastrophe, if catastrophe there was planned to be. The latter—well, the choice was certainly small. One thing, however, he realised, was plain—he must show neither fear nor hesitancy.

"My watch must have gained," he observed quietly, turning the hands back without looking up. "It seems I have certainly missed that train and shall be obliged to throw myself upon your hospitality. But, believe me, I had no intention of putting you out to any such extent."

"I'm delighted," the other said. "Defer to the judgment of an older man and make yourself comfortable for the night. There's a bitter storm outside, and you don't put me out at all. On the contrary it's a great pleasure. I have so little contact with the outside world that it's really a god-send to have you."

The man's face changed as he spoke. His manner was cordial and sincere. Shorthouse began to feel ashamed of his doubts and to read between the lines of his employer's warning. He took off his coat and the two men moved to the armchairs beside the fire.

"You see," Garvey went on in a lowered voice, "I understand your hesitancy perfectly. I didn't know Sidebotham all those years without knowing a good deal about him—perhaps more than you do. I've no doubt, now, he filled your mind with all sorts of nonsense about me—probably told you that I was the greatest villain unhung, eh? and all that sort of thing? Poor fellow! He was a fine sort before his mind became unhinged. One of his fancies used to be that everybody else was insane, or just about to become insane. Is he still as bad as that?"

"Few men," replied Shorthouse, with the manner of making a great confidence, but entirely refusing to be drawn, "go through his experiences and reach his age without entertaining delusions of one kind or another."

"Perfectly true," said Garvey. "Your observation is evidently keen."

"Very keen indeed," Shorthouse replied, taking his cue neatly; "but, of course, there are some things"—and here he looked cautiously over his shoulder—"there are some things one cannot talk about too circumspectly."

"I understand perfectly and respect your reserve."

There was a little more conversation and then Garvey got up and excused himself on the plea of superintending the preparation of the bedroom.

"It's quite an event to have a visitor in the house, and I want to make you as comfortable as possible," he said. "Marx will do better for a little supervision. And," he added with a laugh as he stood in the doorway, "I want you to carry back a good account to Sidebotham."

2

The tall form disappeared and the door was shut. The conversation of the past few minutes had come somewhat as a revelation to the secretary. Garvey seemed in full possession of normal instincts. There was no doubt as to the sincerity of his manner and intentions. The suspicions of the first hour began to vanish like mist before the sun. Sidebotham's portentous warnings and the mystery with which he surrounded the whole episode had been allowed to unduly influence his mind. The loneliness of the situation and the bleak nature of the surroundings had helped to complete the illusion. He began to be ashamed of his suspicions and a change commenced gradually to be wrought in his thoughts. Anyhow a dinner and a bed were preferable to six miles in the dark, no dinner, and a cold train into the bargain.

Garvey returned presently. "We'll do the best we can for you," he said, dropping into the deep armchair on the other side of the fire. "Marx is a good servant if you watch him all the time. You must always stand over a Jew, though, if you want things done properly. They're tricky and uncertain unless they're working for their own interest. But Marx might be worse, I'll admit. He's been with me for nearly twenty years—cook, valet, housemaid, and butler all in one. In the old days, you know, he was a clerk in our office in Chicago."

Garvey rattled on and Shorthouse listened with occasional remarks thrown in. The former seemed pleased to have somebody to talk to and the sound of his own voice was evidently sweet music in his ears. After a few minutes, he crossed over to the sideboard and again took up the decanter of whisky, holding it to the light. "You will join me this time," he said pleasantly, pouring out two glasses, "it will give us an appetite for dinner," and this time Shorthouse did not refuse. The liquor was mellow and soft and the men took two glasses apiece.

"Excellent," remarked the secretary.

"Glad you appreciate it," said the host, smacking his lips. "It's very old whisky, and I rarely touch it when I'm alone. But this," he added, "is a special occasion, isn't it?"

Shorthouse was in the act of putting his glass down when something drew his eyes suddenly to the other's face. A strange note in the man's voice caught his attention and communicated alarm to his nerves. A new light shone in Garvey's eyes and there flitted momentarily across his strong features the shadow of something that set the secretary's nerves tingling. A mist spread before his eyes and the unaccountable belief rose strong in him that he was staring into the visage of an untamed animal. Close to his heart there was something that was wild, fierce, savage. An involuntary shiver ran over him and seemed to dispel the strange fancy as suddenly as it had come. He met the other's eye with a smile, the counterpart of which in his heart was vivid horror.

"It *is* a special occasion," he said, as naturally as possible, "and, allow me to add, very special whisky."

Garvey appeared delighted. He was in the middle of a devious tale describing how the whisky came originally into his possession when the door opened behind them and a grating voice announced that dinner was ready. They followed the cassocked form of Marx across the dirty hall, lit only by the shaft of light that followed them from the library door, and entered a small room where a single lamp stood upon a table laid for dinner. The walls were destitute of pictures, and the windows had Venetian blinds without curtains. There was no fire in the grate, and when the men sat down facing each other Shorthouse noticed that, while his own cover was laid with its due proportion of glasses and cutlery, his companion had nothing before him but a soup plate, without fork, knife, or spoon beside it.

"I don't know what there is to offer you," he said; "but I'm sure

Marx has done the best he can at such short notice. I only eat one course for dinner, but pray take your time and enjoy your food."

Marx presently set a plate of soup before the guest, yet so loathsome was the immediate presence of this old Hebrew servitor, that the spoonfuls disappeared somewhat slowly. Garvey sat and watched him.

Shorthouse said the soup was delicious and bravely swallowed another mouthful. In reality his thoughts were centred upon his companion, whose manners were giving evidence of a gradual and curious change. There was a decided difference in his demeanour, a difference that the secretary *felt* at first, rather than saw. Garvey's quiet self-possession was giving place to a degree of suppressed excitement that seemed so far inexplicable. His movements became quick and nervous, his eye shifting and strangely brilliant, and his voice, when he spoke, betrayed an occasional deep tremor. Something unwonted was stirring within him and evidently demanding every moment more vigorous manifestation as the meal proceeded.

Intuitively Shorthouse was afraid of this growing excitement, and while negotiating some uncommonly tough pork chops he tried to lead the conversation on to the subject of chemistry, of which in his Oxford days he had been an enthusiastic student. His companion, however, would none of it. It seemed to have lost interest for him, and he would barely condescend to respond. When Marx presently returned with a plate of steaming eggs and bacon the subject dropped of its own accord.

"An inadequate dinner dish," Garvey said, as soon as the man was gone; "but better than nothing, I hope."

Shorthouse remarked that he was exceedingly fond of bacon and eggs, and, looking up with the last word, saw that Garvey's face was twitching convulsively and that he was almost wriggling in his chair. He quieted down, however, under the secretary's gaze and observed, though evidently with an effort—

"Very good of you to say so. Wish I could join you, only I never eat such stuff. I only take one course for dinner."

Shorthouse began to feel some curiosity as to what the nature of this one course might be, but he made no further remark and contented himself with noting mentally that his companion's excitement seemed to be rapidly growing beyond his control. There was something uncanny about it, and he began to wish he had chosen the alternative of the walk to the station.

"I'm glad to see you never speak when Marx is in the room," said

Garvey presently. "I'm sure it's better not. Don't you think so?"

He appeared to wait eagerly for the answer.

"Undoubtedly," said the puzzled secretary.

"Yes," the other went on quickly. "He's an excellent man, but he has one drawback—a really horrid one. You may—but, no, you could hardly have noticed it yet."

"Not drink, I trust," said Shorthouse, who would rather have discussed any other subject than the odious Jew.

"Worse than that a great deal," Garvey replied, evidently expecting the other to draw him out. But Shorthouse was in no mood to hear anything horrible, and he declined to step into the trap.

"The best of servants have their faults," he said coldly.

"I'll tell you what it is if you like," Garvey went on, still speaking very low and leaning forward over the table so that his face came close to the flame of the lamp, "only we must speak quietly in case he's listening. I'll tell you what it is—if you think you won't be frightened."

"Nothing frightens me," he laughed. (Garvey must understand that at all events.) "Nothing can frighten me," he repeated.

"I'm glad of that; for it frightens *me* a good deal sometimes."

Shorthouse feigned indifference. Yet he was aware that his heart was beating a little quicker and that there was a sensation of chilliness in his back. He waited in silence for what was to come.

"He has a horrible predilection for vacuums," Garvey went on presently in a still lower voice and thrusting his face farther forward under the lamp.

"Vacuums!" exclaimed the secretary in spite of himself. "What in the world do you mean?"

"What I say of course. He's always tumbling into them, so that I can't find him or get at him. He hides there for hours at a time, and for the life of me I can't make out what he does there."

Shorthouse stared his companion straight in the eyes. What in the name of Heaven was he talking about?

"Do you suppose he goes there for a change of air, or—or to escape?" he went on in a louder voice.

Shorthouse could have laughed outright but for the expression of the other's face.

"I should not think there was much air of any sort in a vacuum," he said quietly.

"That's exactly what *I* feel," continued Garvey with ever growing excitement. "That's the horrid part of it. How the devil does he live there? You see—"

"Have you ever followed him there?" interrupted the secretary. The other leaned back in his chair and drew a deep sigh.

"Never! It's impossible. You see I can't follow him. There's not room for two. A vacuum only holds one comfortably. Marx knows that. He's out of my reach altogether once he's fairly inside. He knows the best side of a bargain. He's a regular Jew."

"That is a drawback to a servant, of course—" Shorthouse spoke slowly, with his eyes on his plate.

"A drawback," interrupted the other with an ugly chuckle, "I call it a draw-in, that's what I call it."

"A draw-in does seem a more accurate term," assented Shorthouse. "But," he went on, "I thought that nature abhorred a vacuum. She used to, when I was at school—though perhaps—it's so long ago—"

He hesitated and looked up. Something in Garvey's face—something he had *felt* before he looked up—stopped his tongue and froze the words in his throat. His lips refused to move and became suddenly dry. Again the mist rose before his eyes and the appalling shadow dropped its veil over the face before him. Garvey's features began to burn and glow. Then they seemed to coarsen and somehow slip confusedly together. He stared for a second—it seemed only for a second—into the visage of a ferocious and abominable animal; and then, as suddenly as it had come, the filthy shadow of the beast passed off, the mist melted out, and with a mighty effort over his nerves he forced himself to finish his sentence.

"You see it's so long since I've given attention to such things," he stammered. His heart was beating rapidly, and a feeling of oppression was gathering over it.

"It's my peculiar and special study on the other hand," Garvey resumed. "I've not spent all these years in my laboratory to no purpose, I can assure you. Nature, I know for a fact," he added with unnatural warmth, "does *not* abhor a vacuum. On the contrary, she's uncommonly fond of 'em, much too fond, it seems, for the comfort of my little household. If there were fewer vacuums and more abhorrence we should get on better—a damned sight better in my opinion."

"Your special knowledge, no doubt, enables you to speak with authority," Shorthouse said, curiosity and alarm warring with other mixed feelings in his mind; "but how *can* a man tumble into a vacuum?"

"You may well ask. That's just it. How can he? It's preposterous and I can't make it out at all. Marx knows, but he won't tell me. Jews know more than we do. For my part I have reason to believe—" He stopped and listened. "Hush! here he comes," he added, rubbing his hands together as if in glee and fidgeting in his chair.

Steps were heard coming down the passage, and as they approached the door Garvey seemed to give himself completely over to an excitement he could not control. His eyes were fixed on the door and he began clutching the tablecloth with both hands. Again his face was screened by the loathsome shadow. It grew wild, wolfish. As through a mask, that concealed, and yet was thin enough to let through a suggestion of, the beast crouching behind, there leaped into his countenance the strange look of the animal in the human—the expression of the were-wolf, the monster. The change in all its loathsomeness came rapidly over his features, which began to lose their outline. The nose flattened, dropping with broad nostrils over thick lips. The face rounded, filled, and became squat. The eyes, which, luckily for Shorthouse, no longer sought his own, glowed with the light of untamed appetite and bestial greed. The hands left the cloth and grasped the edges of the plate, and then clutched the cloth again.

"This is *my* course coming now," said Garvey, in a deep guttural voice. He was shivering. His upper lip was partly lifted and showed the teeth, white and gleaming.

A moment later the door opened and Marx hurried into the room and set a dish in front of his master. Garvey half rose to meet him, stretching out his hands and grinning horribly. With his mouth he made a sound like the snarl of an animal. The dish before him was steaming, but the slight vapour rising from it betrayed by its odour that it was not born of a fire of coals. It was the natural heat of flesh warmed by the fires of life only just expelled.

The moment the dish rested on the table Garvey pushed away his own plate and drew the other up close under his mouth. Then he seized the food in both hands and commenced to tear it with his teeth, grunting as he did so. Shorthouse closed his eyes, with a feeling of nausea. When he looked up again the lips and jaw of the man opposite were stained with crimson. The whole man was transformed. A feasting tiger, starved and ravenous, but without a tiger's grace—this was what he watched for several minutes, transfixed with horror and disgust.

Marx had already taken his departure, knowing evidently what was not good for the eyes to look upon, and Shorthouse knew at last that he was sitting face to face with a madman.

The ghastly meal was finished in an incredibly short time and nothing was left but a tiny pool of red liquid rapidly hardening. Garvey leaned back heavily in his chair and sighed. His smeared face, withdrawn now from the glare of the lamp, began to resume its normal appearance. Presently he looked up at his guest and said in his natural voice—

"I hope you've had enough to eat. You wouldn't care for this, you know," with a downward glance.

Shorthouse met his eyes with an inward loathing, and it was impossible not to show some of the repugnance he felt. In the other's face, however, he thought he saw a subdued, cowed expression. But he found nothing to say.

"Marx will be in presently," Garvey went on. "He's either listening, or in a vacuum."

"Does he choose any particular time for his visits?" the secretary managed to ask.

"He generally goes after dinner; just about this time, in fact. But he's not gone yet," he added, shrugging his shoulders, "for I think I hear him coming."

Shorthouse wondered whether vacuum was possibly synonymous with wine cellar, but gave no expression to his thoughts. With chills of horror still running up and down his back, he saw Marx come in with a basin and towel, while Garvey thrust up his face just as an animal puts up its muzzle to be rubbed.

"Now we'll have coffee in the library, if you're ready," he said, in the tone of a gentleman addressing his guests after a dinner party.

Shorthouse picked up the bag, which had lain all this time between his feet, and walked through the door his host held open for him. Side by side they crossed the dark hall together, and, to his disgust, Garvey linked an arm in his, and with his face so close to the secretary's ear that he felt the warm breath, said in a thick voice—

"You're uncommonly careful with that bag, Mr. Shorthouse. It surely must contain something more than the bundle of papers."

"Nothing but the papers," he answered, feeling the hand burning upon his arm and wishing he were miles away from the house and its abominable occupants.

"Quite sure?" asked the other with an odious and suggestive chuckle. "Is there any meat in it, fresh meat—raw meat?"

The secretary felt, somehow, that at the least sign of fear the beast on his arm would leap upon him and tear him with his teeth.

"Nothing of the sort," he answered vigorously. "It wouldn't hold enough to feed a cat."

"True," said Garvey with a vile sigh, while the other felt the hand upon his arm twitch up and down as if feeling the flesh. "True, it's too small to be of any real use. As you say, it wouldn't hold enough to feed a cat."

Shorthouse was unable to suppress a cry. The muscles of his fingers, too, relaxed in spite of himself and he let the black bag drop with a bang to the floor. Garvey instantly withdrew his arm and turned with a quick movement. But the secretary had regained his control as suddenly as he had lost it, and he met the maniac's eyes with a steady and aggressive glare.

"There, you see, it's quite light. It makes no appreciable noise when I drop it." He picked it up and let it fall again, as if he had dropped it for the first time purposely. The ruse was successful.

"Yes. You're right," Garvey said, still standing in the doorway and staring at him. "At any rate it wouldn't hold enough for two," he laughed. And as he closed the door the horrid laughter echoed in the empty hall.

They sat down by a blazing fire and Shorthouse was glad to feel its warmth. Marx presently brought in coffee. A glass of the old whisky and a good cigar helped to restore equilibrium. For some minutes the men sat in silence staring into the fire. Then, without looking up, Garvey said in a quiet voice—

"I suppose it was a shock to you to see me eat raw meat like that. I must apologise if it was unpleasant to you. But it's all I can eat and it's the only meal I take in the twenty-four hours."

"Best nourishment in the world, no doubt; though I should think it might be a trifle strong for some stomachs."

He tried to lead the conversation away from so unpleasant a subject, and went on to talk rapidly of the values of different foods, of vegetarianism and vegetarians, and of men who had gone for long periods without any food at all. Garvey listened apparently without interest and had nothing to say. At the first pause he jumped in eagerly.

"When the hunger is really great on me," he said, still gazing into the fire, "I simply cannot control myself. I must have raw meat—the first I can get—" Here he raised his shining eyes and Shorthouse felt his hair beginning to rise.

"It comes upon me so suddenly too. I never can tell when to expect it. A year ago the passion rose in me like a whirlwind and Marx was out and I couldn't get meat. I had to get something or I should have bitten myself. Just when it was getting unbearable my dog ran out from beneath the sofa. It was a spaniel."

Shorthouse responded with an effort. He hardly knew what he was saying and his skin crawled as if a million ants were moving over it.

There was a pause of several minutes.

"I've bitten Marx all over," Garvey went on presently in his strange quiet voice, and as if he were speaking of apples; "but he's bitter. I doubt if the hunger could ever make me do it again. Probably that's what first drove him to take shelter in a vacuum." He chuckled hideously as he thought of this solution of his attendant's disappearances.

Shorthouse seized the poker and poked the fire as if his life depended on it. But when the banging and clattering was over Garvey continued his remarks with the same calmness. The next sentence, however, was never finished. The secretary had got upon his feet suddenly.

"I shall ask your permission to retire," he said in a determined voice; "I'm tired tonight; will you be good enough to show me to my room?"

Garvey looked up at him with a curious cringing expression behind which there shone the gleam of cunning passion.

"Certainly," he said, rising from his chair. "You've had a tiring journey. I ought to have thought of that before."

He took the candle from the table and lit it, and the fingers that held the match trembled.

"We needn't trouble Marx," he explained. "That beast's in his vacuum by this time."

3

They crossed the hall and began to ascend the carpetless wooden stairs. They were in the well of the house and the air cut like ice. Garvey, the flickering candle in his hand throwing his face into strong outline, led the way across the first landing and opened a door near the mouth of a dark passage. A pleasant room greeted the visitor's eyes, and he rapidly took in its points while his host walked over and lit two candles that stood on a table at the foot of the bed. A fire burned brightly in the grate. There were two windows, opening like doors, in the wall opposite, and a high canopied bed occupied most of the space on the right. Panelling ran all round the room reaching nearly to the ceiling and gave a warm and cosy appearance to the whole; while the portraits that stood in alternate panels suggested somehow the atmosphere of an old country house in England. Shorthouse was agreeably surprised.

"I hope you'll find everything you need," Garvey was saying in the doorway. "If not, you have only to ring that bell by the fireplace. Marx won't hear it of course, but it rings in my laboratory, where I spend most of the night."

Then, with a brief goodnight, he went out and shut the door after him. The instant he was gone Mr. Sidebotham's private secretary did a peculiar thing. He planted himself in the middle of the room with his back to the door, and drawing the pistol swiftly from his hip pocket levelled it across his left arm at the window. Standing motionless in this position for thirty seconds he then suddenly swerved right round and faced in the other direction, pointing his pistol straight at the keyhole of the door. There followed immediately a sound of shuffling outside and of steps retreating across the landing.

"On his knees at the keyhole," was the secretary's reflection. "Just as I thought. But he didn't expect to look down the barrel of a pistol and it made him jump a little."

As soon as the steps had gone downstairs and died away across the hall, Shorthouse went over and locked the door, stuffing a piece of crumpled paper into the second keyhole which he saw immediately above the first. After that, he made a thorough search of the room. It hardly repaid the trouble, for he found nothing unusual. Yet he was glad he had made it. It relieved him to find no one was in hiding under the bed or in the deep oak cupboard; and he hoped sincerely it was not the cupboard in which the unfortunate spaniel had come to its vile death.

The French windows, he discovered, opened on to a little balcony. It looked on to the front, and there was a drop of less than twenty feet to the ground below. The bed was high and wide, soft as feathers and covered with snowy sheets—very inviting to a tired man; and beside the blazing fire were a couple of deep armchairs.

Altogether it was very pleasant and comfortable; but, tired though he was, Shorthouse had no intention of going to bed. It was impossible to disregard the warning of his nerves. They had never failed him before, and when that sense of distressing horror lodged in his bones he knew there was something in the wind and that a red flag was flying over the immediate future. Some delicate instrument in his being, more subtle than the senses, more accurate than mere presentiment, had seen the red flag and interpreted its meaning.

Again it seemed to him, as he sat in an armchair over the fire, that his movements were being carefully watched from somewhere; and, not knowing what weapons might be used against him, he felt that his real safety lay in a rigid control of his mind and feelings and a stout refusal to admit that he was in the least alarmed.

The house was very still. As the night wore on the wind dropped. Only occasional bursts of sleet against the windows reminded him that the elements were awake and uneasy. Once or twice the windows rattled and the rain hissed in the fire, but the roar of the wind in the chimney grew less and less and the lonely building was at last lapped in a great stillness. The coals clicked, settling themselves deeper in the grate, and the noise of the cinders dropping with a tiny report into the soft heap of accumulated ashes was the only sound that punctuated the silence.

In proportion as the power of sleep grew upon him the dread of the situation lessened; but so imperceptibly, so gradually, and so insinuatingly that he scarcely realised the change. He thought he was as wide awake to his danger as ever. The successful exclusion of horrible mental pictures of what he had seen he attributed to his rigorous control, instead of to their true cause, the creeping over him of the soft influences of sleep. The faces in the coals were so soothing; the armchair was so comfortable; so sweet the breath that gently pressed upon his eyelids; so subtle the growth of the sensation of safety. He settled down deeper into the chair and in another moment would have been asleep when the red flag began to shake violently to and fro and he sat bolt upright as if he had been stabbed in the back.

Someone was coming up the stairs. The boards creaked beneath a stealthy weight.

Shorthouse sprang from the chair and crossed the room swiftly, taking up his position beside the door, but out of range of the keyhole. The two candles flared unevenly on the table at the foot of the bed. The steps were slow and cautious—it seemed thirty seconds between each one—but the person who was taking them was very close to the door. Already he had topped the stairs and was shuffling almost silently across the bit of landing.

The secretary slipped his hand into his pistol pocket and drew back further against the wall, and hardly had he completed the movement when the sounds abruptly ceased and he knew that somebody was standing just outside the door and preparing for a careful observation through the keyhole.

He was in no sense a coward. In action he was never afraid. It was the waiting and wondering and the uncertainty that might have loosened his nerves a little. But, somehow, a wave of intense horror swept over him for a second as he thought of the bestial maniac and his attendant Jew; and he would rather have faced a pack of wolves than have to do with either of these men.

Something brushing gently against the door set his nerves tingling afresh and made him tighten his grasp on the pistol. The steel was cold and slippery in his moist fingers. What an awful noise it would make when he pulled the trigger! If the door were to open how close he would be to the figure that came in! Yet he knew it was locked on the inside and could not possibly open. Again something brushed against the panel beside him and a second later the piece of crumpled paper fell from the keyhole to the floor, while the piece of thin wire that had accomplished this result showed its point for a moment in the room and was then swiftly withdrawn.

Somebody was evidently peering now through the keyhole, and realising this fact the spirit of attack entered into the heart of the beleaguered man. Raising aloft his right hand he brought it suddenly down with a resounding crash upon the panel of the door next the keyhole—a crash that, to the crouching eavesdropper, must have seemed like a clap of thunder out of a clear sky. There was a gasp and a slight lurching against the door and the midnight listener rose startled and alarmed, for Shorthouse plainly heard the tread of feet across the landing and down the stairs till they were lost in the silences of the hall. Only, this time, it seemed to him there were four feet instead of two.

Quickly stuffing the paper back into the keyhole, he was in the act of walking back to the fireplace when, over his shoulder, he caught sight of a white face pressed in outline against the outside of the window. It was blurred in the streams of sleet, but the white of the moving eyes was unmistakable. He turned instantly to meet it, but the face was withdrawn like a flash, and darkness rushed in to fill the gap where it had appeared.

"Watched on both sides," he reflected.

But he was not to be surprised into any sudden action, and quietly walking over to the fireplace as if he had seen nothing unusual he stirred the coals a moment and then strolled leisurely over to the window. Steeling his nerves, which quivered a moment in spite of his will, he opened the window and stepped out on to the balcony. The wind, which he thought had dropped, rushed past him into the room and extinguished one of the candles, while a volley of fine cold rain burst all over his face. At first he could see nothing, and the darkness came close up to his eyes like a wall. He went a little farther on to the balcony and drew the window after him till it clashed. Then he stood and waited.

But nothing touched him. No one seemed to be there. His eyes got accustomed to the blackness and he was able to make out the iron railing, the dark shapes of the trees beyond, and the faint light coming from the other window. Through this he peered into the room, walking the length of the balcony to do so. Of course he was standing in a shaft of light and whoever was crouching in the darkness below could plainly see him. *Below?*—That there should be anyone *above* did not occur to him until, just as he was preparing to go in again, he became aware that something was moving in the darkness over his head. He looked up, instinctively raising a protecting arm, and saw a long black line swinging against the dim wall of the house. The shutters of the window on the next floor, whence it depended, were thrown open and moving backwards and forwards in the wind. The line was evidently a thickish cord, for as he looked it was pulled in and the end disappeared in the darkness.

Shorthouse, trying to whistle to himself, peered over the edge of the balcony as if calculating the distance he might have to drop, and then calmly walked into the room again and closed the window behind him, leaving the latch so that the lightest touch would cause it to fly open. He relit the candle and drew a straight-backed chair up to the table. Then he put coal on the fire and stirred it up into a royal blaze. He would willingly have folded the shutters over those staring windows at his back. But that was out of the question. It would have been to cut off his way of escape.

Sleep, for the time, was at a disadvantage. His brain was full of blood and every nerve was tingling. He felt as if countless eyes were upon him and scores of stained hands were stretching out from the corners and crannies of the house to seize him. Crouching figures, figures of hideous Jews, stood everywhere about him where shelter was, creeping forward out of the shadows when he was not looking and retreating swiftly and silently when he turned his head. Wherever he looked, other eyes met his own, and though they melted away under his steady, confident gaze, he knew they would wax and draw in upon him the instant his glances weakened and his will wavered.

Though there were no sounds, he knew that in the well of the house there was movement going on, *and preparation*. And this knowledge, inasmuch as it came to him irresistibly and through other and more subtle channels than those of the senses kept the sense of horror fresh in his blood and made him alert and awake.

But, no matter how great the dread in the heart, the power of sleep will eventually overcome it. Exhausted nature is irresistible, and as the minutes wore on and midnight passed, he realised that nature was vigorously asserting herself and sleep was creeping upon him from the extremities.

To lessen the danger he took out his pencil and began to draw the articles of furniture in the room. He worked into elaborate detail the cupboard, the mantelpiece, and the bed, and from these he passed on to the portraits. Being possessed of genuine skill, he found the occupation sufficiently absorbing. It kept the blood in his brain, and that kept him awake. The pictures, moreover, now that he considered them for the first time, were exceedingly well painted. Owing to the dim light, he centred his attention upon the portraits beside the fireplace. On the right was a woman, with a sweet, gentle face and a figure of great refinement; on the left was a full-size figure of a big handsome man with a full beard and wearing a hunting costume of ancient date.

From time to time he turned to the windows behind him, but the vision of the face was not repeated. More than once, too, he went to the door and listened, but the silence was so profound in the house that he gradually came to believe the plan of attack had been abandoned. Once he went out on to the balcony, but the sleet stung his face and he only had time to see that the shutters above were closed, when he was obliged to seek the shelter of the room again.

In this way the hours passed. The fire died down and the room grew chilly. Shorthouse had made several sketches of the two heads and was beginning to feel overpoweringly weary. His feet and his hands were cold and his yawns were prodigious. It seemed ages and ages since the steps had come to listen at his door and the face had watched him from the window. A feeling of safety had somehow come to him. In reality he was exhausted. His one desire was to drop upon the soft white bed and yield himself up to sleep without any further struggle.

He rose from his chair with a series of yawns that refused to be stifled and looked at his watch. It was close upon three in the morning. He made up his mind that he would lie down with his clothes on and get some sleep. It was safe enough, the door was locked on the inside and the window was fastened. Putting the bag on the table near his pillow he blew out the candles and dropped with a sense of careless and delicious exhaustion upon the soft mattress. In five minutes he was sound asleep.

There had scarcely been time for the dreams to come when he found himself lying sideways across the bed with wide open eyes staring into the darkness. Someone had touched him, and he had writhed away in his sleep as from something unholy. The movement had awakened him.

The room was simply black. No light came from the windows and the fire had gone out as completely as if water had been poured upon it. He gazed into a sheet of impenetrable darkness that came close up to his face like a wall.

His first thought was for the papers in his coat and his hand flew to the pocket. They were safe; and the relief caused by this discovery left his mind instantly free for other reflections.

And the realisation that at once came to him with a touch of dismay was, that during his sleep some definite *change* had been effected in the room. He felt this with that intuitive certainty which amounts to positive knowledge. The room was utterly still, but the corroboration that was speedily brought to him seemed at once to fill the darkness with a whispering, secret life that chilled his blood and made the sheet feel like ice against his cheek.

Hark! This was it; there reached his ears, in which the blood was already buzzing with warning clamour, a dull murmur of something that rose indistinctly from the well of the house and became audible to him without passing through walls or doors. There seemed no solid surface between him, lying on the bed, and the landing; between the landing and the stairs, and between the stairs and the hall beyond.

He knew that the door of the room *was standing open*! Therefore it had been opened from the *inside*. Yet the window was fastened, also on the inside.

Hardly was this realised when the conspiring silence of the hour was broken by another and a more definite sound. A step was coming along the passage. A certain bruise on the hip told Shorthouse that the pistol in his pocket was ready for use and he drew it out quickly and cocked it. Then he just had time to slip over the edge of the bed and crouch down on the floor when the step halted on the threshold of the room. The bed was thus between him and the open door. The window was at his back.

He waited in the darkness. What struck him as peculiar about the steps was that there seemed no particular desire to move stealthily. There was no extreme caution. They moved along in rather a slipshod way and sounded like soft slippers or feet in stockings. There was something clumsy, irresponsible, almost reckless about the movement.

For a second the steps paused upon the threshold, but only for a second. Almost immediately they came on into the room, and as they passed from the wood to the carpet Shorthouse noticed that they became wholly noiseless. He waited in suspense, not knowing whether the unseen walker was on the other side of the room or was close upon him. Presently he stood up and stretched out his left arm in front of him, groping, searching, feeling in a circle; and behind it he held the pistol, cocked and pointed, in his right hand. As he rose a bone cracked in his knee, his clothes rustled as if they were newspapers, and his breath seemed loud enough to be heard all over the room. But not a sound came to betray the position of the invisible intruder.

Then, just when the tension was becoming unbearable, a noise relieved the gripping silence. It was wood knocking against wood, and it came from the farther end of the room. The steps had moved over to the fireplace. A sliding sound almost immediately followed it and then silence closed again over everything like a pall.

For another five minutes Shorthouse waited, and then the suspense became too much. He could not stand that open door! The candles were close beside him and he struck a match and lit them, expecting in the sudden glare to receive at least a terrific blow. But nothing happened, and he saw at once that the room was entirely empty. Walking over with the pistol cocked he peered out into the darkness of the landing and then closed the door and turned the key. Then he searched the room—bed, cupboard, table, curtains, everything that could have concealed a man; but found no trace of the intruder. The owner of the footsteps had disappeared like a ghost into the shadows of the night. But for one fact he might have imagined that he had been dreaming: *the bag had vanished*!

There was no more sleep for Shorthouse that night. His watch pointed to 4 a.m. and there were still three hours before daylight. He sat down at the table and continued his sketches. With fixed determination he went on with his drawing and began a new outline of the man's head. There was something in the expression that continually evaded him. He had no success with it, and this time it seemed to him that it was the eyes that brought about his discomfiture. He held up his pencil before his face to measure the distance between the nose and the eyes, and to his amazement he saw that a change had come over the features. The eyes were no longer open. *The lids had closed!*

For a second he stood in a sort of stupefied astonishment. A push would have toppled him over. Then he sprang to his feet and held a candle close up to the picture. The eyelids quivered, the eyelashes trembled. Then, right before his gaze, the eyes opened and looked straight into his own. Two holes were cut in the panel and this pair of eyes, human eyes, just fitted them.

As by a curious effect of magic, the strong fear that had governed him ever since his entry into the house disappeared in a second. Anger rushed into his heart and his chilled blood rose suddenly to boiling point. Putting the candle down, he took two steps back into the room and then flung himself forward with all his strength against the painted panel. Instantly, and before the crash came, the eyes were withdrawn, and two black spaces showed where they had been. The old huntsman was eyeless. But the panel cracked and split inwards like a sheet of thin cardboard; and Shorthouse, pistol in hand, thrust an arm through the jagged aperture and, seizing a human leg, dragged out into the room—the Jew!

Words rushed in such a torrent to his lips that they choked him. The old Hebrew, white as chalk, stood shaking before him, the bright pistol barrel opposite his eyes, when a volume of cold air rushed into the room, and with it a sound of hurried steps. Shorthouse felt his arm knocked up before he had time to turn, and the same second Garvey, who had somehow managed to burst open the window came between him and the trembling Marx. His lips were parted and his eyes rolled strangely in his distorted face.

"Don't shoot him! Shoot in the air!" he shrieked. He seized the Jew by the shoulders.

"You damned hound," he roared, hissing in his face. "So I've got you at last. That's where your vacuum is, is it? I know your vile hiding-place at last." He shook him like a dog. "I've been after him all night," he cried, turning to Shorthouse, "all night, I tell you, and I've got him at last."

Garvey lifted his upper lip as he spoke and showed his teeth. They shone like the fangs of a wolf. The Jew evidently saw them too, for he gave a horrid yell and struggled furiously.

Before the eyes of the secretary a mist seemed to rise. The hideous shadow again leaped into Garvey's face. He foresaw a dreadful battle, and covering the two men with his pistol he retreated slowly to the door. Whether they were both mad, or both criminal, he did not pause to inquire. The only thought present in his mind was that the sooner he made his escape the better.

Garvey was still shaking the Jew when he reached the door and turned the key, but as he passed out on to the landing both men stopped their struggling and turned to face him. Garvey's face, bestial, loathsome, livid with anger; the Jew's white and grey with fear and horror;—both turned towards him and joined in a wild, horrible yell that woke the echoes of the night. The next second they were after him at full speed.

Shorthouse slammed the door in their faces and was at the foot of the stairs, crouching in the shadow, before they were out upon the landing. They tore shrieking down the stairs and past him, into the hall; and, wholly unnoticed, Shorthouse whipped up the stairs again, crossed the bedroom and dropped from the balcony into the soft snow.

As he ran down the drive he heard behind him in the house the yells of the maniacs; and when he reached home several hours later Mr. Sidebotham not only raised his salary but also told him to buy a new hat and overcoat, and send in the bill to him.

The Dance of Death

Browne went to the dance feeling genuinely depressed, for the doctor had just warned him that his heart was weak and that he must be exceedingly careful in the matter of exertion.

"Dancing?" he asked, with that assumed lightness some natures affect in the face of a severe shock—the plucky instinct to conceal pain.

"Well—in moderation, perhaps," hummed the doctor. "Not *wildly*," he added, with a smile that betrayed something more than mere professional sympathy.

At any other time, Browne would probably have laughed, but the doctor's serious manner put a touch of ice on the springs of laughter. At the age of twenty-six one hardly realises death; life is still endless; and it is only old people who have "hearts" and such-like afflictions. So it was that the professional *dictum* came as a real shock; and with it too, as a sudden revelation, came that little widening of sympathy for others that is part of every deep experience as the years roll up and pass.

At first, he thought of sending an excuse. He went about carefully, making the 'buses stop dead before he got out, and going very slowly up steps.

Then gradually he grew more accustomed to the burden of his dread secret: the commonplace events of the day; the hated drudgery of the office, where he was an underpaid clerk; the contact with other men who bore similar afflictions with assumed indifference; the fault-finding of the manager, making him fearful of his position—all this helped to reduce the sense of first alarm, and, instead of sending an excuse, he went to the dance, as we have seen, feeling deeply depressed, and moving all the time as if he carried in his side a brittle glass globe that the least jarring might break into a thousand pieces.

The spontaneous jollity natural to a boy and girl dance served, however, to emphasise vividly the contrast of his own mood, and to make him very conscious again of his little hidden source of pain. But, though he would gladly have availed himself of a sympathetic ear among the many there whom he knew intimately, he nevertheless exercised the restraint natural to his character, and avoided any reference to the matter that bulked so largely in his consciousness. Once or twice, he was tempted, but a prevision of the probable conversation that would ensue stopped him always in time: "Oh, I *am* so sorry, Mr. Browne, and you mustn't dance too hard, you know," and then his careless laugh as he remarked that it didn't matter a bit, and his little joke as he whirled his partner off for another spin.

He knew, of course, there was nothing very sensational about being told that one's heart was weak. Even the doctor had smiled a little; and he now recalled more than one acquaintance who had the same trouble and made light of it. Yet it sounded in Browne's life a note of profound and sinister gloom. It snatched beyond his reach at one fell swoop all that he most loved and enjoyed, destroying a thousand dreams, and painting the future a dull drab colour without hope. He was an idealist at heart, hating the sordid routine of the life he led as a business underling. His dreams were of the open air, of mountains, forests, and great plains, of the sea, and of the lonely places of the world.

Wind and rain spoke intimately to his soul, and the storms of heaven, as he heard them raging at night round his high room in Bloomsbury, stirred savage yearnings that haunted him for days afterwards with the voices of the desert. Sometimes during the lunch hour, when he escaped temporarily from the artificial light and close air of his high office stool, to see the white clouds sailing by overhead, and to hear the wind singing in the wires, it set such a fever in his blood that for the remainder of the afternoon he found it impossible to concentrate on his work, and thus exasperated the loud-voiced manager almost to madness.

Having no expectations, and absolutely no practical business ability, he was fortunate, however, in having a "place" at all, and the hard fact that promotion was unlikely made him all the more careful to keep his dreams in their place, to do his work as well as possible, and to save what little he could.

His holidays were the only points of light in an otherwise dreary existence. And one day, when he should have saved enough, he looked forward vaguely to a life close to Nature, perhaps a shepherd on a hundred hills, a dweller in the woods, within sound of his beloved trees and waters, where the smell of the earth and camp fire would be ever in his nostrils, and the running stream always ready to bear his boat swiftly away into happiness.

And now the knowledge that he had a weak heart came to spoil everything. It shook his dream to the very foundations. It depressed him utterly. Any moment the blow might fall. It might catch him in the water, swimming, or half-way up the mountain, or midway in one of his lonely tramps, just when his enjoyment depended most upon his being reckless and forgetful of bodily limitations—that freedom of the spirit in the wilderness he so loved. He might even be forced to spend his holiday, to say nothing of the dream of the far future, in some farmhouse "*quietly*" instead of gloriously in the untrodden wilds. The thought made him angry with pain. All day he was haunted and dismayed, and all day he heard the wind whispering among branches and the water lapping somewhere against sandy banks in the sun.

The dance was a small subscription affair, hastily arranged and happily informal. It took place in a large hall that was used in the daytime as a gymnasium, but the floor was good and the music more than good. Foils and helmets hung round the walls, and high up under the brown rafters were ropes, rings, and trapezes coiled away out of reach, their unsightliness further concealed by an array of brightly coloured flags. Only the light was not of the best, for the hall was very long, and the gallery at the far end loomed in a sort of twilight that was further deepened by the shadows of the flags overhead. But its benches afforded excellent sitting-out places, where strong light was not always an essential to happiness, and no one dreamed of finding fault

At first, he danced cautiously, but by degrees the spirit of the time and place relieved his depression and helped him to forget. He had probably exaggerated the importance of his malady. Lots of other fellows, even as young as he was, had weak hearts and thought nothing of it. All the time, however, there was an undercurrent of sadness and disappointment not to be denied. Something had gone out of life. A note of darkness had crept in. He found his partners dull, and they no doubt found him still duller.

Yet this dance, with nothing apparently to distinguish it from a hundred others, stood out in all his experience with an indelible red mark against it. It is a common trick of Nature—and a profoundly significant one—that, just when despair is deepest, she waves a wand before the weary eyes and does her best to waken an impossible hope. Her idea, presumably, being to keep her victim going actively to the very end of the chapter, lest through indifference he should lose something of the lesson she wishes to teach.

Thus, it was that, midway in the dance, Browne's listless glance fell upon a certain girl whose appearance instantly galvanised him into a state of keenest possible desire. A flash of white light entered his heart and set him all on fire to know her. She attracted him tremendously She was dressed in pale green, and always danced with the same man— a man about his own height and colouring, whose face, however, he never could properly see. They sat out together much of the time—always in the gallery where the shadows were deepest. The girl's face he saw clearly, and there was something about her that simply lifted him bodily out of himself and sent strange thrills of delight coursing over him like shocks of electricity.

Several times their eyes met, and when this happened, he could not tear his glance away. She fascinated him, and all the forces in his being merged into a single desire to be with her, to dance with her, speak with her, and to know her name. Especially he wondered who the man was she so favoured; he reminded him so oddly of himself. No one knows precisely what he himself looks like, but this tall dark figure, whose face he never could contrive to see, started the strange thought in him that it was his own double.

In vain he sought to compass an introduction to this girl. No one seemed to know her. Her dress, her hair, and a certain wondrous slim grace made him think of a young tree waving in the wind; of ivy leaves; of something that belonged to the life of the woods rather than to ordinary humanity. She possessed him, filling his thoughts with wild woodland dreams. Once, too, he was certain when their eyes met that she smiled at him, and the call was so well-nigh irresistible that he almost dropped his partner's arm to run after her.

But it seemed impossible to obtain an introduction from anyone.

"Do you know who that girl is over there?" he asked one of his partners while sitting out a square dance, half exhausted with his exertions; "the one up there in the gallery?"

"In pink?"

"No, the one in green, I mean."

"Oh, next to the wallflower lady in red!"

"*In* the gallery, not *under* it," he explained impatiently.

"I can't see up there. It's so dark," returned the girl after a careful survey through glasses. I don't think I see anyone at all."

"It is rather dark," he remarked.

"Why? Do you know who she is?" she asked foolishly.

He did not like to insist. It seemed so rude to his partner. But this sort of thing happened once or twice. Evidently no one knew this girl in green, or else he described her so inaccurately that the people he asked looked at someone else instead.

"In that green sort of ivy-looking dress," he tried another.

"With the rose in her hair and the red nose? Or the one sitting out?"

After that he gave it up finally. His partners seemed to sniff a little when he asked. Evidently *la désirée* was not a popular maiden. Soon after, too, she disappeared and he lost sight of her. Yet the thought that she might have gone home made his heart sink into a sort of horrible blackness.

He lingered on much later than he intended in the hope of getting an introduction, but at last, when he had filled all his engagements, or nearly all, he made up his mind to slip out and go home. It was already late, and he had to be in the office—that hateful office—punctually at nine o'clock. He felt tired, awfully tired, more so than ever before at a dance. It was, of course, his weak heart. He still dawdled a little while, however, hoping for another glimpse of the sylph in green, hungering for a last look that he could carry home with him and perhaps mingle with his dreams. The mere thought of her filled him with pain and joy, and a sort of rarefied delight he had never known before. But he could not wait for ever, and it was already close upon two o'clock in the morning. His rooms were only a short distance down the street; he would light a cigarette and stroll home. No; he had forgotten for a moment; *without* a cigarette: the doctor had been very stern on that point

He was in the act of turning his back on the whirl of dancing figures, when the flags at the far end of the room parted for an instant in the moving air, and his eye rested upon the gallery just visible among the shadows.

A great pain ran swiftly through his heart as he looked.

There were only two figures seated there: the tall dark man, who was his double, and the, ivy girl in green. She was looking straight at him down the length of the room, and even at that distance he could see that she smiled.

He stopped short. The flags waved back again and hid the picture, but on the instant, he made up his mind to act. There, among all this dreary crowd of dancing dolls, was someone he really wanted to know, to speak with, to touch—someone who drew him beyond all he had ever known, and made his soul cry aloud. The room was filled with automatic lay-figures, but here was someone alive. He must know her. It was impossible to go home without speech, utterly impossible.

A fresh stab of pain, worse than the first, gave him momentary pause. He leant against the wall for an instant just under the clock, where the hands pointed to two, waiting for the swooning blackness to go. Then he passed on, disregarding it utterly; It supplied him, in truth, with the extra little impetus he needed to set the will into vigorous action, for it reminded him forcibly of what *might* happen. His time might be short; he had known few enough of the good things of life; he would seize what he could. He had no introduction, but—to the devil with the conventions. The risk was nothing. To meet her eyes at close quarters, to hear her voice, to know something of the perfume of that hair and dress—what was the risk of a snub compared to that?

He slid down the side of the long room, dodging the dancers as best he could. The tall man, he noted, had left the gallery, but the girl sat on alone. He made his way quickly up the wooden steps, light as air, trembling with anticipation. His heart beat like a quick padded hammer, and the blood played a tambourine in his ears. It was odd he did not meet the tall man on the stairs, but doubtless there was another exit from the gallery that he had not observed. He topped the stairs and turned the corner. By Jove, she was still there, a few feet in front of him, sitting with her arms upon the railing, peering down upon the dancers below. His eyes swam for a moment, and something clutched at the very roots of his being.

But he did not hesitate. He went up quite close past the empty seats, meaning to ask naturally and simply if he might beg for the pleasure of a dance. Then, when he was within a few feet of her side, the girl suddenly turned and faced him, and the words died away on his lips. They seemed absolutely foolish and inadequate.

"Yes, I am ready," she said quietly, looking straight into his eyes; "but what a long time you were in coming. Was it such a great effort to *leave?*"

The form of the question struck him as odd, but he was too happy to pause. He became transfigured with joy. The sound of her voice instantly drowned all the clatter of the ball-room, and seemed to him the only thing in the whole world. It did not break on the consonants like most human speech. It flowed smoothly; it was the sound of wind among branches, of water running over pebbles. It swept into him and caught him away, so that for a moment he saw his beloved woods and hills and seas. The stars were somewhere in it too and the murmur of the plains.

By the gods! Here was a girl he could speak with in the words of silence; she stretched every string in his soul and then played on them. His spirit expanded with life and happiness. She would listen gladly to all that concerned him. To her he could talk openly about his poor broken heart, for she would sympathise. Indeed, it was all he could do to prevent himself running forward at once with his arms outstretched to take her. There was a perfume of earth and woods about her.

"Oh, I am so *awfully* glad—" he began lamely, his eyes on her face. Then, remembering something of earthly manners, he added:

"My name—er—is——"

Something unusual—something indescribable—in her gesture stopped him. She had moved to give him space at her side.

"Your name!" she laughed, drawing her green skirts with a soft rustle like leaves along the bench to make room; "but you need no name now, you know!"

Oh, the wonder of it! She understood him. He sat down with a feeling that he had been flying in a free wind and was resting among the tops of trees. The room faded out temporarily.

"But my name, if you like to know, is Issidy," she said, still smiling.

"Miss Issidy," he stammered, making another attempt at the forms of worldly politeness.

"Not *Miss* Issidy," she laughed aloud merrily; It surely was the sound of wind in poplars. "Issidy is my first name; so, if you call me anything, you must call me that"

The name was pure music in his ears, but though he blundered about in his memory to find his own, it had utterly vanished; for the life of him he could not recollect what his friends called him. He stared a moment, vaguely wondering, almost beside himself with delight No other girls he had known—ye heavens above! there were no longer any other girls! He had never known any other girl than this one. Here was his universe, framed in a green dress, with a voice of sea and wind, eyes like the sun, and movements of bending grasses. All else was mere shadow and fantasy. For the first time in his existence, he was alive, *and knew that he was alive.*

"I was sure you would come to me," she was saying. "You couldn't help yourself." Her eyes were always on his face.

"I was afraid at first—"

"But your thoughts," she interrupted softly, "your thoughts were up here with me all the time."

"You knew that!" he cried, delighted.

"I felt them," she replied simply. "They—you kept me company, for I have been alone here all the evening. I know no one else here—yet"

Her words amazed him. He was just going to ask who the tall dark man was, when he saw that she was rising to her feet and that she wanted to dance.

"But my heart—" he stammered.

"It won't hurt your poor heart to dance with me, you know," she laughed. "You may trust me. I shall know how to take care of it."

Browne felt simply ecstatic; it was too wonderful to be true; it was impossible—this meeting in London, at an ordinary dull dance, in the twentieth century. He would wake up presently from a dream of silver and gold. Yet he felt even then that she was drawing his arm about her waist for the dance, and with that first magical touch he almost lost consciousness and passed with her into a state of pure spirit.

It puzzled him for a moment how they reached the floor so quickly and found themselves among the whirling couples. He had no recollection of coming down the stairs. But meanwhile he was dancing on wings, and the girl in green beside him seemed to fly too, and as he pressed her to his heart, he found it impossible to think of anything else in the world but that—that and his astounding happiness.

And the music was within them, rather than without; indeed, they seemed to make their own music out of their swift whirling movements, for it never ceased and he never grew tired. His heart had ceased to pain him. Other curious things happened, too, but he hardly noticed them; or, rather, they no longer seemed strange. In that crowded ballroom they never once touched other people. His partner required no steering. She made no sound. Then suddenly he realised that his own feet made no sound either. They skimmed the floor with noiseless feet like spirits dancing. No one else appeared to take the least notice of them. Most of the faces seemed, indeed, strange to him now, as though he had not seen them before, but once or twice he could have sworn that he passed couples who were dancing almost as happily and lightly as themselves, couples he had known in past years, couples who were *dead*.

Gradually the room emptied of its original comers, and others filled their places, silently, with airy graceful movements and happy faces, till the whole floor at length was covered with the soundless feet and whirling forms of those who had already left the world. And, as the artificial light faded away, there came in its place a soft white light that filled the room with beauty and made all the faces look radiant. And, once, as they skimmed past a mirror, he saw that the girl beside him was not there—that he seemed to be dancing alone, clasping no one; yet when he glanced down, there was her magical face at his shoulder and he felt her little form pressing up against him.

Such dancing, too, he had never even dreamed about, for it was like swinging with the tree-tops in the winds.

Then they danced farther out, ever swifter and swifter, past the shadows beneath the gallery, under the motionless hanging flags—and out into the night. The walls were behind them. They were off their feet and the wind was in their hair. They were rising, rising, rising towards the stars.

He felt the cool air of the open sky on his cheeks, and when he looked down, as they cleared the summit of the dark-lying hills, he saw that Issidy had melted away into himself and they had become one being. And he knew then that his heart would never pain him again on earth, or cause him to fear for any of his beloved dreams.

★★★★★★★★★★

But the manager of the "hateful office" only knew two days later why Browne had not turned up to his desk, nor sent any word to explain his absence. He read it in the paper—how he had dropped down dead at a dance, suddenly stricken by heart disease. It happened just before two o'clock in the morning.

"Well," thought the manager, "he's no loss to us anyhow. He had no real business instincts. Smith will do his work much better—and for less money too."

With Intent to Steal

To sleep in a lonely barn when the best bedrooms in the house were at our disposal, seemed, to say the least, unnecessary, and I felt that some explanation was due to our host.

But Shorthouse, I soon discovered, had seen to all that; our enterprise would be tolerated, not welcomed, for the master kept this sort of thing down with a firm hand. And then, how little I could get this man, Shorthouse, to tell me. There was much I wanted to ask and hear, but he surrounded himself with impossible barriers. It was ludicrous; he was surely asking a good deal of me, and yet he would give so little in return, and his reason—that it was for my good—may have been perfectly true, but did not bring me any comfort in its train. He gave me sops now and then, however, to keep up my curiosity, till I soon was aware that there were growing up side by side within me a genuine interest and an equally genuine fear; and something of both these is probably necessary to all real excitement.

The barn in question was some distance from the house, on the side of the stables, and I had passed it on several of my journeyings to and fro wondering at its forlorn and untarred appearance under a *régime* where everything was so spick and span; but it had never once occurred to me as possible that I should come to spend a night under its roof with a comparative stranger, and undergo there an experience belonging to an order of things I had always rather ridiculed and despised.

At the moment I can only partially recall the process by which Shorthouse persuaded me to lend him my company. Like myself, he was a guest in this autumn house-party, and where there were so many to chatter and to chaff, I think his taciturnity of manner had appealed to me by contrast, and that I wished to repay something of what I owed. There was, no doubt, flattery in it as well, for he was more than twice my age, a man of amazingly wide experience, an explorer of all the world's corners where danger lurked, and—most subtle flattery of all—by far the best shot in the whole party, our host included.

At first, however, I held out a bit.

"But surely this story you tell," I said, "has the parentage common to all such tales—a superstitious heart and an imaginative brain—and has grown now by frequent repetition into an authentic ghost story? Besides, this head gardener of half a century ago," I added, seeing that he still went on cleaning his gun in silence, "who was he, and what positive information have you about him beyond the fact that he was found hanging from the rafters, dead?"

"He was no mere head gardener, this man who passed as such," he replied without looking up, "but a fellow of splendid education who used this curious disguise for his own purposes. Part of this very barn, of which he always kept the key, was found to have been fitted up as a complete laboratory, with *athanor, alembic, cucurbite,* and other appliances, some of which the master destroyed at once—perhaps for the best—and which I have only been able to guess at—"

"Black Arts," I laughed.

"Who knows?" he rejoined quietly. "The man undoubtedly possessed knowledge—dark knowledge—that was most unusual and dangerous, and I can discover no means by which he came to it—no ordinary means, that is. But I *have* found many facts in the case which point to the exercise of a most desperate and unscrupulous will; and the strange disappearances in the neighbourhood, as well as the bones found buried in the kitchen garden, though never actually traced to him, seem to me full of dreadful suggestion."

I laughed again, a little uncomfortably perhaps, and said it reminded one of the story of Giles de Rays, *Maréchal* of France, who was said to have killed and tortured to death in a few years no less than one hundred and sixty women and children for the purposes of necromancy, and who was executed for his crimes at Nantes. But Shorthouse would not "rise," and only returned to his subject.

"His suicide seems to have been only just in time to escape arrest," he said.

"A magician of no high order then," I observed sceptically, "if suicide was his only way of evading the country police."

"The police of London and St. Petersburg rather," returned Shorthouse; "for the headquarters of this pretty company was somewhere in Russia, and his apparatus all bore the marks of the most skilful foreign make. A Russian woman then employed in the household—governess, or something—vanished, too, about the same time and was never caught. She was no doubt the cleverest of the lot. And, remember, the object of this appalling group was not mere vulgar gain, but a kind of knowledge that called for the highest qualities of courage and intellect in the seekers."

I admit I was impressed by the man's conviction of voice and manner, for there is something very compelling in the force of an earnest man's belief, though I still affected to sneer politely.

"But, like most Black Magicians, the fellow only succeeded in compassing his own destruction—that of his tools, rather, and of escaping himself."

"So that he might better accomplish his objects *elsewhere and otherwise*," said Shorthouse, giving, as he spoke, the most minute attention to the cleaning of the lock.

"Elsewhere and otherwise," I gasped.

"As if the shell he left hanging from the rafter in the barn in no way impeded the man's spirit from continuing his dreadful work under new conditions," he added quietly, without noticing my interruption. "The idea being that he sometimes revisits the garden and the barn, chiefly the barn—"

"The barn!" I exclaimed; "for what purpose?"

"Chiefly the barn," he finished, as if he had not heard me, "that is, when there is anybody in it."

I stared at him without speaking, for there was a wonder in me how he would add to this.

"When he wants fresh material, that is—he comes to steal from the living."

"Fresh material!" I repeated aghast. "To steal from the living!" Even then, in broad daylight, I was foolishly conscious of a creeping sensation at the roots of my hair, as if a cold breeze were passing over my skull.

"The strong vitality of the living is what this sort of creature is supposed to need most," he went on imperturbably, "and where he has worked and thought and struggled before is the easiest place for him to get it in. The former conditions are in some way more easily reconstructed—" He stopped suddenly, and devoted all his attention to the gun. "It's difficult to explain, you know, rather," he added presently, "and, besides, it's much better that you should not know till afterwards."

I made a noise that was the beginning of a score of questions and of as many sentences, but it got no further than a mere noise, and Shorthouse, of course, stepped in again.

"Your scepticism," he added, "is one of the qualities that induce me to ask you to spend the night there with me."

"In those days," he went on, in response to my urging for more information, "the family were much abroad, and often travelled for years at a time. This man was invaluable in their absence. His wonderful knowledge of horticulture kept the gardens—French, Italian, English—in perfect order. He had *carte blanche* in the matter of expense, and of course selected all his own underlings. It was the sudden, unexpected return of the master that surprised the amazing stories of the countryside before the fellow, with all his cleverness, had time to prepare or conceal."

"But is there no evidence, no more recent evidence, to show that something is likely to happen if we sit up there?" I asked, pressing him yet further, and I think to his liking, for it showed at least that I was interested. "Has anything happened there lately, for instance?"

Shorthouse glanced up from the gun he was cleaning so assiduously, and the smoke from his pipe curled up into an odd twist between me and the black beard and oriental, suntanned face. The magnetism of his look and expression brought more sense of conviction to me than I had felt hitherto, and I realised that there had been a sudden little change in my attitude and that I was now much more inclined to go in for the adventure with him. At least, I thought, with such a man, one would be safe in any emergency; for he is determined, resourceful, and to be depended upon.

"There's the point," he answered slowly; "for there has apparently been a fresh outburst—an attack almost, it seems,—quite recently. There is evidence, of course, plenty of it, or I should not feel the interest I do feel, but—" he hesitated a moment, as though considering how much he ought to let me know, "but the fact is that three men this summer, on separate occasions, who have gone into that barn after nightfall, have been *accosted*—"

"Accosted?" I repeated, betrayed into the interruption by his choice of so singular a word.

"And one of the stablemen—a recent arrival and quite ignorant of the story—who had to go in there late one night, saw a dark substance hanging down from one of the rafters, and when he climbed up, shaking all over, to cut it down—for he said he felt sure it was a corpse—

the knife passed through nothing but air, and he heard a sound up under the eaves as if someone were laughing. Yet, while he slashed away, and afterwards too, the thing went on swinging there before his eyes and turning slowly with its own weight, like a huge joint on a spit. The man declares, too, that it had a large bearded face, and that the mouth was open and drawn down like the mouth of a hanged man."

"Can we question this fellow?"

"He's gone—gave notice at once, but not before I had questioned him myself very closely."

"Then this was quite recent?" I said, for I knew Shorthouse had not been in the house more than a week.

"Four days ago," he replied. "But, more than that, only three days ago a couple of men were in there together in full daylight when one of them suddenly turned deadly faint. He said that he felt an overmastering impulse to hang himself; and he looked about for a rope and was furious when his companion tried to prevent him—"

"But he did prevent him?"

"Just in time, but not before he had clambered on to a beam. He was very violent."

I had so much to say and ask that I could get nothing out in time, and Shorthouse went on again.

"I've had a sort of watching brief for this case," he said with a smile, whose real significance, however, completely escaped me at the time, "and one of the most disagreeable features about it is the deliberate way the servants have invented excuses to go out to the place, and always after dark; some of them who have no right to go there, and no real occasion at all—have never been there in their lives before probably—and now all of a sudden have shown the keenest desire and determination to go out there about dusk, or soon after, and with the most paltry and foolish excuses in the world. Of course," he added, "they have been prevented, but the desire, stronger than their superstitious dread, and which they cannot explain, is very curious."

"Very," I admitted, feeling that my hair was beginning to stand up again.

"You see," he went on presently, "it all points to volition—in fact to deliberate arrangement. It is no mere family ghost that goes with every ivied house in England of a certain age; it is something real, and something very malignant."

He raised his face from the gun barrel, and for the first time his eye caught mine in the full. Yes, he was very much in earnest. Also, he knew a great deal more than he meant to tell.

"It's worth tempting—and fighting, *I* think," he said; "but I want a companion with me. Are you game?" His enthusiasm undoubtedly caught me, but I still wanted to hedge a bit.

"I'm very sceptical," I pleaded.

"All the better," he said, almost as if to himself. "You have the pluck; I have the knowledge—"

"The knowledge?"

He looked round cautiously as if to make sure that there was no one within earshot.

"I've been in the place myself," he said in a lowered voice, "quite lately—in fact only three nights ago—the day the man turned queer."

I stared.

"But—I was obliged to come out—"

Still I stared.

"Quickly," he added significantly.

"You've gone into the thing pretty thoroughly," was all I could find to say, for I had almost made up my mind to go with him, and was not sure that I wanted to hear too much beforehand.

He nodded. "It's a bore, of course, but I must do everything thoroughly—or not at all."

"That's why you clean your own gun, I suppose?"

"That's why, when there's any danger, I take as few chances as possible," he said, with the same enigmatical smile I had noticed before; and then he added with emphasis, "And that is also why I ask you to keep me company now."

Of course, the shaft went straight home, and I gave my promise without further ado.

Our preparations for the night—a couple of rugs and a flask of black coffee—were not elaborate, and we found no difficulty, about ten o'clock, in absenting ourselves from the billiard-room without attracting curiosity. Shorthouse met me by arrangement under the cedar on the back lawn, and I at once realised with vividness what a difference there is between making plans in the daytime and carrying them out in the dark. One's common-sense—at least in matters of this sort—is reduced to a minimum, and imagination with all her attendant sprites usurps the place of judgment.

Two and two no longer make four—they make a mystery, and the mystery loses no time in growing into a menace. In this particular case, however, my imagination did not find wings very readily, for I knew that my companion was the most *unmovable* of men—an unemotional, solid block of a man who would never lose his head, and in any conceivable state of affairs would always take the right as well as the strong course. So my faith in the man gave me a false courage that was nevertheless very consoling, and I looked forward to the night's adventure with a genuine appetite.

Side by side, and in silence, we followed the path that skirted the East Woods, as they were called, and then led across two hay fields, and through another wood, to the barn, which thus lay about half a mile from the Lower Farm. To the Lower Farm, indeed, it properly belonged; and this made us realise more clearly how very ingenious must have been the excuses of the Hall servants who felt the desire to visit it.

It had been raining during the late afternoon, and the trees were still dripping heavily on all sides, but the moment we left the second wood and came out into the open, we saw a clearing with the stars overhead, against which the barn outlined itself in a black, lugubrious shadow. Shorthouse led the way—still without a word—and we crawled in through a low door and seated ourselves in a soft heap of hay in the extreme corner.

"Now," he said, speaking for the first time, "I'll show you the inside of the barn, so that you may know where you are, and what to do, in case anything happens."

A match flared in the darkness, and with the help of two more that followed I saw the interior of a lofty and somewhat rickety-looking barn, erected upon a wall of grey stones that ran all round and extended to a height of perhaps four feet. Above this masonry rose the wooden sides, running up into the usual vaulted roof, and supported by a double tier of massive oak rafters, which stretched across from wall to wall and were intersected by occasional uprights. I felt as if we were inside the skeleton of some antediluvian monster whose huge black ribs completely enfolded us. Most of this, of course, only sketched itself to my eye in the uncertain light of the flickering matches, and when I said I had seen enough, and the matches went out, we were at once enveloped in an atmosphere as densely black as anything that I have ever known. And the silence equalled the darkness.

We made ourselves comfortable and talked in low voices. The rugs, which were very large, covered our legs; and our shoulders sank into a really luxurious bed of softness. Yet neither of us apparently felt sleepy. I certainly didn't, and Shorthouse, dropping his customary brevity that fell little short of gruffness, plunged into an easy run of talking that took the form after a time of personal reminiscences. This rapidly became a vivid narration of adventure and travel in far countries, and at any other time I should have allowed myself to become completely absorbed in what he told. But, unfortunately, I was never able for a single instant to forget the real purpose of our enterprise, and consequently I felt all my senses more keenly on the alert than usual, and my attention accordingly more or less distracted.

It was, indeed, a revelation to hear Shorthouse unbosom himself in this fashion, and to a young man it was of course doubly fascinating; but the little sounds that always punctuate even the deepest silence out of doors claimed some portion of my attention, and as the night grew on I soon became aware that his tales seemed somewhat disconnected and abrupt—and that, in fact, I heard really only part of them.

It was not so much that I actually heard other sounds, but that I *expected* to hear them; this was what stole the other half of my listening. There was neither wind nor rain to break the stillness, and certainly there were no physical presences in our neighbourhood, for we were half a mile even from the Lower Farm; and from the Hall and stables, at least a mile. Yet the stillness was being continually broken—perhaps *disturbed* is a better word—and it was to these very remote and tiny disturbances that I felt compelled to devote at least half my listening faculties.

From time to time, however, I made a remark or asked a question, to show that I was listening and interested; but, in a sense, my questions always seemed to bear in one direction and to make for one issue, namely, my companion's previous experience in the barn when he had been obliged to come out "quickly."

Apparently I could not help myself in the matter, for this was really the one consuming curiosity I had; and the fact that it was better for me not to know it made me the keener to know it all, even the worst.

Shorthouse realised this even better than I did. I could tell it by the way he dodged, or wholly ignored, my questions, and this subtle sympathy between us showed plainly enough, had I been able at the time to reflect upon its meaning, that the nerves of both of us were in a very sensitive and highly-strung condition. Probably, the complete confidence I felt in his ability to face whatever might happen, and the extent to which also I relied upon him for my own courage, prevented the exercise of my ordinary powers of reflection, while it left my senses free to a more than usual degree of activity.

Things must have gone on in this way for a good hour or more, when I made the sudden discovery that there was something unusual in the conditions of our environment. This sounds a roundabout mode of expression, but I really know not how else to put it. The discovery almost rushed upon me. By rights, we were two men waiting in an alleged haunted barn for something to happen; and, as two men who trusted one another implicitly (though for very different reasons), there should have been two minds keenly alert, with the ordinary senses in active co-operation. Some slight degree of nervousness, too, there might also have been, but beyond this, nothing. It was therefore with something of dismay that I made the sudden discovery that there *was* something more, and something that I ought to have noticed very much sooner than I actually did notice it.

The fact was—Shorthouse's stream of talk was wholly unnatural. He was talking with a purpose. He did not wish to be cornered by my questions, true, but he had another and a deeper purpose still, and it grew upon me, as an unpleasant deduction from my discovery, that this strong, cynical, unemotional man by my side was talking—and had been talking all this time—to gain a particular end. And this end, I soon felt clearly, was to *convince himself*. But, of what?

For myself, as the hours wore on towards midnight, I was not anxious to find the answer; but in the end it became impossible to avoid it, and I knew as I listened, that he was pouring forth this steady stream of vivid reminiscences of travel—South Seas, big game, Russian exploration, women, adventures of all sorts—*because he wished the past to reassert itself to the complete exclusion of the present.* He was taking his precautions. He was afraid.

I felt a hundred things, once this was clear to me, but none of them more than the wish to get up at once and leave the barn. If Shorthouse was afraid already, what in the world was to happen to me in the long hours that lay ahead? . . . I only know that, in my fierce efforts to deny to myself the evidence of his partial collapse, the strength came that enabled me to play my part properly, and I even found myself helping him by means of animated remarks upon his stories, and by more or less judicious questions.

I also helped him by dismissing from my mind any desire to enquire into the truth of his former experience; and it was good I did so, for had he turned it loose on me, with those great powers of convincing description that he had at his command, I verily believe that I should never have crawled from that barn alive. So, at least, I felt at the moment. It was the instinct of self-preservation, and it brought sound judgment.

Here, then, at least, with different motives, reached, too, by opposite ways, we were both agreed upon one thing, namely, that temporarily we would forget. Fools we were, for a dominant emotion is not so easily banished, and we were for ever recurring to it in a hundred ways direct and indirect. A real fear cannot be so easily trifled with, and while we toyed on the surface with thousands and thousands of words—mere words—our sub-conscious activities were steadily gaining force, and would before very long have to be properly acknowledged. We could not get away from it. At last, when he had finished the recital of an adventure which brought him near enough to a horrible death, I admitted that in my uneventful life I had never yet been face to face with a real fear. It slipped out inadvertently, and, of course, without intention, but the tendency in him at the time was too strong to be resisted. He saw the loophole, and made for it full tilt.

"It is the same with all the emotions," he said. "The experiences of others never give a complete account. Until a man has deliberately turned and faced for himself the fiends that chase him down the years, he has no knowledge of what they really are, or of what they can do. Imaginative authors may write, moralists may preach, and scholars may criticise, but they are dealing all the time in a coinage of which they know not the actual value. Their listener gets a sensation—but not the true one.

"Until you have faced these emotions," he went on, with the same race of words that had come from him the whole evening, "and made them your own, your slaves, you have no idea of the power that is in them—hunger, that shows lights beckoning beyond the grave; thirst, that fills with mingled ice and fire; passion, love, loneliness, revenge, and—" He paused for a minute, and though I knew we were on the brink I was powerless to hold him. ". . . . *and fear,*" he went on—"fear . . . I think that death from fear, or madness from fear, must sum up in a second of time the total of all the most awful sensations it is possible for a man to know."

"Then you have yourself felt something of this fear," I interrupted; "for you said just now—"

"I do not mean physical fear," he replied; "for that is more or less a question of nerves and will, and it is imagination that makes men cowards. I mean an *absolute* fear, a physical fear one might call it, that reaches the soul and withers every power one possesses."

He said a lot more, for he, too, was wholly unable to stem the torrent once it broke loose; but I have forgotten it; or, rather, mercifully I did not hear it, for I stopped my ears and only heard the occasional words when I took my fingers out to find if he had come to an end. In due course he did come to an end, and there we left it, for I then knew positively what he already knew: that somewhere here in the night, and within the walls of this very barn where we were sitting, there was waiting Something of dreadful malignancy and of great power. Something that we might both have to face ere morning, and Something that he had already tried to face once and failed in the attempt.

The night wore slowly on; and it gradually became more and more clear to me that I could not dare to rely as at first upon my companion, and that our positions were undergoing a slow process of reversal. I thank Heaven this was not borne in upon me too suddenly; and that I had at least the time to readjust myself somewhat to the new conditions. Preparation was possible, even if it was not much, and I sought by every means in my power to gather up all the shreds of my courage, so that they might together make a decent rope that would stand the strain when it came. The strain would come, that was certain, and I was thoroughly well aware—though for my life I cannot put into words the reasons for my knowledge—that the massing of the material against us was proceeding somewhere in the darkness with determination and a horrible skill besides.

Shorthouse meanwhile talked without ceasing. The great quantity of hay opposite—or straw, I believe it actually was—seemed to deaden the sound of his voice, but the silence, too, had become so oppressive that I welcomed his torrent and even dreaded the moment when it would stop. I heard, too, the gentle ticking of my watch. Each second uttered its voice and dropped away into a gulf, as if starting on a journey whence there was no return. Once a dog barked somewhere in the distance, probably on the Lower Farm; and once an owl hooted close outside and I could hear the swishing of its wings as it passed overhead.

Above me, in the darkness, I could just make out the outline of the barn, sinister and black, the rows of rafters stretching across from wall to wall like wicked arms that pressed upon the hay. Shorthouse, deep in some involved yarn of the South Seas that was meant to be full of cheer and sunshine, and yet only succeeded in making a ghastly mixture of unnatural colouring, seemed to care little whether I listened or not. He made no appeal to me, and I made one or two quite irrelevant remarks which passed him by and proved that he was merely uttering sounds. He, too, was afraid of the silence.

I fell to wondering how long a man could talk without stopping. . . . . . .Then it seemed to me that these words of his went falling into the same gulf where the seconds dropped, only they were heavier and fell faster. I began to chase them. Presently one of them fell much faster than the rest, and I pursued it and found myself almost immediately in a land of clouds and shadows. They rose up and enveloped me, pressing on the eyelids. . . . It must have been just here that I actually fell asleep, somewhere between twelve and one o'clock, because, as I chased this word at tremendous speed through space, I knew that I had left the other words far, very far behind me, till, at last, I could no longer hear them at all. The voice of the story-teller was beyond the reach of hearing; and I was falling with ever increasing rapidity through an immense void.

A sound of whispering roused me. Two persons were talking under their breath close beside me. The words in the main escaped me, but I caught every now and then bitten-off phrases and half sentences, to which, however, I could attach no intelligible meaning. The words were quite close—at my very side in fact—and one of the voices sounded so familiar, that curiosity overcame dread, and I turned to look. I was not mistaken; *it was Shorthouse whispering*. But the other person, who must have been just a little beyond him, was lost in the darkness and invisible to me. It seemed then that Shorthouse at once turned up his face and looked at me and, by some means or other that caused me no surprise at the time, I easily made out the features in the darkness. They wore an expression I had never seen there before; he seemed distressed, exhausted, worn out, and as though he were about to give in after a long mental struggle. He looked at me, almost beseechingly, and the whispering of the other person died away.

"They're at me," he said.

I found it quite impossible to answer; the words stuck in my throat. His voice was thin, plaintive, almost like a child's.

"I shall have to go. I'm not as strong as I thought. They'll call it suicide, but, of course, it's really murder." There was real anguish in his voice, and it terrified me.

A deep silence followed these extraordinary words, and I somehow understood that the Other Person was just going to carry on the conversation—I even fancied I saw lips shaping themselves just over my friend's shoulder—when I felt a sharp blow in the ribs and a voice, this time a deep voice, sounded in my ear. I opened my eyes, and the wretched dream vanished. Yet it left behind it an impression of a strong and quite unusual reality.

"*Do* try not to go to sleep again," he said sternly. "You seem exhausted. Do you feel so?" There was a note in his voice I did not welcome,—less than alarm, but certainly more than mere solicitude.

"I do feel terribly sleepy all of a sudden," I admitted, ashamed.

"So you may," he added very earnestly; "but I rely on you to keep awake, if only to watch. You have been asleep for half an hour at least—and you were so still—I thought I'd wake you—"

"Why?" I asked, for my curiosity and nervousness were altogether too strong to be resisted. "Do you think we are in danger?"

"I think *they* are about here now. I feel my vitality going rapidly—that's always the first sign. You'll last longer than I, remember. Watch carefully."

The conversation dropped. I was afraid to say all I wanted to say. It would have been too unmistakably a confession; and intuitively I realised the danger of admitting the existence of certain emotions until positively forced to. But presently Shorthouse began again. His voice sounded odd, and as if it had lost power. It was more like a woman's or a boy's voice than a man's, and recalled the voice in my dream.

"I suppose you've got a knife?" he asked.

"Yes—a big clasp knife; but why?" He made no answer. "You don't think a practical joke likely? No one suspects we're here," I went on. Nothing was more significant of our real feelings this night than the way we toyed with words, and never dared more than to skirt the things in our mind.

"It's just as well to be prepared," he answered evasively. "Better be quite sure. See which pocket it's in—so as to be ready."

I obeyed mechanically, and told him. But even this scrap of talk proved to me that he was getting further from me all the time in his mind. He was following a line that was strange to me, and, as he distanced me, I felt that the sympathy between us grew more and more strained. *He knew more*; it was not that I minded so much—but that he was willing to *communicate less*. And in proportion as I lost his support, I dreaded his increasing silence. Not of words—for he talked more volubly than ever, and with a fiercer purpose—but his silence in giving no hint of what he must have known to be really going on the whole time.

The night was perfectly still. Shorthouse continued steadily talking, and I jogged him now and again with remarks or questions in order to keep awake. He paid no attention, however, to either.

About two in the morning a short shower fell, and the drops rattled sharply on the roof like shot. I was glad when it stopped, for it completely drowned all other sounds and made it impossible to hear anything else that might be going on. Something *was* going on, too, all the time, though for the life of me I could not say what. The outer world had grown quite dim—the house-party, the shooters, the billiard-room, and the ordinary daily incidents of my visit. All my energies were concentrated on the present, and the constant strain of watching, waiting, listening, was excessively telling.

Shorthouse still talked of his adventures, in some Eastern country now, and less connectedly. These adventures, real or imaginary, had quite a savour of the Arabian Nights, and did not by any means make it easier for me to keep my hold on reality. The lightest weight will affect the balance under such circumstances, and in this case the weight of his talk was on the wrong scale. His words were very rapid, and I found it overwhelmingly difficult not to follow them into that great gulf of darkness where they all rushed and vanished. But that, I knew, meant sleep again. Yet, it was strange I should feel sleepy when at the same time all my nerves were fairly tingling.

Every time I heard what seemed like a step outside, or a movement in the hay opposite, the blood stood still for a moment in my veins. Doubtless, the unremitting strain told upon me more than I realised, and this was doubly great now that I knew Shorthouse was a source of weakness instead of strength, as I had counted. Certainly, a curious sense of languor grew upon me more and more, and I was sure that the man beside me was engaged in the same struggle. The feverishness of his talk proved this, if nothing else. It was dreadfully hard to keep awake.

But this time, instead of dropping into the gulf, I saw something come up out of it! It reached our world by a door in the side of the barn furthest from me, and it came in cautiously and silently and moved into the mass of hay opposite. There, for a moment, I lost it, but presently I caught it again higher up. It was clinging, like a great bat, to the side of the barn. Something trailed behind it, I could not make out what. . . . It crawled up the wooden wall and began to move out along one of the rafters. A numb terror settled down all over me as I watched it. The thing trailing behind it was apparently a rope.

The whispering began again just then, but the only words I could catch seemed without meaning; it was almost like another language. The voices were above me, under the roof. Suddenly I saw signs of active movement going on just beyond the place where the thing lay upon the rafter. There was something else up there with it! Then followed panting, like the quick breathing that accompanies effort, and the next minute a black mass dropped through the air and dangled at the end of the rope.

Instantly, it all flashed upon me. I sprang to my feet and rushed headlong across the floor of the barn. How I moved so quickly in the darkness I do not know; but, even as I ran, it flashed into my mind that I should never get at my knife in time to cut the thing down, or else that I should find it had been taken from me. Somehow or other—the Goddess of Dreams knows how—I climbed up by the hay bales and swung out along the rafter. I was hanging, of course, by my arms, and the knife was already between my teeth, though I had no recollection of how it got there.

It was open. The mass, hanging like a side of bacon, was only a few feet in front of me, and I could plainly see the dark line of rope that fastened it to the beam. I then noticed for the first time that it was swinging and turning in the air, and that as I approached it seemed to move along the beam, so that the same distance was always maintained between us. The only thing I could do—for there was no time to hesitate—was to jump at it through the air and slash at the rope as I dropped.

I seized the knife with my right hand, gave a great swing of my body with my legs and leaped forward at it through the air. Horrors! It was closer to me than I knew, and I plunged full into it, and the arm with the knife missed the rope and cut deeply into some substance that was soft and yielding. But, as I dropped past it, the thing had time to turn half its width so that it swung round and faced me—and I could have sworn as I rushed past it through the air, that it had the features of Shorthouse.

The shock of this brought the vile nightmare to an abrupt end, and I woke up a second time on the soft hay-bed to find that the grey dawn was stealing in, and that I was exceedingly cold. After all I had failed to keep awake, and my sleep, since it was growing light, must have lasted at least an hour. A whole hour off my guard!

There was no sound from Shorthouse, to whom, of course, my first thoughts turned; probably his flow of words had ceased long ago, and he too had yielded to the persuasions of the seductive god. I turned to wake him and get the comfort of companionship for the horror of my dream, when to my utter dismay I saw that the place where he had been was vacant. He was no longer beside me.

It had been no little shock before to discover that the ally in whom lay all my faith and dependence was really frightened, but it is quite impossible to describe the sensations I experienced when I realised he had gone altogether and that I was alone in the barn. For a minute or two my head swam and I felt a prey to a helpless terror. The dream, too, still seemed half real, so vivid had it been! I was thoroughly frightened—hot and cold by turns—and I clutched the hay at my side in handfuls, and for some moments had no idea in the world what I should do.

This time, at least, I was unmistakably awake, and I made a great effort to collect myself and face the meaning of the disappearance of my companion. In this I succeeded so far that I decided upon a thorough search of the barn, inside and outside. It was a dreadful undertaking, and I did not feel at all sure of being able to bring it to a conclusion, but I knew pretty well that unless something was done at once, I should simply collapse.

But, when I tried to move, I found that the cold, and fear, and I know not what else unholy besides, combined to make it almost impossible. I suddenly realised that a tour of inspection, during the whole of which my back would be open to attack, was not to be thought of. My will was not equal to it. Anything might spring upon me any moment from the dark corners, and the growing light was just enough to reveal every movement I made to any who might be watching. For, even then, and while I was still half dazed and stupid, I knew perfectly well that someone was watching me all the time with the utmost intentness. I had not merely awakened; I had *been* awakened.

I decided to try another plan; I called to him. My voice had a thin weak sound, far away and quite unreal, and there was no answer to it. Hark, though! There was something that might have been a very faint voice near me!

I called again, this time with greater distinctness, "Shorthouse, where are you? can you hear me?"

There certainly was a sound, but it was not a voice. Something was moving. It was someone shuffling along, and it seemed to be outside the barn. I was afraid to call again, and the sound continued. It was an ordinary sound enough, no doubt, but it came to me just then as something unusual and unpleasant. Ordinary sounds remain ordinary only so long as one is not listening to them; under the influence of intense listening they become unusual, portentous, and therefore extraordinary. So, this common sound came to me as something uncommon, disagreeable. It conveyed, too, an impression of stealth. And with it there was another, a slighter sound.

Just at this minute the wind bore faintly over the field the sound of the stable clock, a mile away. It was three o'clock; the hour when life's pulses beat lowest; when poor souls lying between life and death find it hardest to resist. Vividly I remember this thought crashing through my brain with a sound of thunder, and I realised that the strain on my nerves was nearing the limit, and that something would have to be done at once if I was to reclaim my self-control at all.

When thinking over afterwards the events of this dreadful night, it has always seemed strange to me that my second nightmare, so vivid in its terror and its nearness, should have furnished me with no inkling of what was really going on all this while; and that I should not have been able to put two and two together, or have discovered sooner than I did *what* this sound was and *where* it came from. I can well believe that the vile scheming which lay behind the whole experience found it an easy trifle to direct my hearing amiss; though, of course, it may equally well have been due to the confused condition of my mind at the time and to the general nervous tension under which I was undoubtedly suffering.

But, whatever the cause for my stupidity at first in failing to trace the sound to its proper source, I can only say here that it was with a shock of unexampled horror that my eye suddenly glanced upwards and caught sight of the figure moving in the shadows above my head among the rafters. Up to this moment I had thought that it was somebody outside the barn, crawling round the walls till it came to a door; and the rush of horror that froze my heart when I looked up and saw that it was Shorthouse creeping stealthily along a beam, is something altogether beyond the power of words to describe.

He was staring intently down upon me, and I knew at once that it was he who had been watching me.

This point was, I think, for me the climax of feeling in the whole experience; I was incapable of any further sensation—that is any further sensation in the same direction. But here the abominable character of the affair showed itself most plainly, for it suddenly presented an entirely new aspect to me. The light fell on the picture from a new angle, and galvanised me into a fresh ability to feel when I thought a merciful numbness had supervened. It may not sound a great deal in the printed letter, but it came to me almost as if it had been an extension of consciousness, for the Hand that held the pencil suddenly touched in with ghastly effect of contrast the element of the ludicrous. Nothing could have been worse just then.

Shorthouse, the masterful spirit, so intrepid in the affairs of ordinary life, whose power increased rather than lessened in the face of danger—this man, creeping on hands and knees along a rafter in a barn at three o'clock in the morning, watching me all the time as a cat watches a mouse! Yes, it was distinctly ludicrous, and while it gave me a measure with which to gauge the dread emotion that caused his aberration, it stirred somewhere deep in my interior the strings of an empty laughter.

One of those moments then came to me that are said to come sometimes under the stress of great emotion, when in an instant the mind grows dazzlingly clear. An abnormal lucidity took the place of my confusion of thought, and I suddenly understood that the two dreams which I had taken for nightmares must really have been sent me, and that I had been allowed for one moment to look over the edge of what was to come; the Good was helping, even when the Evil was most determined to destroy.

I saw it all clearly now. Shorthouse had overrated his strength. The terror inspired by his first visit to the barn (when he had failed) had roused the man's whole nature to win, and he had brought me to divert the deadly stream of evil. That he had again underrated the power against him was apparent as soon as he entered the barn, and his wild talk, and refusal to admit what he felt, were due to this desire not to acknowledge the insidious fear that was growing in his heart.

But, at length, it had become too strong. He had left my side in my sleep—had been overcome himself, perhaps, first in *his* sleep, by the dreadful impulse. He knew that I should interfere, and with every movement he made, he watched me steadily, for the mania was upon him and he was *determined to hang himself.* He pretended not to hear me calling, and I knew that anything coming between him and his purpose would meet the full force of his fury—the fury of a maniac, of one, for the time being, truly possessed.

For a minute or two I sat there and stared. I saw then for the first time that there was a bit of rope trailing after him, and that this was what made the rustling sound I had noticed. Shorthouse, too, had come to a stop. His body lay along the rafter like a crouching animal. He was looking hard at me. That whitish patch was his face.

I can lay claim to no courage in the matter, for I must confess that in one sense I was frightened almost beyond control. But at the same time the necessity for decided action, if I was to save his life, came to me with an intense relief. No matter what animated him for the moment, Shorthouse was only a *man*; it was flesh and blood I had to contend with and not the intangible powers. Only a few hours before I had seen him cleaning his gun, smoking his pipe, knocking the billiard balls about with very human clumsiness, and the picture flashed across my mind with the most wholesome effect.

Then I dashed across the floor of the barn and leaped upon the hay bales as a preliminary to climbing up the sides to the first rafter. It was far more difficult than in my dream. Twice I slipped back into the hay, and as I scrambled up for the third time I saw that Shorthouse, who thus far had made no sound or movement, was now busily doing something with his hands upon the beam. He was at its further end, and there must have been fully fifteen feet between us. Yet I saw plainly what he was doing; he was fastening the rope to the rafter. *The other end, I saw, was already round his neck!*

This gave me at once the necessary strength, and in a second I had swung myself on to a beam, crying aloud with all the authority I could put into my voice—

"You fool, man! What in the world are you trying to do? Come down at once!"

My energetic actions and words combined had an immediate effect upon him for which I blessed Heaven; for he looked up from his horrid task, stared hard at me for a second or two, and then came wriggling along like a great cat to intercept me. He came by a series of leaps and bounds and at an astonishing pace, and the way he moved somehow inspired me with a fresh horror, for it did not seem the natural movement of a human being at all, but more, as I have said, like that of some lithe wild animal.

He was close upon me. I had no clear idea of what exactly I meant to do. I could see his face plainly now; he was grinning cruelly; the eyes were positively luminous, and the menacing expression of the mouth was most distressing to look upon. Otherwise it was the face of a chalk man, white and dead, with all the semblance of the living human drawn out of it. Between his teeth he held my clasp knife, which he must have taken from me in my sleep, and with a flash I recalled his anxiety to know exactly which pocket it was in.

"Drop that knife!" I shouted at him, "and drop after it yourself—"

"Don't you dare to stop me!" he hissed, the breath coming between his lips across the knife that he held in his teeth. "Nothing in the world can stop me now—I have promised—and I must do it. I can't hold out any longer."

"Then drop the knife and I'll help you," I shouted back in his face. "I promise—"

"No use," he cried, laughing a little, "I must do it and you can't stop me."

I heard a sound of laughter, too, somewhere in the air behind me. The next second Shorthouse came at me with a single bound.

To this day I cannot quite tell how it happened. It is still a wild confusion and a fever of horror in my mind, but from somewhere I drew more than my usual allowance of strength, and before he could well have realised what I meant to do, I had his throat between my fingers. He opened his teeth and the knife dropped at once, for I gave him a squeeze he need never forget. Before, my muscles had felt like so much soaked paper; now they recovered their natural strength, and more besides. I managed to work ourselves along the rafter until the hay was beneath us, and then, completely exhausted, I let go my hold and we swung round together and dropped on to the hay, he clawing at me in the air even as we fell.

The struggle that began by my fighting for his life ended in a wild effort to save my own, for Shorthouse was quite beside himself, and had no idea what he was doing. Indeed, he has always averred that he remembers nothing of the entire night's experiences after the time when he first woke me from sleep. A sort of deadly mist settled over him, he declares, and he lost all sense of his own identity. The rest was a blank until he came to his senses under a mass of hay with me on the top of him.

It was the hay that saved us, first by breaking the fall and then by impeding his movements so that I was able to prevent his choking me to death.

The Old Man of Visions

1

The image of Teufelsdröckh, sitting in his watchtower "alone with the stars," leaped into my mind the moment I saw him; and the curious expression of his eyes proclaimed at once that here was a being who allowed the world of small effects to pass him by, while he himself dwelt among the eternal verities. It was only necessary to catch a glimpse of the bent grey figure, so slight yet so tremendous, to realise that he carried staff and wallet, and was travelling alone in a spiritual region, uncharted, and full of wonder, difficulty, and fearful joy.

The inner eye perceived this quite as clearly as the outer was aware of his Hebraic ancestry; but along what winding rivers, through what haunted woods, by the shores of what singing seas he pressed forward towards the mountains of his goal, no one could guess from a mere inspection of that wonderful old face.

To have stumbled upon such a figure in the casual way I did seemed incredible to me even at the time, yet I at once caught something of the uplifting airs that followed this inhabitant of a finer world, and I spent days—and considered them well spent—trying to get into conversation with him, so that I might know something more than the thin disguise of his holding a reader's ticket for the Museum Library.

To reach the stage of intimacy where actual speech is a hindrance to close understanding, one need not in some cases have spoken at all, thus by merely setting my mind, and above all, my imagination, into tune with his, and by steeping myself so much in his atmosphere that I absorbed and then gave back to him with my own stamp the forces he exhaled, it was at length possible to persuade those vast-seeing eyes to turn in my direction; and our glances having once met, I simply rose when he rose, and followed him out of the little smoky restaurant so closely up the street that our clothes brushed, and I thought I could even catch the sound of his breathing.

Whether, having already weighed me, he accepted the office, or whether he was grateful for the arm to lean upon, with his many years' burden, I do not know; but the sympathy between us was such that, without a single word, we walked up that foggy London street to the door of his lodging in Bloomsbury, while I noticed that at the touch of his arm the noise of the town seemed to turn into deep singing, and even the hurrying passers-by seemed bent upon noble purposes; and though he barely reached to my shoulder, and his grey beard almost touched my glove as I bent my arm to hold his own, there was something immense about his figure that sent him with towering stature above me and filled my thoughts with enchanting dreams of grandeur and high beauty.

But it was only when the door had closed on him with a little rush of wind, and I was walking home alone, that I fully realised the shock of my return to earth; and on reaching my own rooms I shook with laughter to think I had walked a mile and a half with a complete stranger without uttering a single syllable. Then the laughter suddenly hushed as I caught my face in the glass with the expression of the soul still lingering about the eyes and forehead, and for a brief moment my heart leaped to a sort of noble fever in the blood, leaving me with the smart of the soul's wings stirring beneath the body's crushing weight. And when it passed, I found myself dwelling upon the only words he had spoken when I left him at the door:

"I am the Old Man of Visions, and I am *at your service*."

I think he never had a name—at least, it never passed his lips, and perhaps lay buried with so much else of the past that he clearly deemed unimportant. To me, at any rate, he became simply the Old Man of Visions, and to the little waiting-maid and the old landlady he was known simply as "Mister"—Mister, neither more nor less. The impenetrable veil that hung over his past never lifted for any vital revelations of his personal history, though he evidently knew all countries of the world, and had absorbed into his heart and brain the experience of all possible types of human nature; and there was an air about him not so much of "Ask me no questions," as "Do not ask me, for I cannot answer you *in words*."

He could satisfy, but not in mere language; he would reveal, but by the wonderful words of silence only; for he was the Old Man of Visions, and visions need no words, being swift and of the spirit

Moreover, the landlady—poor, dusty, faded woman—the landlady stood in awe, and disliked being probed for information in a passageway down which he might any moment tread, for she could only tell me, "He just came in one night, years ago, and he's been here ever since!" And more than that I never knew. "Just came in— one night—years ago." This adequately explained him, for where he came *from*, or was journeying *to*, was something quite beyond the scope of ordinary limited language.

I pictured him suddenly turning aside from the stream of unimportant events, quietly stepping out of the world of straining, fighting, and shouting, and moving to take his rightful place among the forces of the still, spiritual region where he belonged by virtue of long pain and difficult attainment. For he was unconnected with any conceivable network of relations, friends, or family, and his terrible aloofness could not be disturbed by any one unless with his permission and by his express wish. Nor could he be imagined as "belonging" to any definite set of souls. He was apart from the world—and above it.

But it was only when I began to creep a little nearer to him, and our strange, silent intimacy passed from mental to spiritual, that I began really to understand more of this wonderful Old Man of Visions.

Steeped in the tragedy, and convulsed with laughter at the comedy, of life, he yet lived there in his high attic wrapped in silence as in a golden cloud; and so seldom did he actually speak to me that each time the sound of his voice, that had something elemental in it—something of winds and waters—thrilled me with the power of the first time. He lived, like Teufelsdröckh, "alone with the stars," and it seemed impossible, more and more, to link him on anywhere into practical dealings with ordinary men and women. Life somehow seemed to pass below him. Yet the small, selfish spirit of the recluse was far from him, and he was tenderly and deeply responsive to pain and suffering, and more particularly to genuine yearning for the far things of beauty. The unsatisfied longings of others could move him at once to tears.

"My relations with men are perfect," he said one night as we neared his dwelling. "I give them all sympathy out of my stores of knowledge and experience, and they give to me what kindness I need. My outer shell lies within impenetrable solitude, for only so can my inner life move freely along the paths and terraces that are thronged with the beings to whom I belong." And when I asked him how he maintained such deep sympathy with humanity, and had yet absolved himself apparently from action as from speech, he stopped against an area railing and turned his great eyes on to my face, as though their fires could communicate his thought without the husk of words:

"I have peered too profoundly into life and beyond it," he murmured, "to wish to express in language what I *know*. Action is not for all, always; and I am in touch with the cisterns of thought that lie behind action. I ponder the mysteries. What I may solve is not lost for lack either of speech or action, for the true mystic is ever the true man of action, and my thought will reach others as soon as they are ready for it in the same way that it reached you. All who strongly yearn must, sooner or later, find me and be comforted."

His eyes shifted from my face towards the stars, softly shining above the dark museum roof, and a moment later he had disappeared into the hall-way of his house

"An old poet who has strayed afield and lost his way," I mused; but through the door where he had just vanished the words came back to me as from a great distance: "A priest, rather, who has begun to find his way."

For a space I stood, pondering on his face and words:—that mercilessly intelligent look of the Hebrew woven in with the expression of the sadness of a whole race, yet touched with the glory of the spirit; and his utterance—that he had passed through all the traditions and no longer needed a formal, limited creed to hold to. I forget how I reached my own door several miles away, but it seemed to me that I flew.

In this way, and by unregistered degrees, we came to know each other better, and he accepted me and took me into his life. Always wrapped in the great calm of his delightful silence, he taught me more, and told me more, than could ever lie within the confines of mere words; and in moments of need, no matter when or where, I always knew exactly how to find him, reaching him in a few seconds by some swift way that disdained the means of ordinary locomotion.

Then at last one day he gave me the key of his house. And the first time I found my way into his eyry, and realised that it was a haven I could always fly to when the yearnings of the heart and soul struggled vainly for recompense, the full meaning and importance of the Old Man of Visions became finally clear to me.

2

The room, high up creaky, darkened stairs in the ancient house, was bare and fireless, looking through a single patched window across a tumbled sea of roofs and chimneys; yet there was that in it which instantly proclaimed it a little holy place out of the world, a temple in which someone with spiritual vitality had worshipped, prayed, wept, and sung.

It was dusty and unswept, yet it was utterly *unsoiled*; and the Old Man of Visions who lived there, for all his shabby and stained garments, his uncombed beard and broken shoes, stood within its door revealed in his real self, moving in a sort of divine whiteness, iridescent, shining. And here, in this attic (lampless and unswept), high up under the old roofs of Bloomsbury, the window scarred with rain and the corners dropping cobwebs, I heard his silver whisper issue from the shadows:

"Here you may satisfy your soul's desire and may commune with the Invisibles; only, to find the Invisibles, you must first be able to lose yourself."

Ah! through that stained window-pane, the sight leaping at a single bound from black roofs up to the stars, what pictures, dreams, and visions the Old Man has summoned to my eyes! Distances, measureless and impossible hitherto, became easy, and from the oppression of dead bricks and the market-place he transported me in a moment to the slopes of the Mountains of Dream; leading me to little places near the summits where the pines grew thinly and the stars were visible through their branches, fading into the rose of dawn; where the winds tasted of the desert, and the voices of the wilderness fled upward with a sound of wings and falling streams.

At his word houses melted away, and the green waves of all the seas flowed into their places; forests waved themselves into the coastline of dull streets; and the power of the old earth, with all her smells and flowers and wild life, thrilled down among the dead roofs and caught me away into freedom among the sunshine of meadows and the music of sweet pipings. And with the divine deliverance came the crying of sea-gulls, the glimmer of reedy tarns, the whispering of wind among grasses, and the healing scorch of a real sun upon the skin.

And poetry such as was never known or heard before clothed all he uttered, yet even then took no form in actual words, for it was of the substance of aspiration and yearning, voicing adequately all the busy, high-born dreams that haunt the soul yet never live in the uttered line. He breathed it about him in the air so that it filled my being. It was part of him—beyond words; and it sang my own longings, and sang them perfectly so that I was satisfied; for my own mood never failed to touch him instantly and to waken the right response. In its essence it was spiritual—the mystic poetry of heaven; still, the love of humanity informed it, for star-fire and heart's blood were about equally mingled there, while the mystery of unattainable beauty moved through it like a white flame.

With other dreams and longings, too, it was the same; and all the most beautiful ideas that ever haunted a soul undowered with expression here floated with satisfied eyes and smiling lips before one—floated in silence, unencumbered, unlimited, unrestrained by words.

In this dim room, never made ugly by artificial light, but always shadowy in a kind of gentle dusk, the Old Man ofVisions had only to lead me to the window to bring peace. Music, that rendered the soul fluid, as it poured across the old roofs into the room, was summoned by him at need; and when one's wings beat sometimes against the prison walls and the yearning for escape oppressed the heart, I have heard the little room rush and fill with the sound of trees, wind among grasses, whispering branches, and lapping waters. The very odours of space and mountain-side came too, and the looming of noble hills seemed visible overhead against the stars, as though the ceiling had suddenly become transparent.

For the Old Man ofVisions had the power of instantly satisfying an ideal when once that ideal created a yearning that could tear and burn its way out with sufficient force to set the will a-moving

3

But as the time passed and I came to depend more and more upon the intimacy with my strange old friend, new light fell upon the nature and possibilities of our connection. I discovered, for instance, that though I held the key to his dwelling, and was familiar with the way, he was nevertheless not always available. Two things, in different fashion, rendered him inaccessible, or mute; and, for the first, I gradually learned that when life was prosperous, and the body singing loud, I could not find my way to his house. No amount of wandering, calculation, or persevering effort enabled me even to find the street again. With any burst of worldly success, however fleeting, the Old Man of Visions somehow slipped away into remote shadows and became unreal and misty.

A merely passing desire to be with him, to seek his inspiration by a glimpse through that magic windowpane, resulted only in vain and tiresome pacing to and fro along ugly streets that produced weariness and depression; and after these periods it became, I noticed, less and less easy to discover the house, to fit the key in the door, or, having gained access to the temple, to the visions I *thought* I craved for.

Often, in this way, have I searched in vain for days, but only succeeded in losing myself in the murky purlieus of a quite strange Bloomsbury; stopping outside numberless counterfeit doors, and struggling vainly with locks that knew nothing of my little shining key.

But, on the other hand, pain, loneliness, sorrow—the merest whisper of spiritual affliction—and, lo, in a single moment the difficult geography became plain, and without hesitation, when I was unhappy or distressed, I found the way to his house as by a bird's instinctive flight, and the key slipped into the lock as though it loved it and was returning home.

The other cause to render him inaccessible, though not so determined—since it never concealed the way to the house— was even more distressing, for it depended wholly on myself; and I came to know how the least ugly action, involving a depreciation of ideals, so confused the mind that, when I got into the house, with difficulty, and found him in the little room after much searching, he was able to do or say scarcely anything at all for me. The mirror facing the door then gave back, I saw, no proper reflection of his person, but only a faded and wavering shadow with dim eyes and stooping, indistinct outline, and I even fancied I could see the pattern of the wall and shape of the furniture *through* his body, as though he had grown semi-transparent.

"You must not expect yearnings to weigh," came his whisper, like wind far overhead, "unless you lend to them *your own* substance; and your own substance you cannot both keep and lend. If you would know the Invisibles, forget yourself."

And later, as the years slipped away one after another into the mists, and the frontier between the real and the unreal began to shift amazingly with his teachings, it became more and more clear to me that he belonged to a permanent region that, with all the changes in the world's history, has itself never altered in any essential particular. This immemorial Old Man of Visions, as I grew to think of him, had existed always; he was old as the sea and coeval with the stars; and he dwelt beyond time and space, reaching out a hand to all those who, weary of the shadows and illusions of practical life, really call to him with their heart of hearts. To me, indeed, the touch of sorrow was always near enough to prevent his becoming often inaccessible, and after a while even his voice became so living that I sometimes heard it calling to me in the street and in the fields.

Oh, wonderful Old Man of Visions! Happy the days of disaster, since they taught me how to know you, the Unraveller of Problems, the Destroyer of Doubts, who bore me ever away with soft flight down the long, long vistas of the heart and soul!

And his loneliness in that temple attic under the stars, his loneliness, too, had a meaning I did not fail to understand later, and why he was always available for me and seemed to belong to no other.

"To everyone who finds me," he said, with the strange smile that wrapped his whole being and not his face alone, "to everyone I am the same, and yet different. I am not really ever alone. The whole world, nay"—his voice rose to a singing cry—"the whole universe lies in this room, or just beyond that windowpane; for here past and future meet and all real dreams find completeness. But remember," he added—and there was a sound as of soft wind and rain in the room with his voice—"no true dream can ever be shared, and should you seek to explain me to another you must lose me beyond recall. You have never asked my name, nor must you ever tell it Each must find me in his own way."

Yet one day, for all my knowledge and his warnings, I felt so sure of my intimacy with this immemorial being, that I spoke of him to a friend who was, I had thought, so much a part of myself that it seemed no betrayal. And my friend, who went to search and found nothing, returned with the fool's laughter on his face, and swore that no street or number existed, for he had looked in vain, and had repeatedly asked the way.

And, from that day to this, the Old Man of Visions has neither called to me nor let his place be found; the streets are strange and empty, and I have even lost the little shining key.

May Day Eve

1

It was in the spring when I at last found time from the hospital work to visit my friend, the old folk-lorist, in his country isolation, and I rather chuckled to myself, because in my bag I was taking down a book that utterly refuted all his tiresome pet theories of magic and the powers of the soul.

These theories were many and various, and had often troubled me. In the first place, I scorned them for professional reasons, and, in the second, because I had never been able to argue quite well enough to convince or to shake his faith, in even the smallest details, and any scientific knowledge I brought to bear only fed him with confirmatory data. To find such a book, therefore, and to know that it was safely in my bag, wrapped up in brown paper and addressed to him, was a deep and satisfactory joy, and I speculated a good deal during the journey how he would deal with the overwhelming arguments it contained against the existence of any important region outside the world of sensory perceptions.

Speculative, too, I was whether his visionary habits and absorbing experiments would permit him to remember my arrival at all, and I was accordingly relieved to hear from the solitary porter that the "professor" had sent a "veeckle" to meet me, and that I was thus free to send my bag and walk the four miles to the house across the hills.

It was a calm, windless evening, just after sunset, the air warm and scented, and delightfully still. The train, already sinking into distance, carried away with it the noise of crowds and cities and the last suggestions of the stressful life behind me, and from the little station on the moorland I stepped at once into the world of silent, growing things, tinkling sheep-bells, shepherds, and wild, desolate spaces.

My path lay diagonally across the turfy hills. It slanted a mile or so to the summit, wandered vaguely another two miles among gorse-bushes along the crest, passed Tom Bassett's cottage by the pines, and then dropped sharply down on the other side through rather thin woods to the ancient house where the old folk-lorist lived and dreamed himself into his impossible world of theory and fantasy. I fell to thinking busily about him during the first part of the ascent, and convinced myself, as usual, that, but for his generosity to the poor, and his benign aspect, the peasantry must undoubtedly have regarded him as a wizard who speculated in souls and had dark dealings with the world of faery.

The path I knew tolerably well. I had already walked it once before—a winter's day some years ago—and from the cottage onward felt sure of my way; but for the first mile or so there were so many cross cattle-tracks, and the light had become so dim that I felt it wise to inquire more particularly. And this I was fortunately able to do of a man who with astonishing suddenness rose from the grass where he had been lying behind a clump of bushes, and passed a few yards in front of me at a high pace downhill toward the darkening valley.

He was in such a state of hurry that I called out loudly to him, fearing to be too late, but on hearing my voice he turned sharply, and seemed to arrive almost at once beside me. In a single instant he was standing there, quite close, looking, with a smile and a certain expression of curiosity, I thought, into my face. I remember thinking that his features, pale and wholly untanned, were rather wonderful for a countryman, and that the eyes were those of a foreigner; his great swiftness, too, gave me a distinct sensation—something almost of a start—though I knew my vision was at fault at the best of times, and of course especially so in the deceptive twilight of the open hillside.

Moreover—as the way often is with such instructions—the words did not stay in my mind very clearly after he had uttered them, and the rapid, panther-like movements of the man as he quickly vanished down the hill again left me with little more than a sweeping gesture indicating the line I was to follow. No doubt his sudden rising from behind the gorse-bush, his curious swiftness, and the way he peered into my face, and even touched me on the shoulder, all combined to distract my attention somewhat from the actual words he used; and the fact that I was travelling at a wrong angle, and should have come out a mile too far to the right, helped to complete my feeling that his gesture, pointing the way, was sufficient.

On the crest of the ridge, panting a little with the unwonted exertion, I lay down to rest a moment on the grass beside a flaming yellow gorse-bush. There was still a good hour before I should be looked for at the house; the grass was very soft, the peace and silence soothing. I lingered, and lit a cigarette. And it was just then, I think, that my subconscious memory gave back the words, the actual words, the man had spoken, and the heavy significance of the personal pronoun, as he had emphasised it in his odd foreign voice, touched me with a sense of vague amusement: "The safest way *for you* now," he had said, as though I was so obviously a townsman and might be in danger on the lonely hills after dark.

And the quick way he had reached my side, and then slipped off again like a shadow down the steep slope, completed a definite little picture in my mind. Then other thoughts and memories rose up and formed a series of pictures, following each other in rapid succession, and forming a chain of reflections undirected by the will and without purpose or meaning. I fell, that is, into a pleasant reverie.

Below me, and infinitely far away, it seemed, the valley lay silent under a veil of blue evening haze, the lower end losing itself among darkening hills whose peaks rose here and there like giant plumes that would surely nod their great heads and call to one another once the final shadows were down. The village lay, a misty patch, in which lights already twinkled. A sound of rooks faintly cawing, of seagulls crying far up in the sky, and of dogs barking at a great distance rose up out of the general murmur of evening voices. Odours of farm and field and open spaces stole to my nostrils, and everything contributed to the feeling that I lay on the top of the world, nothing between me and the stars, and that all the huge, free things of the earth—hills, valleys, woods, and sloping fields—lay breathing deeply about me.

A few seagulls—in daytime hereabouts they fill the air—still circled and wheeled within range of sight, uttering from time to time sharp, petulant cries; and far in the distance there was just visible a shadowy line that showed where the sea lay.

Then, as I lay gazing dreamily into this still pool of shadows at my feet, something rose up, something sheet-like, vast, imponderable, off the whole surface of the mapped-out country, moved with incredible swiftness down the valley, and in a single instant climbed the hill where I lay and swept by me, yet without hurry, and in a sense without speed. Veils in this way rose one after another, filling the cups between the hills, shrouding alike fields, village, and hillside as they passed, and settled down somewhere into the gloom behind me over the ridge, or slipped off like vapour into the sky.

Whether it was actually mist rising from the surface of the fast-cooling ground, or merely the earth giving up her heat to the night, I could not determine. The coming of the darkness is ever a series of mysteries. I only know that this indescribable vast stirring of the landscape seemed to me as though the earth were unfolding immense sable wings from her sides, and lifting them for silent, gigantic strokes so that she might fly more swiftly from the sun into the night. The darkness, at any rate, did drop down over everything very soon afterward, and I rose up hastily to follow my pathway, realising with a degree of wonder strangely new to me the magic of twilight, the blue open depths into the valley below, and the pale yellow heights of the watery sky above.

I walked rapidly, a sense of chilliness about me, and soon lost sight of the valley altogether as I got upon the ridge proper of these lonely and desolate hills.

It could not have been more than fifteen minutes that I lay there in reverie, yet the weather, I at once noticed, had changed very abruptly, for mist was seething here and there about me, rising somewhere from smaller valleys in the hills beyond, and obscuring the path, while overhead there was plainly a sound of wind tearing past, far up, with a sound of high shouting. A moment before it had been the stillness of a warm spring night, yet now everything had changed; wet mist coated me, raindrops smartly stung my face, and a gusty wind, descending out of cool heights, began to strike and buffet me, so that I buttoned my coat and pressed my hat more firmly upon my head.

The change was really this—and it came to me for the first time in my life with the power of a real conviction—that everything about me seemed to have become suddenly *alive*.

It came oddly upon me—prosaic, matter-of-fact, materialistic doctor that I was—this realisation that the world about me had somehow stirred into life; oddly, I say, because Nature to me had always been merely a more or less definite arrangement of measurement, weight, and colour, and this new presentation of it was utterly foreign to my temperament. A valley to me was always a valley; a hill, merely a hill; a field, so many acres of flat surface, grass or ploughed, drained well or drained ill; whereas now, with startling vividness, came the strange, haunting idea that after all they could be something more than valley, hill, and field; that what I had hitherto perceived by these names were only the veils of something that lay concealed within, something alive. In a word, that the poetic sense I had always rather sneered at, in others, or explained away with some shallow physiological label, had apparently suddenly opened up in myself without any obvious cause.

And, the more I puzzled over it, the more I began to realise that its genesis dated from those few minutes of reverie lying under the gorse-bush (reverie, a thing I had never before in all my life indulged in!), or, now that I came to reflect more accurately, from my brief interview with that wild-eyed, swift-moving, shadowy man of whom I had first inquired the way.

I recalled my singular fancy that veils were lifting off the surface of the hills and fields, and a tremor of excitement accompanied the memory. Such a thing had never before been possible to my practical intelligence, and it made me feel suspicious—suspicious about myself. I stood still a moment—I looked about me into the gathering mist, above me to the vanishing stars, below me to the hidden valley, and then sent an urgent summons to my individuality, as I had always known it, to arrest and chase these undesirable fancies.

But I called in vain. No answer came. Anxiously, hurriedly, confusedly, too, I searched for my normal self, but could not find it; and this failure to respond induced in me a sense of uneasiness that touched very nearly upon the borders of alarm.

I pushed on faster and faster along the turfy track among the gorse-bushes with a dread that I might lose the way altogether, and a sudden desire to reach home as soon as might be. Then, without warning, I emerged unexpectedly into clear air again, and the vapour swept past me in a rushing wall and rose into the sky. Anew I saw the lights of the village behind me in the depths, here and there a line of smoke rising against the pale yellow sky, and stars overhead peering down through thin wispy clouds that stretched their wind-signs across the night.

After all, it had been nothing but a stray bit of sea-fog driving up from the coast, for the other side of the hills, I remembered, dipped their chalk cliffs straight into the sea, and strange lost winds must often come a-wandering this way with the sharp changes of temperature about sunset. None the less, it was disconcerting to know that mist and storm lay hiding within possible reach, and I walked on smartly for a sight of Tom Bassett's cottage and the lights of the Manor House in the valley a short mile beyond.

The clearing of the air, however, lasted but a very brief while, and vapour was soon rising about me as before, hiding the path and making bushes and stone walls look like running shadows. It came, driven apparently, by little independent winds up the many side gullies, and it was very cold, touching my skin like a wet sheet. Curious great shapes, too, it assumed as the wind worked to and fro through it: forms of men and animals; grotesque, giant outlines; ever shifting and running along the ground with silent feet, or leaping into the air with sharp cries as the gusts twisted them inwardly and lent them voice.

More and more I pushed my pace, and more and more darkness and vapour obliterated the landscape. The going was not otherwise difficult, and here and there cowslips glimmered in patches of dancing yellow, while the springy turf made it easy to keep up speed; yet in the gloom I frequently tripped and plunged into prickly gorse near the ground, so that from shin to knee was soon a-tingle with sharp pain. Odd puffs and spits of rain stung my face, and the periods of utter stillness were always followed by little shouting gusts of wind, each time from a new direction. Troubled is perhaps too strong a word, but flustered I certainly was; and though I recognised that it was due to my being in an environment so remote from the town life I was accustomed to, I found it impossible to stifle altogether the feeling of malaise that had crept into my heart, and I looked about with increasing eagerness for the lighted windows of Bassett's cottage.

More and more, little pinpricks of distress and confusion accumulated, adding to my realisation of being away from streets and shop-windows, and things I could classify and deal with. The mist, too, distorted as well as concealed, played tricks with sounds as well as with sights. And, once or twice, when I stumbled upon some crouching sheep, they got up without the customary alarm and hurry of sheep, and moved off slowly into the darkness, but in such a singular way that I could almost have sworn they were not sheep at all, but human beings crawling on all-fours, looking back and grimacing at me over their shoulders as they went.

On these occasions—for there were more than one—I never could get close enough to feel their woolly wet backs, as I should have liked to do; and the sound of their tinkling bells came faintly through the mist, sometimes from one direction, sometimes from another, sometimes all round me as though a whole flock surrounded me; and I found it impossible to analyse or explain the idea I received that they were *not* sheep-bells at all, but something quite different.

But mist and darkness, and a certain confusion of the senses caused by the excitement of an utterly strange environment, can account for a great deal. I pushed on quickly. The conviction that I had strayed from the route grew, nevertheless, for occasionally there was a great commotion of seagulls about me, as though I had disturbed them in their sleeping-places. The air filled with their plaintive cries, and I heard the rushing of multitudinous wings, sometimes very close to my head, but always invisible owing to the mist. And once, above the swishing of the wet wind through the gorse-bushes, I was sure I caught the faint thunder of the sea and the distant crashing of waves rolling up some steep-throated gully in the cliffs. I went cautiously after this, and altered my course a little away from the direction of the sound.

Yet, increasingly all the time, it came to me how the cries of the sea-birds sounded like laughter, and how the everlasting wind blew and drove about me with a purpose, and how the low bushes persistently took the shape of stooping people, moving stealthily past me, and how the mist more and more resembled huge protean figures escorting me across the desolate hills, silently, with immense footsteps. For the inanimate world now touched my awakened poetic sense in a manner hitherto unguided, and became fraught with the pregnant messages of a dimly concealed life. I readily understood, for the first time, how easily a superstitious peasantry might people their world, and how even an educated mind might favour an atmosphere of legend. I stumbled along, looking anxiously for the lights of the cottage.

Suddenly, as a shape of writhing mist whirled past, I received so direct a stroke of wind that it was palpably a blow in the face. Something swept by with a shrill cry into the darkness. It was impossible to prevent jumping to one side and raising an arm by way of protection, and I was only just quick enough to catch a glimpse of the sea-gull as it raced past, with suddenly altered flight, beating its powerful wings over my head. Its white body looked enormous as the mist swallowed it. At the same moment a gust tore my hat from my head and flung the flap of my coat across my eyes. But I was well-trained by this time, and made a quick dash after the retreating black object, only to find on overtaking it that I held a prickly branch of gorse. The wind combed my hair viciously.

Then, out of a corner of my eye, I saw my hat still rolling, and grabbed swiftly at it; but just as I closed on it, the real hat passed in front of me, turning over in the wind like a ball, and I instantly released my first capture to chase it. Before it was within reach, another one shot between my feet so that I stepped on it. The grass seemed covered with moving hats, yet each one, when I seized it, turned into a piece of wood, or a tiny gorse-bush, or a black rabbit hole, till my hands were scored with prickles and running blood. In the darkness, I reflected, all objects looked alike, as though by general conspiracy. I straightened up and took a long breath, mopping the blood with my handkerchief. Then something tapped at my feet, and on looking down, there was the hat within easy reach, and I stooped down and put it on my head again. Of course, there were a dozen ways of explaining my confusion and stupidity, and I walked along wondering which to select. My eyesight, for one thing—and under such conditions why seek further? It was nothing, after all, and the dizziness was a momentary effect caused by the effort and stooping.

But for all that, I shouted aloud, on the chance that a wandering shepherd might hear me; and of course, no answer came, for it was like calling in a padded room, and the mist suffocated my voice and killed its resonance.

It was really very discouraging: I was cold and wet and hungry; my legs and clothes torn by the gorse, my hands scratched and bleeding; the wind brought water to my eyes by its constant buffeting, and my skin was numb from contact with the chill mist. Fortunately, I had matches, and after some difficulty, by crouching under a wall, I caught a swift glimpse of my watch, and saw that it was but little after eight o'clock. Supper I knew was at nine, and I was surely over half-way by this time.

But here again was another instance of the way everything seemed in a conspiracy against me to appear otherwise than ordinary, for in the gleam of the match my watch-glass showed as the face of a little old grey man, uncommonly like the folk-lorist himself, peering up at me with an expression of whimsical laughter. My own reflection it could not possibly have been, for I am clean-shaven, and this face looked up at me through a running tangle of grey hair. Yet a second and third match revealed only the white surface with the thin black hands moving across it.

2

And it was at this point, I well remember, that I reached what was for me the true heart of the adventure, the little fragment of real experience I learned from it and took back with me to my doctor's life in London, and that has remained with me ever since, and helped me to a new sympathetic insight into the intricacies of certain curious mental cases I had never before really understood.

For it was sufficiently obvious by now that a curious change had been going forward in me for some time, dating, so far as I could focus my thoughts sufficiently to analyse, from the moment of my speech with that hurrying man of shadow on the hillside. And the first deliberate manifestation of the change, now that I looked back, was surely the awakening in my prosaic being of the "poetic thrill"; my sudden amazing appreciation of the world around me as something alive. From that moment the change in me had worked ahead subtly, swiftly. Yet, so natural had been the beginning of it, that although it was a radically new departure for my temperament, I was hardly aware at first of what had actually come about; and it was only now, after so many encounters, that I was forced at length to acknowledge it.

It came the more forcibly too, because my very commonplace ideas of beauty had hitherto always been associated with sunshine and crude effects; yet here this new revelation leaped to me out of wind and mist and desolation on a lonely hillside, out of night, darkness, and discomfort. New values rushed upon me from all sides. Everything had changed, and the very simplicity with which the new values presented themselves proved to me how profound the change, the readjustment, had been.

In such trivial things the evidence had come that I was not aware of it until repetition forced my attention: the veils rising from valley and hill; the mountain tops as personalities that shout or murmur in the darkness; the crying of the sea birds and of the living, purposeful wind; above all, the feeling that Nature about me was instinct with a life differing from my own in degree rather than in kind; everything, from the conspiracy of the gorse-bushes to the disappearing hat, showed that a fundamental attitude of mind in me had changed—and changed, too, without my knowledge or consent.

Moreover, at the same time the deep sadness of beauty had entered my heart like a stroke; for all this mystery and loveliness, I realised poignantly was utterly independent and careless of *me*, as me; and that while I must pass, decay, grow old, these manifestations would remain for ever young and unalterably potent. And thus, gradually had I become permeated with the recognition of a region hitherto unknown to me, and that I had always depreciated in others and especially, it now occurred to me, in my friend the old folk-lorist.

Here surely, I thought, was the beginning of conditions which, carried a little further, must become pathogenic. That the change was real and pregnant I had no doubt whatever. My consciousness was expanding and I had caught it in the very act. I had of course read much concerning the changes of personality, swift, kaleidoscopic—had come across something of it in my practice—and had listened to the folk-lorist holding forth like a man inspired upon ways and means of reaching concealed regions of the human consciousness, and opening it to the knowledge of things called magical, so that one became free of a larger universe. But it was only now for the first time, on these bare hills, in touch with the wind and the rain, that I realised in how simple a fashion the frontiers of consciousness could shift this way and that, or with what touch of genuine awe the certainty might come that one stood on the borderland of new, untried, perhaps dangerous, experiences.

At any rate, it did now come to me that my consciousness had shifted its frontiers very considerably, and that whatever might happen must seem not abnormal, but quite simple and inevitable, and of course utterly true. This very simplicity, however, doing no violence to my being, brought with it none the less a sense of dread and discomfort; and my dim awareness that unknown possibilities were about me in the night puzzled and distressed me perhaps more than I cared to admit.

3

All this that takes so long to describe became apparent to me in a few seconds. What I had always despised ascended the throne.

But with the finding of Bassett's cottage, as a signpost close to home, my former *sang-froid*, my stupidity, would doubtless return, and my relief was therefore considerable when at length a faint gleam of light appeared through the mist, against which the square dark shadow of the chimney-line pointed upwards. After all, I had not strayed so very far out of the way. Now I could definitely ascertain where I was wrong.

Quickening my pace, I scrambled over a broken stone wall, and almost ran across the open bit of grass to the door. One moment the black outline of the cottage was there in front of me, and the next, when I stood actually against it—there was nothing! I laughed to think how utterly I had been deceived. Yet not utterly, for as I groped back again over the wall, the cottage loomed up a little to the left, with its windows lighted and friendly, and I had only been mistaken in my angle of approach after all. Yet again, as I hurried to the door, the mist drove past and thickened a second time—and the cottage was not where I had seen it!

My confusion increased a lot after that. I scrambled about in all directions, rather foolishly hurried, and over countless stone walls it seemed, and completely dazed as to the true points of the compass. Then suddenly, just when a kind of despair came over me, the cottage stood there solidly before my eyes, and I found myself not two feet from the door. Was ever mist before so deceptive? And there, just behind it, I made out the row of pines like a dark wave breaking through the night. I sniffed the wet resinous odour with joy, and a genuine thrill ran through me as I saw the unmistakable yellow light of the windows. At last, I was near home and my troubles would soon be over.

A cloud of birds rose with shrill cries off the roof and whirled into the darkness when I knocked with my stick on the door, and human voices, I was almost certain, mingled somewhere with them, though it was impossible to tell whether they were within the cottage or outside. It all sounded confusedly with a rush of air like a little whirlwind, and I stood there rather alarmed at the clamour of my knocking. By way, too, of further proof that my imagination had awakened, the significance of that knocking at the door set something vibrating within me that most surely had never vibrated before, so that I suddenly realised with what atmosphere of mystical suggestion is the mere act of knocking surrounded—*knocking at a door*—both for him who knocks, wondering what shall be revealed on opening, and for him who stands within, waiting for the summons of the knocker. I only know that I hesitated a lot before making up my mind to knock a second time.

And, anyhow, what happened subsequently came in a sort of haze. Words and memory both failed me when I try to record it truthfully, so that even the faces are difficult to visualise again, the words almost impossible to hear.

Before I knew it the door was open and before I could frame the words of my first brief question, I was within the threshold, and the door was shut behind me.

I had expected the little dark and narrow hallway of a cottage, oppressive of air and odour, but instead I came straight into a room that was full of light and full of—people. And the air tasted like the air about a mountain-top.

To the end I never saw what produced the light, nor understood how so many men and women found space to move comfortably to and fro, and pass each other as they did, within the confines of those four walls. An uncomfortable sense of having intruded upon some private gathering was, I think, my first emotion; though how the poverty-stricken country-side could have produced such an assemblage puzzled me beyond belief. And my second emotion—if there was any division at all in the wave of wonder that fairly drenched me—was feeling a sort of glory in the presence of such an atmosphere of splendid and vital *youth*. Everything vibrated, quivered, shook about me, and I almost felt myself as an aged and decrepit man by comparison.

I know my heart gave a great fiery leap as I saw them, for the faces that met me were fine, vigorous, and comely, while burning everywhere through their ripe maturity shone the ardours of youth and a kind of deathless enthusiasm. Old, yet eternally young they were, as rivers and mountains count their years by thousands, yet remain ever youthful; and the first effect of all those pairs of eyes lifted to meet my own was to send a whirlwind of unknown thrills about my heart and make me catch my breath with mingled terror and delight. A fear of death, and at the same time a sensation of touching something vast and eternal that could never die, surged through me.

A deep hush followed my entrance as all turned to look at me. They stood, men and women, grouped about a table, and something about them—not their size alone—conveyed the impression of being *gigantic*, giving me strangely novel realisations of freedom, power, and immense existence more or less than human.

I can only record my thoughts and impressions as they came to me and as I dimly now remember them. I had expected to see old Tom Bassett crouching half asleep over a peat fire, a dim lamp on the table beside him, and instead this assembly of tall and splendid men and women stood there to greet me, and stood in silence. It was little wonder that at first the ready question died upon my lips, and I almost forgot the words of my own language.

"I thought this was Tom Bassett's cottage!" I managed to ask at length, and looked straight at the man nearest me across the table. He had wild hair falling about his shoulders and a face of clear beauty. His eyes, too, like all the rest, seemed shrouded by something veil-like that reminded me of the shadowy man of whom I had first inquired the way. They were *shaded*—and for some reason I was glad they were.

At the sound of my voice, unreal and thin, there was a general movement throughout the room, as though everyone changed places, passing each other like those shapes of fluid sort I had seen outside in the mist. But no answer came. It seemed to me that the mist even penetrated into the room about me and spread inwardly over my thoughts.

"Is this the way to the Manor House?" I asked again, louder, fighting my inward confusion and weakness. "Can *no one* tell me?"

Then apparently everyone began to answer at once, or rather, not to answer directly, but to speak to each other in such a way that I could easily overhear. The voices of the men were deep, and of the women wonderfully musical, with a slow rhythm like that of the sea, or of the wind through the pine-trees outside. But the unsatisfactory nature of what they said only helped to increase my sense of confusion and dismay.

"Yes," said one; "Tom Bassett *was* here for a while with the sheep, but his home was not here."

"He asks the way to a house when he does not even know the way to his own mind!" another voice said, sounding overhead it seemed.

"And could he recognise the signs if we told him?" came in the singing tones of a woman's voice close behind me.

And then, with a noise more like running water, or wind in the wings of birds, than anything else I could liken it to, came several voices together:

"And what sort of way does he seek? The splendid way, or merely the easy?"

"Or the short way of fools!"

"But he must have *some* credentials, or he never could have got as far as this," came from another.

A laugh ran round the room at this, though what there was to laugh at I could not imagine. It sounded like wind rushing about the hills. I got the impression too that the roof was somehow open to the sky, for their laughter had such a spacious quality in it, and the air was so cool and fresh, and moving about in currents and waves.

"It was I who showed him the way," cried a voice belonging to someone who was looking straight into my face over the table. "It was the safest way for him once he had got so far——"

I looked up and met his eye, and the sentence remained unfinished. It was the hurrying, shadowy man of the hillside. He had the same shifting outline as the others now, and the same veiled and shaded eyes, and as I looked the sense of terror stirred and grew in me. I had come in to ask for help, but now I was only anxious to be free of them all and out again in the rain and darkness on the moor. Thoughts of escape filled my brain, and I searched quickly for the door through which I had entered. But nowhere could I discover it again. The walls were bare; not even the windows were visible. And the room seemed to fill and empty of these figures as the waves of the sea fill and empty a cavern, crowding one upon another, yet never occupying more space, or less. So, the coming and going of these men and women always evaded me.

And my terror became simply a terror that the veils of their eyes might lift, and that they would look at me with their clear, naked sight. I became horribly aware of their eyes. It was not that I felt them evil, but that I feared the new depths in me their merciless and terrible insight would stir into life. My consciousness had expanded quite enough for one night! I must escape at all costs and claim my own self again, however limited. I must have sanity, even if with limitations, but sanity at any price.

But meanwhile, though I tried hard to find my voice again, there came nothing but a thin piping sound that was like reeds whistling where winds meet about a corner. My throat was contracted, and I could only produce the smallest and most ridiculous of noises. The power of movement, too, was far less than when I first came in, and every moment it became more difficult to use my muscles, so that I stood there, stiff and awkward, face to face with this assemblage of shifting, wonderful people.

"And now," continued the voice of the man who had last spoken, "and now the safest way for him will be through the other door, where he shall see that which he may more easily understand."

With a great effort I regained the power of movement, while at the same time a burst of anger and a determination to be done with it all and to overcome my dreadful confusion drove me forward.

He saw me coming, of course, and the others indeed opened up and made a way for me, shifting to one side or the other whenever I came too near them, and never allowing me to touch them. But at last, when I was close in front of the man, ready both to speak and act, he was no longer there. I never saw the actual change—but instead of a man it was a woman! And when I turned with amazement, I saw that the other occupants walking like figures in some ancient ceremony, were moving slowly toward the far end of the room. One by one, as they filed past, they raised their calm, passionless faces to mine, immensely vital, proud, austere, and then, without further word or gesture, they opened the door I had lost and disappeared through it one by one into the darkness of the night beyond. And as they went it seemed that the mist swallowed them up and a gust of wind caught them away, and the light also went with them, leaving me alone with the figure who had last spoken.

Moreover it was just here that a most disquieting thought flashed through my brain with unreasoning conviction, shaking my personality, as it were, to the foundations: *viz.*, that I had hitherto been spending my life in the pursuit of false knowledge, in the mere classifying and labelling of effects, the analysis of results, scientific so called; whereas it was the folk-lorist, and such like, who with their dreams and prayers were all the time on the path of real knowledge, the trail of causes; that the one was merely adding to the mechanical comfort and safety of the body, ultimately degrading the highest part of man, and never advancing the type, while the other—but then I had never yet believed in a soul—and now was no time to begin, terror or no terror. Clearly, my thoughts were wandering.

4

It was at this moment the sound of the purring first reached me—deep, guttural purring—that made me think at once of some large concealed animal. It was precisely what I had heard many a time at the Zoological Gardens, and I had visions of cows chewing the cud, or horses munching hay in a stall outside the cottage. It was certainly an animal sound, and one of pleasure and contentment.

Semi-darkness filled the room. Only a very faint moonlight, struggling through the mist, came through the window, and I moved back instinctively toward the support of the wall against my back. Somewhere, through openings, came the sound of the night driving over the roof, and far above I had visions of those everlasting winds streaming by with clouds as large as continents on their wings. Something in me wanted to sing and shout, but something else in me at the same time was in a very vivid state of unreasoning terror. I felt immense, yet tiny, confident, yet timid; a part of huge, universal forces, yet an utterly small, personal, and very limited being.

In the corner of the room on my right stood the woman. Her face was hid by a mass of tumbling hair, that made me think of living grasses on a field in June. Thus, her head was partially turned from me, and the moonlight, catching her outline, just revealed it against the wall like an impressionist picture. Strange hidden memories stirred in the depths of me, and for a moment I felt that I knew all about her. I stared about me quickly, nervously, trying to take in everything at once. Then the purring sound grew much louder and closer, and I forgot my notion that this woman was no stranger to me and that

I knew her as well as I knew myself. That purring thing was in the room close beside me. Between us two, indeed, it was, for I now saw that her arm nearest to me was raised, and that she was pointing to the wall in front of us.

Following the direction of her hand, I saw that the wall was transparent, and that I could see through a portion of it into a small square space beyond, as though I was looking through gauze instead of bricks. This small inner space was lighted, and on stooping down I saw that it was a sort of cupboard or cell-like cage let into the wall. The thing that purred was there in the centre of it.

I looked closer. It was a being, apparently a *human* being, crouched down in its narrow cage, feeding. I saw the body stooping over a quantity of coarse-looking, piled-up substance that was evidently food. It was like a man huddled up. There it squatted, happy and contented, with the minimum of air, light, and space, dully satisfied with its prisoned cage behind the bars, utterly unconscious of the vast world about it, grunting with pleasure, purring like a great cat, scornfully ignorant of what might lie beyond. The cell, moreover, I saw was a perfect masterpiece of mechanical contrivance and inventive ingenuity—the very last word in comfort, safety and scientific skill. I was in the act of trying to fit in my memory some of the details of its construction and arrangement, when I made a chance noise, and at once became too agitated to note carefully what I saw. For at the noise the creature turned, and I saw that it *was* a human being—a man.

I was aware of a face close against my own as it pressed forward, but a face with embryonic features impossible to describe and utterly loathsome, with eyes, ears, nose and skin, only just sufficiently alive and developed to transfer the minimum of gross sensation to the brain. The mouth, however, was large and thick-lipped, and the jaws were still moving in the act of slow mastication.

I shrank back, shuddering with mingled pity and disgust, and at the same moment the woman beside me called me softly *by my own name*. She had moved forward a little so that she stood quite close to me, full in the thin stream of moonlight that fell across the floor, and I was conscious of a swift transition from hell to heaven as my gaze passed from that embryonic visage to a countenance so refined, so majestic, so divinely sensitive in its strength, that it was like turning from the face of a devil to look upon the features of a goddess.

At the same instant I was aware that both beings—the creature and the woman—were moving rapidly toward me.

A pain like a sharp sword dived deep down into me and twisted horribly through my heart, for as I saw them coming, I realised in one swift moment of terrible intuition that they had their life in me, that they were born of my own being, and were indeed *projections of myself.* They were portions of my consciousness projected outwardly into objectivity, and their degree of reality was just as great as that of any other part of me.

With a dreadful swiftness they rushed toward me, and in a single second had merged themselves into my own being; and I understood in some marvellous manner beyond the possibility of doubt that they were symbolic of my own soul: the dull animal part of me that had hitherto acknowledged nothing beyond its cage of minute sensations, and the higher part, almost out of reach, and in touch with the stars, that for the first time had feebly awakened into life during my journey over the hill.

5

I forget altogether how it was that I escaped, whether by the window or the door. I only know I found myself a moment later making great speed over the moor, followed by screaming birds and shouting winds, straight on the track downhill toward the Manor House. Something must have guided me, for I went with the instinct of an animal, having no uncertainties as to turnings, and saw the welcome lights of windows before I had covered another mile. And all the way I felt as though a great sluice gate had been opened to let a flood of new perceptions rush like a sea over my inner being, so that I was half ashamed and half delighted, partly angry, yet partly happy.

Servants met me at the door, several of them, and I was aware at once of an atmosphere of commotion in the house. I arrived breathless and hatless, wet to the skin, my hands scratched and my boots caked with mud.

"We made sure you were lost, sir," I heard the old butler say, and I heard my own reply, faintly, like the voice of someone else:

"I thought so too."

A minute later I found myself in the study, with the old folk-lorist standing opposite. In his hands he held the book I had brought down for him in my bag, ready addressed. There was a curious smile on his face.

"It never occurred to me that you would dare to *walk*—tonight of all nights," he was saying.

I stared without a word. I was bursting with the desire to tell him something of what had happened and try to be patient with his explanations, but when I sought for words and sentences my story seemed suddenly flat and pointless, and the details of my adventure began to evaporate and melt away, and seemed hard to remember.

"I had an exciting walk," I stammered, still a little breathless from running. "The weather was all right when I started from the station."

"The weather is all right still," he said, "though you may have found some evening mist on the top of the hills. But it's not that I meant."

"What then?"

"I meant," he said, still laughing quizzically, "that you were a very brave man to walk tonight over the enchanted hills, because this is May Day eve, and on May Day eve, you know, *They* have power over the minds of men, and can put glamour upon the imagination——"

"Who—'*they*?' What do you mean?"

He put my book down on the table beside him and looked quietly for a moment into my eyes, and as he did so the memory of my adventure began to revive in detail, and I thought quickly of the shadowy man who had shown me the way first. What could it have been in the face of the old folk-lorist that made me think of this man? A dozen things ran like flashes through my excited mind, and while I attempted to seize them, I heard the old man's voice continue. He seemed to be talking to himself as much as to me.

"The elemental beings you have always scoffed at, of course; they who operate ceaselessly behind the screen of appearances, and who fashion and mould the moods of the mind. And an extremist like you—for extremes are always dangerously weak—is their legitimate prey."

"Pshaw!" I interrupted him, knowing that my manner betrayed me hopelessly, and that he had guessed much. "Any man may have subjective experiences, I suppose——"

Then I broke off suddenly. The change in his face made me start; it had taken on for the moment so exactly the look of the man on the hillside. The eyes gazing so steadily into mine had shadows in them, I thought.

"*Glamour!*" he was saying, "all glamour! One of them must have come very close to you, or perhaps touched you." Then he asked sharply, "Did you meet anyone? Did you speak with anyone?"

"I came by Tom Bassett's cottage," I said. "I didn't feel quite sure of my way and I went in and asked."

"All glamour," he repeated to himself, and then aloud to me, "and as for Bassett's cottage, it was burnt down three years ago, and nothing stands there now but broken, roofless walls——"

He stopped because I had seized him by the arm. In the shadows of the lamp-lit room behind him I thought I caught sight of dim forms moving past the book-shelves. But when my eye tried to focus them, they faded and slipped away again into ceiling and walls. The details of the hill-top cottage, however, started into life again at the sight, and I seized my friend's arm to tell him. But instantly, when I tried, it all faded away again as though it had been a dream, and I could recall nothing intelligible to repeat to him.

He looked at me and laughed.

"They always obliterate the memory afterward," he said gently, "so that little remains beyond a mood, or an emotion, to show how profoundly deep their touch has been. Though sometimes part of the change remains and becomes permanent—as I hope in your case it may."

Then, before I had time to answer, to swear, or to remonstrate, he stepped briskly past me and closed the door into the hall, and then drew me aside farther into the room. The change that I could not understand was still working in his face and eyes.

"If you have courage enough left to come with me," he said, speaking very seriously, "we will go out again and see more. Up till midnight, you know, there is still the opportunity, and with me perhaps you won't feel so—so——"

It was impossible somehow to refuse; everything combined to make me go. We had a little food and then went out into the hall, and he clapped a wide-awake on his gray hairs. I took a cloak and seized a walking-stick from the stand. I really hardly knew what I was doing. The new world I had awakened to seemed still a-quiver about me.

As we passed out on to the gravel drive the light from the hall windows fell upon his face, and I saw that the change I had been so long observing was nearing its completeness, for there breathed about him that keen, wonderful atmosphere of eternal youth I had felt upon the inmates of the cottage. He seemed to have gone back forty years; a veil was gathering over his eyes; and I could have sworn that somehow his stature had increased, and that he moved beside me with a vigour and power I had never seen in him before.

And as we began to climb the hill together in silence, I saw that the stars were clear overhead and there was no mist, that the trees stood motionless without wind, and that beyond us on the summit of the hills there were lights dancing to and fro, appearing and disappearing like the inflection of stars in water.

Miss Slumbubble—and Claustrophobia

Miss Daphne Slumbubble was a nervous lady of uncertain age who invariably went abroad in the spring. It was her one annual holiday, and she slaved for it all the rest of the year, saving money by the many sad devices known only to those who find their incomes after forty "barely enough," and always hoping that something would one day happen to better her dreary condition of cheap tea, tin loaves, and weekly squabbles with the laundress.

This spring holiday was the only time she really lived in the whole year, and she half starved herself for months immediately after her return, so as to put by quickly enough money for the journey in the following year. Once those six pounds were safe, she felt better. After that she only had to save so many sums of four *francs*, each four *francs* meaning another day in the little cheap *pension* she always went to on the flowery slopes of the Alps of Valais.

Miss Slumbubble was exceedingly conscious of the presence of men. They made her nervous and afraid. She thought in her heart that all men were untrustworthy, not excepting policemen and clergymen, for in her early youth she had been cruelly deceived by a man to whom she had unreservedly given her heart. He had suddenly gone away and left her without a word of explanation, and some months later had married another woman and allowed the announcement to appear in the papers. It is true that he had hardly once spoken to Daphne.

But that was nothing. For the way he looked at her, the way he walked about the room, the very way he avoided her at the tea-parties where she used to meet him at her rich sister's house—indeed, everything he did or left undone, brought convincing proof to her fluttering heart that he loved her secretly, and that he knew she loved him. His near presence disturbed her dreadfully, so much so that she invariably spilt her tea if he came even within scenting-distance of her; and once, when he crossed the room to offer her bread and butter, she was so certain the very way he held the plate interpreted his silent love, that she rose from her chair, looked straight into his eyes—and took the whole plate in a state of delicious confusion!

But all this was years ago, and she had long since learned to hold her grief in subjection and to prevent her life being too much embittered by the treachery—she felt it *was* treachery—of one man. She still, however, felt anxious and self-conscious in the presence of men, especially of silent, unmarried men, and to some extent it may be said that this fear haunted her life. It was shared, however, with other fears, probably all equally baseless. Thus, she lived in constant dread of fire, of railway accidents, of runaway cabs, and of being locked into a small, confined space. The former fears she shared, of course, with many other persons of both sexes, but the latter, the dread of confined spaces, was entirely due, no doubt, to a story she had heard in early youth to the effect that her father had once suffered from that singular nervous malady, *claustrophobia* (the fear of closed spaces), the terror of being caught in a confined place without possibility of escape.

Thus, it was clear that Miss Daphne Slumbubble, this good, honest soul with jet flowers in her bonnet and rows of coloured photographs of Switzerland on her bedroom mantelpiece, led a life unnecessarily haunted.

The thought of the annual holiday, however, compensated for all else. In her lonely room behind Warwick Square, she stewed through the dusty heat of summer, fought her way pluckily through the freezing winter fogs, and then, with the lengthening days, worked herself steadily into a fever heat of joyous anticipation as she counted the hours to the taking of her ticket in the first week of May. When the day came her happiness was so great that she wished for nothing else in the world. Even her name ceased to trouble her, for once on the other side of the Channel it sounded quite different on the lips of the foreigners, while in the little *pension* she was known as "Mlle. Daphné," and the mere sound brought music into her heart. The odious surname belonged to the sordid London life. It had nothing to do with the glorious days that Mlle. Daphné spent among the mountain tops.

The platform at Victoria was already crowded when she arrived a good hour before the train started, and got her tiny faded trunk weighed and labelled. She was so excited that she talked unnecessarily to anyone who would listen—to anyone in station uniform, that is.

Already in fancy she saw the blue sky above the shining snow peaks, heard the tinkling cow-bells, and sniffed the odours of pinewood and sawmill. She imagined the cheerful *table d'hôte* room with its wooden floor and rows of chairs; the diligence winding up the hot white road far below; the fragrant *café complet* in her bedroom at 7.30—and then the long mornings with sketch-book and poetry-book under the forest shade, the clouds trailing slowly across the great cliffs, and the air always humming with the echoes of falling water.

"And you feel sure the passage will be calm, do you?" she asked the porter for the third time, as she bustled to and fro by his side.

"Well, there ain't no wind *'ere*, at any rate, Miss," he replied cheerfully, putting her small box on a barrow.

"Such a lot of people go by this train, don't they?" she piped.

"Oh, a tidy few. This is the season for foreign parts, I suppose."

"Yes, yes; and the trains on the other side will be very full, too, I dare say," she said, following him down the platform with quick, pattering footsteps, chirping all the way like a happy bird.

"Quite likely, Miss."

"I shall go in a 'Ladies only,' you know. I always do every year. I think it's safer, isn't it?"

"I'll see to it all for yer, Miss," replied the patient porter. "But the train ain't in yet, not for another 'arf hour or so."

"Oh, thank you, then I'll be here when it comes. 'Ladies only,' remember, and second class, and a corner seat facing the engine—no, back to the engine, I mean; and I do hope the Channel will be smooth. Do you think the wind?"

But the porter was out of hearing by this time, and Miss Slumbubble went wandering about the platform watching the people arrive, studying the blue and yellow advertisements of the *Côte d'azur*, and waggling her jet beads with delight—with passionate delight—as she thought of her own little village in the high Alps where the snow crept down to a few hundred feet above the church and the meadows were greener than any in the whole wide world.

"I've put yer wraps in a 'Lidies only,' Miss," said the porter at length, when the train came in," and you've got the corner back to the engine all to yerself, an' quite comfortable. Thank you, Miss." He touched his cap and pocketed his sixpence, and the fussy little traveller went off to take up her position outside the carriage door for another half hour before the train started. She was always very nervous about trains; not only fearful of possible accidents to the engine and carriages, but of untoward happenings to the occupants of corridor-less compartments during long journeys without stops. The mere sight of a railway station, with its smoke and whistling and luggage, was sufficient to set her imagination in the direction of possible disaster.

The careful porter had piled all her belongings neatly in the corner for her: three newspapers, a magazine and a novel, a little bag to carry food in, two bananas and a Bath bun in paper, a bundle of wraps tied with a long strap, an umbrella, a bottle of Yanatas, an opera-glass (for the mountains), and a camera. She counted them all over, rearranged them a little differently, and then sighed a bit, partly from excitement, partly by way of protest at the delay.

A number of people came up and eyed the compartment critically and seemed on the point of getting in, but no one actually took possession. One lady put her umbrella in the corner, and then came tearing down the platform a few minutes later to take it away again, as though she had suddenly heard the train was not to start at all. There was much bustling to and fro, and a good deal of French was audible, and the sound of it thrilled Miss Daphne with happiness, for it was another delightful little anticipation of what was to come. Even the language sounded like a holiday, and brought with it a whiff of mountains and the subtle pleasures of sweet freedom.

Then a fat Frenchman arrived and inspected the carriage, and attempted to climb in. But she instantly pounced upon him in courageous dismay.

"*Mais, c'est pour dames, m'sieur!*" she cried, pronouncing it "dam."

"Oh, damn!" he exclaimed in English; "I didn't notice." And the rudeness of the man—it was the fur coat over his arm made her think he was French—set her all in a flutter, so that she jumped in and took her seat hurriedly, and spread her many parcels in a protective and prohibitive way about her.

For the tenth time she opened her black beaded bag and took out her purse and made sure her ticket was in it, and then counted over her belongings.

"I *do* hope," she murmured, "I do hope that stupid porter *has* put in my luggage all right, and that the Channel won't be rough. Porters *are* so stupid. One ought never to lose sight of them till the luggage is actually in. I think I'd better pay the extra fare and go first class on the boat if it is rough. I can carry all my own packages, I think."

At that moment the man came for tickets. She searched everywhere for her own, but could not find it

"I'm certain I had it a moment ago," she said breathlessly, while the man stood waiting at the open door. "I know I had it—only this very minute. Dear me, what *can* I have done with it? Ah! here it is!"

The man took so long examining the little tourist cover that she was afraid something must be wrong with it, and when at last he tore out a leaf and handed back the rest a sort of panic seized her.

"It's all right, isn't it, guard? I mean I'm all right, am I not?" she asked.

The guard closed the door and locked it

"All right for Folkestone, ma'am," he said, and was gone.

There was much whistling and shouting and running up and down the platform, and the inspector was standing with his hand raised and the whistle at his lips, waiting to blow and looking cross. Suddenly her own porter flew past with an empty barrow. She dashed her head out of the window and hailed him.

"You're sure you put my luggage in aren't, you?" she cried. The man did not or would not hear, and as the train moved slowly off, she bumped her head against an old lady standing on the platform who was looking the other way and waving to someone in a front carriage.

"Ooh!" cried Miss Slumbubble, straightening her bonnet, "you really should look where you're looking, madam!"—and then, realising she had said something foolish, she withdrew into the carriage and sank back in a fluster on the cushions.

"Oh!" she gasped again, "oh dear! I'm actually off at last. It's too good to be true. Oh, that horrid London!"

Then she counted her money over again, examined her ticket once more, and touched each of her many packages with a long finger in a cotton glove, saying, "*That's* there, and that, and that, and—*that!*" And then turning and pointing at herself she added, with a little happy laugh, "*and that!*"

The train gathered speed, and the dirty roofs and sea of ugly chimneys flew by as the dreary miles of depressing suburbs revealed themselves through the windows. She put all her parcels up in the rack and then took them all down again; and after a bit she put a few up—a carefully selected few that she would not need till Folkestone—and arranged the others, some upon the seat beside her, and some opposite. The paper bag of bananas she kept in her lap, where it grew warmer and warmer and more and more dishevelled in appearance.

"Actually, off at last!" she murmured again, catching her breath a little in her joy. "Paris, Berne, Thun, Frutigen," she gave herself a little hug that made the jet beads rattle; "then the long diligence journey up those gorgeous mountains," she knew every inch of the way, "and a clear fifteen days at the *pension*, or even eighteen days, if I can get the cheaper room. Wheeeee! Can it be true? Can it be really true?" In her happiness she made sounds just like a bird.

She looked out of the window, where green fields had replaced the rows of streets. She opened her novel and tried to read. She played with the newspapers in a vain attempt to keep her eye on any one column. It was all in vain. A scene of wild beauty held her inner eye and made all else dull and uninteresting. The train sped on—slowly enough to her—yet every moment of the journey, every turn of the creaking wheels that brought her nearer, every little detail of the familiar route, became a source of keenest anticipatory happiness to her. She no longer cared about her name, or her silent and faithless lover of long ago, or of anything in the world but the fact that her absorbing little annual passion was now once again in a fair way to be gratified.

Then, quite suddenly, Miss Slumbubble realised her actual position, and felt afraid, unreasonably afraid. For the first time she became conscious that she was alone, alone in the compartment of an express train, and not even of a corridor express train.

Hitherto the excitement of getting off had occupied her mind to the exclusion of everything else, and if she had realised her solitude at all, she had realised it pleasurably. But now, in the first pause for breath as it were, when she had examined her packages, counted her money, glared at her ticket, and all the rest of it for the twentieth time, she leaned back in her seat and knew with a distinct shock that she was alone in a railway carriage on a comparatively long journey, alone for the first time in her life in a rattling, racing, shrieking train. She sat bolt upright and tried to collect herself a little.

Of all the emotions, that of fear is probably the least susceptible to the power of suggestion, certainly of *auto*-suggestion; and of vague fear that has no obvious cause this is especially true. With a fear of known origin one can argue, humour it, pacify, turn on the hose of ridicule—in a word, *suggest* that it depart; but with a fear that rises stealthily out of no comprehensible causes the mind finds itself at a complete loss. The mere assertion "I am not afraid" is as useless and empty as the subtler kind of suggestion that lies in affecting to ignore it altogether. Searching for the cause, moreover, tends to confuse the mind, and searching in vain, to terrify.

Miss Slumbubble pulled herself sharply together, and began to search for what made her afraid, but for a long time she searched in vain.

At first, she searched externally: she thought perhaps it had something to do with one of her packages, and she placed them all out in a row on the seat in front of her and examined each in turn, bananas, camera, food bag, black bead bag, &c. &c. But she discovered nothing among them to cause alarm.

Then she searched internally: her thoughts, her rooms in London, her *pension*, her money, ticket, plans in general, her future, her past, her health, her religion, anything and everything among the events of her inner life she passed in review, yet found nothing that could have caused this sudden sense of being troubled and afraid.

Moreover, as she vainly searched, her fear increased. She got into a regular nervous flurry.

"I declare if I'm not all in a perspiration!" she exclaimed aloud, and shifted down the dirty cushions to another place, looking anxiously about her as she did so. She probed everywhere in her thoughts to find the reason of her fear, but could think of nothing. Yet in her soul there was a sense of growing distress.

She found her new seat no more comfortable than the one before it, and shifted in turn into all the corners of the carriage, and down the middle as well, till at last, she had tried every possible part of it. In each place she felt less at ease than in the one before. She got up and looked into the empty racks, under the seats, beneath the heavy cushions, which she lifted with difficulty. Then she put all the packages back again into the rack, dropping several of them in her nervous hurry, and being obliged to kneel on the floor to recover them from under the seats. This made her breathless.

Moreover, the dust got into her throat and made her cough. Her eyes smarted and she grew uncomfortably warm. Then, quite accidentally, she caught sight of her reflection in the coloured picture of Boulogne under the rack, and the appearance she presented added greatly to her dismay. She looked so unlike herself, and wore such an odd expression. It was almost like the face of another person altogether.

The sense of alarm, once wakened, is fed by anything and everything, from a buzzing fly to a dark cloud in the sky. The woman collapsed on to the seat behind her in a distressing fluster of nervous fear.

But Miss Daphne Slumbubble had pluck. She was not so easily dismayed after all. She had read somewhere that terror was sometimes dispersed by the loud and strong affirmation of one's own name. She believed much that she read, provided it was plainly and vigorously expressed, and she acted at once on this knowledge.

"I am Daphne Slumbubble!" she affirmed in a firm, confident tone of voice, sitting stiffly on the edge of the seat, "I am not afraid—of anything." She added the last two words as an afterthought. "I am Daphne Slumbubble, and I have paid for my ticket, and know where I am going, and my luggage is in the van, and I have all my smaller things here!" She enumerated them one by one; she omitted nothing.

Yet the sound of her own voice, and especially of her own name, added apparently to her distress. It sounded oddly, like a voice outside the carriage. Everything seemed suddenly to have become strange, and unfamiliar, and unfriendly. She moved across to the opposite corner and looked out of the window: trees, fields, and occasional country houses flew past in endless swift succession. The country looked charming; she saw rooks flying and farm-horses moving laboriously over the fields. What in the world was there to feel afraid of? What in the world made her so restless and fidgety and frightened? Once again, she examined her packages, her ticket, her money. All was right.

Then she dashed across to the window and tried to open it. The sash stuck. She pulled and pulled in vain. The sash refused to yield. She ran to the other window, with a like result. Both were closed. Both refused to open. Her fear grew. She was locked in! The windows would not open. Something was wrong with the carriage. She suddenly recalled the way everyone had examined it and refused to enter. There must be something the matter with the carriage—something she had omitted to observe. Terror ran like a flame through her. She trembled and was ready to cry.

She ran up and down between the cushioned seats like a bird in a cage, casting wild glances at the racks and under the seats and out of the windows. A sudden panic took her, and she tried to open the door. It was locked. She flew to the other door. That, too, was locked. Good Heavens, both were locked! She was locked in. She was a prisoner. She was caught in a closed space. The mountains were out of her reach—the free open woods—the wide fields, the scented winds of heaven. She was caught, hemmed in, celled, restricted like a prisoner in a dungeon. The thought maddened her. The feeling that she could not reach the open spaces of sky and forest, of field and blue horizon, struck straight into her soul and touched all that she held most dear. She screamed. She ran down between the cushioned seats and screamed aloud.

Of course, no one heard her. The thunder of the train killed the feeble sound of her voice. Her voice was the cry of the imprisoned person.

Then quite suddenly she understood what it all meant. There was nothing wrong with the carriage, or with her parcels, or with the train. She sat down abruptly upon the dirty cushions and faced the position there and then. It had nothing to do with her past or her future, her ticket or her money, her religion or her health. It was something else entirely. She knew what it was, and the knowledge brought icy terror at once. She had at last labelled the source of her consternation, and the discovery increased rather than lessened her distress.

It was the fear of closed spaces. It was *claustrophobia!*

There could no longer be any doubt about it; She was shut in. She was enclosed in a narrow space from which she could not escape. The walls and floor and ceiling shut her in implacably. The doors were fastened; the windows were sealed, there was no escape.

"That porter *might* have told me!" she exclaimed inconsequently, mopping her face. Then the foolishness of the saying dawned upon her, and she thought her mind must be going. That was the effect of claustrophobia, she remembered: the mind went, and one said and did foolish things. Oh, to get out into a free open space, uncornered! Here she was trapped, horribly trapped.

"The guard man should never have locked me in—never!" she cried, and ran up and down between the seats, throwing her weight first against the door and then against the other. Of course, fortunately, neither of them yielded.

Thinking food might calm her, perhaps, she took down the banana bag and peeled the squashy over ripe fruit, munching it with part of the Bath bun from the other bag, and sitting midway on the forward seat. Suddenly the right-hand window dropped with a bang and a rattle. It had only been stuck after all, and her efforts, aided by the shaking of the train, had completed its undoing, or rather its unclosing. Miss Slumbubble shrieked, and dropped her banana and bun.

But the shock passed in a moment when she saw what had happened, and that the window was open and the sweet air pouring in from the flying fields. She rushed up and put her head out. This was followed by her hand, for she meant to open the door from the outside if possible. Whatever happened, the one imperative thing was that she must get into open space. The handle turned easily enough, but the door was locked higher up and she could not make it budge. She put her head farther out, so that the wind tore the jet bonnet off her head and left it twirling in the dusty whirlwind on the line far behind, and this sensation of the air whistling past her ears and through her flying hair somehow or other managed to make her feel wilder than ever. In fact, she completely lost her head, and began to scream at the top of her voice:

"I'm locked in! I'm a prisoner! Help, help!" she yelled.

A window opened in the next compartment and a young man put his head out.

"What the deuce is the matter? Are you being murdered?" he shouted down the wind.

"I'm locked in! I'm locked in!" screamed the hatless lady, wrestling furiously with the obdurate door handle.

"Don't open the door!" cried the young man anxiously.

"I can't, you idiot! I can't!"

"Wait a moment and I'll come to you. Don't try to get out. I'll climb along the foot-board. Keep calm, madam, keep calm. I'll save you."

He disappeared from view. Good Heavens! he meant to crawl out and come to her carriage by the window! A man, a *young* man, would shortly be in the compartment with her. Locked in, too! No, it was impossible. That was worse than the claustrophobia, and she could not endure such a thing for a moment. The young man would certainly kill her and steal all her packages.

She ran once or twice frantically up and down the narrow floor. Then she looked out of the window.

"Oh, bless my heart and soul!" she cried out, "he's out already!"

The young man, evidently thinking the lady was being assaulted, had climbed out of the window and was pluckily coming to her rescue. He was already on the foot-board, swinging by the brass bars on the side of the coach as the train rocked down the line at a fearful pace.

But Miss Slumbubble took a deep breath and a sudden determination. She did, in fact, the only thing left to her to do. She pulled the communication cord once, twice, three times, and then drew the window up with a sudden snap just before the young man's head appeared round the corner of the sash. Then, stepping backwards, she trod on the slippery banana bag and fell flat on her back upon the dirty floor between the seats.

The train slackened speed almost immediately and came to a stop. Miss Slumbubble still sat on the floor, staring in a dazed fashion at her toes. She realised the enormity of her offence, and was thoroughly frightened. She had actually pulled the cord!—the cord that is meant to be seen but not touched, the little chain that meant a £5 fine and all sorts of dire consequences.

She heard voices shouting and doors opening, and a moment later a key rattled near her head, and she saw the guard swinging up on to the steps of the carriage. The door was wide open, and the young man from the next compartment was explaining volubly what he seen and heard.

"I thought it was murder," he was saying.

But the guard pushed quickly into the carriage and lifted the panting and dishevelled lady on to the seat.

"Now, what's all this about? Was it you that pulled the cord, ma'am?" he asked somewhat roughly. "It's serious stoppin' a train like this, you know, a mail train."

Now Miss Daphne did not mean to tell a lie. It was not deliberate, that is to say. It seemed to slip out of its own accord as the most natural and obvious thing to say. For she was terrified at what she had done, and *had* to find a good excuse. Yet how in the world could she describe to this stupid and hurried official all she had gone through? Moreover, he would be so certain to think she was merely drunk.

"It was a man," she said, falling back instinctively upon her natural enemy. "There's a man somewhere!" She glanced round at the racks and under the seats. The guard followed her eyes.

"I don't see no man," he declared; "all I know is you've stopped the mail train without any visible or reasonable cause. "I'll be obliged with your name and address, ma'am, if you please," he added, taking a dirty note-book from his pocket and wetting the blunt pencil in his mouth.

"Let me get air—at once," she said. "I must have air first. Of course, you shall have my name. The whole affair is disgraceful." She was getting her wits back. She moved to the door.

"That may be, ma'am," the man said, "but I've my duty to perform, and I must report the facts, and then get the train on as quick as possible. You must stay in the carriage, please. We've been waiting 'ere a bit too long already."

Miss Slumbubble met her fate calmly. She realised it was not fair to keep all the passengers waiting while she got a little fresh air. There was a brief confabulation between the two guards, which ended by the one who had first come taking his seat in her carriage, while the other blew his whistle and the train started off again and flew at great speed the remaining miles to Folkestone.

"Now I'll take the name and address, if you please, ma'am," he said politely. "*Daphny*, yes, thank you , Daphny without a hef, all right, thank you."

He wrote it all down laboriously while the hatless little lady sat opposite, indignant, excited, ready to be voluble the moment she could think what was best to say, and above all fearful that her holiday would be delayed, if not prevented altogether.

Presently the guard looked up at her and put his note-book away in an inner pocket. It was just after he had entered the number of the carriage.

"You see, ma'am," he explained with sudden suavity, "this communication cord is only for cases of real danger, and if I report this, as I should do, it means a 'eavy fine. You must 'ave just pulled it as a sort of hexperiment, didn't you?"

Something in the man's voice caught her ear; there was a change in it; his manner, too, had altered somehow. He suddenly seemed to have become apologetic. She was quick to notice the change, though she could not understand what caused it. It began, she fancied, from the moment he entered the number of the carriage in his notebook.

"It's the delay to the train I've got to explain," he continued, as if speaking to himself, "and I can't put it all on to the engine-driver—"

"Perhaps we shall make it up and there won't be any delay," ventured Miss Slumbubble, carefully smoothing her hair and rearranging the stray hairpins.

"——and I don't want to get no one into any kind of trouble, least of all myself," he continued, wholly ignoring the interruption. Then he turned round in his seat and stared hard at his companion with rather a worried, puzzled expression of countenance and a shrug of the shoulders that was distinctly apologetic. Plainly, she thought, he was preparing the way for a compromise—for a tip!

The train was slackening speed; already it was in the cutting where it reverses and is pushed backwards on to the pier. Miss Slumbubble was desperate. She had never tipped a man before in her life except for obvious and recognised services, and this seemed to her like compounding a felony, or some such dreadful thing. Yet so much was at stake: she might be detained at Folkestone for days before the matter came into court, to say nothing of a £5 fine, which meant that her holiday would be utterly stopped. The blue and white mountains swam into her field of vision, and she heard the wind in the pine forest.

"Perhaps you would give this to your wife," she said timidly, holding out a sovereign.

The guard looked at it and shook his head.

"I 'aven't got a wife, exackly," he said; "but it isn't money I want. What I want is to 'ush this little matter up as quietly as possible. I may lose my job over this—but if you'll agree to say nothing about it, I think I can square the driver and t'other guard."

"*I* won't say anything, *of course*," stammered the astonished lady. "But I don't think I quite understand—"

"You couldn't understand either till I tell you," he replied, looking greatly relieved; "but the fac' is, I never noticed the carriage till I come to put the number down, and then I see it's the very one—the very same number—"

"What number?"

He stared at her for a moment without speaking. Then he appeared to take a great decision.

"Well, I'm in your 'ands anyhow, ma'am, and I may as well tell you the lot, and then we both 'elps the other out It's this way, you see. You ain't the first to try and jump out of this carriage—not by a long ways. It's been done before by a good number—"

"Gracious!"

"But the first who did it was that German woman, Binckmann—"

"Binckmann, the woman who was found on the line last year, and the carriage door open?" cried Miss Slumbubble, aghast.

"That's her. This was the carriage she jumped from, and they tried to say it was murder, but couldn't find anyone who could have done it, and then they said she must have been crazy. And since then, this carriage was said to be 'aunted, because so many other people tried to do the same thing and throw theirselves out too, till the company changed the number—"

"To this number?" cried the excited spinster, pointing to the figures on the door.

"That's it, ma'am. And if you look, you'll see this number don't follow on with the others. Even then the thing didn't stop, and we got orders to let no one in. That's where I made my mistake. I left the door unlocked, and they put you in. If this gets in the papers I'll be dismissed for sure. The company's awful strict about that."

"I'm terrified!" exclaimed Miss Slumbubble, "for that's exactly what I felt—"

"That you'd got to jump out, you mean?" asked the guard.

"Yes. The terror of being shut in."

"That's what the doctors said Binckmann had—the fear of being shut up in a tight place. They gave it some long name, but that's what it was: she couldn't abide being closed in. Now, here we are at the pier, ma'am, and, if you'll allow me, I'll help you to carry your little bits of luggage."

"Oh, thank you, guard, thank you," she said faintly, taking his proffered hand and getting out with infinite relief on to the platform.

"Tchivalry ain't dead yet, Miss," he replied gallantly, as he loaded himself up with her packages and led the way down to the steamer.

Ten minutes later the deep notes of the syren echoed across the pier, and the paddles began to churn the green sea. And Miss Daphne Slumbubble, hatless but undismayed, went abroad to flutter the remnants of her faded youth before the indifferent foreigners in the cheap *pension* among the Alps.

The Woman's Ghost Story

"Yes," she said, from her seat in the dark corner, "I'll tell you an experience if you care to listen. And, what's more, I'll tell it briefly, without trimmings—I mean without unessentials. That's a thing story-tellers never do, you know," she laughed. "They drag in all the unessentials and leave their listeners to disentangle; but I'll give you just the essentials, and you can make of it what you please. But on one condition: that at the end you ask no questions, because I can't explain it and have no wish to."

We agreed. We were all serious. After listening to a dozen prolix stories from people who merely wished to "talk" but had nothing to tell, we wanted "essentials."

"In those days," she began, feeling from the quality of our silence that we were with her, "in those days I was interested in psychic things, and had arranged to sit up alone in a haunted house in the middle of London. It was a cheap and dingy lodging-house in a mean street, unfurnished. I had already made a preliminary examination in daylight that afternoon, and the keys from the caretaker, who lived next door, were in my pocket. The story was a good one—satisfied me, at any rate, that it was worth investigating; and I won't weary you with details as to the woman's murder and all the tiresome elaboration as to *why* the place was alive. Enough that it was.

"I was a good deal bored, therefore, to see a man, whom I took to be the talkative old caretaker, waiting for me on the steps when I went in at 11 p.m., for I had sufficiently explained that I wished to be there alone for the night.

"'I wished to show you *the* room,' he mumbled, and of course I couldn't exactly refuse, having tipped him for the temporary loan of a chair and table.

"'Come in, then, and let's be quick,' I said.

"We went in, he shuffling after me through the unlighted hall up to the first floor where the murder had taken place, and I prepared myself to hear his inevitable account before turning him out with the half-crown his persistence had earned. After lighting the gas I sat down in the armchair he had provided—a faded, brown plush armchair—and turned for the first time to face him and get through with the performance as quickly as possible. And it was in that instant I got my first shock. The man was not the caretaker. It was not the old fool, Carey, I had interviewed earlier in the day and made my plans with. My heart gave a horrid jump.

"'Now who are *you*, pray?' I said. 'You're not Carey, the man I arranged with this afternoon. Who are you?'

"I felt uncomfortable, as you may imagine. I was a 'psychical researcher,' and a young woman of new tendencies, and proud of my liberty, but I did not care to find myself in an empty house with a stranger. Something of my confidence left me. Confidence with women, you know, is all humbug after a certain point. Or perhaps you don't know, for most of you are men. But anyhow my pluck ebbed in a quick rush, and I felt afraid.

"'Who are you?' I repeated quickly and nervously. The fellow was well dressed, youngish and good-looking, but with a face of great sadness. I myself was barely thirty. I am giving you essentials, or I would not mention it Out of quite ordinary things comes this story. I think that's why it has value.

"'No,' he said; 'I'm the man who was frightened to death.'

"His voice and his words ran through me like a knife, and I felt ready to drop. In my pocket was the book I had bought to make notes in. I felt the pencil sticking in the socket. I felt, too, the extra warm things I had put on to sit up in, as no bed or sofa was available—a hundred things dashed through my mind, foolishly and without sequence or meaning, as the way is when one is really frightened. Unessentials leaped up and puzzled me, and I thought of what the papers might say if it came out, and what my 'smart' brother-in-law would think, and whether it would be told that I had cigarettes in my pocket, and was a free-thinker."

"'The man who was frightened to death!'" I repeated aghast

"'That's me,' he said stupidly.

"I stared at him just as you would have done—any one of you men now listening to me—and felt my life ebbing and flowing like a sort of hot fluid. You needn't laugh! That's how I felt. Small things, you know, touch the mind with great earnestness when terror is there—*real ter-*

ror. But I might have been at a middle-class tea-party, for all the ideas I had: they were so ordinary!"

"'But I thought you were the caretaker I tipped this afternoon to let me sleep here!' I gasped. 'Did—did Carey send you to meet me?'

"'No,' he replied in a voice that touched my boots somehow. 'I am the man who was frightened to death. And what is more, I am frightened *now!*'

"'So am I!' I managed to utter, speaking instinctively. 'I'm simply terrified.'

"'Yes,' he replied in that same odd voice that seemed to sound within me. 'But you are still in the flesh, and I—*am not!*'

"I felt the need for vigorous self-assertion. I stood up in that empty, unfurnished room, digging the nails into my palms and clenching my teeth. I was determined to assert my individuality and my courage as a new woman and a free soul.

"'You mean to say you are not in the flesh!' I gasped. 'What in the world are you talking about?'

"The silence of the night swallowed up my voice. For the first time I realised that darkness was over the city; that dust lay upon the stairs; that the floor above was untenanted and the floor below empty. I was alone in an unoccupied and haunted house, unprotected, and a woman. I chilled. I heard the wind round the house, and knew the stars were hidden. My thoughts rushed to policemen and omnibuses, and everything that was useful and comforting. I suddenly realised what a fool I was to come to such a house alone. I was icily afraid I thought the end of my life had come. I was an utter fool to go in for psychical research when I had not the necessary nerve.

"'Good God!' I gasped. 'If you're not Carey, the man I arranged with, who are you?'

"I was really stiff with terror. The man moved slowly towards me across the empty room. I held out my arm to stop him, getting up out of my chair at the same moment, and he came to a halt just opposite to me, a smile on his worn, sad face.

"'I told you who I am,' he repeated quietly with a sigh, looking at me with the saddest eyes I have ever seen, 'and I am frightened *still.*'

"By this time, I was convinced that I was entertaining either a rogue or a madman, and I cursed my stupidity in bringing the man in without having seen his face. My mind was quickly made up, and I knew what to do. Ghosts and psychic phenomena flew to the winds. If I angered the creature my life might pay the price. I must humour him till I got to the door, and then race for the street. I stood bolt upright and faced him. We were about of a height, and I was a strong, athletic woman who played hockey in winter and climbed Alps in summer. My hand itched for a stick, but I had none,

"'Now, of course, I remember,' I said with a sort of stiff smile that was very hard to force. 'Now I remember your case and the wonderful way you behaved. . . . .'

"The man stared at me stupidly, turning his head to watch me as I backed more and more quickly to the door. But when his face broke into a smile, I could control myself no longer. I reached the door in a run, and shot out on to the landing. Like a fool, I turned the wrong way, and stumbled over the stairs leading to the next storey. But it was too late to change. The man was after me, I was sure, though no sound of footsteps came; and I dashed up the next flight, tearing my skirt and banging my ribs in the darkness, and rushed headlong into the first room I came to. Luckily the door stood ajar, and, still more fortunate, there was a key in the lock. In a second I had slammed the door, flung my whole weight against it, and turned the key.

"I was safe, but my heart was beating like a drum. A second later it seemed to stop altogether, for I saw that there was someone else in the room besides myself. A man's figure stood between me and the windows, where the street lamps gave just enough light to outline his shape against the glass. I'm a plucky woman, you know, for even then I didn't give up hope, but I may tell you that I have never felt so vilely frightened in all my born days. I had locked myself in with him!

"The man leaned against the window, watching me where I lay in a collapsed heap upon the floor. So, there were two men in the house with me, I reflected. Perhaps other rooms were occupied too! What could it all mean? But, as I stared something changed in the room, or in me—hard to say which—and I realised my mistake, so that my fear, which had so far been physical, at once altered its character and became *psychical*. I became afraid in my soul instead of in my heart, and I knew immediately who this man was.

"'How in the world did you get up here?' I stammered to him across the empty room, amazement momentarily stemming my fear.

"'Now, let me tell you,' he began, in that odd far-away voice of his that went down my spine like a knife. 'I'm in different space, for one thing, and you'd find me in any room you went into; for according to your way of measuring, I'm *all over the house*. Space is a bodily condition, but I am out of the body, and am not affected by space. It's my condition that keeps me here. I want something to change my condition for me, for then I could get away. What I want is sympathy. Or, really, more than sympathy; I want affection—I want love!'

"While he was speaking, I gathered myself slowly upon my feet. I wanted to scream and cry and laugh all at once, but I only succeeded in sighing, for my emotion was exhausted and a numbness was coming over me. I felt for the matches in my pocket and made a movement towards the gas jet.

"'I should be much happier if you didn't light the gas,' he said at once, 'for the vibrations of your light hurt me a good deal. You need not be afraid that I shall injure you. I can't touch your body to begin with, for there's a great gulf fixed, you know; and really this half-light suits me best. Now, let me continue what I was trying to say before. You know, so many people have come to this house to see me, and most of them have seen me, and one and all have been terrified. If only, oh! if only someone would be *not* terrified, but kind and loving to me! Then, you see, I might be able to change my condition and get away.'

"His voice was so sad that I felt tears start somewhere at the back of my eyes; but fear kept all else in check, and I stood shaking and cold as I listened to him.

"'Who are you then? Of course, Carey didn't send you, I know now,' I managed to utter. My thoughts scattered dreadfully and I could think of nothing to say. I was afraid of a stroke.

"'I know nothing about Carey, or who he is,' continued the man quietly, 'and the name my body had I have forgotten, thank God; but I am the man who was frightened to death in this house ten years ago, and I have been frightened ever since, and am frightened still; for the succession of cruel and curious people who come to this house to see the ghost, and thus keep alive its atmosphere of terror, only helps to render my condition worse. If only someone would be kind to me—*laugh*, speak gently and rationally with me, cry if they like, pity, comfort, soothe me—anything but come here in curiosity and tremble as you are now doing in that corner. Now, madam, won't you take pity on me?' His voice rose to a dreadful cry. 'Won't you step out into the middle of the room and try to love me a little?'

"A horrible laughter came gurgling up in my throat as I heard him, but the sense of pity was stronger than the laughter, and I found myself actually leaving the support of the wall and approaching the centre of the floor.

"'By God!' he cried, at once straightening up against the window, 'you have done a kind act. That's the first attempt at sympathy that has been shown me since I died, and I feel better already. In life, you know, I was a misanthrope. Everything went wrong with me, and I came to hate my fellow men so much that I couldn't bear to see them even. Of course, like begets like, and this hate was returned. Finally, I suffered from horrible delusions, and my room became haunted with demons that laughed and grimaced, and one night I ran into a whole cluster of them near the bed—and the fright stopped my heart and killed me. It's hate and remorse, as much as terror, that clogs me so thickly and keeps me here. If only someone could feel pity, and sympathy, and perhaps a little love for me, I could get away and be happy. When you came this afternoon to see over the house, I watched you, and a little hope came to me for the first time. I saw you had courage, originality, resource—*love*. If only I could touch your heart, without frightening you, I knew I could perhaps tap that love you have stored up in your being there, and thus borrow the wings for my escape!'

"Now I must confess my heart began to ache a little, as fear left me and the man's words sank their sad meaning into me. Still, the whole affair was so incredible, and so touched with unholy quality, and the story of a woman's murder I had come to investigate had so obviously nothing to do with this thing, that I felt myself in a kind of wild dream that seemed likely to stop at any moment and leave me somewhere in bed after a nightmare.

"Moreover, his words possessed me to such an extent that I found it impossible to reflect upon anything else at all, or to consider adequately any ways and means of action or escape.

"I moved a little nearer to him in the gloom, horribly frightened, of course, but with the beginnings of a strange determination in my heart

"'You women,' he continued, his voice plainly thrilling at my approach, 'you wonderful women, to whom life often brings no opportunity of spending your great love, oh, if you only could know how many of us simply yearn for it! It would save our souls, if you but knew. Few might find the chance that you now have, but if you only spent your love freely, without definite object, just letting it flow openly for all who need, you would reach hundreds and thousands of souls like me, and *release us!* Oh, madam, I ask you again to feel with me, to be kind and gentle— and if you can to love me a little!'

"My heart did leap within me and this time the tears did come, for I could not restrain them. I laughed too, for the way he called me 'madam' sounded so odd, here in this empty room at midnight in a

London street, but my laughter stopped dead and merged in a flood of weeping when I saw how my change of feeling affected him. He had left his place by the window and was kneeling on the floor at my feet, his hands stretched out towards me, and the first signs of a kind of glory about his head.

"'Put your arms round me and kiss me, for the love of God!' he cried. 'Kiss me, oh, kiss me, and I shall be freed! You have done so much already—now do this!'

"I stuck there, hesitating, shaking, my determination on the verge of action, yet not quite able to compass it. But the terror had almost gone.

"'Forget that I'm a man and you're a woman,' he continued in the most beseeching voice I ever heard. 'Forget that I'm a ghost, and come out boldly and press me to you with a great kiss, and let your love flow into me. Forget yourself just for one minute and do a brave thing! Oh, *love me, love me, love me!* and I shall be free!'

"The words, or the deep force they somehow released in the centre of my being, stirred me profoundly, and an emotion infinitely greater than fear surged up over me and carried me with it across the edge of action. Without hesitation I took two steps forward towards him where he knelt, and held out my arms. Pity and love were in my heart at that moment, genuine pity, I swear, and genuine love. I forgot myself and my little tremblings in a great desire to help another soul.

"'I love you! poor, aching, unhappy thing! I love you,' I cried through hot tears; 'and I am not the least bit afraid in the world.'

"The man uttered a curious sound, like laughter, yet not laughter, and turned his face up to me. The light from the street below fell on it, but there was another light, too, shining all round it that seemed to come from the eyes and skin. He rose to his feet and met me, and in that second I folded him to my breast and kissed him full on the lips again and again."

All our pipes had gone out, and not even a skirt rustled in that dark studio as the story-teller paused a moment to steady her voice, and put a hand softly up to her eyes before going on again.

"Now, what can I say, and how can I describe to you, all you sceptical men sitting there with pipes in your mouths, the amazing sensation I experienced of holding an intangible, impalpable thing so closely to my heart that it touched my body with equal pressure all the way down, and then melted away somewhere into my very being? For it was like seizing a rush of cool wind and feeling a touch of burning fire the moment it had struck its swift blow and passed on. A series of shocks ran all over and all through me; a momentary ecstasy of flaming sweetness and wonder thrilled down into me; my heart gave another great leap— and then I was alone.

"The room was empty. I turned on the gas and struck a match to prove it. All fear had left me, and something was singing round me in the air and in my heart like the joy of a spring morning in youth. Not all the devils or shadows or hauntings in the world could then have caused me a single tremor.

"I unlocked the door and went all over the dark house, even into kitchen and cellar and up among the ghostly attics. But the house was empty. Something had left it. I lingered a short hour, analysing, thinking, wondering—you can guess what and how, perhaps, but I won't detail, for I promised only essentials, remember—and then went out to sleep the remainder of the night in my own flat, locking the door behind me upon a house no longer haunted.

"But my uncle, Sir Henry, the owner of the house, required an account of my adventure, and of course I was in duty bound to give him some kind of a true story. Before I could begin, however, he held up his hand to stop me.

"'First,' he said, 'I wish to tell you a little deception I ventured to practise on you. So many people have been to that house and seen the ghost that I came to think the story acted on their imaginations, and I wished to make a better test. So, I invented for their benefit another story, with the idea that if you did see anything, I could be sure it was not due merely to an excited imagination.'

"'Then what you told me about a woman having been murdered, and all that, was not the true story of the haunting?'

"'It was not. The true story is that a cousin of mine went mad in that house, and killed himself in a fit of morbid terror following upon years of miserable *hypochondriasis*. It is his figure that investigators see.'

"'That explains, then,' I gasped—

"'Explains what?'

"I thought of that poor struggling soul, longing all these years for escape, and determined to keep my story for the present to myself.

"'Explains, I mean, why I did not see the ghost of the murdered woman,' I concluded.

"'Precisely,' said Sir Henry, 'and why, if you had seen anything, it would have had value, inasmuch as it could not have been caused by the imagination working upon a story you already knew.'"

The Insanity of Jones

(A Study in Reincarnation)

1

Adventures come to the adventurous, and mysterious things fall in the way of those who, with wonder and imagination, are on the watch for them; but the majority of people go past the doors that are half ajar, thinking them closed, and fail to notice the faint stirrings of the great curtain that hangs ever in the form of appearances between them and the world of causes behind.

For only to the few whose inner senses have been quickened, perchance by some strange suffering in the depths, or by a natural temperament bequeathed from a remote past, comes the knowledge, not too welcome, that this greater world lies ever at their elbow, and that any moment a chance combination of moods and forces may invite them to cross the shifting frontier.

Some, however, are born with this awful certainty in their hearts, and are called to no apprenticeship, and to this select company Jones undoubtedly belonged.

All his life he had realised that his senses brought to him merely a more or less interesting set of sham appearances; that space, as men measure it, was utterly misleading; that time, as the clock ticked it in a succession of minutes, was arbitrary nonsense; and, in fact, that all his sensory perceptions were but a clumsy representation of *real* things behind the curtain—things he was for ever trying to get at, and that sometimes he actually did get at.

He had always been tremblingly aware that he stood on the borderland of another region, a region where time and space were merely forms of thought, where ancient memories lay open to the sight, and where the forces behind each human life stood plainly revealed and he could see the hidden springs at the very heart of the world. Moreover, the fact that he was a clerk in a fire insurance office, and did his work with strict attention, never allowed him to forget for one moment that, just beyond the dingy brick walls where the hundred men scribbled with pointed pens beneath the electric lamps, there existed this glorious region where the important part of himself dwelt and moved and had its being.

For in this region, he pictured himself playing the part of a spectator to his ordinary workaday life, watching, like a king, the stream of events, but untouched in his own soul by the dirt, the noise, and the vulgar commotion of the outer world.

And this was no poetic dream merely. Jones was not playing prettily with idealism to amuse himself. It was a living, working belief. So convinced was he that the external world was the result of a vast deception practised upon him by the gross senses, that when he stared at a great building like St. Paul's he felt it would not very much surprise him to see it suddenly quiver like a shape of jelly and then melt utterly away, while in its place stood all at once revealed the mass of colour, or the great intricate vibrations, or the splendid sound—the spiritual idea—which it represented in stone.

For something in this way, it was that his mind worked.

Yet, to all appearances, and in the satisfaction of all business claims, Jones was normal and unenterprising. He felt nothing but contempt for the wave of modern psychism. He hardly knew the meaning of such words as "clairvoyance" and "clairaudience." He had never felt the least desire to join the Theosophical Society and to speculate in theories of astral-plane life, or elementals.

He attended no meetings of the Psychical Research Society, and knew no anxiety as to whether his "*aura*" was black or blue; nor was he conscious of the slightest wish to mix in with the revival of cheap occultism which proves so attractive to weak minds of mystical tendencies and unleashed imaginations.

There were certain things he *knew*, but none he cared to argue about; and he shrank instinctively from attempting to put names to the contents of this other region, knowing well that such names could only limit and define things that, according to any standards in use in the ordinary world, were simply undefinable and illusive.

So that, although this was the way his mind worked, there was clearly a very strong leaven of common sense in Jones. In a word, the man the world and the office knew as Jones *was* Jones. The name summed him up and labelled him correctly—John Enderby Jones.

Among the things that he *knew*, and therefore never cared to speak or speculate about, one was that he plainly saw himself as the inheritor of a long series of past lives, the net result of painful evolution, always as himself, of course, but in numerous different bodies each determined by the behaviour of the preceding one.

The present John Jones was the last result to date of all the previous thinking, feeling, and doing of John Jones in earlier bodies and in other centuries. He pretended to no details, nor claimed distinguished ancestry, for he realised his past must have been utterly commonplace and insignificant to have produced his present; but he was just as sure he had been at this weary game for ages as that he breathed, and it never occurred to him to argue, to doubt, or to ask questions.

And one result of this belief was that his thoughts dwelt upon the past rather than upon the future; that he read much history, and felt specially drawn to certain periods whose spirit he understood instinctively as though he had lived in them; and that he found all religions uninteresting because, almost without exception, they start from the present and speculate ahead as to what men shall become, instead of looking back and speculating why men have got here as they are.

In the insurance office he did his work exceedingly well, but without much personal ambition. Men and women, he regarded as the impersonal instruments for inflicting upon him the pain or pleasure he had earned by his past workings, for chance had no place in his scheme of things at all; and while he recognised that the practical world could not get along unless every man did his work thoroughly and conscientiously, he took no interest in the accumulation of fame or money for himself, and simply, therefore, did his plain duty, with indifference as to results.

In common with others who lead a strictly impersonal life, he possessed the quality of utter bravery, and was always ready to face any combination of circumstances, no matter how terrible, because he saw in them the just working-out of past causes, he had himself set in motion which could not be dodged or modified. And whereas the majority of people had little meaning for him, either by way of attraction or repulsion, the moment he met someone with whom he felt his past had been *vitally* interwoven his whole inner being leapt up instantly and shouted the fact in his face, and he regulated his life with the utmost skill and caution, like a sentry on watch for an enemy whose feet could already be heard approaching.

Thus, while the great majority of men and women left him uninfluenced—since he regarded them as so many souls merely passing with him along the great stream of evolution—there were, here and there, individuals with whom he recognised that his smallest intercourse was of the gravest importance. These were persons with whom he knew in every fibre of his being he had accounts to settle, pleasant or otherwise, arising out of dealings in past lives; and into his relations with these few, therefore, he concentrated as it were the efforts that most people spread over their intercourse with a far greater number.

By what means he picked out these few individuals only those conversant with the startling processes of the subconscious memory may say, but the point was that Jones believed the main purpose, if not quite the entire purpose, of his present incarnation lay in his faithful and thorough settling of these accounts, and that if he sought to evade the least detail of such settling, no matter how unpleasant, he would have lived in vain, and would return to his next incarnation with this added duty to perform.

For according to his beliefs there was no Chance, and could be no ultimate shirking, and to avoid a problem was merely to waste time and lose opportunities for development.

And there was one individual with whom Jones had long understood clearly, he had a very large account to settle, and towards the accomplishment of which all the main currents of his being seemed to bear him with unswerving purpose. For, when he first entered the insurance office as a junior clerk ten years before, and through a glass door had caught sight of this man seated in an inner room, one of his sudden overwhelming flashes of intuitive memory had burst up into him from the depths, and he had seen, as in a flame of blinding light, a symbolical picture of the future rising out of a dreadful past, and he had, without any act of definite volition, marked down this man for a real account to be settled.

"With *that* man I shall have much to do," he said to himself, as he noted the big face look up and meet his eye through the glass. "There is something I cannot shirk—a vital relation out of the past of both of us."

And he went to his desk trembling a little, and with shaking knees, as though the memory of some terrible pain had suddenly laid its icy hand upon his heart and touched the scar of a great horror. It was a moment of genuine terror when their eyes had met through the glass door, and he was conscious of an inward shrinking and loathing that seized upon him with great violence and convinced him in a single second that the settling of this account would be almost, perhaps, more than he could manage.

The vision passed as swiftly as it came, dropping back again into the submerged region of his consciousness; but he never forgot it, and the whole of his life thereafter became a sort of natural though undeliberate preparation for the fulfilment of the great duty when the time should be ripe.

In those days—ten years ago—this man was the Assistant Manager, but had since been promoted as Manager to one of the company's local branches; and soon afterwards Jones had likewise found himself transferred to this same branch. A little later, again, the branch at Liverpool, one of the most important, had been in peril owing to mismanagement and defalcation, and the man had gone to take charge of it, and again, by mere chance apparently, Jones had been promoted to the same place.

And this pursuit of the Assistant Manager had continued for several years, often, too, in the most curious fashion; and though Jones had never exchanged a single word with him, or been so much as noticed indeed by the great man, the clerk understood perfectly well that these moves in the game were all part of a definite purpose. Never for one moment did he doubt that the Invisibles behind the veil were slowly and surely arranging the details of it all so as to lead up suitably to the climax demanded by justice, a climax in which himself and the Manager would play the leading *roles*.

"It is inevitable," he said to himself, "and I feel it may be terrible; but when the moment comes, I shall be ready, and I pray God that I may face it properly and act like a man."

Moreover, as the years passed, and nothing happened, he felt the horror closing in upon him with steady increase, for the fact was Jones hated and loathed the Manager with an intensity of feeling he had never before experienced towards any human being. He shrank from his presence, and from the glance of his eyes, as though he remembered to have suffered nameless cruelties at his hands; and he slowly began to realise, moreover, that the matter to be settled between them was one of very ancient standing, and that the nature of the settlement was a discharge of accumulated punishment which would probably be very dreadful in the manner of its fulfilment.

When, therefore, the chief cashier one day informed him that the man was to be in London again—this time as General Manager of the head office—and said that he was charged to find a private secretary for him from among the best clerks, and further intimated that the selection had fallen upon himself, Jones accepted the promotion quietly, fatalistically, yet with a degree of inward loathing hardly to be described.

For he saw in this merely another move in the evolution of the inevitable Nemesis which he simply dared not seek to frustrate by any personal consideration; and at the same time he was conscious of a certain feeling of relief that the suspense of waiting might soon be mitigated. A secret sense of satisfaction, therefore, accompanied the unpleasant change, and Jones was able to hold himself perfectly well in hand when it was carried into effect and he was formally introduced as private secretary to the General Manager.

Now the Manager was a large, fat man, with a very red face and bags beneath his eyes. Being short-sighted, he wore glasses that seemed to magnify his eyes, which were always a little bloodshot. In hot weather a sort of thin slime covered his cheeks, for he perspired easily. His head was almost entirely bald, and over his turn-down collar his great neck folded in two distinct reddish collops of flesh. His hands were big and his fingers almost massive in thickness.

He was an excellent business man, of sane judgment and firm will, without enough imagination to confuse his course of action by showing him possible alternatives; and his integrity and ability caused him to be held in universal respect by the world of business and finance. In the important regions of a man's character, however, and at heart, he was coarse, brutal almost to savagery, without consideration for others, and as a result often cruelly unjust to his helpless subordinates.

In moments of temper, which were not infrequent, his face turned a dull purple, while the top of his bald head shone by contrast like white marble, and the bags under his eyes swelled till it seemed they would presently explode with a pop. And at these times he presented a distinctly repulsive appearance.

But to a private secretary like Jones, who did his duty regardless of whether his employer was beast or angel, and whose mainspring was principle and not emotion, this made little difference. Within the narrow limits in which any one *could* satisfy such a man, he pleased the General Manager; and more than once his piercing intuitive faculty, amounting almost to clairvoyance, assisted the chief in a fashion that served to bring the two closer together than might otherwise have been the case, and caused the man to respect in his assistant a power of which he possessed not even the germ himself. It was a curious relationship that grew up between the two, and the cashier, who enjoyed the credit of having made the selection, profited by it indirectly as much as anyone else.

So, for some time the work of the office continued normally and very prosperously. John Enderby Jones received a good salary, and in the outward appearance of the two chief characters in this history there was little change noticeable, except that the Manager grew fatter and redder, and the secretary observed that his own hair was beginning to show rather greyish at the temples.

There were, however, two changes in progress, and they both had to do with Jones, and are important to mention.

One was that he began to dream evilly. In the region of deep sleep, where the possibility of significant dreaming first develops itself, he was tormented more and more with vivid scenes and pictures in which a tall thin man, dark and sinister of countenance, and with bad eyes, was closely associated with himself. Only the setting was that of a past age, with costumes of centuries gone by, and the scenes had to do with dreadful cruelties that could not belong to modern life as he knew it.

The other change was also significant, but is not so easy to describe, for he had in fact become aware that some new portion of himself, hitherto unawakened, had stirred slowly into life out of the very depths of his consciousness. This new part of himself amounted almost to another personality, and he never observed its least manifestation without a strange thrill at his heart.

For he understood that it had begun to *watch* the Manager!

2

It was the habit of Jones, since he was compelled to work among conditions that were utterly distasteful, to withdraw his mind wholly from business once the day was over. During office hours he kept the strictest possible watch upon himself, and turned the key on all inner dreams, lest any sudden uprush from the deeps should interfere with his duty. But, once the working day was over, the gates flew open, and he began to enjoy himself.

He read no modern books on the subjects that interested him, and, as already said, he followed no course of training, nor belonged to any society that dabbled with half-told mysteries; but, once released from the office desk in the Manager's room, he simply and naturally entered the other region, because he was an old inhabitant, a rightful denizen, and because he belonged there. It was, in fact, really a case of dual personality; and a carefully drawn agreement existed between Jones-of-the-fire-insurance-office and Jones-of-the-mysteries, by the terms of which, under heavy penalties, neither region claimed him out of hours.

For the moment he reached his rooms under the roof in Bloomsbury, and had changed his city coat to another, the iron doors of the office clanged far behind him, and in front, before his very eyes, rolled up the beautiful gates of ivory, and he entered into the places of flowers and singing and wonderful veiled forms. Sometimes he quite lost touch with the outer world, forgetting to eat his dinner or go to bed, and lay in a state of trance, his consciousness working far out of the body.

And on other occasions he walked the streets on air, half-way between the two regions, unable to distinguish between incarnate and discarnate forms, and not very far, probably, beyond the *strata* where poets, saints, and the greatest artists have moved and thought and found their inspiration.

But this was only when some insistent bodily claim prevented his full release, and more often than not he was entirely independent of his physical portion and free of the real region, without let or hindrance.

One evening he reached home utterly exhausted after the burden of the day's work. The Manager had been more than usually brutal, unjust, ill-tempered, and Jones had been almost persuaded out of his settled policy of contempt into answering back. Everything seemed to have gone amiss, and the man's coarse, underbred nature had been in the ascendant all day long: he had thumped the desk with his great fists, abused, found fault unreasonably, uttered outrageous things, and behaved generally as he actually was—beneath the thin veneer of acquired business varnish.

He had done and said everything to wound all that was woundable in an ordinary secretary, and though Jones fortunately dwelt in a region from which he looked down upon such a man as he might look down on the blundering of a savage animal, the strain had nevertheless told severely upon him, and he reached home wondering for the first time in his life whether there was perhaps a point beyond which he would be unable to restrain himself any longer.

For something out of the usual had happened. At the close of a passage of great stress between the two, every nerve in the secretary's body tingling from undeserved abuse, the Manager had suddenly turned full upon him, in the corner of the private room where the safes stood, in such a way that the glare of his red eyes, magnified by the glasses, looked straight into his own.

And at this very second that other personality in Jones—the one that was ever *watching*—rose up swiftly from the deeps within and held a mirror to his face.

A moment of flame and vision rushed over him, and for one single second—one merciless second of clear sight—he saw the Manager as the tall dark man of his evil dreams, and the knowledge that he had suffered at his hands some awful injury in the past crashed through his mind like the report of a cannon.

It all flashed upon him and was gone, changing him from fire to ice, and then back again to fire; and he left the office with the certain conviction in his heart that the time for his final settlement with the man, the time for the inevitable retribution, was at last drawing very near.

According to his invariable custom, however, he succeeded in putting the memory of all this unpleasantness out of his mind with the changing of his office coat, and after dozing a little in his leather chair before the fire, he started out as usual for dinner in the Soho French restaurant, and began to dream himself away into the region of flowers and singing, and to commune with the Invisibles that were the very sources of his real life and being.

For it was in this way that his mind worked, and the habits of years had crystallised into rigid lines along which it was now necessary and inevitable for him to act.

At the door of the little restaurant, he stopped short, a half-remembered appointment in his mind. He had made an engagement with someone, but where, or with whom, had entirely slipped his memory. He thought it was for dinner, or else to meet just after dinner, and for a second it came back to him that it had something to do with the office, but whatever it was, he was quite unable to recall it, and a reference to his pocket engagement book showed only a blank page. Evidently, he had even omitted to enter it; and after standing a moment vainly trying to recall either the time, place, or person, he went in and sat down.

But though the details had escaped him, his subconscious memory seemed to know all about it, for he experienced a sudden sinking of the heart, accompanied by a sense of foreboding anticipation, and felt that beneath his exhaustion there lay a centre of tremendous excitement. The emotion caused by the engagement was at work, and would presently cause the actual details of the appointment to reappear.

Inside the restaurant the feeling increased, instead of passing: someone was waiting for him somewhere—someone whom he had definitely arranged to meet. He was expected by a person that very night and just about that very time. But by whom? Where? A curious inner trembling came over him, and he made a strong effort to hold himself in hand and to be ready for anything that might come.

And then suddenly came the knowledge that the place of appointment was this very restaurant, and, further, that the person he had promised to meet was already here, waiting somewhere quite close beside him.

He looked up nervously and began to examine the faces round him. The majority of the diners were Frenchmen, chattering loudly with much gesticulation and laughter; and there was a fair sprinkling of clerks like himself who came because the prices were low and the food good, but there was no single face that he recognised until his glance fell upon the occupant of the corner seat opposite, generally filled by himself.

"There's the man who's waiting for me!" thought Jones instantly.

He knew it at once. The man, he saw, was sitting well back into the corner, with a thick overcoat buttoned tightly up to the chin. His skin was very white, and a heavy black beard grew far up over his cheeks. At first the secretary took him for a stranger, but when he looked up and their eyes met, a sense of familiarity flashed across him, and for a second or two Jones imagined he was staring at a man he had known years before.

For, barring the beard, it was the face of an elderly clerk who had occupied the next desk to his own when he first entered the service of the insurance company, and had shown him the most painstaking kindness and sympathy in the early difficulties of his work. But a moment later the illusion passed, for he remembered that Thorpe had been dead at least five years. The similarity of the eyes was obviously a mere suggestive trick of memory.

The two men stared at one another for several seconds, and then Jones began to act *instinctively*, and because he had to. He crossed over and took the vacant seat at the other's table, facing him; for he felt it was somehow imperative to explain why he was late, and how it was he had almost forgotten the engagement altogether.

No honest excuse, however, came to his assistance, though his mind had begun to work furiously.

"Yes, you *are* late," said the man quietly, before he could find a single word to utter. "But it doesn't matter. Also, you had forgotten the appointment, but that makes no difference either."

"I knew—that there was an engagement," Jones stammered, passing his hand over his forehead; "but somehow—"

"You will recall it presently," continued the other in a gentle voice, and smiling a little. "It was in deep sleep last night we arranged this, and the unpleasant occurrences of today have for the moment obliterated it."

A faint memory stirred within him as the man spoke, and a grove of trees with moving forms hovered before his eyes and then vanished again, while for an instant the stranger seemed to be capable of self-distortion and to have assumed vast proportions, with wonderful flaming eyes.

"Oh!" he gasped. "It was there—in the other region?"

"Of course," said the other, with a smile that illumined his whole face. "You will remember presently, all in good time, and meanwhile you have no cause to feel afraid."

There was a wonderful soothing quality in the man's voice, like the whispering of a great wind, and the clerk felt calmer at once. They sat a little while longer, but he could not remember that they talked much or ate anything.

He only recalled afterwards that the head waiter came up and whispered something in his ear, and that he glanced round and saw the other people were looking at him curiously, some of them laughing, and that his companion then got up and led the way out of the restaurant.

They walked hurriedly through the streets, neither of them speaking; and Jones was so intent upon getting back the whole history of the affair from the region of deep sleep, that he barely noticed the way they took. Yet it was clear he knew where they were bound for just as well as his companion, for he crossed the streets often ahead of him, diving down alleys without hesitation, and the other followed always without correction.

The pavements were very full, and the usual night crowds of London were surging to and fro in the glare of the shop lights, but somehow no one impeded their rapid movements, and they seemed to pass through the people as if they were smoke.

And, as they went, the pedestrians and traffic grew less and less, and they soon passed the Mansion House and the deserted space in front of the Royal Exchange, and so on down Fenchurch Street and within sight of the Tower of London, rising dim and shadowy in the smoky air.

Jones remembered all this perfectly well, and thought it was his intense preoccupation that made the distance seem so short. But it was when the Tower was left behind and they turned northwards that he began to notice how altered everything was, and saw that they were in a neighbourhood where houses were suddenly scarce, and lanes and fields beginning, and that their only light was the stars overhead.

And, as the deeper consciousness more and more asserted itself to the exclusion of the surface happenings of his mere body during the day, the sense of exhaustion vanished, and he realised that he was moving somewhere in the region of causes behind the veil, beyond the gross deceptions of the senses, and released from the clumsy spell of space and time.

Without great surprise, therefore, he turned and saw that his companion had altered, had shed his overcoat and black hat, and was moving beside him absolutely *without sound*. For a brief second, he saw him, tall as a tree, extending through space like a great shadow, misty and wavering of outline, followed by a sound like wings in the darkness; but, when he stopped, fear clutching at his heart, the other resumed his former proportions, and Jones could plainly see his normal outline against the green field behind.

Then the secretary saw him fumbling at his neck, and at the same moment the black beard came away from the face in his hand.

"Then you *are* Thorpe!" he gasped, yet somehow without overwhelming surprise.

They stood facing one another in the lonely lane, trees meeting overhead and hiding the stars, and a sound of mournful sighing among the branches.

"I am Thorpe," was the answer in a voice that almost seemed part of the wind. "And I have come out of our far past to help you, for my debt to you is large, and in this life, I had but small opportunity to repay."

Jones thought quickly of the man's kindness to him in the office, and a great wave of feeling surged through him as he began to remember dimly the friend by whose side he had already climbed, perhaps through vast ages of his soul's evolution.

"To help me *now?*" he whispered.

"You will understand me when you enter into your real memory and recall how great a debt I have to pay for old faithful kindnesses of long ago," sighed the other in a voice like falling wind.

"Between us, though, there can be no question of *debt*," Jones heard himself saying, and remembered the reply that floated to him on the air and the smile that lightened for a moment the stern eyes facing him.

"Not of debt, indeed, but of privilege."

Jones felt his heart leap out towards this man, this old friend, tried by centuries and still faithful. He made a movement to seize his hand. But the other shifted like a thing of mist, and for a moment the clerk's head swam and his eyes seemed to fail.

"Then you are *dead?*" he said under his breath with a slight shiver.

"Five years ago, I left the body you knew," replied Thorpe. "I tried to help you then instinctively, not fully recognising you. But now I can accomplish far more."

With an awful sense of foreboding and dread in his heart, the secretary was beginning to understand.

"It has to do with—with—?"

"Your past dealings with the Manager," came the answer, as the wind rose louder among the branches overhead and carried off the remainder of the sentence into the air.

Jones's memory, which was just beginning to stir among the deepest layers of all, shut down suddenly with a snap, and he followed his companion over fields and down sweet-smelling lanes where the air was fragrant and cool, till they came to a large house, standing gaunt and lonely in the shadows at the edge of a wood. It was wrapped in utter stillness, with windows heavily draped in black, and the clerk, as he looked, felt such an overpowering wave of sadness invade him that his eyes began to burn and smart, and he was conscious of a desire to shed tears.

The key made a harsh noise as it turned in the lock, and when the door swung open into a lofty hall, they heard a confused sound of rustling and whispering, as of a great throng of people pressing forward to meet them.

The air seemed full of swaying movement, and Jones was certain he saw hands held aloft and dim faces claiming recognition, while in his heart, already oppressed by the approaching burden of vast accumulated memories, he was aware of the *uncoiling of something* that had been asleep for ages.

As they advanced, he heard the doors close with a muffled thunder behind them, and saw that the shadows seemed to retreat and shrink away towards the interior of the house, carrying the hands and faces with them. He heard the wind singing round the walls and over the roof, and its wailing voice mingled with the sound of deep, collective breathing that filled the house like the murmur of a sea; and as they walked up the broad staircase and through the vaulted rooms, where pillars rose like the stems of trees, he knew that the building was crowded, row upon row, with the thronging memories of his own long past.

"This is the *House of the Past*," whispered Thorpe beside him, as they moved silently from room to room; "the house of *your* past. It is full from cellar to roof with the memories of what you have done, thought, and felt from the earliest stages of your evolution until now.

"The house climbs up almost to the clouds, and stretches back into the heart of the wood you saw outside, but the remoter halls are filled with the ghosts of ages ago too many to count, and even if we were able to waken them you could not remember them now. Someday, though, they will come and claim you, and you must know them, and answer their questions, for they can never rest till they have exhausted themselves again through you, and justice has been perfectly worked out.

"But now follow me closely, and you shall see the particular memory for which I am permitted to be your guide, so that you may know and understand a great force in your present life, and may use the sword of justice, or rise to the level of a great forgiveness, according to your degree of power."

Icy thrills ran through the trembling clerk, and as he walked slowly beside his companion, he heard from the vaults below, as well as from more distant regions of the vast building, the stirring and sighing of the serried ranks of sleepers, sounding in the still air like a chord swept from unseen strings stretched somewhere among the very foundations of the house.

Stealthily, picking their way among the great pillars, they moved up the sweeping staircase and through several dark corridors and halls, and presently stopped outside a small door in an archway where the shadows were very deep.

"Remain close by my side, and remember to utter no cry," whispered the voice of his guide, and as the clerk turned to reply he saw his face was stern to whiteness and even shone a little in the darkness.

The room they entered seemed at first to be pitchy black, but gradually the secretary perceived a faint reddish glow against the farther end, and thought he saw figures moving silently to and fro.

"Now watch!" whispered Thorpe, as they pressed close to the wall near the door and waited. "But remember to keep absolute silence. It is a torture scene."

Jones felt utterly afraid, and would have turned to fly if he dared, for an indescribable terror seized him and his knees shook; but some power that made escape impossible held him remorselessly there, and with eyes glued on the spots of light he crouched against the wall and waited.

The figures began to move more swiftly, each in its own dim light that shed no radiance beyond itself, and he heard a soft clanking of chains and the voice of a man groaning in pain. Then came the sound of a door closing, and thereafter Jones saw but one figure, the figure of an old man, naked entirely, and fastened with chains to an iron framework on the floor.

His memory gave a sudden leap of fear as he looked, for the features and white beard were familiar, and he recalled them as though of yesterday.

The other figures had disappeared, and the old man became the centre of the terrible picture. Slowly, with ghastly groans; as the heat below him increased into a steady glow, the aged body rose in a curve of agony, resting on the iron frame only where the chains held wrists and ankles fast.

Cries and gasps filled the air, and Jones felt exactly as though they came from his own throat, and as if the chains were burning into his own wrists and ankles, and the heat scorching the skin and flesh upon his own back. He began to writhe and twist himself.

"Spain!" whispered the voice at his side, "and four hundred years ago."

"And the purpose?" gasped the perspiring clerk, though he knew quite well what the answer must be.

"To extort the name of a friend, to his death and betrayal," came the reply through the darkness.

A sliding panel opened with a little rattle in the wall immediately above the rack, and a face, framed in the same red glow, appeared and looked down upon the dying victim. Jones was only just able to choke a scream, for he recognised the tall dark man of his dreams. With horrible, gloating eyes he gazed down upon the writhing form of the old man, and his lips moved as in speaking, though no words were actually audible.

"He asks again for the name," explained the other, as the clerk struggled with the intense hatred and loathing that threatened every moment to result in screams and action. His ankles and wrists pained him so that he could scarcely keep still, but a merciless power held him to the scene.

He saw the old man, with a fierce cry, raise his tortured head and spit up into the face at the panel, and then the shutter slid back again, and a moment later the increased glow beneath the body, accompanied by awful writhing, told of the application of further heat. There came the odour of burning flesh; the white beard curled and burned to a crisp; the body fell back limp upon the red-hot iron, and then shot up again in fresh agony; cry after cry, the most awful in the world, rang out with deadened sound between the four walls; and again, the panel slid back creaking, and revealed the dreadful face of the torturer.

Again, the name was asked for, and again it was refused; and this time, after the closing of the panel, a door opened, and the tall thin man with the evil face came slowly into the chamber. His features were savage with rage and disappointment, and in the dull red glow that fell upon them he looked like a very prince of devils. In his hand he held a pointed iron at white heat.

"Now the murder!" came from Thorpe in a whisper that sounded as if it was outside the building and far away.

Jones knew quite well what was coming, but was unable even to close his eyes. He felt all the fearful pains himself just as though he were actually the sufferer; but now, as he stared, he felt something more besides; and when the tall man deliberately approached the rack and plunged the heated iron first into one eye and then into the other, he heard the faint fizzing of it, and felt his own eyes burst in frightful pain from his head.

At the same moment, unable longer to control himself, he uttered a wild shriek and dashed forward to seize the torturer and tear him to a thousand pieces. Instantly, in a flash, the entire scene vanished; darkness rushed in to fill the room, and he felt himself lifted off his feet by some force like a great wind and borne swiftly away into space.

When he recovered his senses, he was standing just outside the house and the figure of Thorpe was beside him in the gloom. The great doors were in the act of closing behind him, but before they shut, he fancied he caught a glimpse of an immense veiled figure standing upon the threshold, with flaming eyes, and in his hand a bright weapon like a shining sword of fire.

"Come quickly now—all is over!" Thorpe whispered.

"And the dark man—?" gasped the clerk, as he moved swiftly by the other's side.

"In this present life is the Manager of the company."

"And the victim?"

"Was yourself!"

"And the friend he—*I* refused to betray?"

"I was that friend," answered Thorpe, his voice with every moment sounding more and more like the cry of the wind. "You gave your life in agony to save mine."

"And again, in this life, we have all three been together?"

"Yes. Such forces are not soon or easily exhausted, and justice is not satisfied till all have reaped what they sowed."

Jones had an odd feeling that he was slipping away into some other state of consciousness. Thorpe began to seem unreal. Presently he would be unable to ask more questions. He felt utterly sick and faint with it all, and his strength was ebbing.

"Oh, quick!" he cried, "now tell me more. Why did I see this? What must I do?"

The wind swept across the field on their right and entered the wood beyond with a great roar, and the air round him seemed filled with voices and the rushing of hurried movement.

"To the ends of justice," answered the other, as though speaking out of the centre of the wind and from a distance, "which sometimes is entrusted to the hands of those who suffered and were strong. One wrong cannot be put right by another wrong, but your life has been so worthy that the opportunity is given to—"

The voice grew fainter and fainter, already it was far overhead with the rushing wind.

"You may punish or—" Here Jones lost sight of Thorpe's figure altogether, for he seemed to have vanished and melted away into the wood behind him. His voice sounded far across the trees, very weak, and ever rising.

"Or if you can rise to the level of a great forgiveness—"

The voice became inaudible.... The wind came crying out of the wood again.

★★★★★★★★★★

Jones shivered and stared about him. He shook himself violently and rubbed his eyes. The room was dark, the fire was out; he felt cold and stiff. He got up out of his armchair, still trembling, and lit the gas.

Outside the wind was howling, and when he looked at his watch, he saw that it was very late and he must go to bed.

He had not even changed his office coat; he must have fallen asleep in the chair as soon as he came in, and he had slept for several hours. Certainly, he had eaten no dinner, for he felt ravenous.

3

Next day, and for several weeks thereafter, the business of the office went on as usual, and Jones did his work well and behaved outwardly with perfect propriety. No more visions troubled him, and his relations with the Manager became, if anything, somewhat smoother and easier.

True, the man *looked* a little different, because the clerk kept seeing him with his inner and outer eye promiscuously, so that one moment he was broad and red-faced, and the next he was tall, thin, and dark, enveloped, as it were, in a sort of black atmosphere tinged with red. While at times a confusion of the two sights took place, and Jones saw the two faces mingled in a composite countenance that was very horrible indeed to contemplate.

But, beyond this occasional change in the outward appearance of the Manager, there was nothing that the secretary noticed as the result of his vision, and business went on more or less as before, and perhaps even with a little less friction.

But in the rooms under the roof in Bloomsbury it was different, for there it was perfectly clear to Jones that Thorpe had come to take up his abode with him. He never saw him, but he knew all the time he was there.

Every night on returning from his work he was greeted by the well-known whisper, "Be ready when I give the sign!" and often in the night he woke up suddenly out of deep sleep and was aware that Thorpe had that minute moved away from his bed and was standing waiting and watching somewhere in the darkness of the room. Often, he followed him down the stairs, though the dim gas jet on the landings never revealed his outline; and sometimes he did not come into the room at all, but hovered outside the window, peering through the dirty panes, or sending his whisper into the chamber in the whistling of the wind.

For Thorpe had come to stay, and Jones knew that he would not get rid of him until he had fulfilled the ends of justice and accomplished the purpose for which he was waiting.

Meanwhile, as the days passed, he went through a tremendous struggle with himself, and came to the perfectly honest decision that the "level of a great forgiveness" was impossible for him, and that he must therefore accept the alternative and use the secret knowledge placed in his hands—and execute justice. And once this decision was arrived at, he noticed that Thorpe no longer left him alone during the day as before, but now accompanied him to the office and stayed more or less at his side all through business hours as well.

His whisper made itself heard in the streets and in the train, and even in the Manager's room where he worked; sometimes warning, sometimes urging, but never for a moment suggesting the abandonment of the main purpose, and more than once so plainly audible that the clerk felt certain others must have heard it as well as himself.

The obsession was complete. He felt he was always under Thorpe's eye day and night, and he knew he must acquit himself like a man when the moment came, or prove a failure in his own sight as well in the sight of the other.

And now that his mind was made up, nothing could prevent the carrying out of the sentence. He bought a pistol, and spent his Saturday afternoons practising at a target in lonely places along the Essex shore, marking out in the sand the exact measurements of the Manager's room.

Sundays he occupied in like fashion, putting up at an inn overnight for the purpose, spending the money that usually went into the savings bank on travelling expenses and cartridges. Everything was done very thoroughly, for there must be no possibility of failure; and at the end of several weeks, he had become so expert with his six-shooter that at a distance of 25 feet, which was the greatest length of the Manager's room, he could pick the inside out of a halfpenny nine times out of a dozen, and leave a clean, unbroken rim.

There was not the slightest desire to delay. He had thought the matter over from every point of view his mind could reach, and his purpose was inflexible. Indeed, he felt proud to think that he had been chosen as the instrument of justice in the infliction of so well-deserved and so terrible a punishment. Vengeance may have had some part in his decision, but he could not help that, for he still felt at times the hot chains burning his wrists and ankles with fierce agony through to the bone.

He remembered the hideous pain of his slowly roasting back, and the point when he thought death *must* intervene to end his suffering, but instead new powers of endurance had surged up in him, and awful further stretches of pain had opened up, and unconsciousness seemed farther off than ever.

Then at last the hot irons in his eyes. . . . It all came back to him, and caused him to break out in icy perspiration at the mere thought of it . . . the vile face at the panel . . . the expression of the dark face. . . . His fingers worked. His blood boiled. It was utterly impossible to keep the idea of vengeance altogether out of his mind.

Several times he was temporarily baulked of his prey. Odd things happened to stop him when he was on the point of action. The first day, for instance, the Manager fainted from the heat. Another time when he had decided to do the deed, the Manager did not come down to the office at all.

And a third time, when his hand was actually in his hip pocket, he suddenly heard Thorpe's horrid whisper telling him to wait, and turning, he saw that the head cashier had entered the room noiselessly without his noticing it. Thorpe evidently knew what he was about, and did not intend to let the clerk bungle the matter.

He fancied, moreover, that the head cashier was watching him. He was always meeting him in unexpected corners and places, and the cashier never seemed to have an adequate excuse for being there. His movements seemed suddenly of particular interest to others in the office as well, for clerks were always being sent to ask him unnecessary questions, and there was apparently a general design to keep him under a sort of surveillance, so that he was never much alone with the Manager in the private room where they worked. And once the cashier had even gone so far as to suggest that he could take his holiday earlier than usual if he liked, as the work had been very arduous of late and the heat exceedingly trying.

He noticed, too, that he was sometimes followed by a certain individual in the streets, a careless-looking sort of man, who never came face to face with him, or actually ran into him, but who was always in his train or omnibus, and whose eye he often caught observing him over the top of his newspaper, and who on one occasion was even waiting at the door of his lodgings when he came out to dine.

There were other indications too, of various sorts, that led him to think something was at work to defeat his purpose, and that he must act at once before these hostile forces could prevent.

And so, the end came very swiftly, and was thoroughly approved by Thorpe.

It was towards the close of July, and one of the hottest days London had ever known, for the City was like an oven, and the particles of dust seemed to burn the throats of the unfortunate toilers in street and office. The portly Manager, who suffered cruelly owing to his size, came down perspiring and gasping with the heat. He carried a light-coloured umbrella to protect his head.

"He'll want something more than that, though!" Jones laughed quietly to himself when he saw him enter.

The pistol was safely in his hip pocket, every one of its six chambers loaded.

The Manager saw the smile on his face, and gave him a long steady look as he sat down to his desk in the corner. A few minutes later he touched the bell for the head cashier—a single ring—and then asked Jones to fetch some papers from another safe in the room upstairs.

A deep inner trembling seized the secretary as he noticed these precautions, for he saw that the hostile forces were at work against him, and yet he felt he could delay no longer and must act that very morning, interference or no interference. However, he went obediently up in the lift to the next floor, and while fumbling with the combination of the safe, known only to himself, the cashier, and the Manager, he again heard Thorpe's horrid whisper just behind him:

"You must do it today! You must do it today!"

He came down again with the papers, and found the Manager alone. The room was like a furnace, and a wave of dead heated air met him in the face as he went in. The moment he passed the doorway he realised that he had been the subject of conversation between the head cashier and his enemy.

They had been discussing him. Perhaps an inkling of his secret had somehow got into their minds. They had been watching him for days past. They had become suspicious.

Clearly, he must act now, or let the opportunity slip by perhaps for ever. He heard Thorpe's voice in his ear, but this time it was no mere whisper, but a plain human voice, speaking out loud.

"Now!" it said. "Do it now!"

The room was empty. Only the Manager and himself were in it.

Jones turned from his desk where he had been standing, and locked the door leading into the main office. He saw the army of clerks scribbling in their shirtsleeves, for the upper half of the door was of glass. He had perfect control of himself, and his heart was beating steadily.

The Manager, hearing the key turn in the lock, looked up sharply.

"What's that you're doing?" he asked quickly.

"Only locking the door, sir," replied the secretary in a quite even voice.

"Why? Who told you to—?"

"The voice of Justice, sir," replied Jones, looking steadily into the hated face.

The Manager looked black for a moment, and stared angrily across the room at him. Then suddenly his expression changed as he stared, and he tried to smile. It was meant to be a kind smile evidently, but it only succeeded in being frightened.

"That *is* a good idea in this weather," he said lightly, "but it would be much better to lock it on the *outside*, wouldn't it, Mr. Jones?"

"I think not, sir. You might escape me then. Now you can't."

Jones took his pistol out and pointed it at the other's face. Down the barrel he saw the features of the tall dark man, evil and sinister. Then the outline trembled a little and the face of the Manager slipped back into its place. It was white as death, and shining with perspiration.

"You tortured me to death four hundred years ago," said the clerk in the same steady voice, "and now the dispensers of justice have chosen me to punish you."

The Manager's face turned to flame, and then back to chalk again. He made a quick movement towards the telephone bell, stretching out a hand to reach it, but at the same moment Jones pulled the trigger and the wrist was shattered, splashing the wall behind with blood.

"That's *one* place where the chains burnt," he said quietly to himself. His hand was absolutely steady, and he felt that he was a hero.

The Manager was on his feet, with a scream of pain, supporting himself with his right hand on the desk in front of him, but Jones pressed the trigger again, and a bullet flew into the other wrist, so that the big man, deprived of support, fell forward with a crash on to the desk.

"You damned madman!" shrieked the Manager. "Drop that pistol!"

"That's *another* place," was all Jones said, still taking careful aim for another shot.

The big man, screaming and blundering, scrambled beneath the desk, making frantic efforts to hide, but the secretary took a step forward and fired two shots in quick succession into his projecting legs, hitting first one ankle and then the other, and smashing them horribly.

"Two more places where the chains burnt," he said, going a little nearer.

The Manager, still shrieking, tried desperately to squeeze his bulk behind the shelter of the opening beneath the desk, but he was far too large, and his bald head protruded through on the other side. Jones caught him by the scruff of his great neck and dragged him yelping out on to the carpet. He was covered with blood, and flopped helplessly upon his broken wrists.

"Be quick now!" cried the voice of Thorpe.

There was a tremendous commotion and banging at the door, and Jones gripped his pistol tightly. Something seemed to crash through his brain, clearing it for a second, so that he thought he saw beside him a great veiled figure, with drawn sword and flaming eyes, and sternly approving attitude.

"Remember the eyes! Remember the eyes!" hissed Thorpe in the air above him.

Jones felt like a god, with a god's power. Vengeance disappeared from his mind. He was acting impersonally as an instrument in the hands of the Invisibles who dispense justice and balance accounts. He bent down and put the barrel close into the other's face, smiling a little as he saw the childish efforts of the arms to cover his head. Then he pulled the trigger, and a bullet went straight into the right eye, blackening the skin. Moving the pistol two inches the other way, he sent another bullet crashing into the left eye. Then he stood upright over his victim with a deep sigh of satisfaction.

The Manager wriggled convulsively for the space of a single second, and then lay still in death.

There was not a moment to lose, for the door was already broken in and violent hands were at his neck. Jones put the pistol to his temple and once more pressed the trigger with his finger.

But this time there was no report. Only a little dead click answered the pressure, for the secretary had forgotten that the pistol had only six chambers, and that he had used them all. He threw the useless weapon on to the floor, laughing a little out loud, and turned, without a struggle, to give himself up.

"I *had* to do it," he said quietly, while they tied him. "It was simply my duty! And now I am ready to face the consequences, and Thorpe will be proud of me. For justice has been done and the gods are satisfied."

He made not the slightest resistance, and when the two policemen marched him off through the crowd of shuddering little clerks in the office, he again saw the veiled figure moving majestically in front of him, making slow sweeping circles with the flaming sword, to keep back the host of faces that were thronging in upon him from the Other Region.

www.ingramcontent.com/pod-product-compliance
Lightning Source LLC
Chambersburg PA
CBHW020553310726
48979CB00008B/1193/J
* 9 7 8 1 9 1 5 2 3 4 9 0 2 *